Blood and Chaos

Song of the King's Heart

Book Two

Nicole Sallak Anderson

Literary Wanderlust | Denver, Colorado

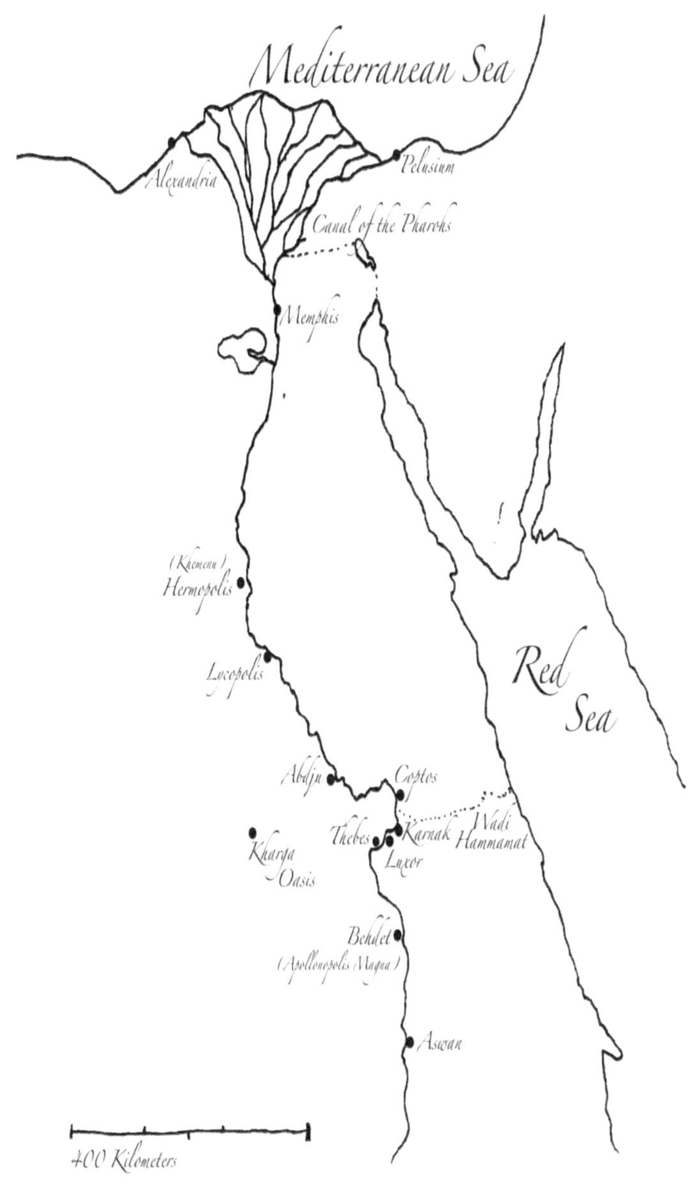

Mediterranean Sea
Alexandria
Pelusium
Canal of the Pharohs
Memphis
(Khemenu)
Hermopolis
Lycopolis
Abdju
Coptos
Karnak
Wadi Hammamat
Thebes
Luxor
Kharga Oasis
Behdet
(Apollonepolis Magna)
Aswan
Red Sea
400 Kilometers

List of Characters

Adikhalamani: King of Kush and Meroe during the Great Egyptian Revolt. Sent troops to aid Horwenefer.

Agathoclea: Ptolemy IV Philopater's mistress. Sister of Agathocles.

Agathocles: Favorite and advisor of Ptolemy IV Philopater.

Alexa: Daughter of Tyia. Priestess of Isis. Mother of Sethe and spiritual companion to Chanax.

Anen: Daughter of Silus and Ruia.

Ankhmaat: First born son of Ankhmakis and Weret.

Ankhmakis: Second son of Pharaoh Horwenefer and Queen Keket. Father of Helena with his spiritual companion, Natasa. Father of Ankhmaat with his sister-wife, Weret. General of the rebellion. Known to the Greeks as Chaonnophris. Pharaonic name is Ankhwenefer.

Ansel: One of Ankhmakis's guards. Greek heritage.

Antonius: Friend of Senmen during his training in Memphis. Greek heritage.

Arsinoe III: Queen of Egypt 220–204 BCE. Sister and wife of Ptolemy IV Philopater and mother of Ptolemy V Epiphanes.

Baktre: Eldest daughter of Bithiah and Chanax.

Bastyre: Royal Midwife of Behdet. Teacher of medicine and herbalism.

Bithiah: Second daughter of Pharaoh Horwenefer and his second queen, Mafuane. Married to Chanax. Mother of Baktre, Panas, and Hor. Has an affair with her half-brother Nefermaat, her true love.

Chanax: Third son of Pharaoh Horwenefer and Queen Keket. Priest of Set and father of Sethe with his spiritual companion, Alexa. Father to Baktre, Panas, and Hor with his sister-wife Bithiah.

Corinna: Nursemaid of Nefermaat and Natasa. Mother of Eleni with her husband, Hecataeus.

Dardre: High priest of Meroe.

Djed: Metakryon's assistant in Memphis.

Eleni: Natasa's younger half-sister. Daughter of Corinna and Vizier Hecataeus.

Ennaeus: Assistant of Vizier Hecataeus. Appointed by Ptolemy III Euergetes.

Epiphanes: Son of Ptolemy IV Philopater and Queen Arsinoe III. Fifth Ptolemy to take the throne.

Hecataeus: Greek vizier of Behdet, originally assigned by Ptolemy III Euergetes to spy on the royals of Behdet. After the death of Euergetes, betrays Ptolemy IV Philopater and helps Horwenefer procure an army and launch the rebellion. Father of Natasa with the high priestess Neferu-ankh-maat. Father of Eleni with his wife, Corinna.

Helena: Holy child of the temple. Daughter of Ankhmakis and Natasa.

Hor: Second son of Chanax and Bithiah.

Horpais: Second son of Silus and Ruia.

Horwenefer: Pharaoh of Upper Egypt from 205–199 BCE. Father of Silus, Ankhmakis, and Senmen with Keket. Father of Ruia, Bithiah, and Weret with Mafuane. Father of Nefermaat with his spiritual companion the high priestess Neferu-ankh-maat. Launched the rebellion against the Ptolemaic Empire in 205 BCE. Known to the Greeks as Haronnophris. Also known as Hugronaphor.

Ikui: Weapons trainer and master smithy for the rebellion.

Isidor: High priest of Set in Behdet. Mentor to Chanax. Spiritual companion of the high priestess Neferu-ankh-maat.

Had an affair with Queen Keket for decades.

Iu-Amon: High priest of the Houses of Healing.

Kawit: Daughter of Tyia. Priestess of Isis. Spiritual companion to Silus.

Keket: High queen of Upper Egypt. Married to Pharaoh Horwenefer. Mother of Silus, Ankhmakis, and Senmen. Had an affair with the High Priest Isidor for decades.

Khaleme: General of the Kush (Ethiopian) army. Sent by King Adikhalamani to support the Egyptian Revolt.

Kyros: Greek military officer hired by Vizier Hecataeus to train and build the rebel army.

Mafuane: Priestess of Isis. Second queen of Pharaoh Horwenefer. Mother of Ruia, Bithiah, and Weret. Died giving birth to Weret.

Metakryon: High priest of Memphis and the Lower Kingdom of Egypt. Head of the cult of Set and training in Memphis.

Min: Son of the priest Zethus and a royal nursemaid. Twin brother of Pontius. Ankhmakis's captain of the guard.

Natasa: Daughter of High Priestess Neferu-ankh-maat and Vizier Hecataeus. Heir to the temple of Isis. Mother of Helena and spiritual companion of Ankhmakis.

Neferu-ankh-maat: High priestess of Isis in Behdet. Spiritual companion to Pharaoh Horwenefer and High Priest Isidor. Mother of Nefermaat with Horwenefer. Mother of Natasa with Vizier Hecataeus.

Nefermaat: Son of High Priestess Neferu-ankh-maat and Pharaoh Horwenefer. Royal Guard. Has an affair with Bithiah.

Panas: First son of Chanax and Bithiah.

Pistias: Greek sailor commissioned by Hecataeus to help him flee the country. Owns a mongoose named Belladonna.

Pontius: Son of the priest Zethus and a royal nursemaid. Twin brother of Min. Guards the Princes of Behdet.

Philopater: Fourth king of the Ptolemaic Empire. Reigned from 221–204 BCE. Pharaoh when the Great Revolt of 205 BCE was launched. Father of Epiphanes with his wife, Queen Arsinoe III.

Qeny: Friend of Senmen during his training in Memphis. Native Egyptian.

Ruia: Eldest daughter of Pharaoh Horwenefer and his second queen, Mafuane. Mother of Senui, Horpais, and Anen with her husband and half-brother, Silus.

Sebastos: Horse trainer and master falconer of Behdet.

Setep: High priest of Thebes and the Upper Kingdom of Egypt.

Sethe: Holy child of the temple. Son of Priest Chanax and

Priestess Alexa.

Silus: Eldest son of Pharaoh Horwenefer and Queen Keket. Father of Senui, Horpais, and Anen with his sister-wife Ruia. His spiritual companion is Kawit.

Sosibuis: Favorite and advisor of Ptolemy IV Philopater.

Tyia: Priestess of Isis and assistant to the high priestess Neferu-ankh-maat. Mother of Kawit and Alexa.

Weret: Youngest daughter of Pharaoh Horwenefer and his second queen, Mafuane. Married to her half-brother, Ankhmakis. Mother of Ankhmaat.

Zethus: Elder priest of Horus. Father to Min and Pontius.

Song of the King's Heart: *Blood and Chaos* is a work of fiction. Names, characters, places, and incidents are the products of the author's imagination and have been used fictitiously. Any resemblance to actual events, locales, or persons, living or dead, is entirely coincidental.

Published in the United States by Literary Wanderlust LLC, Denver, Colorado.
https//www.LiteraryWanderlust.com

ISBN Print: 978-1-942856-64-1
ISBN Digital: 978-1-942856-70-2
Cover design: Pozo Mitsuma

Printed in the United States of America

Acknowledgments

While I wrote all three *Song of the King's Heart* novels at once, it has taken years to refine each one into its own story. This time around, it is my editor, Kylee Howells, who gets all the credit. A novel is better with an editor, and I'm glad she's mine.

Many thanks also to my publisher, Susan Brooks. The publishing process for *Origins* showed me just how professional Literary Wanderlust is. From the cover design to the reviews and all the support, I'm truly grateful.

To my loved ones: my husband, who sometimes takes second fiddle to this project; Jackson, who lent me a copy of *The Tale of Sinuhe* and *Herodotus's Histories* (yeah, he's a Reedie); and Michael, who has shared me the most with Ankhmakis.

And of course, to my crew—Regan, Jillian, and Maureen. You listened when I needed it. Thank you so much.

Dear Reader

There's not a lot of historical data about my hero, and as such I was allowed to create his world from scratch. Yet I still wanted to tell his story with some sort of accuracy, particularly as it came to the war he waged.

There is one document I found very helpful—a lecture given by Willy Clarysse at The Center for the Tebtunis Papyri at the University of California Berkeley on March 16, 2004. Using tax receipts, stele, letters, and slave sales, Clarysse was able to pull together a rudimentary timeline for the Great Egyptian Revolt. While I didn't follow everything he suggests, and my dates of 200 BCE don't exactly match—this is after all speculation on all of our parts—the following novel tries to honor as many of the dates and events as possible. *Blood and Chaos* is about the wars Ankhmakis waged both on the battlefield and within his court. The courtly drama was mine to create, yet I wanted the battlefield to be driven by history as much as possible.

As promised in *Origins*, the Wands of Horus make their appearance in *Blood and Chaos*. Ankhmakis's story is a tragedy, but the wands bring us hope that beyond the chaos of humanity, there is the aspiration of what Walt Whitman once called, "the song of the universal." There are many legends

about the wands, and I hope that Natasa's story is one that
will satisfy the more esoteric reader.

Sincerely,
Nicole Sallak Anderson

For the Golden Child, who is always misunderstood.

PART ONE

The Great Egyptian Revolt

"The Divine Plan is the evolution of consciousness. Every living thing in the universe lives for this Divine Plan in their own unique way, contributing in freedom and love. Possibilities and potentialities abound, and each occurs when the time is right, one state causing another to occur, like raindrops on a still pond. All are one, all are unique, and all are working toward the Divine Plan—to shepherd consciousness forth to perfection.

"The freedom of the individual is this—to enter the dance on the material plane eyes open, striving to live from the highest self, keeping the connection to Spirit open, and working toward understanding one's place in the web of life, or to enter the body eyes closed, ignorant to the Divine Plan and thus choosing suffering, karma, and pain. Saints and Messiahs are those who choose the first, and those who live in fear, greed, war, and destruction choose the latter. They refuse to see their connection to the web of life.

"Of all beings in the universe, whether trees, animals, mountains, rivers, stars, or planets, only humans make the choice to remain asleep. The rest are awake and aware of their role in the manifestation of the cosmic dance. Only humans fail to remain open. Only humans refuse to see.

"Thus, the origin of evil is not outside of yourselves—it is your own creation, and only you can put an end to it."

~ "Destiny" by Finnian, Scribe of the North.

1

Too Long

"The war against the Egyptians started shortly after the battle at Raphia in 217 BCE in which Ptolemy IV, by gaining an unexpected victory on the Seleucid Antiochus III, managed to keep control over Palestine. By arming the Egyptians for his war against Antiochus, Ptolemy had an excellent idea for the short term, but he did not consider the future. Priding themselves upon their victory at Raphia, the soldiers were no longer disposed to obey orders, but they sought out a leader and figurehead, in the opinion that they could come up for themselves.

And shortly afterward, they did indeed do so."

~ Polybius, Historiae V 107.1 and XIV 107.1

The Nile River, northwest of Panopolis 204 BCE

The prince of Behdet gazed across the Nile River at the city of Panopolis, its bonfires flickering like beacons in the dark night. A hot wind caressed his sunburnt face. He turned to see his enemy's army spread out before him, torchlights zigzagging across an island downriver like ants on honey, protecting their city with their mighty arsenal of archers and ships. He wanted control of the island, needed it, if he were ever to return home to his lover's arms.

"This war is taking too long," he hissed under his breath.

"My lord," Min, his personal guard, answered. "It has been a year. It took our greatest ancestor, Pharaoh Amhose I, nineteen years to banish the Hyksos filth from our lands. Prior to his victory, his father and grandfather also battled for independence. Their line of kings fought for over thirty years to take Egypt unto back unto native hands. Our war is young. Be patient."

Ankhmakis turned to his friend and captain, his lips curled. "I don't want this to take three generations, Min. I will not leave this task to my heirs. I will march upon Alexandria and kill Ptolemy IV with my own hands. We should at least be to Memphis by now. Instead we're in Panopolis, held back by their army. For the second time, the Inundation is at our backs. If we don't hurry, we'll be trapped here when the river floods. Such a failure can't happen again."

He recalled the first Akhet of the war, when he and his troops had failed to take Panopolis and had been forced to spend four miserable months stuck in Abdju, surrounded by flood waters and unable to navigate their navy in either direction. It had taken most of Perit to regroup and ready themselves to continue their quest north. This Akhet he preferred to spend at home in Behdet, in the comforts of his chambers, his warm bath, and his lover's passionate embrace.

"Which is why we must take it tonight. I understand, my lord," Min agreed.

"Yes," Ankhmakis said, squinting to see farther into the black night surrounding them. "Tonight, under Khon's dark blessing, we will destroy the island, and Panopolis will be ours. They've relocated most of their troops to the island. If we can take it, the remaining soldiers in the city will be overwhelmed. Upon victory, we will establish a naval blockade to hold the line and return to Behdet to train the Ethiopians during the floods."

"And return to Natasa," Min said, his crooked smile so wide it shone even under the cover of darkness.

Ankhmakis thought of Natasa waiting for him in Behdet. He'd gone without her touch for over a year, and his constant ache for her was unbearable. Their child was an infant when he'd ridden off to war. How old was she now? Did she look like her mother? Could she walk? His throat constricted as he fought back the pain of their physical separation.

"Go," he commanded his captain. "This is the darkest hour of the night. The time is now. Send the signal."

"Yes, my lord," Min replied as he slid into the inky-black night, leaving the prince alone on the banks of the river.

Ankhmakis wore nothing but a linen kilt around his lean waist. He strapped a dagger to his right calf and picked up his wooden stave, twirling it in the air before planting a tip in the sand. His rebellion had shooters of their own, called the megau, but tonight's mission needed his strong-arm fighters, the nakhtu-aa. Forty-two of his best nakhtu-aa approached without sound from the south. Soon they would swim to the island before them, spreading out in formation to encircle the shoreline.

Pharaoh Horwenefer's army had been trying to claim Panopolis since the start of Shemu, the harvesting season, but the Ptolemaic army on the island was situated to guard both the city and the river itself. Their ships blocked all water passage, rendering Ankhmakis's navy impotent, and Ptolemy's archers numbered several hundred, capable of shooting at the Egyptian land army from every direction.

Ankhmakis's older brother, Silus, had attacked Panopolis from the desert side to the east. His troops had managed to scale the wall, but they were overrun within the city by enemy soldiers arriving on Greek ships at the western entrance, trapping them and slaughtering Silus's soldiers. Silus had been taken for ransom, and now sat in the dungeon awaiting their father's negotiations. Tonight's mission was Pharaoh Horwenefer's answer.

"Men," Ankhmakis whispered as his nakhtu-aa drew within hearing range, "this is our last chance. If we fail, the war may be lost. We must take the island by stealth."

He looked out once more at the island, surrounded on all sides by makeshift docks and Greek battleships. Getting past the docks—there were several of them surrounding the island—was a formidable task. One which many of his men, and perhaps even himself, wouldn't survive.

Shaking the doubt from his mind, he turned back to the nakhtu-aa.

"We'll swim to our positions, encircling the entire circumference of the island. Climb out under the cover of the docks to get on land. Don't try to enter from the shoreline. It's too risky, even under the dark moon. Rely on the cover of the ships to slip in through the cracks. Kill anyone who sees you. Be swift and silent. Their navy must remain unaware of our presence for as long as possible. Continue on foot, crawling in the sand if you must, under the cover of shadow, until you get to the military camp at the center of the island. Remain in hiding until you hear my signal. Nefermaat, Pontius, Min, Kyros, and I will infiltrate the camp first, putting the ones still walking out of their misery. If our spies have done their job, the men should be dropping dead within the hour."

He paused, considering the camp cooks he'd bribed—

three women whose children he now kept under lock-and-key in the pharaoh's headquarters in Thebes. If they wanted their children returned to their arms, they had no choice but to help him poison the army. A pinch of henbane in the stew should take out most of the men, leaving only the inner-most guards and the captain of the island himself to battle.

"When we've breached their inner sanctum, we'll call for you to join the fight. The pharaoh waits upriver aboard his ships for our signal to take the harbors. With most of their archers dead, their sailors will have no means to stand against us."

The nakhtu-aa murmured their pleasure, and Ankhmakis felt his chest swell. Many he'd trained one-on-one, each one an expert at hand-to-hand combat. They couldn't carry their swords and shields; both were too heavy to swim the deep waters. Wooden staves, the weapons of his ancestors, were to be used tonight.

After Ptolemy the First had secured Egypt from the rest of Alexander the Great's Diadokhoi in 312 BCE, he'd stripped the native population of its armaments, armories, and military system. He had allowed them only the wooden stave, and over the generations the native men of Egypt had become very skilled with the club. Ankhmakis tipped his face to the dark sky, closed his eyes, and gave thanks to his father, whose efforts in the Battle of Raphia had enabled the natives to become an armed population. Pharaoh Horwenefer's army was the first in two hundred years to hold real weapons, master the bow and arrow, throw the javelin, and feel the sting of the sickled khopesh sword—the sword of the great kings of old.

Turning to his men, he gave his final instructions: "Stay alert. Swim as swiftly as the serpent Apophis, without making so much as a ripple. Give thanks to the night god Khons and ask him to remain hidden so none of his light will give away our actions to our enemies."

The men nodded their agreement and Ankhmakis headed into the water. A chill raced across his skin as the dark river swelled around his feet, each step guiding him deeper into its depths. He focused on his abdomen, taking several deep breaths, igniting the power of his soul. As the energy traveled up his spine, he sent his Ka out in six directions and found her, ready to be his eyes and ears.

"*Natasa,*" he said within his heart, yet silent to the world around him. "*Are you ready?*"

"*Yes, my love,*" she answered. The rush of passion filled his every cell. He mated his sexual desire and the thrill of battle, becoming invincible as he swam across the river, extending his Ka toward the island and covering it with his energetic field.

Being twin flames, Ankhmakis and Natasa were capable of sending their Ba out from their bodies to the other's surroundings, granting her the power to travel to battle with him, going beyond him and gathering the crucial information he needed for such risky missions. Their connection was part of his military success. Ankhmakis knew it had something to do with the fact they shared one Ba—a single spirit which had split into two bodies—one male and one female.

It made for the greatest lovemaking he had ever known, but more than this, when in Natasa's arms, Ankhmakis felt whole and one with the entire cosmos. To be in her embrace was to be complete, and her love made life worthwhile. To have two minds gave them the advantage over others in the court. The astral travel they had perfected during their sex now served as the connection that not only helped him in battle, but also enabled them to be together even when miles apart.

"The soldiers in the harbors don't yet sense your arrival," she reported. *"Most of them are on land, gambling and drinking. Some are whoring in their quarters on the ships. A few of the guards are alert and yet still remain unaware of the forty men now swimming through the channels."*

"Good," he replied. *"What about the men in the camp at the center of the island?"*

"Still awake, but your female spies huddle together in a corner. They were successful at putting the henbane in the evening meal and are now terrified of being discovered."

"The men still roam the camp? Are you sure?"

"Yes, but they are sluggish. One tries to force himself upon a serving girl and is, well, unsuccessful. Part of his body has stopped working already." She giggled.

"Natasa, this is war. Could you be a bit more serious?"

"Danger," she warned. *"Some of your men have arrived at their positions upriver. A guard has noticed something amiss."*

Ankhmakis swam faster, allowing Natasa's voice to fade to the background in his mind as he focused on matters at hand. He glided along in the water, hearing the voices of the Greek soldiers on the boats and along the shoreline. There were more of them than he'd expected. He should have sent Natasa out earlier to check, but she was busy in Behdet, raising their daughter and instructing future priestesses of Isis in the temple. Her mother, High Priestess Neferu-ankh-maat, expected her daughter to perform her temple duties to the best of her abilities. Ankhmakis didn't want to tax Natasa more than he had to.

He swam up beside the wooden hull of a ship and hovered there a moment, treading water and covered in the boat's shadow. The men here were laughing, playing the lute, and from the rhythmic sounds of their footfalls, dancing. He continued to swim until he found a landing free of any vessel. Ankhmakis glided his slick body into position under the dock and climbed up one of the pilings, the wood slimy under his grip. He froze at the sound of approaching footsteps. Holding his breath, he clung to the piling, still as a statue in one of his ancestor's tombs, waiting until the guard passed above him and back onto the shore.

Droplets of water dripped from his body as he climbed up onto the wooden dock, the night air causing his wet muscles to shiver. Clutching his stave in his hands, he strode toward the shore, where he could see a few men sitting by a fire outside a makeshift shed. Taking mental notes, he observed the shoddy buildings along the shore, thrown together in obvious haste. It appeared the Greeks didn't think the war was going to last much longer and felt there was no need for a permanent garrison.

Tonight, Ankhmakis would teach them how wrong they were. The prince smiled as he approached the men. Their heads flinched up from the fire at the sound of his footsteps, eyes narrowing as they glared at him. His wet hair hung in curtains around his face, and his white linen skirt clung to his groin, leaving nothing to the imagination.

"What?" a man dressed in a Macedonian shift cried as he rose from his chair.

"Evening, gentlemen," Ankhmakis said as he lifted his stave above his head and slammed it into the man's skull.

The soldier thumped to the ground, and Ankhmakis turned to meet the other two as they rose from their positions. Ankhmakis felt the warmth of his enemy's blood under his feet as he stepped forward to meet them in combat. They drew their swords, but not quick enough, allowing Ankhmakis to get in close and ram his stave into one set of ribs with a cracking sound. He spun and thrust the end of his wooden weapon into the third man's throat. The soldier's eyes rolled back into his head as his neck snapped. The enemy's sword fell from his hand before he could even get in one swing. Within moments, all was silent.

Ankhmakis dropped his stave and grasped the sword from the ground. The grip felt foreign to his palm, and the blade was too straight, but it would do. He continued up the path away from the docks, leaving the men there to their merriment. He had a general to defeat.

The island was a sandhill, barren and flat. There was nowhere to hide, and Ankhmakis fell to his belly to crawl like the mighty crocodile god Sobek toward his goal. The sand scraped against his naked chest, but he ignored the sensation, and instead focused on the mission at hand. As he approached the military encampment, it was evident the poison part of his plan had worked. Collapsed upon the ground, faces pale and tongues bulging, were several archers who had been stationed at this point on the perimeter. Part of Ankhmakis was thrilled at the fact his plan had been successful, yet another part was disappointed. He'd wanted a fight. Moments later, he got his wish as a group of new guards ran to their fallen comrade's aid.

"What is this?" an archer cried out. In one smooth motion, the enemy swung his bow from his shoulder, cocked, and released an arrow. Ankhmakis had mere seconds to tumble out of the way. The arrow swished past his cheek. A second arrow flew toward him, and he jumped behind a supply wagon to take cover.

"This wasn't supposed to happen," he said out loud.

"There are four of them," Natasa answered. *"Rip out the seat of the wagon to use as a shield and get closer."*

He peeked above the wagon and arrows flew above his head. Cursing, he ducked back down. In the distance he could hear skirmishes breaking out across the camp. His men had arrived too soon.

"No, you're right on time," Natasa answered. *"Most of the Greeks are falling dead inside the camp. What you see here are the general's personal guards. They have different servants and different food. They expect poison."*

"I assumed they would," Ankhmakis answered. *"Does the general know we're here?"*

"He is sending out his men to stop you. I can see around seventy."

Ankhmakis considered the odds. Seventy of their best against forty of his nakhtu-aa. Another set of arrows struck the ground near his feet—time to move. He dropped the sword to the ground and gripped the wagon, expanding his Ka over, under, and around it. He visualized the space beneath the wagon growing taller, lifting it from the ground. The cart felt light as a feather.

The shock of seeing a man lift the wagon distracted the soldiers for a moment, granting Ankhmakis time to gain the upper hand. He thrust the cart at them, missing by a long shot, but forcing them to lose their formation. He snatched the knife tied to his calf and threw it at the front archer, meeting his mark in the center of his forehead. Sprinting toward them as fast as he could, he shortened the distance granting the archers their security and swung his sword at their bows, splintering them into pieces. The men turned to flee, but Ankhmakis, now under the spell of battle lust, raced forward to grab a soldier and sliced his sword through the man's torso.

His dying screams of pain filled the air. Ankhmakis leaped over the fallen body and chased the last man right into the camp, where he found his nakhtu-aa engaged in combat.

The men kicked up sand as they fought, and in spite of the violence, Ankhmakis found the fighting to be a beautiful, dangerous desert dance. Eager to be a part of the skirmish, the prince threw himself into the battle, his sword meeting flesh, and his own body burning in pain as he took various blows. The smell of blood penetrated his senses, and he tasted iron in his mouth. Swallowing down a bit of horror, he inhaled and felt the desire for the fight deep within his warrior's soul. To his delight, the Greek general approached, crowned in a golden helmet and with an emerald green cape fluttering over his shoulder.

Ankhmakis lifted his sword and pointed it at the man, looking down his blade, which glowed in the firelight in spite of the blood now covering it. His chest clenched as he squeezed the hilt tighter. This was the man who had kept him at bay for months. This was the man who had stopped his army's momentum. This man was the reason Ankhmakis was still eating slop rather than dining in the halls of Alexandria in victory. This man was the reason he slept alone in a tent instead of in his royal chambers beside Natasa, her warm flesh like silk against his body.

"You," Ankhmakis cried as he charged.

Ankhmakis launched himself into the air toward his target, and the man's eyes went wide at the bold maneuver. Ankhmakis knew this man was a man of war—most of Philopater's army had spent the past decade on the Syrian plains, fighting Antiochus III. Ankhmakis and his Egyptian men were the novices in this situation. Yet they had something the Greeks didn't. For all their strategic glory, these Macedonian men knew nothing of the Alchemies of Horus and as such, fought as if blindfolded. Ankhmakis had been trained to draw upon the unseen forces of the world, and this made him more than a potential usurper. He was a general to be reckoned with in his own right.

As Ankhmakis landed in the sand before his target, the general swung at him, and the rebel prince struggled to raise his sword in time to block it. The sound of metal on metal clashed and clanged as the two men thrust and parried. Around them, men from both sides fell, one-by-one, onto the sandy field. Ankhmakis's bare feet slipped in the dirt, now soft and sticky with blood. He fell to his knees and rolled, causing the Greek general to miss his next strike, his sword burrowing into the moist ground instead of Ankhmakis's flesh. As his enemy struggled to tug his sword free from the earth, Ankhmakis grabbed him from behind and yanked his prisoner into his chest, placing his stolen Macedonian sword at the general's throat.

"Looks like I've caught myself a prize," Ankhmakis hissed into the man's ear.

He struggled to hold his foe as he glanced around, taking inventory of the situation. Most of the enemy soldiers were either poisoned, dead from battle, or lying wounded upon the ground, crying out in misery. The few survivors had been rounded up by his men and stood, hands tied, by a great bonfire in the center of the camp. Ankhmakis himself had twenty-two nakhtu-aa fighters left.

A vision from Natasa flashed in his mind—hordes of Greek soldiers were heading from the docks toward them. It meant they would soon be ransacked, yet the shoreline would be left unprotected—his mission had succeeded.

"Min, send the signal to the pharaoh. We've secured the

camp. It's time for his ships to take the docks."

"Yes, sir," Min answered as he ran out of the camp.

"Nefermaat," he said to his half-brother. "Arm the rest of our men with the Greek's bows and arrows to secure the perimeter. The soldiers from the harbor will be here soon, and we must hold them back till the pharaoh arrives."

"What about them?" Nefermaat asked, shrugging his still wet head toward the captured soldiers at the center of camp.

Ankhmakis tightened his grip around the general. He had at most twenty of his own men left. He'd lost half. Not enough to guard the prisoners of war and fight the others now on their way, their footsteps and war cries now all too near.

"What must be done, must be done," he said, his voice thick. "Kill them."

He drew his sword across the general's neck, and agony filled his soul as Natasa severed their connection.

He dropped the man to the ground, panting ragged breaths. Nefermaat tossed him a composite bow and quiver filled with arrows, taken from the island's armory. Ankhmakis heard the clamor of the new soldiers arriving and turned to face them, their shadows lumbering toward him in the dark.

"To the perimeter," he screamed to his men, who sprinted to form a circle facing outward to face the enemy.

In the distance, a flare flew in the sky, and he knew his father's ships were on their way. With the hundreds of Greek archers now dead on the island, the dock men had been forced to leave their posts to defend the army camp. Pharaoh Horwenefer would gain control of the docks and then the whole island. All Ankhmakis had to do was survive until his father's ships arrived. Drawing on the energy around him, he nocked an arrow, connecting to his target. He freed the string and felt satisfaction as one of the Greeks running toward him fell to the ground. Within moments he'd taken down several more.

"*What must be done, must be done,*" he said again in his mind, wishing Natasa could understand.

His beloved didn't reply.

2

Broken

The Queen of Behdet had been young when she was forced to take her place at her brother's side to rule the people. Her father's death had stolen not only her heart, but also her life from her. As the sole female born of the high queen, when her father, the king of Behdet, died without warning, Keket became her younger brother's wife, and the one to carry the burden of the line of kings.

Behdet, Egypt 204 BCE

The high queen of Upper Egypt paced the tomb-like room. Normally, when High Priest Isidor summoned her to his secret quarters, she was greeted by a warm fire and libations. Tonight, nothing but a torch in the wall awaited her. Not even Isidor was present. His absence was very unlike him.

Keket hadn't seen him in private for weeks, and the separation was destroying her. She'd done something wrong, and he was punishing her, yet the exact nature of her failing was unknown. Their illegal love affair had been tumultuous on many levels. Despite the fact that she was the high queen, Isidor had been her lover for decades, and Keket needed him to find joy in her otherwise joyless life. Her marriage to Horwenefer—she was still getting used to his Pharaonic name—had been forced upon her, and the man's touch disgusted her. When he had left to launch the civil war against the Ptolemaic Empire, Keket had assumed it would provide more time for her to indulge in Isidor's sexual favor. The opposite had happened, and instead of igniting their illicit affair, she'd seen Isidor less and less since the war began. It appeared her lover was sending her a message.

Keket hugged herself as goosebumps formed upon her dark arms—the room was cold. Waiting for Isidor was driving her mad. Where was he? She wandered over to the heavy chest in the corner. Hesitating a moment, she lifted the lid and saw the various implements the high priest used to teach her the discipline needed for his type of Anit-Shadya, the magic of ecstasy. No one else in the temple practiced the same sex magic they did, not even his precious Neferu-ankh-maat, the high priestess of Isis and spiritual companion of both her husband and Isidor—Keket hated the whore. Keket smiled as she considered the fact that she, the high queen of Upper Egypt, was the only one with whom Isidor could be honest about his sexuality. He liked it rough and enjoyed hurting her, something the pious Neferu-ankh-maat would never allow. Keket wasn't sure why she needed the pain, but she did. It made her feel alive. She eyed the flails, ropes, chains, and small riding crop and recalled how exhilarating his aggressive attentions felt.

"Ah, my queen, I'm sorry to have kept you waiting."

Startled, she turned at Isidor's voice, letting the chest slam shut. Her resolve to appear regal before him weakened as she drank in his handsome face, bald head shining in the firelight, and gaze focused upon her like a falcon upon his prey. No one had ever made her feel so alive, yet simultaneously vulnerable. No one ever would.

"Isidor?" she breathed, her chest rising and falling as he moved to her side. "What's going on? Why are your tools still in the chest?"

"Don't you mean toys, my dear?" he replied, running a finger along the chest, his relaxed grin making her blush.

"Toys don't hurt," she replied.

"They do if the pain leads to pleasure," he answered, turning away to shut the thick, wooden door to the room and locking it, as was his habit. His private chambers were soundproof, and no one, not even the guards, knew they existed.

"Please," he continued, "have a seat."

"Why haven't you started a fire?" Keket demanded. "It's cold in here."

"Because we won't be long," he answered. He sat on the silk and animal skin-covered sedan and leaned back, gesturing to the empty place beside him. "Please, Keket, take a seat. We have much to discuss."

The high queen's heart sank. He hadn't called her for sex. Yet, she did as he said, for obedience to his command had been bred into her after decades of sexual servitude. Isidor had started teaching her when he performed her First Rites after her sixteenth birthday. She'd been a very faithful pupil.

"My lord," she began, "I don't understand."

"Of course you don't," he said in a soft voice, as if preparing her for something painful, "and I can see why. It is my custom to send for you to enjoy your body, but bliss isn't on the agenda tonight."

"I see," she whispered.

"No, you don't, but I will make it clear. My dear Keket,

I'm sorry to say this, but you and I will no longer engage in our lessons."

She gasped, pain searing her heart, as if he'd reached into her breast and was squeezing the organ in his hand. She looked at his calm face and noticed a smirk forming upon his full, luscious lips. Keket fought back the tears forming under her painted eyelids. "Have I done something wrong, Lord Isidor?"

"Yes, Keket, you have, and I'm very, very angry with you."

Keket's vision faded to black as if she'd fainted, so great was her fear. Had he discovered her dark secret? The one she'd kept for decades? The secret she'd killed for in order keep it from him and the pharaoh, for the truth would upend everything any of them had ever worked for.

"You're angry, my lord?" she whispered, her words trembling from her lips.

"How dare you let Horwenefer give Natasa the golden wand?"

As she realized Isidor wasn't talking about her horrible secret, Keket laughed. She recalled the gift her husband had given Natasa at Ankhmakis's wedding to Weret as a boon for being their middle son's spiritual companion. It had been a year since the event; why would Isidor mention it now?

"The wand? Is that all?" She was giddy, grateful he hadn't discovered her terrible truth. The wand was nothing compared to the surreptitious events she'd concealed all these years. She thanked the goddess silently, unable to hide her relief from her furious lover.

Isidor glared at her, his nostrils flaring. "You promised to steal it from him and give it to me. How dare you fail at this one simple task?"

"Isidor, I had no idea he was going to present it Natasa as

a gift. Why do you care?”

"I warned you before your sons’ weddings that the time had come for you to steal the wand, yet you didn’t. I’ve asked you several times since the event to get it back from the girl and you’ve failed.”

"Isidor, please, I didn’t realize the object’s importance,” she begged. "How could you abandon our love for such a simple mistake?”

"Your failure was not a simple mistake,” Isidor said, his voice shaking and increasing in volume. He rose from his place and towered over her. "I told you I had to have it. You promised you would steal it for me, but now your son’s half-breed whore has one of the last Wands of Horus, and I can’t take it from her without exposing myself.”

"Don’t be dramatic. Have her mother get it for you. The high priestess will do whatever you ask, am I right?” Keket put her hand on her hips as she stood to face him. Now she was the one getting impatient. Neferu-ankh-maat was Natasa’s mother—she could demand her daughter give the wand to Isidor. "I don’t see why this is a crisis.”

"You wouldn’t, Keket, because you’re too small minded. I have been searching for the golden wand for decades. When you told me about it, I knew the wand should be mine. I have given you my attention for years, and when I ask you to do one small thing, you fail.”

"Isidor, how important could the wand be?” Keket demanded.

He stood closer and sneered. "The one who commands the Wands of Horus has the power to create any conditions he chooses. Your ignorant husband has no idea of their potential, or he wouldn’t have given one to his son’s concubine. You were supposed to listen to me without failure.”

Isidor stood so close she could smell his sweat. Her desire and fear of him made her woozy. "I'm sorry, my lord," she whispered, placing her fingertips upon his bare chest. His skin was hotter than the midday sun. "I will do anything to make up for it."

"There is nothing you can do," he hissed, slapping her hands away as if disgusted by her touch. "I've been waiting for three seasons, and you've come up empty handed. Now, please go and never expect me to call for you again."

Keket sniffled and ran her hand across her eyes, smearing her dark eyeliner. Anger welled up within her. "How foolish I've been. You've been using me, haven't you?"

"Using you? No, my lady. You and I have been experimenting." He laughed as he sat back down on his settee. "It's been fun, don't you think? Yet, it appears I wasn't strict enough in my education."

Keket looked down upon him, lounging on his sofa, arm slung behind his head. The candlelight illuminated his sculpted arms and body. Desire coursed through her body, and she straddled him, lifting her skirt. Rather than grow hard as he once had, his entire body stiffened.

"Isidor, you can't mean this."

"Keket," he answered, staring at her without emotion, "I only speak the truth. You've disappointed me. It's over."

"I've never let you down before," she begged.

"I've made up my mind. Besides, you're getting a bit too old for me. I've found a younger student. A servant girl. Much less dangerous than taking the pharaoh's wife, don't you think? No one will notice the bruises and marks."

"Too old?" Keket couldn't believe it. "I'm younger than Neferu-ankh-maat, and you still enjoy Shadya with her."

"Ah, but I love Neferu-ankh-maat, more than anything in

the entire world. Now please, get off me, and take yourself from my chambers. You know the way out."

The pain of heartbreak filled Keket's soul, crushing her as if he'd stepped on her chest, her breath caught under her breast as her lungs failed her. Nothing had ever hurt her in this way. Isidor had been her sole companion in the entire royal complex. The one she'd trusted above all others, the only person who had shown her any interest.

She'd lost her reason to live.

Keket rose from Isidor's lap, and the room spun around her. Never had she been so vulnerable. Not even the day she'd been forced to marry her younger brother had reduced her to such agony. She looked down at her lover and cringed at his cold expression.

"Isidor?" she whispered.

"My queen, please leave before you make a fool of yourself."

She turned, her body heavy, and allowed her feet to carry her to the door. As if she were already dead, the high queen of Upper Egypt opened the thick door to the priest's secret study and began the long walk down the cold, stone corridor. One foot, and then the other. It took incredible strength to keep from collapsing to the floor. After struggling to walk for what seemed like eternity, she found the door leading outside. Heaving it open, the cool, evening desert air met her face, and she risked a breath. Over and over she gasped for air, as if she were drowning in her sorrow. She got as far as her personal royal gardens before she gave in to the pain and fell under the starry night sky, sobbing for her aching heart.

Keket was alone in this world of kings and priests. A world where men made the rules and women were expected to be complicit. Never had she been given a choice, never had she been asked what she wanted—and now she wanted two things very, very much.

First, she wanted someone to love her.

Second, she wanted Neferu-ankh-maat to suffer as she suffered.

Her first wish was impossible, for the pharaoh would never love her, and no man other than Isidor would dare risk taking her as a lover. But her second wish was in her power as the high queen, and she would hurt Neferu-ankh-maat, if it was the last thing she did.

3

The King's Invisible Hands

"Oh, my soul, foolish to belittle the sorrow which is due to life, you who constrain me toward death, when I have not come to it... Is this pain? It would be of sweet relief, if the gods drove off the heaviness of my body!"

~ The Dialogue of a Man and His Soul, late Twelfth Dynasty manuscript

Behdet, Egypt 204 BCE

The High Priestess Neferu-ankh-maat hid in the small alcove. She'd never set foot in the Temple of Horus, nor had she been allowed to take part in a ceremony within its walls. This was the domain of Isidor and the god of chaos, Set—women were not allowed. She heard footsteps in the distance and crouched lower in her hiding place, tugging the brown hood tighter around her head.

Spying was hard for her, yet she'd been trained to make herself invisible. Using her concentration, she became smaller, reducing her energy field bit by bit, until she was sure no one could sense her presence. Isidor and a group of men entered the temple and proceeded toward the altar. They wore the red robes of the cult of Set, and their faces were covered, but she knew at least one of them was Chanax, the youngest prince and Isidor's acolyte. The men filed in behind their master and formed a circle around him. One of them stepped forward, holding a small, light-skinned boy. The boy was gagged and bound and struggled as he was dragged toward the stone altar.

"Secure him," Isidor said.

The red-robed figure heaved the victim upon the altar, and the others joined him in tying the fitful child to the stone surface. Neferu-ankh-maat fought the urge to try to save him— she couldn't interrupt. She needed to see everything. Gone were the days of speculation. After years of enduring this cult, she needed to see what her lover and spiritual companion was up to when he wasn't at her side.

Neferu-ankh-maat's heart pounded in her chest. She'd loved Isidor since childhood, and for as long as she could recall being alive, he'd been by her side. Their Anit-Shadya ceremony was powerful and their wisdom great. Yet his training as a young man in Memphis had changed him, and the cult he grew within the Temple of Horus was dark and dangerous. In spite of decades of Anit-Shadya, she'd never been able to penetrate his mind and discover what evil he was up to in the bowels of his temple. Her mother had taught her that chaos and love didn't mix. Yet because of her love for him, she'd chosen to ignore Isidor's work—until now.

She recalled the moment when she'd first suspected him. On the night before Pharaoh Horwenefer had launched the war, they'd taken Anit-Shadya, the ceremony of purest pleasure, together. In the throes of Anit-Shadya, a person was as powerful as the gods, and yet also vulnerable to psychic attack, should anyone be bold enough to invade such a sacred moment. On the night before the war began, Isidor had been so bold. Not to attack her, but the king himself.

As Horwenefer climaxed in Neferu-ankh-maat's embrace, she'd felt Isidor's presence for the first time during her lovemaking with the king. Isidor had shared her sexually without jealousy or concern for decades. Unlike her daughter's father, Vizier Hecataeus, Isidor had understood her duty to the Pharaoh Horwenefer and never once made her feel guilty or ashamed for her work. Yet on that night, she'd caught Isidor weaving his Ka into their bliss energetically, trying to access the king. For what purpose? Why would he do such a dangerous thing as to attempt energetic magic against the pharaoh during Anit-Shadya? He had to know she'd notice the action. Yet a year later, he still hadn't explained himself, and rather than approach Isidor face-to-face, Neferu-ankh-maat decided to go inside his realm herself and discover his plan.

Isidor ripped the gag from his victim and forced the Greek child to take a drink from a goblet. The boy quieted and fell limp under the ropes. Isidor turned to the other men—eleven in total—and raised his arms to the vaulted ceiling.

"My brothers," he began. "Welcome to Behdet, your new home. You met in Memphis as children and classmates under Metakryon, and suffered together at the hands of Philopater, the defiler. Through years of study, you have become powerful men. Chanax has trained you in the dark arts, and now the time has come for you to do the great work of winning this war." He took a place in the circle and raised his arms to the statue of Horus. "Memphis requests we eliminate Philopater, as his part in this story is over. I take it you hate him as much as Chanax does?"

The men murmured a resounding yes, and Isidor smiled. "Good, let us use your hate, together as a group, to end his life. Each of you has taken an oath to Set, the one and true god, and has passed the test. Together, you will eliminate the last Ptolemy to rule our lands, and you will inherit everlasting life."

The men bowed to Isidor and chanted in a slow, methodical tone, their voices quiet and yet intense and powerful. Neferu-ankh-maat watched the forms of hate and anger take shape between the men at the center of their circle. "See your hate," Isidor commanded, his smooth, deep voice resonating upon the stone walls. "Feel your desire for death. We shall take the beating heart and pierce it."

The other men continued to chant as Isidor left the circle and strode toward the altar, his back straight and shoulders down. He stood next to the sacrificial child and raised a dagger above his head. "Our Lord and Master Set, the god of power and life. Take our sacrifice. See how the knife penetrates this boy. May the hate in this room penetrate the heart of Ptolemy IV, Philopater the Defiler in the same way. Free our land from his grip and take Philopater unto everlasting death."

Isidor plunged the knife into the boy's heart and Neferu-ankh-maat flinched. She clutched her robe and fought against her limbs, which were begging her to flee the scene. She had to stay put. The chanting men were louder than her movements, and she remained hidden as Isidor killed the child on the altar and placed a goblet under the body to collect the blood as it poured forth from its victim.

Isidor raised the goblet over his head, the red, glowing firelight reflected in his gaze.

"Lord Set, god of chaos, bless this blood with the power of manifestation." He returned to the circle and took his place among the other men. He drank from the cup and passed it to Chanax, who repeated the action and passed it on. As the goblet made its way around the circle, Isidor guided the men in their hateful meditation.

"See Philopater in your mind's eye, and make his heart seize. Send your hate along your Ka, the ether of life, to he who deserves to die. Let it engulf him in misery."

The men continued to chant and sway. Beads of sweat glistened on Isidor's bald head. He raised his arms high and continued to call out for Ptolemy IV's death over and over.

"Yes," Chanax cried out louder than the others. "Die, Philopater, and rot in agony until the end of time."

The other men cursed the pharaoh in a similar way. They held hands and continued, their chanting and calls approaching a frenzy. As their madness crested its zenith, Isidor's voice boomed out across the hall, "It is finished. Our Lord Set has taken our offering and delivered death unto the man. He will die before our Ra rises from his journey in the night."

The other men dropped their hoods and, in the firelight, Neferu-ankh-maat could see their faces. She didn't recognize any of them, with the exception of Chanax. Each of them looked exhausted, yet they twitched, as if unable to be still, as they gazed upon their leader.

"You come from the north and the south, from every nome in the kingdom," Isidor said. "Pharaoh Horwenefer has given me permission to employ you under my tutelage, as his Invisible Hands. We will eliminate problems for him, like Philopater, as well as spy on the Greek troops and aid him in battle. Together we will create the conditions needed to help him win the war. My home is your home, and if you need anything, please let me know."

"Thank you, Lord Isidor," they replied in unison.

"Now, take some rest. In the morning we will begin working on astrally traveling together to the battlefield. The sword isn't the only weapon in war."

The Invisible Hands bowed and gave their thanks before leaving Isidor alone in the temple. Neferu-ankh-maat watched as he called a servant to take the body from the altar. "Throw him in the burn pile," he said, his face stoic, as if drinking the blood of children was commonplace.

Neferu-ankh-maat felt weak. She'd discovered the truth he'd been hiding, and she wasn't sure she had the strength to face it. Yet she couldn't let him walk away. He had to know she'd caught him. She called on the goddess Isis for strength and took a step forward and into the light.

"Murdering Greek children is the way of Set, is it?" she said, her accusing voice shrill in the empty temple.

Isidor stopped in his tracks and turned to see his accuser. She dropped the hood of her brown robe and revealed herself.

"Now I see what it is you hide from me, in the depths of your heart and mind," she said, her throat tight, glaring at the man she'd once trusted with her life. "This magic will lead us to ruin."

"No," he said, slapping the air with his open hand as if it were her face, as he strode toward her, his robes flowing around his ankles. "You're wrong. You think your magic can lead Egypt to victory? Think again. Chaos will overcome chaos."

Neferu-ankh-maat clenched her fists. "Only love can eliminate chaos."

"Childish dreams," he growled as he stormed closer. She shrank back as his shadow covered her. "You've never understood what is needed here. War is the province of men. How dare you consider its solution?"

Neferu-ankh-maat stood taller and saw him as if for the first time—the anger and malice he'd been hiding from her for years was now apparent. She'd been a fool, and yet her path forward had never been clearer. "You and your circle of Invisible Hands will have no access to the temple of Isis. Is this clear?"

"Are you severing our bond, Neferu-ankh-maat?" he challenged.

"You are unworthy of my embrace."

His mouth twisted, and his eyes glittered like an adder about to strike. "You can leave me, but you will not deny my men their right to a priestess."

"Yes, I will."

"You'd take Alexa from Chanax, a man she's loved since she was a child?"

Neferu-ankh-maat considered what he was saying. It would be wrong to force her priestess, Alexa, to take a new companion. Perhaps her loving arms might be the grace that would keep Chanax from becoming a menace.

Yet if she, the high priestess, hadn't been able to save Isidor from Set's darkness, how could Alexa, barely a woman herself, save Chanax?

The high priestess pursed her lips together and raised her head. "Chanax may remain with Alexa, but none of your other Invisible Hands will be given a spiritual companion. Do I make myself clear?"

Isidor looked down at her from beneath his blood-red hood, his face sallow and flickering under the torchlight of the temple. "Of course, my lady, if I wanted, I could go to the queen and have your desire overturned."

"You wouldn't dare." Neferu-ankh-maat glared at Isidor, and her skin prickled as if she were engulfed in flames. How could he betray her in this way? What had corrupted him?

It mattered not. She couldn't save him. The road he'd

chosen was the road of destruction for Egypt, of this she was sure. She turned and fled from the temple, holding back her tears until the moment she entered her own chambers, shutting Isidor out from her heart and her life, forever.

4

Homecoming

After his father's sudden and unexplained death in 204 BCE, Ptolemy V Epiphanes inherited the throne at the age of five, under the control of his father's regents. By the time he was seven, he would consent to the deaths of not only his mother, but also the regents themselves. Is it any wonder he grew to be a cruel man?

Behdet, Egypt 204 BCE

Natasa stood next to her mother in the royal gardens. Helena struggled in her arms to be put down so she could run and play. Perhaps it had been foolish to bring a toddler to the event? Her chest swelled, as if the sun were glowing beneath her breast. Any moment Ankhmakis and the rest of the army would arrive after being away far too many seasons. She longed to be near him, to know that he was whole and safe. Ever since news of Philopater's death had reached Behdet, she'd been anxious. The war for the throne was now one between man and child, for Philopater's son was just a boy. The timing was perfect for Pharaoh Horwenefer to sack Memphis and take the northern crown while Epiphanes was still young.

Unfortunately, the Inundation had been abundant, the skies pouring rains as if there was no end to Isis's tears. Good for the crops, but not for the moving of troops. Horwenefer sent small groups of men, disguised as merchants, into the north to gather information and assassinate key administrative officials, but the rest of his army remained in Panopolis, waiting until Perit, the planting season, to continue fighting. While frustrating for their mission, the flooding of the Nile gave the pharaoh of Upper Egypt a chance to return to Behdet to greet his people and the court for the first time since launching the war.

Natasa looked to the sky grateful that at the moment, it was clear and sunny. A good omen for the greeting of their king. She swatted away a fly buzzing in her daughter's ear and felt a sudden chill when she caught sight of Weret, Ankhmakis's wife, standing on the dais beside the rest of the royal family. The princess's jewels sparkled in the sunlight as she glared at Helena, her fists clenched at her sides. Natasa gripped her toddler even tighter and allowed her gaze to travel to Weret's flat stomach placed between Bithiah, who held her own daughter above her very pregnant belly, and Ruia, holding her second child, a small boy of one, close to her chest. Ankhmakis's seed hadn't done the job before he'd left for war. Natasa knew what this meant—Weret would demand his time as often as possible.

Temple women plucked their harps and several horns sounded as the watchman called out, "King Horwenefer, Pharaoh of Upper Egypt and beloved of Amon-Re, has arrived."

The dusty streets were thronged with Egyptians placing palm leaves and lotus flowers before their pharaoh as he rode past them upon his great horse. Natasa caught her breath when he entered the garden. Pharaoh Horwenefer glowed like the sun. His pale blue crown sat upon his head, the golden Ureaus snake above his brown hair shone in the sunlight, and a long golden cape depicting the Ibis flowed from his shoulders and across the back of his horse. In his hands he held the hook and flail, given to the pharaoh by the priests of Thebes. Natasa felt the hair on her arms rise as he rode into the courtyard and the people cheered. She looked to her father, who stepped forward and bowed to his lord and master.

"Pharaoh Horwenefer," Hecataeus said as the king dismounted from his horse. "Your beloved City of Behdet welcomes you and congratulates you on your victories. Long live Egypt's finest king."

The crowd roared, and Natasa found herself wanting to clap, yet she held Helena, still squirming in her grasp. Pharaoh Horwenefer strode to the dais and handed his hook and flail to Hecataeus, who took them, and the king bowed once more to his people before approaching the queen.

High Queen Keket stepped forward as two more horses entered the garden, ushering in the princes, Ankhmakis and Silus. Natasa's heart soared, and she didn't even hear what Keket was saying. Her lover scanned the crowd before his passionate gaze fell upon hers. Natasa's insides ached as she recalled his touch. She swooned under his gaze, biting her lip to keep from crying out. It had been excruciating to be separated from him for so long. Now he was near, and she longed to caress him and draw him into her embrace. The air fled from her lungs, and she couldn't breathe—she was drunk in her desire.

Ankhmakis followed his older brother to stand beside their father and receive his mother's welcome before turning to his wife and kissing her on the cheek.

"Behold my family," Horwenefer said, his shoulders back, jaw tilted up toward the sun. "Behold your beautiful city. Behdet is no longer under Greek control. We have secured the Upper Kingdom from Aswan to Abdju, and when the river recedes, we will continue our fight northward. We will not stop until we sack Alexandria and the entire country is under one Egyptian pharaoh."

The crowd cheered again at his words.

Music filled the courtyard and the royals entered their palace. The crowd followed to greet the pharaoh and his princes in the throne room before retiring to a long meal. Natasa walked behind her mother, grateful for the blessed shade of the palace as they entered the great room where their new pharaoh held court. She walked toward the men, her chin held high and heart pounding more with each step. At the end of the hall stood Ankhmakis, handsome in his crown and collar, his sword no longer bloodied but shining in the loving light of Ra pouring through the open windows. As she and her mother approached, Ankhmakis stepped away from Weret's side and against protocol grabbed Natasa and Helena and hugged them close.

"My love," he said, his voice thick in her ear. "I've been gone far too long, and now I can feel you. I can touch you. How sweet it is."

For a moment, the noise and people in the room had vanished, and only the two of them and their child remained. Natasa's pulse raced as he kissed her lips. He took Helena from her arms and lifted her above his head.

"Is this my baby?" he cried. "How can this be? She's huge. Does she walk? Can she talk? How long have we been away?"

Helena struggled in his arms, for he was a stranger after

being gone so long. She turned to Natasa, arms outstretched and crying, "Mama."

"She can talk," Ankhmakis laughed, handing her back.

Natasa heard her mother clear her throat, and the world around them returned in all its harshness. Neferu-ankh-maat placed her arm on Ankhmakis's shoulder, reminding him of his error. The pharaoh, too, looked at his son, a warning in his gaze; Silus was smirking; the princesses were horrified; and Chanax gazed at the ceiling. The queen's look scared Natasa the most—her red, painted lips drawn tight. Her eyes narrowed as she stared down her nose at her middle son.

"Ankhmakis," Queen Keket admonished, "there are others to greet. Mind your place."

He stepped back into the receiving line and the high priestess stepped forward, drawing attention to herself instead.

"Pharaoh Horwenefer," Neferu-ankh-maat said, pressing her palms together in prayer and lowering her gaze to the floor. "You have returned to us, stronger than ever. The gods and goddesses have blessed your pursuit to free Egypt from the hands of the Ptolemys."

"Thank you for your prayers and service, my dear priestesses," the pharaoh answered. "It's good to see both of you."

Natasa and her mother bowed, and Horwenefer touched them on their heads and gave them a blessing. When he was finished, he placed his hands upon Helena's head as well, and they took their place to the side with the other priestesses.

"Why did you let him make a fool of himself?" Neferu-ankh-maat chastised.

"I'm not in control of him," Natasa retorted. She was tired of her mother disdaining her love for Ankhmakis.

"Because you're not in control of yourself."

"What?"

"Men are weak," Neferu-ankh-maat continued. "Their pride and passions control them. If you want him to be proper in court, you must send him a message to behave before you enter the room. Remind him of his place."

"I've missed him so much," Natasa argued.

"It matters not. You must remain neutral in public and remind him to behave through the connection you have. If you're neutral, he's neutral. Save your lust for the night when he's sure to call upon you, or in ceremony, which he must request. Goddess knows the men need her gentle touch after a year of killing. For your safety, you must get him to behave in front of his mother and sister-wife. They hold the keys to your future."

"Mother, you sound so dire," Natasa answered, frowning at her ominous words. "Is there something I don't know?"

"I fear I no longer hold power over the priests," the high priestess said in a low voice. "Which means I no longer hold power over the queen in Horwenefer's absence. I know you hate to hear this, daughter, but your number one goal for the next three months is not to reunite with Ankhmakis. It's to make sure he gets Weret with child."

Natasa held Helena closer. It stung to think of Ankhmakis in Weret's arms, but her mother was correct. Weret would pose less of a threat if she had a baby of her own.

"I understand, Mother. I will encourage him to do his duty."

"It will take more than lecturing. You must also believe in their child and desire a pregnancy as well. Ankhmakis is very influenced by you. More than you realize," Neferu-ankh-maat said. "I say this because I love you. Oh, how I wish Ruia were

Ankhmakis's wife. Everything would be simpler."

Natasa eyed the royal family as they greeted the nobles from the south as well as the people of Behdet. Indeed, of all of them, Ruia was the one who shined the most. Even though she held a heavy baby, she curtsied and smiled and gave each person her attention as they passed her. Ruia was worthy of her station. The rest, including Ankhmakis, were forever scheming against one another.

A line had formed from the great room, through the halls, out the garden, and into the streets. Everyone in the city wanted the pharaoh's blessing, for to be touched by Horwenefer was to be touched by a god. It was going to be a long day.

5

No Man's Land

"Come, let me describe to you the ills of the soldier…"
~ Papyrus Lansing, late New Kingdom

Behdet, Egypt 204 BCE

Hours later, Ankhmakis stood alone in the stable as everyone else in the city slept, exhausted from the morning's festivities as well as the heat. Ra was at his peak, and most of the court was resting. Ankhmakis should have retired to his wife, but he couldn't yet face her. Her questions, demands, and scorn would hurt too much. His feelings were raw and exposed. Off the battlefield, the totality of the past year had begun to sink in. The scent of blood and death filled his nose. His skin burned from it. No amount of washing could make it go away. When killing on the battlefield he'd felt alive, but was now nervous, anxious, and alone. Weret's company would amplify the wounds taking root deep within him. He needed to ground himself back into courtly life before facing her.

In his raw and fragile state, there was only one person he could be near, only one who wouldn't hurt him.

"My lord," Min said as he entered the barn, hot on the heels of Natasa, who was running across the stable toward him, "I fetched the Lady Natasa, as you requested."

As she approached him, time stood still. Her long dark hair hung around her shoulders. She was no longer dressed in her finest, but instead wore a simple, pale linen robe and the golden ring bearing his signet shone bright upon her finger. His heart danced a jig. His skin no longer burned of blood and death but felt clean and light. They were drawn to each other, and after too many seasons apart, they collapsed into a passionate embrace. Ankhmakis took her into his arms and kissed her, searching her soul for traces of his own. She threw her arms around his neck and squeezed him even closer. They continued this way until Ankhmakis felt whole again—her kiss reminding him of who he was—not a prince or a general, but Ankhmakis, lover of Natasa.

Min cleared his throat, breaking the spell. "My lord, would you like me to give the two of you privacy?"

"Min," Ankhmakis answered as he nuzzled Natasa's warm neck, kissing and biting her, causing her to giggle. "I forgot you were still here. You may take your leave."

Min sprinted away and they were alone in the barn.

"We seem to have a habit of rolling in the hay," Natasa said as she shoved him into a pile of the golden-colored grass and lifted up his loincloth.

"Natasa," he groaned as she straddled him, thrusting him inside of her and riding him like a cavalryman on his way into battle.

"Hush," she whispered into his ear, "let me remember you."

Time stood still, or perhaps opened up in all directions. They tumbled to the floor and rolled about without a care in the world, moaning and calling out one another's name. Any one of the stable hands asleep in their quarters was sure to have been awakened, but neither of them cared. Ankhmakis's bliss came in waves, and he beheld Natasa in wonder. His men spoke of sex and often sought out captured women or the local whores after taking a city, but Ankhmakis no longer desired time in a concubine's arms. Natasa was the only woman he wanted. Her touch was salve to his soul. Their pleasure had become an elixir of strength. No other arms could compare. He was as helpless as a fig leaf upon the evening breeze when inside her and yet, at the same time, as powerful as the storm wind itself.

When she'd finished climaxing, Natasa remained astride him for a moment longer, smiling as tears poured down her cheeks. "My love," she cried, "how I feared I would never feel you inside me again, never kiss your lips, or hear the sound of your deep, sweet voice. Your safe return is the greatest of gifts the goddess has ever granted me."

She leaned in to kiss him before sliding from him and standing up, holding out her hand. He took it and stood as well, dusting the hay from his hair and back.

"Nothing could keep me from you, not even war," he said as he brushed her hair behind her ear. "You're my only reason to return to Behdet." She quieted for a moment, and a vision of Weret flashed before him as he read her mind. Their one-to-one communication had grown strong in his absence. His face darkened. "I know what you're thinking."

"Yes, my love," she said, lowering her gaze. "You know how important it is—"

"Don't speak of it," he commanded. "We've discussed it in the past. I will tend to her, I promise."

"I want you to know I will love the children the two of you

have together," she replied, taking his hands in hers. "They will be a part of our family. Your blood is our blood, and I promise to cherish the children who must be born unto Weret sooner than later."

Ankhmakis stood in silence, his heart heavy. In the past this would have made him angry—Natasa was too willing to share him. He recalled what she'd said before he'd left for war and smiled.

"I am you, not yours," he said as he stepped toward her and took her face into his hands.

"And you are me, not mine," she replied.

He kissed her, allowing himself the pleasure of being lost in her essence. He was no longer in Egypt, but in the world of light. The world beyond the world. He drew away and smiled at her beaming face.

"Come, ride with me."

"Where?" she asked.

"To the west."

"Out to the desert? Oh, Ankhmakis, I don't know."

"I know it scares you, but I must ride out and experience its great invincibility, and I don't want to leave your side yet."

She nodded, though she still seemed apprehensive, and Ankhmakis helped her up on top of his horse, Biriq. He took his place in front of her on the saddle cloth. He squeezed his heels, and Biriq trotted out of the stall. The sun was glaring after the dark of the stable, and Natasa wrapped her arms tighter around his torso, her breasts hard against his back. He leaned into her embrace, his body tightening as the vision of her naked body flooded his imagination.

"Hold on tight," he warned as he kicked Biriq, and the horse took off at a canter.

Dust stirred behind them as they made their way past the

amphitheater toward the royal road leading from the city. The city gates were open, and Ankhmakis made his way forward, their speed ever increasing. The wind blew his hair from his face, and he breathed in the pure glory of the ride. They flew past the temples of Isis and Horus and out beyond the masons's dwellings. Farther on they rode until they passed the last of the houses and fields flooded with the life-giving water of the Nile. Birds floated in the pools made by the farmers, delighting in their newfound lakes and eating the unlucky fish that'd been swept up in the rains.

Onward they continued until the road ended, the fields had vanished, and nothing but sand stretched in every direction. The sun beat down upon the golden ocean. To ride west of Behdet was to go to No Man's land—to leave civilization behind. Ankhmakis loved it. He sensed Natasa's fear and sent her confidence and love.

"*Trust me*," he said with his heart.

"*Always.*"

Conversing within their energy field was immediate, as if they already knew the other's answer before the words were spoken. To be in total communion this way was to love beyond words. No matter how hard he tried, Ankhmakis couldn't write a song to do it justice.

He rode the horse this way for at least an hour, knowing the exact location in which to stop. He tugged the reins and fought Biriq's need to continue to run. He turned the brilliant, white horse back toward the way they'd come, the beast's footprints fading under the glare of the sun into the distance.

"My goodness." Natasa gasped as she peeked around his shoulder. "What happened? Where's the city?"

"Somewhere out there," he answered. "We can no longer see it."

"How will we find our way home?" she cried.

"Don't panic. I know what I'm doing. I often ride out to the desert."

"Ankhmakis," she replied, gripping his waist even tighter, "this isn't natural. A sandstorm could come upon us, or we could get lost and never find our way home."

"There's no wind, thus no storm," he answered. "Besides, what if we did get lost? Would it be horrible to fade away into the distance?"

"What do you mean?"

"Why do you think I ride to the west?"

Natasa didn't answer.

Ankhmakis raised his arms to the vast sandscape. "I do it to escape. Out here, I'm outside of time. No one can find me, and no one knows my face. This is the land of freedom, where I can rage, or cry, or sit astride my horse and let my thoughts run away without interruption. The sand has no care for me. The desert herself could swallow me whole and no one would ever find me again. Out here, on the edge of death, I'm alive. I feel this way in your arms, but the desert freedom is different. When I make love to you, I'm home. When I'm out here, there's a risk I'll never come back home. I cherish this risk.

"I've changed, Natasa. I'm no longer a prince of Behdet, but a general of the Egyptian Rebellion. I control thousands of men, and every day of my life has been spent in preparation for this moment. I now know I was born for one reason and one reason alone—to kill."

"Don't say such things," his lover cried.

"It's true, Natasa," he said, his voice beginning to crack. "To have been given to you as a spiritual companion is the only love I've ever known. Everything else has been about war and death. Now the time of battle has arrived, and my entire existence means destruction for thousands. I've killed and maimed so many men and women—children even—I've lost count. Their blood cloaks my dreams and their cries haunt my waking hours. There's nothing between us as my sword cuts them down, and I feel their terror within my heart."

Natasa rested her head upon his shoulder and Ankhmakis felt a hole rip through his soul and open itself to the heavens. His head dropped to his hands. His body shook as the tears poured out of him. Natasa kissed his shoulders and his neck, but he refused to turn around and face her. Instead he hugged himself as she hugged him from behind.

"The slaughter isn't even the worst part," he sobbed, feeling the pain in the back of his throat grow as he recalled the hundreds of men he had killed. "Each time I kill, a part of me enjoys it. To swing the sword and take off a man's arm, or throw an axe and meet your mark, or drive a dozen arrows into your foe—this is a great power and I feel alive in it. I thrive on it in battle. I glory in it."

Natasa shuddered.

"I know you've felt my pleasure as I kill," he continued, the tears now too many to stop. "You withdraw in battle and no longer stay at my side."

"I'm sorry, it's hard for me to endure," she whispered. "I'll try harder to remain by your side."

"No. Don't. I *know* it hurts you to see such violence, and worse to see me delight in it. What sort of a monster have I become? I fear war will end me as I know it, and I'll be lost to it and thus lost to you." She gripped him harder but didn't speak, which made him feel even worse. "I'm ashamed."

"Don't be ashamed," she said as she ran her hands through his hair and massaged his neck and shoulders. "Nothing can make me stop loving you."

"How can you love a man who enjoys such things as murder?"

"Because I can't live without your love. You do what you have to do, and I will do my part. Who knows, perhaps my love will be the light that keeps you whole?"

"I would lose my humanity without you," he admitted. His tears faded. He was empty, yet less vulnerable.

"I admire you, Ankhmakis, and if you lose your light, I will remember it for you. I promise."

He turned, and they sat face-to-face on Biriq's back. Ra descended on the horizon and a cooler breeze danced upon the air. Ankmakis took Natasa's hands in his and smiled. "What did I do to deserve this love?"

"You were born." She smiled back.

He kissed her, breathed in her scent, and sighed. "To be here is bliss," he crooned. He brushed her hair out of her face and gazed into her unusual green eyes. "Truth, beauty, and goodness. This is your way."

He turned from her and kicked Biriq into action. The time had come to ride back to the city, but Ankhmakis had no desire to go and face the court. His season of rest from the battle would be filled with meetings and fortifying Behdet as the center of military operations, as well as the chief medical facility. His father might love Thebes, but he refused to relocate the court there. Thebes was too close to the battle lines. Better to keep his healers, priests, princesses, and their young children out of harm's way. In addition, troops from Nubia and Ethiopia were starting to cross the southern borders to aid them in their quest. Behdet was the perfect central location to train the soldiers before sending them northward to fight. A steady flow of militia men up the Nile from the south meant hours of work preparing their living and training quarters as well as food distribution. Ankhmakis would solve this puzzle, as well as many other logistical problems, as he waited for the Nile to retreat.

Worst of all was his duty to Weret. He forced himself to desire her and see her as worthy of his time. He'd made a promise to Natasa and had to keep it. A pregnant Weret meant safety for her and Helena. The city loomed ahead, and Ankhmakis felt Natasa's relief, but he himself felt dread.

At least he had his nights to himself—hours in Natasa's embrace would be his saving grace. They rode through the town and to the stables. He dismounted and helped Natasa down. She hugged him and smiled.

"Much to my surprise, riding to the desert was wonderful," she admitted. "Please, let's do it again before you leave."

"Of course." He grinned. "As long as you spend your nights in my bed, I will do anything you ask."

"There's nothing I'd love more," she said, the color in her cheeks rising. Ankhmakis felt his own desire rise and an ache build within his groin.

"I must go," she continued. "I'm dancing at the feast, and I need to prepare."

"Yes," he replied, gulping down his need. "What a joy it will be to see you dance again. I'll send Min for you as soon as I can manage to be dismissed this evening."

"I look forward to it, my lord."

He kissed her before letting her go. The stable hands were returning to work and their time alone had ended. As his beloved walked away, Ankhmakis patted Biriq on the back and knew what he had to do next.

"Sebastos," he called out to the stable master. "Brush Biriq down and water him. I have duties to attend to."

"Yes, my lord," Sebastos replied, handing the job over to

a passing stable boy.

Ankhmakis made his way to his chambers. He would bathe, and he would go to Weret.

He had no choice—which made him all the more resentful.

6

A Sister's Pain

"The only active force that arises out of possession is fear of losing the object of possession."
~ Ancient Egyptian Proverb from the temples at Luxor

Three months later, end of the season of Akhet, Behdet Egypt 203 BCE

Weret paced her quarters and glared out the window at beloved Ra, watching the sun god crawl across the sky. Picking up a hand-held plate of gold, polished to show her reflection, she gazed upon herself, noting her soft, rich brown skin, high cheekbones, full, red-painted lips, and eyelids decorated in lapis and lined in kohl. Everyone said she was the most beautiful woman in the kingdom, but what good was her beauty if no one even noticed her existence? Her father noticed her not, so busy was he with his vengeance against the Greeks. Certainly not her half-mother, who had long been more interested in pleasing the priests than caring for the offspring in her charge, nor her sisters, who were busy raising their children. Worst of all, her own husband didn't care enough to be on time for their scheduled mid-afternoon visit.

She plunked herself down on the settee, adjusting her golden arm bands as she did so, cursing the man as her servants fanned her with large palm leaves. Moments later, Ankhmakis burst into her room—dirty, covered in sweat, and panting as if he'd run the whole way to her chambers.

"You're late," she complained as her servants left the room, closing the door behind them. She had food and wine on a small table, flowers in the vases, and jasmine burning in bowls. Yet as he crossed the room to sit upon her bed, it appeared he didn't notice these feminine touches.

"I know, I know," he muttered, distracted as usual, as he removed his dirty sandals from his feet and the sword from his waist. "It's been an intense day. Six hundred men arrived from Aswan today. Twice as many as expected, and thousands more from Kush are on their way. Even with the preparations I've made the past months, we're not going to keep up. They'll be sleeping in the streets. Who's to train them when I leave for Abdju in a few days?" He stood and looked at her. "Do you have a basin? I need to wash up a bit. I've been in the ring with too many men today to count."

Weret pouted, the golden disks on her headpiece clinking as she shook her head. "How dare you be late?"

"What?" he cried. "I got here as soon as I could. What's wrong with you?"

"You've been home three months, correct?" she continued. "Tell me, husband, how much time have you spent with me?"

"I've come here every day at high sun to take rest," he replied through gritted teeth. "Never once have I missed our appointment."

"Oh, Ankhmakis," Weret replied, her lower lip now trembling as she fought her tears. "Why am I an appointment?"

"My entire life is an appointment," he answered, his

handsome face emotionless, making his way to the wash bin and dipping his hands in the ceramic bowl to wash his face. "I'm sure you can see we're at war."

"War has been your excuse since the beginning."

"War is the reason we were married, remember?" He turned, scowling. "What more do you want from me? I've tried very hard to get you pregnant. I thought my efforts would make you happy."

"I want you to spend time with me," she whined, wiping her eyes carefully, so that her eyeliner wouldn't smear. "To take meals together and tell me about your day. I want you to stay after we have sex and hold me. I want you to let me spend the night in your chambers—"

"Enough."

She choked back her tears and looked away, fearing his disdain would lead to harsher words. Ankhmakis was known for his sharp tongue. However, instead of yelling at her, he walked to his things and sat down on the settee to put his sandals back on.

"What are you doing?" Weret ran across the room and threw herself at his feet, grabbing him at the knees. "Don't go, Ankhmakis," she begged. "I'm sorry. Please don't leave."

"Let go of me," he replied. "We're done here."

"Please, I'm not asking for much. You find plenty of time for your whore. How dare you get angry with me for my request? I'm your wife."

Ankhmakis rose and shoved her away from his legs, onto the floor.

"How dare you call her my whore?" he yelled, cracking his neck from side to side, his jaw clenched so tight she could see cords along his neck.

"Oh," Weret said, struggling with her skirt as she made

to stand. "See how you protect her? You claim to be spending time among the men, but I know what you do when you're not in the ring. You ride out with your whore to the west. Natasa spends every night in your chambers, and you still find time to make love to her on Father's boat during the day when you should be using your spare time for me."

"How do you know these things?" he asked, raising his chin and crossing his muscular arms over his bare chest.

"I have spies everywhere, dear husband," she said in a low, threatening voice.

He shrugged. "It matters not if you know of my life. Yes, my spiritual companion and I take ceremony. Our bond is what gives me my strength. I may die on the battlefield and never see her again."

"What about me?" Weret said, her stomach churning as her breath quickened. This wasn't going the way she'd planned. "You might never see me again either."

"Why would I care?" he answered with a toss of his head. "You need to understand something, Weret—I don't need to see you."

"Yes, you do," she exclaimed. "You need me to bear your children. Without an heir you will not take the throne. Would you deny becoming the pharaoh of Egypt because you love your whore more than me?"

Ankhmakis grabbed her and forced her against the wall, his face mere inches from hers. For the first time, Weret feared for her life. "You misunderstand my disdain for you, dear sister. Even if Natasa were dead, I would still refuse your bed and seek instead my comfort from the concubines." He leaned in closer, and her heart pounded against her breast. Her mouth tasted dry. "I've slept with you against my wishes every day this past season. If a child doesn't take, it's not me who has the problem. I've already made one child. Perhaps you're barren? It wouldn't surprise me."

"Ankhmakis, don't say such horrible things," she whined. "You need me to become pharaoh."

"You misunderstand the situation, dear sister. I don't need you. Father doesn't command these lands because of his sons. He commands Upper Egypt because of his army. In the age of war, it is the man who controls the army who wears the crown, and make no mistake about it, Weret, I am the man who controls this army."

He released her and crossed the room to get his sword, scowling as he tugged the scabbard belt tight around his thin, muscular waist. "I will return to the battlefield within the week, but don't expect to see me again for the remainder of my stay in Behdet."

He crossed the room and left, slamming the door behind him. Weret fell to the floor in hysterics, her body rocking as she cried and sobbed. How dare he say these things? How dare he treat her this way? She made to stand but found she couldn't. Her legs were weak, and the room spun as her vision turned dark. Her servants entered the room, asking her what to do. They stood at attention, awaiting her command, yet she was unable to speak as she choked on her tears.

Two of her servants helped her to the bed and another offered her some water, but nothing helped. Her lungs filled with air, and yet she couldn't get enough. Her chest ached as if bound in tight chains. The room continued spinning as terrifying thoughts took over Weret's mind. What if her husband never spoke to her again? Would she die childless, unloved, locked away forever in the lonely cage of servitude to a man incapable of caring?

"Weret," a voice called out. Through her tears, Bithiah's

face appeared above her. "Hush," Bithiah said, the single word enough to break through the fog of terror in Weret's mind.

Her thoughts quieted, and air once more flowed through her lungs. "Bithiah," she groaned. "Sister. It's good to see you."

Bithiah sat on the edge of the bed and handed her a cup of tea. "Here, drink this." Weret grasped the cup from her sister's hand and sipped the hot, bitter liquid. Bithiah clenched and unclenched her hands. "Are you okay?"

"Isn't it apparent I'm not?" Weret answered.

"What happened?"

Weret took a gulp from the earthen mug and felt the tears begin to form again. "Ankhmakis," she sobbed. "He's a horrible husband."

"Yes," Bithiah agreed. "I'm sorry, sister, but you got the worst of them."

"What?" Weret cried. How could Bithiah, the wife of a priest, say such a thing? "You know how the men speak. They think Ankhmakis will be the one to succeed Father. I could be high queen of Egypt someday."

Bithiah raised an eyebrow and folded her hands on top of her huge, pregnant stomach. Weret felt a chill pass through her. "Not without an heir," Bithiah said, her voice soft and mesmerizing. "Silus has two sons. Chanax and Alexa have one son and another of his is on the way any day now. My husband may be a priest, but he's still an heir to the throne."

Bithiah patted her swollen tummy, and Weret felt the panic begin to rise within her once more. "The problem is," Bithiah continued, "you can't keep him in line because you care too much."

"What do you mean? Don't you care for Chanax?"

Bithiah waved her hand in a dismissive gesture, as if swatting away a gnat. "Not a bit. I spend time with him because he teaches me things. I don't care if he loves me, but he has knowledge I need, which is good enough for me."

"But," Weret argued, "what if he loves Alexa more than you?"

"I'm not sure he's capable of love. Chanax is cold, sister, not the type of man a woman can desire. He can love his companion more than I, as long as I get my children and..." Bithiah stopped talking for a moment, her gaze unfocused, before continuing, "Ruia doesn't care either. Silus spends every night with a different woman. Ruia prefers to sleep in her own chambers without the hassle of his snoring. You, sister, your vanity will be the end of you."

Bithiah paused for a moment before gasping as if startled by some revelation. She stared down at Weret, one eyebrow raised and lips pursed. "Why doesn't Ankhmakis care about your lack of pregnancy?"

Weret shrugged. "Because he loves Natasa."

"No." Bithiah shook her head. "His love for her is great and dramatic, but he's too smart to let romance keep him from making you pregnant."

"Oh, but this is what made me upset. He said in times of war, it's not an heir who makes the king, but the army. As general, he's the one who controls the army, so he's going to take the Upper Kingdom from Father."

"Did he say he was going to take it from Father?" Bithiah said, flinching away from Weret, her eyes wide.

"Well," Weret said, hesitating for a moment. She'd been so angry, the entire conversation was now blurry. "I thought he did, but now I'm not sure."

"Before or after Father dies?" Bithiah probed.

"Does it matter?"

"Of course, it does. If he plans on taking it from Father

while he still breathes, it's treason."

Weret's breaths constricted again, and her pulse quickened. Bithiah grabbed her arm and stared at her.

"Yes," Weret said, her voice now a whisper. "He plans to take it while Father still lives."

"We must tell Father," her sister encouraged.

"No." She imagined how angry Ankhmakis would be and her head began to pound.

"Weret," Bithiah continued. "We must tell him. Ankhmakis has been nothing but cruel to you. He must be taught a lesson."

"What will happen to me?"

"Oh, Weret," Bithiah exclaimed. "Father won't punish you. He'll punish Ankhmakis."

"Without Ankhmakis, I'm nothing in the court."

"Nonsense," Bithiah replied. "He won't kill Ankhmakis. He needs him too much. True, he might take away his title and force him into servitude, but you'd be free to be a healer. Not so horrible, is it?"

As Weret considered her sister's words, she saw herself as Iu-Amon's faithful servant, free of the burden of bearing an heir to such a spoiled man and a power surged through her.

"If we don't tell Father," Bithiah continued, "the kingdom is at risk. He must know of Ankhmakis's treachery."

The mere sound of her husband's name made her jaw clench. How dare he treat her the way he did? The time had come to face the idiot and put him in his place. "Yes, we must tell Father. You'll come with me, won't you?"

"Of course, dear sister," Bithiah answered, voice honeyed and calm. "The men are gathered in counsel right now, a perfect place to make Father aware of Ankhmakis's plans."

Weret's confidence faded for a moment, but Bithiah patted her hand. "You can do this," she whispered. "I'll be right by your side."

Weret rose from the bed and forced a smile. "Yes, let's go. But first, let me refresh my makeup."

7

Power Play

"You are worse than the goose of the shore that is busy with mischief. It spends the summer destroying the dates, the winter destroying the seed grain. It spends the balance of the year in pursuit of the cultivators. It does not let seed be cast to the ground without snatching it.... One cannot catch it by snaring. One does not offer it in the temple. The evil, shape-eyed bird that does no work!"

~ Papyrus Lansing, late New Kingdom

Behdet, Egypt 203 BCE

Chanax entered the war room and made his way to Isidor, who stood next to Pharaoh Horwenefer. He bowed to his father, noting the slight changes in his demeanor—the lines on his forehead and around his eyes, his jaundiced skin, the stiffness in his shoulders, and the slight limp he now exhibited. It appeared Isidor's spell was beginning to take its toll on the body of a man whom most had considered immortal. Horwenefer's youth and vitality were legendary. Yet given Isidor's hold over him, it was merely a matter of time before the man, now nearing forty years, fell down and never got up again.

Of course, timing was everything. Isidor couldn't let the pharaoh die until his army took Memphis, and the war was taking longer than they'd hoped. They needed more men.

Chanax nodded to Isidor and beckoned him closer.

"Yes?" Isidor asked as Chanax drew him aside out of earshot from the others in the room. He wanted the rest of the men to remain unaware of Bithiah's plans.

"Something serious is going happen, and I need your help," he said in his master's ear so the pharaoh, Hecataeus, and Ennaeus, who were already present, wouldn't hear.

"What?"

"Bithiah will be interrupting this meeting soon," he explained. "She'll have Weret. They've come to accuse Ankhmakis of treason."

"Impossible," Isidor replied, his voice too loud for Chanax's taste.

"Quiet, please," Chanax continued. He glanced at his father and was relieved to see him deep in conversation with the vizier. "They have reason and proof. There isn't time to explain, but if we work the others in the room in the correct manner, I think we can hurt Ankhmakis in a way we haven't before."

"I see," Isidor said, raising an eyebrow. "Since we can't breach his emotions ourselves, we use the others around him?"

"Yes, and make his life miserable," Chanax said, his mouth turning into a wide grin. "Stir up Father's anger and fear of Ankhmakis. You know he fears that the soldiers love Ankhmakis more than him. I'll take Silus. His outrage at injustice will be helpful, and Bithiah will work Weret."

"How does Bithiah know what to do?" Isidor asked.

"I'm sorry, Master," Chanax replied. "I know I didn't ask, but I've taught her how to attach a cord to other's emotions. Given how insecure the women are about their relationships with the men of the court, she's able to work the queen and Weret the way the Invisible Hands work our enemies. Trust me, it's been very helpful."

"The queen, you say?" Isidor pursed his lips. "Interesting." Ankhmakis and Silus entered the room. "We'll talk about this later."

They took their places around the large table as the pharaoh began the meeting. "Let's get this started. We ride out to war in a few days, and we need to wrap things up here in Behdet. Silus and Ankhmakis, report on the armies from Kush."

Chanax half listened to what was being said, instead focusing his thoughts on Bithiah. She and Weret were approaching and would soon interrupt the meeting. He strummed his fingers on the wooden table as he imagined the look on Ankhmakis's face when the deed was done.

"My lord, Pharaoh Horwenefer," a guard called out. "Your daughters request admittance to this meeting."

"Nonsense," Horwenefer replied, "this is a war counsel. I have no time for women's matters."

"Your Majesty," Isidor suggested, sitting up straight in his seat and clutching his hands upon the table, "they wouldn't be here unless they were bringing important news."

Chanax saw Isidor make the connection between their Kas and begin to feed the pharaoh the form of curiosity.

"They claim they have information critical to your campaign," the guard continued.

"Fine," the pharaoh said with a wave of his hand. "Let them in."

Weret and Bithiah crossed the room, and Ankhmakis gave them a dirty look. Chanax sent a surge of alarm toward Silus, who jerked to attention and took an interest in the women.

"What is it?" Horwenefer said. "Hurry, we haven't got all day."

"Father," Bithiah said as she stepped forward, dragging Weret toward the king, holding her sister's arm and making sure to never break contact. "Weret has something she needs to tell you."

Weret cowered in Bithiah's embrace when she looked into Ankhmakis's face. Bithiah sent the form of anger at her sister as a countermeasure, and Weret grew taller, faced her father, and spoke, her voice steady. "My lord, I've come to inform you of my husband's treason."

The room fell quiet. Hecataeus raised his eyebrows at the princess. Chanax attempted to energetically manipulate the man into silence, but there was no opening. The Greek's energy body was as thick as his skin.

"Weret, treason is a serious accusation," Hecataeus began.

"It's true," the young woman continued, her anger swirling around her like flames. "He told me today he no longer needs to mate with me because he doesn't need an heir."

"Weret," Ankhmakis demanded. "Silence yourself. Our marriage problems have nothing to do with war or treason."

"Been spending too much time with Natasa, eh?" Silus cut in, laughing. "Oh, how the princesses hate our spiritual companions. Jealous, jealous, jealous." He chuckled and poured his second glass of wine in minutes. The longer Chanax worked on him, the more the man drank. His alcoholism would be his undoing. Chanax would make sure of it.

"Enough, Silus," Horwenefer commanded. "Weret, I have to agree with your brothers. I have no patience for such things as women's insecurities."

"No, Father, this isn't about me," Weret said, her face flushed red. "He told me in times of war the one who controls the army controls of the kingdom, and he's the one who controls the army. He plans to use it against you, Father, I swear."

"I never said—" Ankhmakis began.

Chanax hit Silus with an energetic surge of outrage.

"You plan to kill our father and take the throne?" Silus accused, slamming his half full cup on the table. "How dare you?"

"Ankhmakis," Horwenefer shouted, now rising from his seat. Chanax saw Isidor pour anger into the room, infecting every Ka as it sank its tendrils deep into their emotions. "Is this true?"

Ankhmakis rose from his seat and faced his father. "I have no plans whatsoever to take the throne from you."

"You lie." Weret glared at him. "You told me you controlled the army."

"I would never touch my father," Ankhmakis yelled, and Chanax could see his brother's pride begin to swell.

"Why did you say you were the man who controls the army?" Weret snapped.

"Because he plans to use it to kill his brothers," Silus replied. "Am I right?"

Ankhmakis turned on Silus, jaw clenched. "If I have to, I will. I'd never let the war fall into your incompetent hands."

"You do plan on usurping the rightful order of inheritance," Silus yelled.

"If I must," Ankhmakis blurted out.

Chanax watched as his father's face grimaced, turning redder each moment.

"How dare you," Horwenefer's voice boomed and echoed in the stone hall. "Ankhmakis, this has gone too far." Ankhmakis turned to his father and opened his mouth to speak, but Horwenefer raised a hand as if to strike him silent. "The last time I looked, I was pharaoh of Upper Egypt, not you. I will not have you using my hard-earned prize, the army I worked my entire life to procure, as your toy. I will decide who's next in line, and you can be sure it won't be a traitor."

"You can't decide who's pharaoh if you're dead," Ankhmakis said, jaw set, and teeth clenched.

"See, Father," Weret cut in. "He plans to kill you."

"No," Ankhmakis said, striding toward her, fists clenched tight. Chanax saw the form of Ankhmakis's fury surround Weret, and Chanax worried the man might hit her. "You keep mixing up my words, you bitch."

"Stop where you are, young man," Horwenefer commanded. "Don't you dare take another step. I'm well aware of the danger you present to my court. I've seen your skill on the battlefield and the way the men admire you. In order to launch this war, I looked aside. I've seen how you allow Natasa to work through you to spy on the battlefield, and again against my better judgment, I let it be, for the sake of victory, but no longer. You need to be cut down to size. You're not the god Amon-Re here—I am. You will no longer soar above me."

Ankhmakis stared at his father, his posture stiff and shoulders thrown back. Chanax glanced around the table and noticed everyone's faces, from Hecataeus to Silus, were focused on the pair, unable to tear their eyes from the furious men. As Horwenefer squared off to face his middle son, Chanax felt a chill run down his spine.

"How do you plan on reducing me, Father?" Ankhmakis

asked, his head held high.

"You are hereby cut off from the temple of Isis and her priestesses," Horwenefer replied.

"What?" Ankhmakis cried out as if his father had severed his right arm. "Natasa?"

"You heard me," Horwenefer continued. "No more Anit-Shadya. If you seek out Natasa, it will be an act of death for both of you, for she is no longer assigned to you. In addition, no other priestess shall be given to you as companion for as long as I live."

"You can't do this," Ankhmakis yelled.

"He is the pharaoh of Upper Egypt. He can command anything he wants," Isidor said, his voice as smooth and sweet as honey. The pharaoh turned to his high priest. "Give the command," Isidor continued, "and I shall make it temple law. You have the power. The pharaoh is allowed to override the high priestess's decisions, including the assignment of spiritual companions."

"No," Ankhmakis cried out again. "Father, please no."

"Are you sure about this?" Hecataeus jumped in, grabbing the pharaoh by the arm in an attempt to gain his attention. "Why punish him this way? Why not send him south to man the crossing of the Ethiopians or some other menial task? I'm sure a miserable assignment would provide him with an appropriate perspective."

Horwenefer shrugged off Hecataeus's grip and stared at his son, who now trembled uncontrollably, clenching his fists so hard, his knuckles were white. "I'm sure of this. Isidor, make it temple law that Prince Ankhmakis, second born of Pharaoh Horwenefer, may not seek Anit-Shadya from any of the temples of Isis in my kingdom. If he wishes to expand his consciousness and power in this way, he'll have to cross into the Lower Kingdom and beg Ptolemy V's army to let him in. Not that any of the northern temples practice the art of ecstasy anymore."

The silence in the room was too much for even Chanax to bear. He could sense each mind trying to process what had happened. Weret was delighted, Bithiah serene, Hecataeus mortified, Horwenefer furious, and Ankhmakis devastated. Even Chanax hadn't seen this outcome. As the others in the room festered in anger, it dawned on Chanax—after years of waiting and trying to manifest Natasa as his, the opportunity had appeared. As he turned to his father, Isidor shook his head, but Chanax ignored his master.

"Father," Chanax said. "Natasa is the high priestess-in-waiting. She must be bonded to one of your sons, even if it's not Ankhmakis."

Both Ankhmakis and Horwenefer turned to look at him. Chanax ignored his brother's rage and instead looked at his father, his heart full of love and hope.

Silus stepped forward, shoving Chanax aside, and slurred, "I agree, and since I'm the king-in-waiting, she should be mine."

No longer able to contain his anger, Ankhmakis threw himself on his brother, forcing Silus to the ground. Ankhmakis raised his fists and beat Silus's pretty face, striking with such rage, Chanax heard his eldest brother's nose crack under the force. Blood splattered across the fresco-lined floor.

"Guards," Horwenefer called. "Get Ankhmakis off my eldest son."

Four guards, one of which was Min, ran forward and tore the fighting Ankhmakis from Silus. Ankhmakis's narrow gaze glittered, face twisted like a snarled tree, the form of his hate blanketing the room, and Chanax found it hard to breathe.

Never had he seen his brother this angry. Silus moaned from the floor as one of his personal guards helped him get to his feet. He wiped the blood from his mouth and nose.

"You'll pay for that," Silus threatened.

"Take him away," Horwenefer commanded. "Throw him in a cell until he regains his composure."

"You can't do this," Ankhmakis groaned. "Please, Father, I beg it of you. Don't separate us."

"Too late," Horwenefer answered. "I already have. You'll be released when Khons's silver boat graces the sky. Expect to ride out in the morning."

"What about my request?" Silus demanded, his smile laced with lust behind the blood running down his face. "I get Natasa, don't I?"

"Your Majesty," Isidor spoke up, "I think it's a very good idea, and I'm sure the high priestess will agree. She's long thought Natasa's relationship with Ankhmakis was distracting her from her other temple duties."

Chanax turned to his master, sucking in a quick breath. How dare he take this moment from him? Natasa should be his. He opened his mouth to argue when his father spoke, making the decision final.

"Fine," Horwenefer agreed, not even bothering to look at his second-born son. "Natasa will go to Silus." He turned and waved his hand to Ankhmakis, who was still struggling to break free from his captor's grip. It took four guards to hold him back. "Get him out of my sight."

"Father," Ankhmakis screamed as the men dragged him from the room. "Father, don't do this. You'll regret it."

The men managed to get the frenzied prince out the doors, and the room grew silent once more. Silus dabbed his bloodied face with a cloth and poured another glass of wine.

"Well, that was exciting, wasn't it?"

Chanax scowled at him, realizing he hated his eldest brother's smugness, perhaps even more than he hated Ankhmakis for stealing Natasa.

"You two as well," Horwenefer said to the princesses. He wiped his brow as he sat. The argument had weakened him, and Chanax marveled as Isidor took advantage of the moment and drained the pharaoh of his stamina. "You've done great harm. Now get out of here."

Weret pouted at his words, her pleasure at Ankhmakis's punishment vanishing. "Yes, Father."

As the two made their way to the door, Horwenefer sighed and sunk deeper into his chair. "I hope you're happy, Weret," he called out.

Weret turned, her brow wrinkled. "What do you mean?"

"I hope you got what you wanted," he replied.

"I wanted to aid you, Father," she said.

The pharaoh shook his head. "Since birth, it seems, you've demanded much from me. Your mother paid the highest price for your life. The day you were born was the last day I felt alive."

Weret shivered like a hunted mouse under his stern gaze, and Bithiah put her arm around her sister.

"Father," Bithiah reprimanded. "Don't be cruel."

Horwenefer slouched even farther in his throne, as if to make himself disappear. "Get out, everyone. This meeting's adjourned."

8

The Wall

"Mayest thou live and prosper and be hale, my excellent brother, well-equipped, strongly-established, without a wish; thy needs of life and of sustenance satisfied, joy and delight united in thy path."

~ Papyrus Anastasi III, New Kingdom

Behdet, Egypt 203 BCE

Natasa stood in her apartment, fighting back the tears. She couldn't let her mother see her despair.

"While I'm hesitant to agree with Isidor's motives these days," Neferu-ankh-maat said, "I do think this switch will be good for you. Your bond with Ankhmakis is beautiful, but the intensity of your relationship keeps you from digging deeper into the mysteries. Besides, Weret is dangerous. Ruia is the better sister-wife."

"Yes, Mother," Natasa said, denying her desire to strike her mother's face. She searched for Ankhmakis and felt his rage. Ra had not yet set, and he was still caged in the dungeon.

"Besides, Helena has been born, as was prophesized. You and Ankhmakis have completed your great work together.

Now is a time to focus on your inheritance and your place as high priestess someday."

"Helena? What does she have to do with anything?"

"She's the Golden Child," Neferu-ankh-maat replied. "The one foretold to transform Egypt and discover the ancient powers."

"Am I nothing but a womb to give you satisfaction as a seer?"

"No," her mother said, gasping. "Whatever has gotten into you?" Natasa turned her back on her mother and gazed out the window.

"I suggest you remove Ankhmakis's ring," Neferu-ankh-maat advised.

Natasa looked down at her finger and felt her heart break as she took her lover's phoenix from her slim finger and placed it in a small cedar chest, next to the golden wand Horwenefer had given her on Ankhmakis's wedding night, the delicate blue paper flower Ankhmakis bought her years ago in Alexandria, and the bloodstone from Chanax.

Eleni entered the room and placed her hand on Natasa's shoulder. "I feel your sadness, sister," she said. "It's as if the world has forgotten how to love."

"Eleni," Neferu-ankh-maat reprimanded, frowning at them, "love is never forgotten, but our love of the goddess is greater than human love."

Eleni turned to the high priestess and shook her head. "I can see Natasa loves Ankhmakis and not Silus. I've never seen the goddess. How can we love someone we can't see or hug?"

Natasa knew from her mother's pursed lips the high priestess didn't approve of Eleni's observation, but now wasn't the time to discuss philosophy.

"Dearest sister," Natasa croaked, "will you do me a favor?"

"Yes, anything."

Natasa held out the small cedar chest. "This is very important to me. I keep it here, hidden under my desk in this secret place." She placed it under the desktop, sliding it into its hidden location. No one could find it, unless she showed them. "If anything ever happens to me, will you give it to Helena when she's older?"

Eleni cocked her head to the side. "Why would anything happen to you?"

Natasa didn't say what she was thinking—she might not have the will to live anymore without Ankhmakis's touch. To live in the palace, but never be allowed to express her joy at the sound of his voice again, was too hard, and death would be the easier path.

"I need to go," she said instead. "Silus awaits me in the ceremony room."

"Yes," Neferu-ankh-maat replied. "Would you like me to walk with you?"

"No," she answered. "This is something I must do alone, for alone is what I am now."

"Natasa," her mother began, but Natasa raised her hand.

"Don't tell me I'm being dramatic," she hissed. "I'm tired of everyone treating my love for Ankhmakis as unreasonable and unworthy of the goddess. Our love was born of the goddess. Fools and lesser men destroy it at their peril. Horwenefer will pay for his actions today, not by my hand, but through divine order, he will see his folly."

Neferu-ankh-maat gazed at her, arms crossed. Her mouth began to open, and Natasa didn't want her to get the last word. "My truth is mine and mine alone," she said as she walked to the door. "You see the world different than I do. I don't try to change you, so stop trying to change me."

She fled the small apartment and walked out into the quiet evening. The sun was setting low on the horizon. Soon Ankhmakis would be released, and Natasa knew he'd come to find her. It would be too late—Silus had made sure of it. The rocks and sand were cool beneath her bare feet as she crossed the gardens and made her way to the temple of Isis. At least he had the courtesy to call upon her in the ceremony room, rather than his private chambers. She couldn't bear the idea of spending the night with him.

"It's sex," she said to herself. "He has access to my body. Not my soul. I will never have to share my soul with him, or anyone, as long as I live."

This became her mantra as she walked the temple courtyard. Words repeated over and over to harden her heart and enable her to survive the act that awaited her. As she approached the temple of Isis, acolytes were setting fires in the braziers and the pale red setting sun turned the sky bright orange, before fading into the purple of night. She entered the temple and made for the ceremony room. Standing before the great golden doors, she paused, clenching her fists as she gulped down a wave of nausea. She fought against her desire to flee, instead stepping forward to heave open the doors. Silus, wearing nothing but a loincloth, was sitting at the edge of the golden bed. Four guards were stationed at his side. As he rose to greet her, the guards strode past and out the door, letting it fall shut behind them.

"Four guards?" she said as she approached him. "My lord, do you think I'll try to flee?"

"No." He waved his hand at the door. "They're not for you, but for my brother." He pointed to his face, which was swollen and red. "He did this to me earlier. When he's released from the dungeon, I don't want to risk him trying to kill me."

"If you're hurt, we don't have to do this," Natasa offered.

"Nonsense, the law requires us to bond for at least five nights. The rest of the men are heading out tomorrow, and I wish to join them as soon as possible. Can't let Ankhmakis steal my glory on the battlefield, which means we need to get started right away." He rose from the bed and sauntered to a small table to pour two glasses of wine.

"Wine during ceremony?" Natasa frowned. "Drinking spirits isn't allowed."

"It isn't?" He shrugged. "I guess I forgot."

"Don't you and Kawit take ceremony?"

"I've been at war for over a year, Natasa. I don't recall what rituals she made me perform. We never did any of prayer, breathing, or astral travel stuff. Such piety doesn't interest me."

"What does interest you, my prince, and why did you demand me as your spiritual companion when you already have one?"

"As a lord of this land, I can demand a change of companions," he said as he handed her a glass of wine. "Besides, Kawit's Anit-Shadya has become quite boring. I've gone to her once since I've been home and found her lacking. As to why I stepped up to claim you after Father severed your ties to Ankhmakis, isn't it obvious? I did it as revenge. Nothing will tear him apart more than knowing you're now mine."

Natasa's head began to throb. "Why do men need to own a woman's sex?"

"Drink your wine, woman," Silus replied. "You're too serious for me. Can't this be enjoyable? Trust me."

"Why should I trust a man who won't even perform prayer or ceremony?"

"Fine, I promise to follow protocol for you, but not

tonight," he answered as he sucked down his wine and poured himself another glass. He grabbed his lyre and played a light-hearted tune.

"What are you doing?" she asked, giving in and drinking the wine. If he wasn't going to honor the goddess, she wouldn't either. Perhaps she could get him too drunk to have sex.

"Trying to make it easier for you," he said, lowering his gaze.

She looked at him and took in his handsome face. Each of the royal princes were beautiful—like their father. He bit his lower lip as he studied her, and she was surprised by his attempts to make the difficult situation easier for her.

"This can't be easy for you," he continued. "You didn't have much choice in this situation. I'm trying to lighten things up this first time. We can be more serious tomorrow, but tonight, try to relax and let me enjoy your body. Trust me when I say I've wanted you for a very, very long time."

Natasa swallowed the rest of her wine and felt the effects in her legs. She was scared as Silus rose from his seat and dropped his loincloth.

"Whatever power you grant my brother, I want it as my own. Yet, I also want you to feel comfortable. Can you at least try?"

She nodded and held out her goblet. "I think I'll need another glass of wine."

He smiled as he filled her cup. "Of course, my dear priestess."

☦

An hour later, Natasa lay under the prince's arm as he snored, passed out from too much wine and sexual satisfaction. Natasa slipped out from beside him and found her robes in the darkness. She didn't dare light a candle for fear of waking him. In spite of his kindness, her stomach felt ill and her heart heavy. She could no longer smell Ankhmakis on her, as if the physical memory of him had been lost. In order to get through the act and protect Ankhmakis from feeling what was happening, Natasa had closed her heart to her twin, and now felt alone in the world.

She threw on her robe and opened the door. The guards were still there but let her pass. Silus had been honest—they weren't there to keep her from leaving. She walked through the silent courtyard and peered up at the night sky. The stars were glorious, and yet she could no longer hear their song. It felt strange and unnatural. Natasa couldn't bear to live in the world if she remained closed to it. She stopped walking and grounded herself in the earth before opening her heart to the energy around her once more. She sensed the frogs in the pools, the lily pads rustling at the goddess's feet, a cat slinking in the corner and...Ankhmakis.

Rage and anger flooded her entire body, and she startled as he stumbled out of the shadows, distraught and drunk. He held a pitcher in his right hand, and Min was trailing him.

"My lord," Min begged. "This isn't a good idea. There are guards in the temple."

Ankhmakis paid no attention to the man as he strode toward her, his anger permeating the very air she breathed. Natasa tried to read his mind but found a wall around his heart, very similar to Chanax's. She trembled like a child hiding from a beating about to be delivered.

"Finished?" he said, his voice harsh and cutting. She couldn't speak as she gulped down her shame. She wished she could disappear. "As soon as they released me, I ran to your apartment to see you," he continued, slurring his words.

"Corinna told me you'd already left to pleasure Silus."

She wanted to say something, anything, but her mouth wouldn't move.

"What?" Ankhmakis cried. "You're not even going to try to defend yourself? While you've been enjoying a party with my dear brother, I've been out here in agony."

"My lord," Min said, grabbing his shoulder, trying to get his attention. "Please, let's go."

Ankhmakis shrugged off Min's arm and glared at Natasa. "You were quick to let another man slip in between your legs. Weret was right—you are nothing but a whore."

"Ankhmakis," Min shouted. "Stop right now."

Natasa felt despair unlike anything she'd ever known. It flooded her Ka, and with each tear it made in her heart, she built her own wall against her beloved. Brick by brick, placed in neat rows, cutting herself off from him, his hurt, and the cosmos in which she no longer believed. She took the pitcher from Ankhmakis's hand and took a deep sip of wine. He stepped back, his face twisted as if she'd slapped him. She continued to guzzle, allowing the gift of the alcohol to numb her body and her mind.

She swallowed the warm wine and looked to the men— Ankhmakis's hands clenched in rage as Min dragged him away. Natasa raised a hand to stop them.

"No, Min, he's right. I am a whore."

"My lady," Min said, jaw dropping, "don't say such things."

"Why not? One should speak the truth. I was raised to believe my studies in Anit-Shadya and the Alchemies of Horus were for the good of the kingdom and the will of the goddess." She drank again, and to her relief, Ankhmakis remained silent. The world started to spin around her, though she wasn't sure the wine was the cause for her disorientation.

"What a difference a day can make. This morning I woke with the sunrise in the arms of my beloved. And now…"

She trailed off and glanced at Ankhmakis's angry face. She longed for a sign of love from him but received none. "The actions of the men of this court today have taught me a great lesson. My body is nothing more than a pawn for princes to pass around at their whim, like coins on a gambler's table. Winner takes all, am I right, beloved?"

She took another swig from the pitcher and wiped her mouth with the back of her hand. "My body isn't mine. My sex has no meaning beyond a man's pleasure, or perhaps his need to overpower another. It's true, Min. In Pharaoh Horwenefer's kingdom, a priestess of Isis is no freer than a concubine. I was a fool to believe otherwise."

She drank from the pitcher one last time and thrust it at Ankhmakis's stomach. He took it, and his face softened. She resisted the urge to open her heart, choosing instead to indulge in her anger. "I would rather never touch a man again than continue to feel the shame and disgust I now have for my very being."

Min stepped forward and drew her into his arms. "My lady, I'm sorry."

She allowed his embrace for a moment before turning away. "There's nothing you can do. Like me, you have no power here. You serve by command of the pharaoh, and we are objects to these people. Nothing more."

Natasa turned to Ankhmakis, who remained silent, his lower lip trembling. "Goodbye, prince. It's been a pleasure serving you."

As she turned and ran away into the darkness, she placed more bricks around her heart, shutting out her twin flame so completely, she didn't notice him fall to the ground at Min's feet, his hands clutched over his heart. She didn't know he sobbed in the dirt until his guards arrived to take him to his chambers. Instead Natasa returned home and stared out the window until Ra returned, covering the land with his golden light, and the trumpets sounded, announcing the departure of Ankhmakis and his father as they rode out with their new southern allies toward Panopolis in hopes of launching the campaign to drive them past Lycopolis and northward to Alexandria.

Natasa hated Silus for using her body in this way. She hated Ankhmakis for calling her a whore and shaming her for the very work she was born and bred to do. She hated the pharaoh for tearing apart her life with one quick, vengeful declaration, leaving her alone, filthy, and abused. She hated her mother for teaching her that the love of Isis was pure and beautiful. All of them had betrayed her, and her heart beat rapidly as she considered her plight. She no longer loved Behdet, nor the royal family she'd been raised to serve.

Five days later, Silus bid her goodbye and joined the forces en route. He performed true ceremony with her once, though they were unsuccessful at any astral travel. Natasa found she no longer held such power. She felt nothing as the oldest prince returned to war. It mattered not if he lived or died. She hoped war kept him away for years—in her heart and mind, there was no need for her to perform Anit-Shadya, or serve any of the royals, ever again.

She despised them all.

9

Alone

Pharaoh Horwenefer's men surged past Panopolis, and in their wake established bases on either side of the Nile. However, the Greeks held their advancement, and Horwenefer felt the pressure as the priests of Thebes begged him to break through and take Memphis while Ptolemy V Epiphanes was still a child, and his rule vulnerable.

Near Panopolis, Egypt 203 BCE

Ankhmakis stood outside his tent, allowing the cool desert wind to blow upon his sweaty flesh. The stars were brilliant in the sky above. There was music and revelry in the distance—the sounds of men letting go of the horrors of battle. He filled his mug with beer from a keg and walked toward the festivities, hoping to forget the day's killing. He no longer wished to think about his actions. Over and over, he murdered as his father commanded. Death after death. Horwenefer had begun sending him on missions to the Lower Kingdom, deep into enemy territory, to assassinate key administrators and officials, in order to send fear into the Greeks, or gain access to buildings, river ports, and other key locations. The rebellion had become a slow war, a plodding war, and a devious war. Ankhmakis murdered in the dead of night, like a phantom, leaving terror in his wake.

He approached the center of camp and found his men singing, playing instruments, and drinking around a huge bonfire. Women, many of them Greek slaves and concubines taken as the spoils of war, sat upon their laps and pleasured them in various ways. The gathering was situated on the island outside of Panopolis, in the center of the Nile. Ankhmakis recalled the many lives it had cost him to take control of the city and this island. It had felt like a significant victory at the time, adding another thirty miles of territory to their kingdom. Yet thirty miles wasn't enough. He needed to conquer another three hundred miles before he reached the Great Pyramid of Memphis.

"Brother," Nefermaat called out. "You've made it. How goes the mission?"

"The mayor of Lycopolis is dead," Ankhmakis announced as he took his place next to his half-brother and Pontius, Min's twin. "Where's Min?"

"Asleep," Nefermaat answered. "As a married man, he can't handle the temptation of the women."

Ankhmakis nodded, recalling how Min had wed a noblewoman from Thebes. Min found it difficult to be away from her and spent most of his nights alone, away from the revelry.

He looked over Nefermaat's shoulder and eyed a girl with creamy, dark skin and light blue eyes. She was mixed blood—like Natasa. He sucked down his beer and nodded across the fire to the men who were smoking opiates.

"Give your general some peace," he said, wanting nothing more than to stop feeling alive.

The men passed the pipe and he took a long drag, allowing the drug to remove his thoughts of Natasa and his daughter, as well as the mayor and his family whom he'd killed for his father, from his mind. After a few moments, he gazed back at the slave girl.

"Come," he said. Without a word the captive stood, and he could smell the fear on her. She knew well what was about to happen. He took her to his tent and pounded away his anger inside of her before passing out in a drugged daze. At dawn, Min entered the tent and woke him.

"My lord," he said, keeping his gaze lowered. When they were young men, using women in this way had been a pleasurable pastime, but now, Min avoided the concubines and didn't bother to hide his disgust. "Your father requests your presence."

Ankhmakis rose and looked at the girl, still lying in his bed. Wide-eyed, she clutched her robes at her chest with trembling hands. He had no recollection of their sex. Had he been too rough? He wasn't sure. "Leave me," he said. She stood and threw on her robes, skirting Min as she fled.

"Ankhmakis," Min began, "I know why you seek out the young girls."

"Do you?" he replied as he put on a tunic and strapped his sword to his waist. "Please enlighten me because I thought I sought them out to have sex."

"You use them because you're trying to forget Natasa," Min said.

"What if I am?" he said, growling like a caged beast. "She's Silus's companion now, remember? I think I recall him bragging about it the other day. He implied she was one of the wettest women he's ever known."

"Stop," Min cried. "Why do you speak of her this way?

Don't you remember what she said to you? How much she hates what's happened?"

"I remember how much she hates the men of the court. I'm one of those men, remember?"

"She said she hated the behavior of the men of the court," Min clarified.

"Yes, she'd hate my behavior now, wouldn't she? Not sure if she'd hate the fact I take whores to my tent most nights. I think she'd be more upset about the way I killed a man yesterday, and his wife, as well as his small children, in cold blood, with no warning. Yes, Natasa would hate me for slaughtering children."

Ankhmakis left the tent and stomped toward his father's, which was more of a permanent shelter than a tent, complete with a large bed set upon a wooden platform, settees, and several desks covered in maps, protected by twelve guards. Ankhmakis nodded to Pontius and Nefermaat, who stood at either side of the entrance, and gave each a wicked smile as he entered the pharaoh's tent. The king lounged on his throne, wrapped in animal pelts and looking ashen in the pale morning sun. A bald healer stood beside him, offering a steaming brew to heal the pharaoh from his latest malady. Ankhmakis found it strange how often Horwenefer was sick.

"Your Majesty," he said, lifting his chin and refusing either to bow or hide the irritation in his voice. "You called?"

"Yes," Horwenefer answered, sitting straighter in his throne, his body stiff and wary. Dialogue between the two men had been tense and dangerous since Ankhmakis's devastating punishment. "Please, have a seat."

Ankhmakis did so and noticed his head was throbbing. Opiates didn't agree with him, but they aided him in sleep. Insomnia was too frequent a companion these past few months.

"Report," the pharaoh commanded.

"I killed the mayor of Lycopolis," Ankhmakis answered. "As well as his wife and offspring, for good measure. Left their bodies in the throne room as a message."

"A message?" Horwenefer asked. "What sort of message?"

"A warning we're on our way," Ankhmakis replied. "If only we can get past Qau."

"Anything else?"

"I did some investigating. Lycopolis is small, but well-fortified. It's going to take a large amount of megau and cavalry to breach them, as well as ladders, and elephants. Elephants would be nice. You know, like the ones you commanded so spectacularly in Raphia?"

"Ankhmakis, please, now isn't the time for your sarcasm," the pharaoh replied. "Don't you have any more information? In the past, you'd have many helpful details after one of these missions. Your reports have been lacking late."

"Oh, you'd like to know more than what my own eyes can see? Well, dear Father, you're not about to get your wish." Horwenefer glared at his son. Ankhmakis smiled and batted his lashes as he continued, "Spying was Natasa's work. You didn't like it, remember? Made you feel insecure. To ease your ego, you stole her from me and gave her to Silus. Why not send him on these missions? She's in his hands now, not mine."

Ankhmakis stood and made to leave.

"Son," Horwenefer commanded, "you will not talk to me with such disrespect."

"Why not?" He turned back around. "What are you going to do?"

"Hang you for treason and willful behavior," the pharaoh threatened.

"Do it. I dare you." The idea of death was pleasant. A smile graced his face, pulling at dry, sunburned skin. "I'd love to die. I can watch you lose this war from a front row seat in the Halls of Amenti. I have no reason to live now since you've taken the only things I care for. My lover. My daughter. Left me with whores and drugs and death. You want me to respect you? What a fool. Go ahead and kill me. I'd enjoy it."

Horwenefer glared at him. Min shifted in his place.

"There's a commander from Ethiopia I want you to fetch for me," the pharaoh said, pausing as he spoke, as if measuring his every word. "He will arrive in Behdet within the month. I want you to return home, greet him, and deliver him to me in Thebes. Silus will join you."

"Why don't you get him yourself?" Ankhmakis answered, unable to believe his father would make this request.

"Because I have no reason to return to Behdet."

"Neither do I," Ankhmakis retorted.

"You will join your brother. He has things to attend to in Behdet as well."

"Like Natasa?"

"And Ruia. Unlike you, he's a good husband."

Ankhmakis glared at his father and noticed the whites of his eyes were yellow. His skin was wrinkled, and he hid his gray hair with opulent wigs. In addition to illness, age was settling in on the man and making itself at home.

"You need a trip to Behdet more than I, dear Father," he said. "Your Ka could use the sort of regeneration only a night with the high priestess can bestow. And I'm sure you miss the touch of your wife, since you're such an excellent role model when it comes to kind and loving husbands."

Horwenefer stood and made to smack him, but Ankhmakis blocked it and squeezed his father's arm in his angry fist. He might have lost his ability to work with Natasa, but he was still strong and in command of his energy field and the space around him.

"I told you, Father," he whispered in a low tone as he twisted his father's arm in an unnatural position, "you made a mistake when you punished me the way you did. I have nothing to lose now, and thus, nothing to fear. Even you, the pharaoh of the Upper Kingdom, have no power over a man like me. I remain by your side because Egypt needs me, and as long as I fight, those I love live. My participation in your war isn't a sign of loyalty toward you. Don't you ever forget."

He released Horwenefer's arm, and the pharaoh backed away, clutching his robes around his shoulders. The silence crackled with unspoken hate and no one in the room dared even to breathe. After several moments, the king spoke.

"You will go to Behdet and fetch the Ethiopian general. We need him. I'll meet your envoy in Thebes as the harvests of Shemu begin."

"As you command, Your Majesty." Ankhmakis stormed out of the tent and went to hunt down Silus.

"Why do you tempt him in this way?" Min asked as he rushed to catch up. "I know you're consumed by your anger, but it seems like you have a death wish."

"Perhaps I do," Ankhmakis replied. "I don't feel alive anymore. Why not be hung for treason? Yet I know if I die, my father will lose the war, and Egypt will fall. Worse, my people and my daughter will be swept up in the slaughter sure to follow any surrender. It's a horrible thing to be me."

"Stop this nonsense. Stop taking suicide missions. Stop doing the opiates. Stop dragging young girls to your tent at night."

Ankhmakis turned around and took Min by the shoulders.

"Why? Why should I stop?"

"Because," Min said, his voice cracking, "You're a better man than this, Ankhmakis. You have to find a way back to your soul."

"My soul is Natasa's soul," he said, tears now forming. "I can't be whole without her, yet if I connect to my soul, I will long for her and find my way back into her, putting her life at risk. To love myself is to love her. Why do you think she could astral travel hundreds of miles to be with me? Why do you think we could speak to each other without words? Because we're one. Somehow, beyond our two separate bodies, we connect. Our Shadya made it possible to experience oneness in the flesh. Oh, it was the most wonderful thing to be whole..."

His voice trailed off as he gazed at his best friend's face. Min's eyes glistened, and it broke Ankhmakis's heart to see his friend in pain "You must understand, Min, the very thing which makes me human is now a sin punishable by death. The path to my higher impulses ends with her. There's no way to be me without risking her life. Can you imagine it, Min? Trust me, it's better for me to be an animal than to attempt any sort of true wisdom. For in the place of wisdom, there sits the goddess Isis and by her side is Natasa. How do I approach such a place of purity, without falling into her arms? How?"

He jostled Min as he spoke. "I can't be me anymore. In order for Natasa to live, it is I who must die." He released his friend and folded his arms. "Now, come help me find my fiendish brother. We have an errand to run."

"I don't think you should go to Behdet," Min advised.

"Why. Are you afraid I'll hurt Natasa?"

"Of course," Min answered.

"Well," Ankhmakis answered, "I promise I won't go anywhere near her, and after the way I treated her before I shipped out, I imagine she won't want to be anywhere near me. We'll fetch the general and leave."

"What if Silus calls for her and taunts you?"

"I'll ignore him." Min looked at him, frowning. "I promise, I won't break his nose again."

"Don't insult Natasa," Min replied, "or I'll be the one breaking your nose."

Ankhmakis put a hand on his dear friend's shoulder. "What would I do without you?"

"Fail," Min answered, his expression grim.

"Failure is a high possibility right now," Ankhmakis replied. "Only time will tell."

10

Purifying the Temple

When the Persians conquered them in 500 BCE, the priests of Egypt hid their mysteries from the intruders, who for the most part left them alone. The Persians had no interest in Egypt's wisdom. The Greeks, however, took great interest, and from Ptolemy I Soter on, sought to integrate themselves within the temples, in order to know Egypt's power and magic. What the priests gave them was incomplete and missing the most important truth—the world is not matter, but instead energy and vibration. The human who masters these mysteries becomes a god. This information was guarded for centuries—for no Egyptian priest wanted this knowledge to fall into the Greeks's hands.

Behdet, Egypt 203 BCE

"Neferu-ankh-maat," Queen Keket said, her voice sweet like honeycomb on a hot day, a tone the queen had never before uttered in Neferu-ankh-maat's presence. "Please come in."

Dread filled the high priestess's heart as she entered Hecataeus's study, where Isidor and Queen Keket stood waiting by the open window with a view of the valley below. Beyond them, the farmers worked in the fields and boats made their way up and down the river. In a chair by the window sat the high priest of the Houses of Healing, Iu-Amon. He wore a grave look upon his face.

"Good afternoon, my lady," Iu-Amon said, gaze focused on Neferu-ankh-maat, as if the other two weren't in the room.

"Where's Hecataeus?" she asked. It didn't seem right to be in his office without him.

"On his way," Isidor answered. "Would you like something to drink?"

His false manners irritated her. From the triumphant look he wore, she knew he was up to something sinister, yet she couldn't determine what was going on in his evil mind. Even in her astral travels, she was unable to gain access to the events surrounding him. There was much violence and hate, but the specific actions of the Invisible Hands remained veiled. How was he able to protect himself from her in this way?

"No, thank you," she replied, turning as Chanax burst into the room.

"Chanax," the queen said. "It's good to see you."

"Yes, Mother," the younger priest replied. "Where's Hecataeus?"

"I was wondering the same thing," Neferu-ankh-maat said. "It's unlike him to be late."

"We sent him some documentation in advance of this meeting," Isidor explained. "Perhaps he's still analyzing it?"

He winked at Queen Keket, who blushed and batted her eyelashes.

Neferu-ankh-maat had no patience for their games. "Isidor, why are we here?"

"To purify the temple," Hecataeus replied from behind her. He stormed into the room and thrust two sets of scrolls upon the table. "Am I correct, High Priest Isidor?"

"Ah, Vizier," Isidor answered. "I see you read the new laws ahead of time. Thank you. All we need is your stamp on both, and we can be on our way."

"My stamp?" Hecataeus spat, his face a dark, furious red. "You want me to stamp my approval on this corrupt piece of legislation?"

"Vizier," Queen Keket said, her voice raised and high-pitched, "you have no choice but to stamp it. It is the pharaoh's bidding."

"Pharaoh Horwenefer has given me no indication this is the route he wishes to take," Hecataeus argued.

"He doesn't have to," she replied, tossing her hair over her shoulder and pointing to the golden crown upon her brow. "I'm in charge while he's away at war."

"Would someone please tell me what this meeting is about?" Neferu-ankh-maat demanded.

"The priests of Horus and Set have demanded that members of the temple with Greek blood in their pedigree be stripped of their roles and demoted to the lowest level... attendant or page," Hecataeus said, his fists clenched as he nodded to Isidor.

"What?" Neferu-ankh-maat cried. "How dare you suggest such a thing? We'd lose half of our best priests and priestesses, as well as healers."

"The Houses of Healing will be exempt," the queen explained. "The number of wounded soldiers is increasing, and we can't let our warriors die due to a shortage of laborers. Therefore, half-breeds may work in the Houses of Healing in any capacity except high priest or midwife. Those positions will remain pure blooded."

"Iu-Amon?" Neferu-ankh-maat cried out. "You agreed to this?"

He shook his head but remained seated, gazing out the window. "No, I haven't agreed to anything. I will take anyone, regardless of his or her blood, into my service. Why should I care? The purification of the temple? What foolishness."

"You've written a law to strip at least a third of our people in the temples of Horus and Set from their positions of leadership?" Neferu-ankh-maat asked.

"Yes," Queen Keket answered, a smile beaming on her face, "and from the temple of Isis as well. The priestesses who serve our royal men must be of the highest and purest quality."

Neferu-ankh-maat gasped at what the queen was suggesting. "You mean to remove Natasa from her position as high priestess-in-waiting?"

"Indeed," the queen continued. "She's not fit to be a companion to my sons, who are the royal princes of Upper Egypt. It is important that the leadership of this new kingdom be true to our cause."

"No one is more devoted to the goddess than Natasa," Neferu-ankh-maat said.

"How do you know?" Isidor challenged. He pointed at Hecataeus. "How do we know you're not planning to take her to Greece at any moment? We've taught her our deepest mysteries. How easy it would be for our precious knowledge to slip into the wrong hands."

"What complete nonsense." Neferu-ankh-maat scoffed. "If Hecataeus wanted to steal our secrets, he would have a long time ago."

"Stop talking as if I'm not here," Hecataeus demanded. "I have no interest in your religion whatsoever."

"You don't, because you're a heathen," Isidor hissed, "but your daughter is priceless to our enemies. You would be heavily rewarded if you delivered her to the temples in Athens."

"How dare you insult me this way?" Neferu-ankh-maat said. "She is my daughter, born for one reason—to give birth to the goddess herself. How could you strip her of her inheritance? She's the mother of the Golden Child."

"Ha," Isidor said, laughing as he spoke. "You're delusional, Neferu. Helena isn't the Golden Child. Such fantasy. Why in the world would the Messiah of Kemit be a half-breed girl? It has been suggested in Thebes the Golden Child is Horwenefer himself. He's the one risking his life saving us, and our heritage, from the filthy Greeks."

"Horwenefer? He's not the One, Isidor. You know he isn't."

"It doesn't matter what I know," he snapped. "What matters is what the people believe, and they believe in Horwenefer and his son, the brave Ankhmakis. Forget Helena, she's nothing but a female born of a temple union no longer considered valid."

"I won't stamp this," Hecataeus declared, holding up the scroll.

"Yes, you will," Queen Keket answered. "For I've already signed it."

"What about me?" the vizier challenged. "If half-bloods can't hold the highest offices in this kingdom, what are you going to do about the full-blooded Greek vizier you've got?"

Isidor gazed at Hecataeus with an intense, fevered stare, causing Neferu-ankh-maat to take a step back. "It appears Horwenefer made a law before he left insisting that under no circumstances could you be removed, unless he himself signed the order."

"How inconvenient for you," Hecataeus replied.

"It's horrible," Keket insisted. "I don't understand why he'd do such a thing. Why does he protect you in this way?"

"The pharaoh and I have an agreement," Hecataeus answered, his eyes narrow and hands on his hips.

The room fell silent. Neferu-ankh-maat's stomach began to burn. "What is Natasa to do?" she cried. "The temple of Isis is all she knows. She's one of my best teachers. The acolytes revere her."

"Well," Isidor answered. "It's true she's very talented in Anit-Shadya, as both of the elder princes can attest." Neferu-ankh-maat winced at the suggestion in his voice. "We can't let her go to waste," he continued. "Which is why I've reassigned Natasa to my Invisible Hands. None of them have been initiated into the mysteries of Isis. She can teach each one of them of the goddess's touch. There are eleven of them. Her new role should keep her very, very busy."

"Isidor, no," Chanax blurted out, tugging at Isidor's sleeve as if he could overrule his master.

"What you suggest is rape," Neferu-ankh-maat answered. "The priestesses of Isis are not to be passed around like blood in your sacrificial offerings. They share the goddess's touch with one companion at a time. I won't let the darkness of your work taint my daughter."

"You have no choice." He held out a scroll in his hand. She hadn't noticed it before. "I've already signed the order. All I need is the queen to agree to sign it."

"Which of course, I will," Keket replied. A wide smile, as bright as the sun, adorned her face as she took it from his hands.

Neferu-ankh-maat stumbled backward as if drowning in

the wake of evil radiating from the couple. Hecataeus took her in his arms. "They can't do this. Hecataeus, you can't let them do this. It will kill her."

"Stop being so dramatic," Keket insisted. "The whores service many men each day, as my dear husband can attest."

"Enough," Iu-Amon yelled from his corner. He rose from his seat and walked to the queen's side. "Keket, whatever is wrong with you? How could you suggest such a thing?"

She turned to the old priest and a childish look appeared on her face. "My lord, Iu-Amon," she replied, her cheeks flushed, "I was merely suggesting Natasa accept her new place in the court. It's better than death, which is what the Greeks deserve."

"You will not sign Isidor's declaration," Iu-Amon insisted. "You haven't forgotten our arrangement, have you?" He glared at the queen, and she lowered her gaze to the floor.

"No, my lord," she said in a quieter voice.

Neferu-ankh-maat shook violently in Hecataeus's arms, unable to control her feelings of disgust and anger. What was happening? What agreement did the queen have with the old healer?

"Now," Iu-Amon continued, "hand me the scroll."

Queen Keket did as he commanded, and Iu-Amon ripped the papyrus sheet from the wooden handles and tore the document into several pieces, letting them fall to the floor like cypress leaves upon a gentle breeze. He struck the wooden handles together before throwing them at the desk where they thudded against the table and rolled to a stop, striking a clay pitcher.

"She can come and work by my side, if she wishes," Iu-Amon continued. "It will mean a vow of chastity, but the temple of Isis is no longer pure enough for a being such as

Natasa. I think she'll find our celibacy quite liberating."

Neferu-ankh-maat's knees buckled as she stumbled forward and rushed into his arms. "Oh Iu-Amon, yes. What a perfect idea."

"What?" Isidor exclaimed, raising his chin and placing his hands on his hips. "You can't have a half-breed working alongside of you."

"We've already established I can. Your purification of the temple law states Egyptians with Greek blood will still be accepted in the Houses of the Healing, in order to meet the medical demand our army requires. Thus, Natasa can and will work alongside me, if she accepts."

"She will accept," Neferu-ankh-maat replied. "I'm sure of it. Eleni as well. Will you take her under your wing?"

"Indeed," Iu-Amon answered. "It would be a great pleasure to spend my days in such quality company."

He nodded to Hecataeus. "Go ahead and stamp the horrible purification legislation. Send your daughters unto my care. I will protect them from this madness." Iu-Amon stared at Isidor. After a moment, he wrinkled his nose and turned to leave. "There's a reason I rarely leave the healing center," the old man said as he shuffled toward the door. "I don't much enjoy the greed and envy of Pharaoh Horwenefer's court." He turned to the queen and shook his finger at her. "Truth is, I'm not sure it's entirely your fault, dear. Something has been amiss ever since Isidor returned from Memphis as a young man. Don't you agree, Neferu-ankh-maat?"

The high priestess glared at Isidor and Chanax, who stood beside the old healer. Iu-Amon radiated the power of love and neutrality. In contrast, the energy around Isidor and Chanax pulsed with a chaotic rhythm, like shards of glass falling from the sky. They were broken beyond repair.

"Yes, Iu-Amon," she agreed. "Memphis has a way of turning beautiful men into horrible creatures."

She noticed Chanax flinch and drop his head at her words.

"Well," Iu-Amon sighed, "there's nothing to be done about it, is there? I must go. I expect Natasa and Eleni to report tomorrow morning for their pledging ceremony. Men are dying, and I need their help."

"Yes, my lord," Neferu-ankh-maat replied.

When Iu-Amon left the room, there followed a deep silence in which no one spoke. Hecataeus took his stamp and pounded it against the scroll on the table, breaking the spell.

"There, take your unjust law and go purify your temple. Iu-Amon's right. You don't deserve women like Natasa in your service." He handed the scroll to the queen and pointed to the door. "Get out of my office. All three of you."

Neferu-ankh-maat watched as the trio made their way to the door. The queen stopped in the threshold and turned to give Neferu-ankh-maat one last smile, looking like a cat who had stolen his master's cream.

When the door shut, Neferu-ankh-maat let out a deep breath and shuddered. Hecataeus took her in his arms. "What's happening? Why am I losing control of everything?"

"You shouldn't have stopped taking ceremony with Isidor," he said, running a hand through her hair.

"How could I continue, knowing what he does in the bowels of his temple? To think, he wanted to force them upon Natasa. My sweet child, ruined by their evil touch."

"I wouldn't have let it happen. I would have killed Isidor first," Hecataeus replied.

"Thank the goddess for Iu-Amon." She sniffled. "Why didn't I think of making her a healer?"

"He's a clever one, and he's loved Natasa since she was

born," he agreed. "Don't be too hard on yourself. You were upset. They've taken your heir from you."

She frowned. "Yes, I must find a new successor. Truth is, I no longer care about the temple of Isis. I'm not sure I want to be a part of this anymore."

"Do you mean it? I never thought I'd see the day where you denied your station as high priestess."

"Hecataeus," Neferu-ankh-maat whispered. "Egypt is no longer safe for you, Corinna, or the girls."

"I'm well aware our lives are in danger, my dear."

"What do you plan to do?"

"Get us out of here, when the time is right."

"Can I join you?" she asked.

"It would be an act of treason," he replied. "You could never come back. Are you sure you want to abandon your life here?"

"Yes. An Egypt under the influence of Set is no longer my home. I want no part of it."

Her heart felt heavy as she realized the death of her hopes and dreams. She grabbed Hecataeus closer and allowed herself to surrender to her tears.

11

Ancient Alchemy

"Where the south declines toward the setting sun lies the country called Ethiopia, the last inhabited land in that direction. There, gold is obtained in great plenty, huge elephants abound, with wild trees of all sorts, and ebony... and the men are taller, handsomer, and longer lived than anywhere else."

~ Herodotus, Greek Father of History, 420 BC

Behdet, Egypt 203 BCE

Natasa held Helena's tiny hand as they crossed the entrance to the Houses of Healing and made their way toward Iu-Amon's study. In her right arm, she carried her small cedar chest.

"Bee killers," her child said as they passed the fountain.

Natasa smiled at the petite birds playing in the water. "Yes, darling, those are bee killers."

"How can they kill bees?" Helena asked, her high-pitched voice tinkling like bells on the wind. "Do beaks not feel stings?"

"I imagine they don't. You ask so many questions for such a small girl."

Helena had turned three, and it seemed her favorite pastime was to ask why. Every day Natasa was charmed by her, and she cherished her time with her child.

"We're here," Natasa announced as they entered the study. Her mother, father, and Bastyre had also been invited to the meeting.

Helena let go of her mother's hand, toddled up to Neferu-ankh-maat, and climbed into her lap. The high priestess chuckled and held her close while Helena fingered the golden earrings her grandmother wore. Natasa felt a cool breeze on her bald head and rubbed it.

"Welcome, Natasa," Iu-Amon greeted her. "Is something wrong?"

"No," she replied. "I'm still not used to being bald. I miss my hair."

"Yes, well, nothing we can do about it. The soldiers return to us infested with nits and lice. It's easier to shave off their hair, as well as ours, than to battle their infestation. Trust me, you'll get used to it. Now, do you have the golden rod?"

"Yes," she said, holding out the box.

The darkest man Natasa had ever seen walked forward from the shadowed corner. He was tall and muscular and wore a leopard-skin loincloth as well as several large, beaded and golden belts around his waist. Golden rings shone upon his fingers, and his arms were tattooed. He was barefoot, but wore decorative, straw ornaments around his ankles. Most amazing was his face—the whites of his eyes contrasted against his dark skin, and he wore vermillion and chalk paint on his face, forming delicate yellow and white spirals that accented his high cheekbones, raised forehead, and strong jawline.

He bowed and rubbed his own bald head. "I think your baldness is beautiful." He spoke perfect Egyptian with a strong southern accent. "My people believe baldness is a sign of mental clarity and power."

He smiled, revealing teeth as white as alabaster. There was nothing but kindness in his face, and for some reason, it made her shy. She wasn't used to being around someone so powerful yet open.

"Natasa," Iu-Amon said. "This is General Khaleme, warrior and steward of Kush."

Khaleme bowed and held out his hand. "I come in the name of King Adikhalamani, my captain and ruler of Kush." Natasa placed her hand in his and he raised it to his full lips, kissing her palm. "You must be the wand bearer."

Her brows furrowed in confusion. "I'm only a healer."

"You are an initiated priestess of Isis," Iu-Amon added. "Natasa is one of Our Lady's great devotees. Which is the reason I have called you here. Please, take a seat and we'll explain."

Natasa sat beside her mother and watched Khaleme sit beside the old healer. A second Kushman came to stand behind the general.

"Please," Khaleme began, "let me introduce Dardre, the high priest of our temple in Meroe."

The man, face also painted in intricate designs, bowed and remained standing next to Khaleme's seat. Natasa wondered how long it took them to get ready when they awoke in the morning, or if their servants did their faces instead.

"Khaleme has come to help us in the war," Iu-Amon began. "Years ago, right before the rebellion began, Pharaoh Horwenefer presented me with a most wonderful object—a golden wand with the symbol of Isis engraved upon it. It had been passed down within his family for generations, but the exact use of the object was unclear. The only instructions were to guard it from the dark brotherhood and allow it to pass unto pure hands.

"I was unable to discern the object's use, but weeks later, he told me he'd slept with it in his hand and Isis appeared to him in a dream. When he awoke, he understood many things. First, the time for rebellion had come. Second, we were to call for our ancient brothers in Kush to help us. Lastly, he was to give the golden rod to a priestess of Isis, for the goddess demanded it never fall into male hands again—not even one of his own sons.

"He obeyed Our Lady's wisdom and gave it to Natasa as a gift for her service to his middle son. Then he launched the Great Egyptian Revolt, and now the men of Kush, or Ethiopia as the Greeks call it, have begun pouring into our lands to help us. In addition, King Adikhalamani has sent his greatest general to stand beside Pharaoh Horwenefer in his quest to restore the glory of Egypt. It appears this is happening because of the wand Natasa has in her possession."

"I don't understand," she replied. "What would the men of Kush know of it if Horwenefer didn't even know what it's used for? I've been trying to work with it for years, and I agree I've felt a power I can't explain, yet it's nothing I can enter."

"Because the wand is part of a set," Khaleme said, his strong accent making his words even more mysterious. "Please, may I see it?"

Natasa nodded and opened the chest. A deep pain seared in her heart as she brushed aside Ankhmakis's signet and took out the wand. Oh, how she longed to wear her ring, but one simple vow of celibacy had closed the door to Ankhmakis's love and touch forever. As she handed Khaleme the wand, a surge of energy, not unlike bliss, pulsed through her. He smiled, leaving her speechless. His beauty seemed unreal and otherworldly, as if he were Amon-Re himself, peeled from his engraving upon the temple walls to stand before her.

Khaleme took the wand and gazed at it as if it were an object of great importance, passing it from hand-to-hand, and then on to Dardre, who did the same. They spoke to one another in a language Natasa didn't understand as Khaleme took the wand and held it in his right hand. With his left hand, he withdrew from his side pouch a silver wand of the exact same size. He compared the two, and Natasa noted the Ankh symbol on both. A powerful energy unlike any Natasa had ever experienced pulsed through the room.

"What's happening?" she asked.

"This is your wand's sister," Khaleme explained. "They were forged together, thousands of years ago, when the pyramids were first built. Much later, under the reign of our common forefather, King Piye of Kush, this pair found themselves in the hands of his high priest. King Piye used them to rise from Meroe deep in the south and take all of Egypt under Nubian control for seven generations. It's written the Emperor Taharqa, King Piye's descendent, conquered the Syrian Peninsula. Thus, Egypt and Kush were united as one great empire."

He began to move about the room, almost bouncing on the balls of his feet, his hands now animated and gesturing to his audience. Even Helena remained quiet, staring at the man as he continued to speak, her blue eyes open wide.

"Toward the end of his reign, Emperor Taharqa hid the rods, for fear they would fall into the wrong hands. The priesthood could no longer be trusted. When the Nubian dynasty fell, many of our ancestors remained in Egypt and farmed the Nile Valley. The family of Horwenefer stems from this line of kings. They remained in Behdet and farther south, continuing the practices of Anit-Shadya and following the way of the Divine Feminine, in the hopes of keeping our faith alive. But to save Egypt from evil, a pair of brothers, our great-great-great-great-grandfathers, separated the wands, shielding them from the priesthood who was developing the darker magic. One brother kept the golden wand in Behdet and the other took the silver one to Meroe. Thus, many generations later, Horwenefer inherited the male aspect and I, Khaleme, his distant family in Kush, inherited the female aspect. Today, they're reunited."

In silence, Khaleme stood and stepped forward with his left foot, holding the wands in his hands, arms down at his waist. He looked like the ancient statue of Horus in the Temple of Luxor, performing the same action. Natasa felt power dance around him, and to her surprise, she connected to the light of the cosmos for the first time since she'd been cut off from Anit-Shadya with her beloved. The energy wasn't orgasmic, but the purity and frequency were identical. She closed her eyelids and followed the impulse through the veils, which cloaked humans from the realms of light.

"I now understand why Our Lady commanded Horwenefer to give the wand to Natasa," Khaleme said, his voice drawing Natasa back into her body. "This young woman is the one to hold them, and her child is the one to reintroduce them to those who are worthy within our kingdom."

Natasa opened her eyes and stared at the man. She glanced at Helena, who sat upright and quiet in her grandmother's arms. Helena nodded her head at the general. She might be young, but the child understood they were talking about her.

"What do you mean?" Neferu-ankh-maat asked, eagerness visible in her alert, straight-backed posture.

"Our Lady Isis also visited me in a dream," Khaleme

explained. "She said a king worthy of my help had been born in Behdet, and together we could drive the Greeks from these lands and create one unified empire again. In addition, she said a child had been born who would weave the Divine Feminine into our cultures, and I was to deliver the silver wand to the mother of the child. It is with this intent I have come to answer Pharaoh Horwenefer's call—to fight by his side, and to join the wands together once more."

He handed the pair to Natasa, and as she closed her fingers around each one, she merged with the energy of the entire world, and yet she still maintained the clarity of her individual body.

"Stand in places of power within nature, in your bare feet. Hold the silver in your left and the gold in your right. Inside each of these precious metal wands is Kush crystal, crushed into small grains. These will conduct the magnetics of both your Ka and the energy of the earth and allow you to manifest desires, events, and even beings in the physical plane. I understand you're an initiate of the Anit-Shadya of Isis; thus, you already know the paths between the realms and have been prepared for intercourse with the gods in this way."

She nodded and smiled. A joy, equal to the joy she'd felt at Helena's birth, or the first time she kissed Ankhmakis's lips, filled her heart. The wall she'd built in anger to separate from Ankhmakis began to crumble, and a touch of fear pierced her vulnerable soul as she beheld his golden light.

"I no longer practice Shadya," Natasa explained, "for the pharaoh has denied my lover, Ankhmakis, access to the temple of Isis, and I have since taken a vow of celibacy."

"Ankhmakis?" Khaleme asked. "The pharaoh's middle son?"

"Yes," Iu-Amon explained. "Natasa was his spiritual

companion, and Helena is their child."

"I see. They are a divine pair, yes?" Khaleme asked. "I sense this is true. Now the child makes even more sense. Here is a true Osirian and Isis pairing. The perfect male and the perfect female. It's because of your love you are the one to do this work. I'm now eager to meet Prince Ankhmakis tomorrow."

Natasa's head whipped in her father's direction. "Ankhmakis? He's coming to Behdet? Why didn't you tell me?"

"Natasa," Hecataeus warned, "I think it's best you don't see each other."

"Perhaps you're right." Natasa sighed. She was still angry at Ankhmakis for calling her a whore, as well as hurt by his actions and carelessness for her own wellbeing. In many ways, she'd be happier never seeing him again.

Khaleme rose from his seat. "You must excuse me, I'm tired and need to rest. The princes will arrive tomorrow and take me on to Thebes, but I feel in my heart Dardre must remain here and work alongside the high priestess to counter the evil being committed within this court. If outwardly the pharaoh and high priest deny the love of a divine pair, inwardly they seek even worse crimes. Neferu-ankh-maat, Dardre is at your service. Feel free to call upon any of the priests and priestesses of Kush to aid you in the quest of purifying your temple."

"Thank you," Neferu-ankh-maat replied. "I welcome any partnership in honor of Our Lady. I'm very alone now within the temple and its hierarchy."

"Indeed," Khaleme said, nodding, "and now, it's up to you, Natasa, to wield the power of the wands. Learn the secrets needed to reunite our human souls in peace. You must understand—we stand on a precipice. A new era for this great civilization can be born out of divine love, but not if Set is honored in your temples. The pharaoh must choose one, either Our Lady of Love or the Lord of Chaos. If chaos is given too much power, our chance to reclaim Egypt will be lost forever."

Natasa rose from her seat and bowed to Khaleme. "Thank you, sir, for giving me a reason to serve Our Lady once more."

Ever since her forced separation from Ankhmakis she'd felt adrift, no longer wanting the title of high priestess-in-waiting, nor interested in serving the princes of Behdet. The stripping of her titles had angered her, but she'd been considering requesting the peace and solitude of the Houses of Healing. If anything, the queen's xenophobia had given her an excuse to leave her position without angering her mother. Truth be told, if she couldn't be with Ankhmakis, she didn't want to share her body with any man.

The dark warrior turned and left the room, his priest following close behind. Natasa crossed her arms over her chest and held the wands as if they were her own child. She looked to Iu-Amon and her mother. "I will need time each day, in private, to work with the wands. Can you spare me in the infirmary?"

"We will do whatever must be done for you to unlock the message of unity the wands contain," Iu-Amon answered. "Nothing is more important, except this—Isidor and the queen must never discover what you have in your possession. They mustn't know the wands have been reunited. I know for a fact Isidor covets the golden wand and has made many attempts to steal it since Pharaoh Horwenefer gave it to you in front of the entire kingdom. Isidor recovered a silver wand in Memphis long ago and thinks it might pair with yours. They wouldn't work together, even if he had managed to take yours from you, but now that you have a true pair, he'd stop at nothing to get his hands on them. Even murder. Is this clear?"

Natasa nodded, fighting the fear threatening to disturb the newfound bliss the wands granted her.

"Practice in the apiary," he continued. "It is deep within our complex, so remote no one but the beekeepers visit it. There you will be safe to explore the great gift our Kush brothers have given us."

Natasa turned to the midwife. "Bastyre, will you meet me in the apiary later this evening, about an hour before sunset? I would like to begin today, and you are the keeper of the queens. I will need the bee's permission to work in their space."

"It would be an honor, Lady Natasa," Bastyre replied.

"Well," Natasa continued as she placed the wands in the cedar box, which was now becoming quite crowded with precious objects, "it's time for Helena to take a nap. Thank you, Iu-Amon, for everything—from taking me under your care to arranging for the safe transfer of the wands. I don't know what I'd do without you."

"These are troubling times, my lady," Iu-Amon replied. "We need each other if we're to survive."

Natasa ran her hand over her bald head, noting goosebumps had formed. Her teacher was right; these were dark times. She was grateful she now had a mission worthy of her life. She would discover the power of the Wands of Horus, and when she did, Natasa would use them to save Egypt, and crown her beloved as pharaoh of the land.

12

The All-One

"The first concerning the 'secrets': all cognition comes from inside; we are therefore initiated only by ourselves, but the Master gives the keys. The second concerning the 'way': the seeker has need of a Master to guide him and lift him up when he falls, to lead him back to the right way when he strays."

~ Inscription from the temples at Luxor

Behdet, Egypt 203 BCE

Hours later, Natasa met Bastyre in the apiary. The bees droned as the workers from hundreds of hives arrived home with pollen stored in tiny sacks above delicate hind legs. Natasa allowed one to land on her finger and noticed the swollen, yellow pollen packs, like saddle bags on a mule, indicating success.

"Looks like you've had a good day, my lady," she whispered to the insect before it took off for home, flying in a spiral path toward the entrance of its hive.

"Are you ready?" Bastyre asked.

Natasa opened the cedar box and made to grab the wands

but halted at the sight of her beloved's ring. The golden specks in the lapis lazuli phoenix sparkled in the late afternoon sun. It begged to be worn. Natasa placed the ring on her left ring finger and was surprised to connect to Ankhmakis. His signal was faint, his heart full of the despair of a man with no solid bearing on life. As she took the wands in her hands, images once more crossed her vision. Rather than look closer, she sent a wave of peace out around her and traveled beyond his astral emotions, to the place where she and he connected.

She placed her arms at her sides and stepped forward with her left foot, allowing the waning sun to shine upon her face. She sensed the bees's curiosity as many flew out of their hives toward her, and as they entered Natasa's space, they formed a spiral around her, soaring up and down in a lemniscate pattern. Her gaze dropped, and she sensed the power begin to build within her. She extended her consciousness even farther and remembered the day when she was a child in training and had first felt the oneness of the bees. As she opened to their minds, the world appeared as streams of light and impulses. Visions spread out before her in bursts, but she didn't try to understand them. She continued through the images and visions, out of the haze of action and emotion and beyond—to the place of light and dreams—the web of life.

There were no words in this place. Information and wisdom were transferred from the All-One straight into her heart. Natasa felt the bees fly so close to her face they left a breezy trail on her skin. Her ears drank in their droning song, and soon she slipped out of time and place. She no longer knew the garden, nor the earth below her feet. Bastyre disappeared from her vision, as well as the physical world. She was in the realm of light—at once the smallest insect and the greatest star.

Natasa continued farther into the light, found her lover's spirit, and struggled with the various emotions colliding within her breast. Ankhmakis's pain and agony surrounded her, and she knew she needed to forgive him for his failures. She released her anger and united with the pure and powerful form of their love.

"You are me," she whispered as she fell into their Ba and stretched her out her consciousness in all directions, "and I am you. Come to me, my love."

☥

Ankhmakis made his way to the apiary, not knowing why he was drawn to the place. His habit was to seek solitude in the desert before presenting himself to court, but he'd had enough of the sand and his horse after the ride to Behdet. They'd arrived earlier than planned, and rather than get to work, he found himself longing for the peace of the Houses of Healing and the resplendent herb gardens that surrounded the compound. He slipped in through a back gate that hung from its hinges and followed an overgrown path past cypress trees and an olive grove toward the ancient wall bordering the apiary. He hadn't visited this area in years. He was still unsure why he was here, but he continued on toward the rusted, iron gates, as if called by some supernatural force. He nudged the gates open, hoping he'd be alone.

He froze as the breath left his body. Before him stood Natasa, her eyes closed and arms at rest at her side. Ra's rays shone on her face, and golden light radiated around her. Hundreds of bees were encircling her, not touching her, but dancing around her, the way she danced for him as he played the pandura. Her bald head shone under the day's dying sun, and she wore nothing but large golden earrings and a tunic so short, it left little to the imagination. She was stunning, and a rush of love and desire overcame him. His heart pounded in his chest as he whispered aloud, "My goddess, what is she doing?"

"She is working," a low voice replied from behind him.

He jumped around and found Bastyre, the old midwife, standing in the entryway, her hands on her full, round hips. "Don't disturb her."

"Bastyre," he said, "I'm sorry. I was looking for a place to be alone and thought of the apiary. I didn't know she'd be here."

She eyed him for a moment, then shrugged. "Come, follow me."

She walked out of the apiary through the gates and off the path, following the wall to the backside of the complex. Here the olive trees were overgrown to the point they had to duck under them to avoid hitting their heads. Bastyre stopped before the wall, which was covered in old growth vines. She lifted them and revealed a spot in the wall where several bricks were missing.

"You can watch her from here," she said.

He peeked through and saw he was now even closer to Natasa yet hidden by the crumbling wall. He could hear the drone of the bees and see the serenity in her face. She was even more beautiful than he remembered.

"Why is she here? Silus sent for her when we arrived. It's one of the reasons I sought solitude. I didn't want to see them together. He'll be expecting her."

"Well, he'll be disappointed," Bastyre replied, her cheeks now flushed, "for Natasa is no longer a priestess of Isis."

"What?" Ankhmakis answered, raising his eyebrows.

"Your mother stripped her of her titles," Bastyre said,

spittle flying from her mouth as she spoke. "Due to Natasa's Greek blood, she can no longer serve the princes of Behdet as a spiritual companion."

"I don't understand," he replied.

"The purification of the temple," she continued, cracking her knuckles. "Ask your mother. I'm sure she'll delight in telling you about it. It's quite remarkable you've turned out to be such a good man, in spite of your poor inheritance."

He glanced through the hole in the wall at Natasa and felt the rush of desire and sexual need. He wanted nothing more than to be inside her. "I'm not a good man, Bastyre," he replied.

"You're a better man than you think. Someday you'll know it," she answered. He continued to look at Natasa and sighed, content as the midwife continued.

"You know what this means, don't you?"

"What?" he replied, unable to peel his gaze from his beloved as the bees continued to dance around her.

"She's taken a lifelong vow of celibacy," Bastyre explained. "We all do in the Houses of Healing. It's the ancient law."

He whipped his head around and glared at the old woman. "Why would she do such a thing?" he asked, feeling a sense of loneliness even worse than before. The reassignment to Silus was horrible, but something he'd hoped to overturn when he took the kingdom for himself. The vow of celibacy was an ancient ceremony and promise, not a law to be broken or rewritten.

"Because your mother demoted her from spiritual companion to the line of kings and reassigned her to Isidor's Invisible Hands as spiritual companion—all eleven of them."

"Invisible Hands?"

"Yes, a group of men who spend their days hiding deep

within the temple of Set, casting curses and dark magic upon your enemies as well as spying in battle for the pharaoh. They're the real reason Philopater is dead."

Everything now made sense. His father's fear of the power Ankhmakis and Natasa shared on the battlefield had led him to do more than reassign her—he'd created a group to work remotely with him in the same fashion, same as the great kings of old.

"Isidor's Invisible Hands," he whispered.

"Yes, and under the guise of Anit-Shadya, Queen Keket declared Natasa was to become their personal concubine." Bastyre spat at the ground and made a sign to ward off evil before wiping her mouth with her sash. "It broke the girl's heart to be forced to service Silus, but the new assignment would've made her a sex slave. Iu-Amon took her into his service before any of those evil men could touch her, and now she stands before you, working the most holy of magic and safe from Isidor's morbid fascination with the purification of Egypt."

Ankhmakis felt the vein in his neck begin to throb. He clenched his fists, wanting to bash in the ancient wall. Bastyre put her hand on his shoulder. She tugged him closer to her short, full body.

"Natasa is safe now," Bastyre said. "In this place, she is free from Weret's insecurities, your father's fear of you, and your mother's cruel heart. Please, for her sake, and Helena's, don't disturb this fragile peace."

He considered the wise woman's words and knew she spoke the truth.

"Let Natasa be," she begged.

Ankhmakis turned and gazed at his lover. He was torn between the need to run away from her and the desire to tear down the apiary wall and drag her from Behdet. How could his family treat her this way?

"One more thing," Bastyre said as she turned to leave. "Weret is pregnant. About four months along. I confirmed it yesterday. I sense it's a boy, and I'm never wrong about these things. I thought you should know."

Ankhmakis didn't turn around to look at the midwife when she gave him this news. Instead he gazed at Natasa and found himself wanting to connect to her. He expanded his Ka until it touched hers and felt no pain, but joy and peace. Turning inward, he entered into a spiritual embrace with his beloved. She sent him a rush of power, and he was transported to the place of their lovemaking. The pain of war, whores, and drugs spread out around him—he was exposed in her all-knowing sight. He saw himself calling Natasa a whore after she'd been forced to give her body to a man she didn't love, and knew her devastating pain in the moment, a pain she'd carried ever since. He drew away in shame, but the form of her love surrounded him.

"*I love you,*" she said, as clear as if she were speaking out loud by his side, but instead, they were communicating once more within their hearts.

"*I'm not worthy,*" he replied, trying to escape. He wasn't pure enough to unite with her this way. What had he been thinking?

From her place of power, Natasa refused to let him go. She held the upper hand. His sins from the past months marched before his mind's eye, and she shared every moment, from the slaughter of innocent children to his time in a young slave girl's arms. In spite of his evil ways, her love grew greater and stronger around him.

"*I love you,*" she said again.

"I don't understand," he answered. *"How can you love such a man?"*

"I am you. You are me."

His hesitancy released, and he expanded deeper into their Ba. The pain of life disappeared. Beyond his angry actions there was perfection and ease. Why did he fight it?

"Look at me," she commanded.

He obeyed and peeked out at her through the wall. She was gazing at him, the bees now gone and the garden silent. As the sun set, she smiled, and his heart burst into a thousand pieces.

"I called you here," she said, still speaking to his heart.

Ankhmakis's heart pounded within his chest. She was the most beautiful woman in the world. "I miss you," he said out loud.

A single tear traced its way down her cheek, and he wanted nothing more than to hold her in his arms. Instead, he fled from the garden and toward the palace. He knew he should go to Weret and congratulate her and take dinner with his brothers, as well as Hecataeus and the Ethiopian general; however, he was exhausted. He made his way to his chambers and fell into his bed. Within minutes, he was consumed by a deep and peaceful sleep, something he hadn't experienced since before the horrible night when Natasa had been sent to his brother's bed. In the morning, he awoke refreshed, and even though he still no longer cared if he lived or died, he was more himself than he had been in months.

13

Warriors of the Goddess

Hugronaphor chose his Pharaonic name with purpose. The first part, Hor, associated him with the God, Horus, the son of Osiris, the Last God on Earth, who was killed by his wicked brother Set. When Osiris was presented as the divine king on earth, he was often addressed as Wn-nefer, "the good being." Thus, it was this divine name the rebel king used as his throne name—Horwenefer. In short, Hugronaphor chose a Messianic name at the same time when other peoples in the Mediterranean were also expecting their delivery through a Messiah: not only the Jews, but also the Romans. All nations longed for a return to their golden age.

The royal road to Thebes, Egypt 203 BCE

The great Ra rose in the sky, casting a pale morning glow on the army train as it made its way to the royal palace in Thebes. The stay in Behdet had been brief for Ankhmakis— time taken to meet Khaleme, discuss administrative issues with Hecataeus, and show the general from Kush the military training center they'd built for his troops. When the general was satisfied that his men were being treated well, Ankhmakis and Silus headed out northeast to take him, and the first of the Ethiopian troops, to their father.

They rode in silence as Ra rose in the sky, painting pink and gray hues across the desert sands. Ankhmakis had long enjoyed the first hours of the morning, when the army would rise and begin a day's work. After months of sleepless nights, Ra's return to the sky also meant the end of agony. To be alone with one's thoughts in the darkest hours, while all others rested, was nothing short of torture. Yet this morning, Ankhmakis felt alive.

Ankhmakis gazed at Khaleme, who rode beside him, his eyes closed. He wasn't sure if the Ethiopian was asleep or meditating. Something in the way he sat tall and upright suggested the latter. As the sun rose higher in the sky, the painted spirals on the man's face glowed. Ankhmakis found the designs both beautiful and repulsive. Why would anyone decorate himself so elaborately?

He thought of Natasa standing in the apiary. He hadn't spoken to her the rest of the visit, but her love now filled him, like a constant stream of courage, and he smiled and breathed in her adoration.

"I have met your Natasa," Khaleme spoke in his rich, deep, accented voice, startling both Silus and Ankhmakis after such a long period of silence.

"Have you?" Silus asked, thinking the statement was directed at him. "I still can't believe my mother took her from me. The woman is wicked."

Ankhmakis contemplated killing his brother.

"It is a sin against the goddess to govern a woman's sexuality," Khaleme answered. The statement surprised both princes. "It is wrong to buy women to be sex slaves and concubines," the general continued, "but to force a priestess of

Isis to pair with a man she doesn't love is a sin. In my country, the women who are trained in Anit-Shadya choose their companions and have the right to deny anyone unworthy of them."

"Really?" Ankhmakis asked. If Natasa had been granted rights to her own body, she would have prevented his father from punishing him in this way.

"We have found Anit-Shadya provides no benefit to woman, man, or community if the woman doesn't feel safe. The magnetics of her bliss are released by her orgasm, and she can't experience such ecstasy if she's afraid. She must be in love. Anit-Shadya isn't about the man's pleasure; it's about the goddess, and her life-giving gift of abundant energy. The man is necessary only to please the priestess, and ensure she reaches her climax."

"Well I guess I can see why Natasa preferred celibacy, given what position Mother had in store for her," Silus agreed. "Still, she never should have done anything without asking me first. Natasa was mine, given to me by my father."

"It is my opinion, Prince Silus, Natasa should have been asked what she wanted, not you," Khaleme suggested. "Furthermore, I believe if she'd been consulted and given her choice, the way our priestesses are treated, she would have preferred to remain at Prince Ankhmakis's side."

"What?" Silus pouted. "You don't know anything."

"You are wrong, Prince Silus," the general said, his jawline firm and gaze narrowed. "I know very much. Your father sinned against Cosmic Law when he took Natasa from her divine pair and forced her share her body against her will. The king of Meroe would never do such a foolish thing."

Silus made to open his mouth, but after looking at the general's fierce gaze, thought better of it and turned away.

"Honorable men do not use women, and my soldiers are honorable men," Khaleme continued, looking behind him at the two thousand soldiers they were transporting to Thebes, all of them tall, bald, and darker than even the Egyptians, wearing their leopard skins and yellow and white face paint. Stretched out for miles beyond the men rode the baggage train carrying food, weapons, water, and ale.

"Such piety is going to be hard on them," Silus said. "My father's camps are full of whores and captured sex slaves. He believes the soldiers need to blow off steam and provides them with the women and drugs to do so."

"A general's men don't need such things if they believe in their cause." Khaleme shook his head. "Why would your soldiers need to blow off steam, as you put it? A day's fighting or training should be enough to release the anger from the men."

Ankhmakis thought about the war and how the constant violence was affecting him, and his men. "General Khaleme, this war is not like other wars. The clashing of swords occurs within the cities, alongside women and children. Many innocents are killed, and some of us are sent out in secret ahead of the soldiers, to assassinate key leaders and make entry into a city easier for our troops. This war is a bloody, violent puzzle, and the best strategy in the world can't change this fact."

Khaleme listened and remained silent, considering the situation. It seemed like an eternity before he spoke again.

"Assassinations are not the goddess's way. It is a coward's path. I will have many things to discuss with the pharaoh," Khaleme continued. "The men of Kush are warriors, and we know how to kill. Yet we follow the way of the goddess Isis and her consort, Osiris. Why must we kill the civilians when we enter their cities?"

"It is the goal of this war to reclaim Egypt from the Greeks, and we must fight in their cities. That means civilian casualties," Silus demanded. "What choice do we have?"

"The goal of this war is to take the Nile River Valley back into the hands of those who are worthy of it," Khaleme countered. "The Ptolemy royals must be stripped of their titles, but their people have lived among us for centuries. In Kush we know their merchants. There are many types of people in the world, and each has a right to live. My men will not kill civilians."

"It appears your troops are quite limited in their capacity to help us," Silus accused him. "What else do you demand on behalf of your men?"

"They must be allowed to paint their bodies before battle," Khaleme replied, a bright smile upon his decorated face, "and beat their drums as they approach the cities."

"Nonsense," Silus demanded. "Why would you wish to give yourselves away?"

"Because we've found nothing terrifies the light skinned more than facing men they think are savages." Khaleme's smile widened, his teeth blinding in the sunlight shining upon his face. "They are faster to surrender. Trust me, they will flee at the sight of us and our mighty war cries." Khaleme turned his horse around. "If you don't mind, Princes, I will now ride among my men. I have missed them during our separation and wish to know them again."

He rode off toward his army, leaving the brothers alone at the front of the line.

"That man is useless," Silus said, shaking his head as Khaleme rode away.

"No," Ankhmakis replied. "That man is a gift. Father doesn't deserve him, but I'm glad he's here."

14

Fragmentations

In the year 202 BCE, Tlepolemus, the Greek general in charge of the port city of Pelusium, staged a revolt in the Delta in order to secure a position of power over the young pharaoh, Epiphanes. Once the boy was in the general's hands, he was persuaded to give a sign for his mother's killers to be killed themselves. The child king gave consent, more out of fear of his new regent than anything else, and Agathocles and Sosibuis, along with several of their supporters, were violently killed and ripped apart by the Alexandrian mob. Thus, a new military strategy was birthed within the Ptolemaic Empire and Tlepolemus's first order of business was the putting down of the rebel king Horwenefer.

Antaeopolis, Egypt 202 BCE

"Fire," Ankmakis cried to his megau shooters. He stood at the prow of his ship as dozens of arrows flew past his body and into the Greek soldiers on the wall. He yelled to his soldiers, "Prepare the siege engine."

His rowers slowed the ship. Ankhmakis glanced up at the city, amazed they'd built the outer wall this close to the river.

Of course, his ancient ancestors never would have thought a naval vessel this size would attempt to breach it. The shallower waters helped to slow the ship in its approach; however, they risked grounding in the riverbed. If he managed to raise the siege engine, meet his mark, and gain entrance to the city, he didn't care if his ship was banked in the river silt, but if his gambit failed, he would have wasted precious months of labor and handed the Greeks the gift of hard-to-acquire timber. As his megau continued to fire their arrows at the city guards, half his crew anchored the ship, while the others yanked the thick ropes to raise the secret weapon on the prow—a large ladder built into the ship.

The Macedonians were familiar with this technology. In the Library of Alexandria, Ankhmakis had discovered evidence that Alexander's Diadochi had invented ship-mounted siege engines during the forty-year War of the Successors, which had followed their leader's death. This was the first time one had been installed on an Egyptian naval ship, and Ankhmakis prayed to the river god Hapy it would stretch to the wall. The Nile was retreating; thus, even the slightest change in the water levels would thwart his plan.

On land, ten thousand men appeared along the desert outside of the city. The first several rows were dark-skinned men painted from head to toe with bright yellow and white images. They screamed out to their gods in their native language, and their movements were wild as they yelled their battle cries. At first, the Greeks along the city wall sent arrows at the pack of screaming men but fell back as the savages approached the wall, large ladders in their hands. Ankhmakis and his men continued to release arrow after arrow from their ship on the river side of the city. The city of Antaeopolis was well fortified, Ankhmakis knew from previous undercover expeditions, yet it seemed Khaleme's prediction was correct. The sight of the crazed warriors had given him an opening he planned to use.

The ship was anchored into position—they were as close as they could get. He held his breath as the ship-mounted siege ladder climbed higher in the sky, inching its way toward the stone wall, his men grunting under the strain as they tugged the heavy ropes in synch with ordered commands called out by their captain. Behind him, his soldiers lined up in formation, including several Kushmen, ready to climb the ladder as soon as it was secure. Surprised at his action to scale the seawall, the Greeks scuttled toward his location, leaving the desert side of the city vulnerable to the Kushmen. One of the men holding the ladder's rope was struck by a javelin and the ladder hovered in the air as he fell from his post. Time seemed to still as the monstrosity wavered, threatening to fall back onto the ship and Ankhmakis's men. The soldier fell with a thump onto the deck. Ankhmakis yanked the javelin from the dead body and threw it at the wall, striking the lead enemy archer in the head. Satisfied, he grabbed the loose rope himself, heaving with all his might. With a loud crash, the ladder fell and struck its mark—the outer wall of Antaeopolis.

Ankhmakis forced his way through the line to the ladder, slung his bow on his back, and climbed up behind the men of Kush, who jumped onto the fortress screaming like rabid jackals, and into the arms of the Greek soldiers, clearing the way for the rest of the navy. Ankhmakis needed to get inside and open the gates to the city to allow the full army to enter.

As he landed atop the city wall, he drew his sword and sliced a man's head from his body. He continued to mow through the soldiers, darting between the hundreds of skirmishes taking place around him, making for the staircase.

He'd memorized the entire city layout from the maps and knew the shortest path to his goal.

The staircase was protected, but when five Kush warriors charged up behind him, Ankhmakis stepped out of the way and let them attend to their business. The Greek soldiers at the top of the stairs fled to avoid what appeared to be monsters. The men behind them turned and ran down the staircase as well, yelling for their lives. Ankhmakis could make out the words "savages" and "devils" as they fled. He laughed, hacked off the arm of the one who'd remained behind, and made his way down the stairs, beating off the remaining Greeks on the stairs. Seven more men stood before the gatekeeper's entrance. He was pleased to find a chandelier hanging from the high ceiling, filled with lit torches. He cut the flaxen rope that secured the structure with his sword, causing the gatekeepers to either flee or get caught under the massive, flaming iron monstrosity. He darted around the flames as they spread across the wooden floor and slammed his body against the door leading to the gatekeeper's quarters, creating a thin, insignificant crack down its middle.

"Get out of the way," a low voice sounded from behind.

General Khaleme and five giant painted Kush warriors held an enormous log in their hands, which they used to break down the door. As Ankmakis crossed inside the gatekeeper's alcove, he felt pain rush through his entire leg. Glancing down at his body, he discovered an arrow planted through his right thigh. Blood poured out of the wound and each step was excruciating. He fought the urge to collapse and called upon all his strength, channeling it into the wound. He couldn't heal such a severe injury on the spot, but he could dull the pain. As quick as lightning, the ache subsided, and even though he'd regret it later, Ankhmakis continued to fight, killing the archer to his right with one graceful thrust of the sword.

In his injured state, Ankhmakis maimed two more guards, and Khaleme and his men finished the rest, giving him time to stumble to the outer wall and yank the ropes and levers keeping the city gates shut to his troops. Within moments the gates flew open and thousands of painted men, screaming and yelling, poured into Antaeopolis. Behind them ran Egyptian megau, shooting rounds of arrows at the enemy as they advanced, and nakhtu-aa fighters carrying their khopesh swords and axes, and beyond them, the cavalry, led by Silus, kicking up dust as they sped toward the city. Ankhmakis slumped to the ground in pain and agony and hoped the mayor had taken the warning Khaleme insisted on sending ahead of time to evacuate the women and children out of the city.

"You've been hit," Khaleme called as he strode to Ankhmakis, his face pale under his makeup and mouth drawn tight.

"Stupid mistake, didn't think they'd have archers hiding in this small of a room," Ankhmakis replied, glancing at his wound.

It looked horrible—the arrow drove straight through his muscle. Blood was beginning to pool around him, and he grew light-headed.

"We must get you to a healer," Khaleme insisted. "Manu, Archemala." Two young painted Kush men arrived at his side. "Carry him out of the battle and back to the healer's tent," he commanded as he tore a bit of his loincloth and wrapped it around Ankhmakis's leg above the wound. "He needs immediate attention."

Ankhmakis wanted to object, but his energy was draining fast. He turned his field of awareness away from the battle and concentrated on his wound. As the two Kush men picked him up, the world faded. In his last moment of consciousness, someone tugged at his awareness. Natasa's face entered his mind.

"*Help me,*" he called as the world around him turned dark.

☥

One hundred and sixty miles away in Behdet, Natasa's vision blurred and her head spun. She turned to Eleni, who was working by her side, and grabbed her sister's shoulder. "I feel weak. Can you continue without me for a moment?"

Eleni looked at the soldier on the bed and nodded. "I'm wrapping wounds, Natasa, it's not difficult."

"Remember to sing to me sweet as a songbird," the soldier said, giving her a toothless grin. He'd lost his teeth in battle seasons ago.

"Of course." The girl giggled. At eleven years of age, Eleni was still young enough to be charming, but old enough to handle some of the most complex tasks. She'd become a favorite among the surgeons, assisting them as they cleaned, cut, and closed wounds.

Natasa left her sister and walked to a small stool in the corner. She was weak because Ankhmakis was weak. He'd called upon her. As she connected her Ka to his, she watched as he lay upon the ground in a small, brick room while two large, dark men picked him up from the floor. Blood was everywhere. Khaleme was there as well and she could see concern on his face. Ankhmakis head fell back and called to her heart.

"*Help me.*"

Natasa ran to the apiary where she now kept her cedar chest hidden under the north wall of beehives. No one would ever go near such a place. After Iu-Amon's warning, her apartment no longer seemed safe enough from Isidor. Besides, if she walked each morning from her quarters to work holding the box, the priests might see her and become suspicious.

She stood in the center of her secret garden as the sun set, ring on her finger and wands in the correct hands. Taking a step with her left leg she paused, allowing herself to sense the stars, the earth, and the low croon of the frogs along the river. Ankhmakis's injury was a fragmentation in Egypt's history. The outcome of the war hung in the balance. Natasa sent her prayer, not as a request, but as a command to the All-One. She struggled as he struggled between life and death, and as she did, she could feel his heart beat within hers, slow but steady.

"Deliver him unto me so he can heal," she commanded the beings who existed in this realm.

The request issued, she entered back to her own body and consciousness. When she could feel her toes, she looked up at the sky. Natasa smiled at the stars and they sang her soft words of love and respect. She sang in return, and thanked Isis for her gifts.

Natasa's work was done. Either the request would be received, or it wouldn't. Now she had to wait.

15

An Enemy Within the Court

With regards to health, the energetic practices of Ancient Egypt were practical. In the case of injury, the wound was often healed first within the energy of the Ka, which governs the physical body. When the Ka resonates with health, the body responds with homeostasis. Combined with their deep understanding of the physical organs of the body, the Egyptians had huge advantage over the Greeks: Ptolemaic soldiers would be left to die, or limbs amputated, but an Egyptian soldier would often return to battle, healed and even stronger than before.

Behdet, Egypt 202 BCE

Natasa changed the bandages on a young soldier. He was young—fourteen when he'd first gone to battle, and he'd lost his right arm in his valiant efforts. He would never fight again, nor lay bricks like his father before him. His entire life was uncertain.

"Give me your arm," she said.

"I can't, I left it on the battlefield, my lady," the boy said with a shaky laugh. He was trying to be funny, and Natasa felt pity for him.

"The other arm," she said, forcing a smile. "I need to change the bandages."

Along his left arm ran a deep gash, which had been stitched up days prior. She removed the bandage and was relieved it no longer smelled rotten. She cleaned the wound and rubbed castor oil over it before wrapping it back up in crisp, white linen. She hummed a tune, and her patient relaxed and closed his eyes.

When she finished her work, Natasa stood, feeling the bite of exhaustion in her body. Between working among the injured and caring for Helena, she found little time for sleep. As she walked to the next patient, a chill ran across her skin. Ankhmakis's face, cold and pale, flashed in her mind's eye as the bells tolled.

"Prince Ankhmakis arrives. The prince Ankhmakis arrives." The watchman's call echoed through the window.

After waiting for weeks without any information, he'd returned.

Natasa ran to the window and saw a procession coming toward the healing complex. The injured were too numerous to count, body after body being carried by other men not much better off. How had they crossed the desert in such a state? She washed her hands in the basin and fixed the white scarf on her head.

The door burst open and Iu-Amon ran toward her, his robes flowing behind him in his haste. "Make ready a bed," he cried. "Ankhmakis has returned injured and near death, as you foretold."

Her stomach clenched as the men jostled his stretcher into the room and dropped him on the bed nearest the door. Servants set up temporary walls made of palms to give privacy to the prince. She ran to Ankhmakis's side and felt her heart freeze as she took note of the injuries.

His head and chest were covered in sweat, and his hair was matted to his face in grime and dirt. Iu-Amon removed his footgear and lower skirt. She checked the wound in his leg. The arrow had been carved down to a few inches on either end to reduce chance of further injury during the transport across the desert. However, the scabs had cracked, and fresh blood now poured from his injury.

"Why wasn't this treated properly?" she demanded, as she pulled away his filthy bandages. She placed her hand on his forehead and knew he was burning with a high fever.

"Eleni," she commanded, "fetch cool water and cloths to tend to his fever. We can't remove the arrow and treat the wound until he's in a stronger condition."

Eleni nodded and ran out of the room. Natasa sensed the wound wasn't the reason he was near death. She looked at his pale face, blue lips, and eyes rolled back into his head. His tongue wasn't swallowing.

"How long has he been in this state?" she asked Min, as he stumbled into the room. His brow was cinched, and his armor was askew, as if he'd put it on while riding here.

"He was wounded in battle weeks ago, but stabilized after medical aid, so we set out for Behdet with the rest of our injured. The entire trip he was in pain, but still awake when we retired to bed last night. In the morning, we found him like this. Has he lost too much blood?"

She looked back at Ankhmakis and leaned in close to his mouth. The breath was slow, shallow and faint. She looked to Iu-Amon, her heart beating as if inside her head. Gulping as she gasped for air, she clutched her beloved's hand. He was going to die if she didn't do something.

Placing her hands on Ankhmakis's chest, Natasa formed a golden shield around the two of them. The noises of the room disappeared, allowing her to concentrate on his energy systems. His heartbeat was slow, like drums in a funeral procession. Around his body, streams of various colors flowed, not the golden light of health, but the gray light of death. A dark black stream encircled Ankhmakis's heart like an anaconda, trying to squeeze its prey. She'd found the energetic signature of poison and now she was watching as it killed him.

Natasa concentrated on her life force and sent the energy to his heart and through his veins. The space between them faded, and their souls merged, as they had when lovers. She needed to remove the energetic signature of the poison from his Ka, so that the physical body could remove it from his blood.

Natasa tightened her hands over his chest and envisioned herself tugging at the black stream around Ankhmakis's heart. It loosened its grip. She guided the stream into her body and down through her feet, making sure none of it remained within her. To her amazement, the rhythm of his blood now flowed throughout his body, and the energy around his liver grew stronger. She could see his heart beating faster and color returning to his lips. Everyone in the room stood still and quiet as she dropped her chin to her chest.

Ankhmakis opened his eyes, a tired smile gracing his pale face as he recognized her. Natasa let out a deep sigh and placed a hand on his head. He was still feverish, but he was no longer aflame.

"Eleni," she said, wiping her tears, "clean his face. Cool him down."

"Natasa," Ankhmakis croaked as Eleni wiped down his face with a wet rag, his voice a faint whisper, "you came for me."

"Always," she replied as she stroked his scruffy face. She displayed her affection, not caring what the others would think.

"What did you do?" Iu-Amon asked.

She shook her head. "Not now. I'll tell you later." She turned to the other attendants. "Tend to his wounds. Stop the bleeding. Give him an infusion of nettles and iron. Rehydrate him. Min, place several guards. Do not let anyone near him except for Iu-Amon and myself, and any healers in our company."

"Why, my lady?" Min asked.

She gazed at the other men around the bed, each part of Ankhmakis's private guard. "Who else was in your entourage?"

"The princes's guards and the wounded," Min replied.

"No other staff, such as healers, rhapsodists, scribes, or even whores?"

"No."

"Perhaps even the prince's entourage can't be trusted," she suggested.

"We live to protect our prince," Min said, crossing his arms over his armor. "We keep him safe."

"I'm sorry to say this, Min." She sighed, rubbing her forehead. "The arrow wound wasn't killing Ankhmakis. True, it's a severe injury, but not why he was close to death."

Natasa looked at the men before her. Many were unfamiliar, but her brother Nefermaat and Pontius had long been serving Ankhmakis in this fashion. She glared at each man in the room, her gaze hard and appraising, wondering whom it was who had tried to kill their prince.

"Natasa," Ankhmakis asked from the bed, "what are you implying?"

"You were poisoned, my lord," she said, looking Nefermaat in the eye. Did he blink? Shift his feet? She wasn't sure. Natasa turned to look at the prince. "I'm sorry, but someone close to you wants you dead."

His scruffy jaw dropped open, and her heart fluttered. Goddess, she loved this man. Her groin ached—it was unbearable to refrain from kissing his lips.

"Poison," Iu-Amon answered, nodding his head. "How did I not notice? I will set the House of Healing guards as well, to prevent any misunderstandings."

Iu-Amon glanced at each of the prince's guard and then walked to the bed and touched Ankhmakis's head, neck, chest, and his wounded leg. "Once your body has purged the poison, we will remove the arrow," the healer continued. "It will hurt like Hades, but this is standard procedure. We'll stitch up the wound."

"How long before I can go back to the battle?" Ankhmakis asked with the innocence only the ignorant could maintain. "We're close to taking Lycopolis, I can feel it."

Iu-Amon touched Ankhmakis's thigh and the prince winced. "I'm sorry to say this, my prince, but the tendons and the muscle are sliced. It could take months of rehabilitation before you're able to walk, and even under the best circumstances, full function of the leg isn't guaranteed."

"You mean I might never walk again?" Ankhmakis choked.

"I'm sorry, my lord, but it is probable," Iu-Amon replied.

Natasa felt the panic in her lover and took his hand in hers. Iu-Amon inspected the wound and hesitated before speaking again.

"However, there is one method I think will guarantee the best outcome, if you're willing to try it."

"I will do anything, Iu-Amon," Ankhmakis begged.

"Anything to heal."

"It'll still take months," the healer continued. "but if Natasa is your healer, and the two of you practice the Alchemies of Horus together, we can get this wound to heal. You can use your shared energy field to rehabilitate and repair the muscle, under her care."

Natasa stepped back from the priest, clutching her now churning stomach. On one hand, she wanted nothing more than to be by Ankhmakis's side. On the other, the temptation... She glanced at her love, and one look told her he was feeling the same way.

"You see," Iu-Amon continued, "your years of breath work and astral travel, as well as Anit-Shadya, have created a direct path between you. You no longer need to take Shadya to access your power. The meditative exercises alone will do. We healers seek to create this connection with our patients, and when successful, we're able to help them heal themselves. In this case, your ability to connect at a spiritual level would allow Natasa direct access to your Ka, and thus enable her to heal the wound much, much quicker. No other healer, not even I, could do it faster, or with more accuracy. The two of you might be able to even get those tendons to strengthen. At twenty-five years of age, you are still very young and both your Ka and physical body are strong. It's worth trying."

Natasa's breath caught in her chest. How could she spend so much time by his side and not break her vows? She gazed at Ankhmakis and allowed herself to let go of her lust and fear of him. She had to do this—she was the only one who could. Ankhmakis squeezed her hand.

"*I trust you,*" he said via his mind, "*but I don't trust myself.*"

"*We can do this,*" she replied. "*I won't let fear stand in the way.*"

Ankhmakis nodded and looked to Iu-Amon. "Yes," he said to the old healer. "We will do it."

Iu-Amon clapped his hands together. "Wonderful. Natasa, I suggest you go home for the day and rest. If the poison hasn't left too much damage to Ankhmakis's organs, we'll remove the arrow at sunrise tomorrow. We have a prince to heal, but first we need to clean him."

Natasa squeezed Ankhmakis's hand before letting go. "Yes, he does need a bath," she teased. "He looks like a desert Bedouin left out in the sun far too long. I'll see you in the morning, the moment Ra rises in the east."

"Thank you for helping me," Ankhmakis replied, causing the butterflies in her stomach to cartwheel. This wasn't going to be easy.

"It's my pleasure, dear prince."

She left the room, noting Nefermaat and Pontius, as well as Ankhmakis's other guards, and looking for signs of guilt. Min was innocent, but Nefermaat's eyes narrowed as she walked past. He'd never been very kind to her, but why would he turn on his master? A royal guard swore to the death to protect his lord, no matter what his personal opinion of the man.

Someone had poisoned Ankhmakis on the way to Behdet, and she meant to find out whom.

16

The Little Prince

In the Egyptian family, the eldest son was the steward of the father and expected to follow in his footsteps. Younger sons had choices, but the eldest was bound to the rise and fall of his father.

Behdet, Egypt 202 BCE

The moment Iu-Amon ripped the arrow shaft from Ankhmakis's thigh, he passed out due to the intensity of the pain. Hours later, he awoke in the royal wing of the Houses of Healing still in agony. His leg throbbed and pulsed, reminding him of the seriousness of his wound. He made to try to lift his leg, and his sight dimmed as his body rejected the effort and the room spun around him.

"Don't be hasty," a sweet voice warned. "You need to rest. Mama said so."

He turned his head and was delighted to find Helena sitting at the end of his bed, playing with a needle and thread. The sun shone in through the windows, and a young healer strummed a harp in the corner of his room. He breathed in the fresh air and felt a cool breeze upon his head. He rubbed it and wasn't surprised to find he was bald.

"They shaved your hair." Helena giggled, her own black hair tied in a long braid. "Now you look like Mama."

She wrinkled her nose and smiled at him. Her deep blue eyes made him shiver. Helena was still a child, but no longer a baby. Much had changed in the time he'd been gone.

"Come here, my child," he said, opening his arms wide. "Let me hold you. It's been a long time since I last saw you." Helena crawled into his embrace, and he drew her close. Her tiny heart beat a fast pace on his chest. "How old are you now?"

"Four," she replied. "Plus, some."

"Four?" he exclaimed.

She squirmed out of his grip and counted on her fingers. "Yes, four. Hecataeus says so, and he's smart about numbers."

"Well, four is very old." He laughed at her, and she narrowed her eyes at him.

"No," she answered, shaking her head. "Iu-Amon is old. I'm a little girl."

Helena picked up her needle and string and took a piece of cloth in her other chubby hand. She sewed stiches, back and forth, in a delicate pattern.

"What are you doing?" he asked.

"Practicing," she replied, sticking out her tongue a bit as she concentrated on her task.

"For what?"

"To sew people up. I want to be like Mama and Eleni."

Ankhmakis nodded and looked about his private room.

"Where is your mother?" he asked as he glanced at the door, hoping she'd walk in.

"With the other hurting men," Helena answered, continuing her work. "She's very busy. You delivered a lot of broken soldiers to us." She stopped sewing, looked at him, and smiled. "But you will live."

A woman's shrieks filled the hallway, and soon after Min appeared at the door, Weret trailing behind.

"Let me in," the princess demanded, shoving the captain out of the way. "I must see my husband." In her arms she held a chubby, dark-eyed baby boy, and Ankhmakis's stomach dropped.

"Of course, Your Highness," Min said as he bowed, holding up his palms in the air. What Weret wanted, Weret often got.

"Ankhmaat," Helena cried out as Weret approached.

"Yes," Weret said, scowling at Helena as if she were rotten kitchen scraps, "this is Ankhmaat, your son."

She presented the baby, who chewed on a ring of wooden beads and smiled at the sight of Helena. Ankhmakis felt weak. This was his heir. He held out his arms. "May I hold him?" he asked.

Weret placed the boy in his lap, and Helena crawled closer. "He's the best baby, Papa," she cooed. "He has ten toes and ten fingers. I counted the first time I met him, like Bastyre does."

Ankhmakis laughed and looked to Weret. She still wore a slight frown, yet Helena didn't seem to mind. "I take it you spend time together?" he asked.

"The children do," Weret answered, lifting her chin and tossing her hair. "They play together in the garden. They seem to get along very well."

"How many children are there now?"

"Besides your two," she answered, raising a finger for each child, "Ruia has three—she gave birth a month ago—Bithiah has two and a third on the way. Oh, and there's Alexa's boy with Chanax as well. Eight royal children, as of now."

"How old is our son?"

"Ten months."

"Ten months? Have I been gone so long?"

Weret shook her head. "Ankhmakis, you've been gone well over a year."

He looked at his son and felt his heart swell. He'd never wanted the child, but now, as he held the little prince, his lungs felt as if they'd explode. All he wanted was to hold the baby boy closer and never let go.

"This is my son," he said as he kissed his forehead.

Weret's face softened. They hadn't spoken to one another since the dreadful day she'd accused him of treason. Ankhmakis choked down a bit of bile and instead focused on the children.

"I love Ankhmaat." Helena sighed. Weret pursed her lips.

"Why are there so many guards stationed at your door?" Weret asked. "They wouldn't let me in, claiming I wasn't given access. How dare they? I'm your wife."

"I was poisoned," Ankhmakis answered.

"What?" She took a step back. "Who would do such a thing?"

"We don't know," he replied. "Either one of my injured men, or one of my guards. Either one suggests someone within the court wants me dead." He glanced at Ankhmaat, realizing he too could be a target. "We must be careful," he continued. "You and the prince will need protection. I'll have Min recruit a set of guards for you."

"I have guards and servants enough," she replied, dismissing his concern.

He looked her in the eye, narrowing his own. "You will listen to me, Weret. I'll have my son protected."

She was opening her mouth to object, when Natasa entered the room. If Natasa was shocked or put out by Weret's presence, it didn't show. Weret, however, put her hands on her hips and glared at Natasa.

"What are you doing here?" the princess demanded.

"I've been assigned as the prince's main healer," Natasa replied in honeyed tones.

"This will not do," Weret said, waving her finger. "The two of you are to have no contact. It's the law."

With a smirk on her face, Natasa picked up Ankhmakis's hand and felt his pulse. A rush of electricity ran through his body. When she finished taking his vitals, she tilted her head and smiled at Weret. "I understand your concern, but there's no law against me working for the prince when he's sick."

"You've taken a vow of celibacy," Weret cried out. "You can't be his companion anymore."

"Healers aren't spiritual companions. We work in other ways. Trust me, your husband and I will never be lovers again."

A new pain shot through Ankhmakis's heart at her words. The idea of never touching her naked body again felt worse than his injury.

"You wouldn't deny him the very best care, would you, Princess?" Natasa raised an eyebrow.

"Why are you the very best care?" Weret said.

Natasa shrugged. "Why don't you ask High Priest Iu-Amon? He's the one who assigned me."

Ankhmakis felt invisible as the two glared at each other from either side of his bed. Helena sat in silence, observing the women as the baby cooed in Ankhmakis's arms and crunched on the wooden beads he held in his chubby fingers.

"I think I will," Weret exclaimed, a bit of saliva falling out of her mouth. "I won't have you near him."

"Enough," Ankhmakis said, far past losing his patience with his stubborn wife. "You'll do as you're told, woman."

Natasa glanced at the children, avoiding Weret's angry glare. "I think the two of you need some time alone." She lifted Helena from the bed and put her on the ground. "Here, let me take the baby. We'll be in the herb garden. It isn't good for children to be near anger, and the two of you are swimming in it."

Weret made to argue, but Ankhmakis put his son into Natasa's arms. "Yes, I do have some words for my wife. I'll send a guard when I'm ready for our first session."

"Yes, my lord," Natasa replied and left the room with the children.

As soon as they were out of earshot, Weret opened her mouth to speak, but Ankhmakis held up his hand. "You will not make decisions on my behalf," he hissed.

"What?" she argued. "I'm your wife."

"You've proven yourself unworthy of making decisions of any sort," he continued.

"Nonsense, queens are required to make decisions on their husband's behalf. Look at Queen Keket—"

"Weret, I will never let you have such authority. As I said, you've proven you aren't capable."

"What are you talking about? You're not still mad about father's punishment?" she asked. "Natasa would have been taken from you anyway. The purification of the temple requires it."

Ankhmakis's throat burned as if he'd swallowed bitter herbs. The woman was both infuriating and incompetent. "It isn't the fact you somehow managed to convince Father to take the woman of my heart from my side and give her to my brother," he said through clenched teeth. "Such actions are normal behavior for any spoiled girl, and you are a very spoiled girl."

She stepped back, clutching her breast and making him angrier.

"No, Weret, your failing is far greater than petty jealousy," he continued, his words punctuated by his short, angry breaths. "You accused me of treason without giving any thought to what might have happened. Do you know what the punishment should have been for such a crime?"

He allowed his anger to surround him, and she backed away from the bed. He wanted to see her cower. "Death. Father could have killed me. Did you think for once what the consequences of my death would be for our country? You put the entire war effort at risk by accusing the general of the Egyptian army of treason, for your own selfish need to get my attention. Such behavior makes you unworthy of your station. A queen should know better. A queen would investigate further. A queen would take the time to look at the issue from every angle."

Weret's shoulders slumped as she sobbed. "Oh, Ankhmakis, I never thought about it that way."

"Since you were willing to let Father kill me, why do you think I would trust you with any of my care? I will choose for myself, and if I'm unable to speak, my healer, Natasa, will decide my fate for me. Not you. Is this clear?"

"I'm sorry." She sniffled and grasped at his hands. "I wanted you to love me."

"By accusing me of treason?" He wrenched his hand free from her grip. "My dear, you are dumber than I thought."

"Why do you say such cruel things?"

He sighed. Why was he cruel to her? Why couldn't he open his heart? The sweet sounds of children's laughter danced upon the breeze, and he looked out the window at see his son squealing at his sister as she tickled him in the garden. The little prince.

"It's simple, Weret," he said, unable to peel his gaze from the child. He was already in love with the boy. It took a great effort to continue in a kinder tone. "If you want to be a queen, you need to start acting like one. My queen must understand politics and the logistics of war. If you want to be trusted, you need to care more about Egypt than yourself. These are times of war, so make yourself useful. Study under Ennaeus and learn about our efforts. Think before you act, and perhaps, when the war is done, we might be friends. Your behavior is what will determine the outcome."

She sniffled. "Friends? That's it?"

"It's better than enemies," he replied.

"Why can't you love me as you love Natasa?" she begged.

"Weret," he answered, his throat tightened at her words. "Do yourself a favor and don't try to compete for my heart. You can't. It's not because you're not beautiful, it's because Natasa and I were already in love long before Father made you marry me. It's not fair to you, I know, but there's nothing you can do about it. I will never love a woman as I love her because I loved her first."

He took her hand in his. "Right now, I don't trust you with my life, but I do trust you with our son. Let's start there. The two of you shall visit me every day as I sit here in misery trying to heal. Can you do this?"

She nodded, her painted lips pouting like a child's. He wasn't sure she understood his message, but at least it had been said.

"Thank you. Now please, I need you to leave. I have work to do. I'm useless without my leg, and my recovery must be my main focus, for the good of Egypt. Which is why even though it will be very difficult to be near Natasa and remain a gentleman, I will do it. If Iu-Amon thinks she can heal me the fastest, I won't argue. It will be a good lesson in restraint, don't you think?"

He forced himself to smile at his wife, but Weret said nothing. Instead she rubbed her hand across her tear-filled eyes, smearing kohl across her cheeks.

"Min," Ankhmakis called out, ignoring his wife's pain. "Fetch me Natasa."

17

Misfits and Allies

Iu-Amon and Ennaeus had fallen in love the moment the young Greek cleric arrived in Behdet with Hecataeus, the same year of Ankhmakis's birth. Twenty-three years separated the two men in age, but age means nothing to the heart. Divine pairs come in all types.

Behdet, Egypt, mid-Shemu, 202 BCE

"What are you doing, my lord?" Natasa demanded as she entered the prince's room and found him struggling on the floor, Min attempting to heft him back into bed.

She put her hands on her hips and looked down at him, making sure he couldn't see up her skirt. Ankhmakis grinned up from the floor like a boy caught with his hand in the honeypot. She melted at his charm and rushed to his side to assist Min.

"Let me be, I can do it." He pushed them away and grabbed the side of his bed, biceps bulging as he thrust himself back on top of the furniture. As he fidgeted to get comfortable, Natasa re-arranged animal skins around him and leaned him back into his silken pillows.

"You can't walk yet, my lord," she said, trying to be firm with her patient, which was difficult when he was irritated.

"Obviously," he said through clenched teeth, sitting up in the bed. "The wound is healed on the outside now, Natasa, so why is my leg giving out when I put weight on it?"

She placed her hands on his chest and tried to get him to lie back down. "My lord, you need to rest. It's late."

He shook his head, sitting upright. "I can't rest. It's too quiet. I need to be up and about."

"We've made progress. You and I have managed to heal the outer wounds with the slightest amount of scarring in a record two weeks, but the hardest part is yet to come. You need your rest."

"Natasa, I can't stand it. I've got to start training again. Sitting here and looking out the window all night is driving me crazy."

She turned to Min and teased, "Why aren't you entertaining him?"

"He doesn't enjoy my company," Min said, a hint of a smile upon his face. "At least not as much as he enjoys yours."

Natasa gazed at the prince and felt her heart swoon. He was so handsome, even in his irritated state. "I understand your frustration. The scabs have healed, so there's no risk of breaking the skin open with movement. We can begin therapy tomorrow. I promise. It won't be easy—the interior muscles must regrow, lengthen, and strengthen. My lord, the muscle was severed by the arrowhead. Please, stop demanding too much from yourself, or you won't heal."

"I'm bored," he cried out. "Why do you keep calling me 'lord?' My name is Ankhmakis."

She shook her head. "I think it's best to call you by your proper title, the way everyone else does."

"No," he commanded, "it's not. Everyone else is my servant, but you are my love."

From the way he clenched his eyebrows, she could see he was in pain and walked to a cedar table in the corner of the room to pour him a clay mug of wine. She reconsidered and poured two more, one for her and one for Min. To Ankhmakis's mug, she added extra herbs to ease the discomfort as well as reduce the swelling.

"Here," she said, handing him the mug. Their fingers touched as he took it from her, and her heart skipped a beat. He downed it in one gulp.

"Natasa," he said, handing her the empty goblet and nodding to the pitcher, indicating he wanted more, "please call me Ankhmakis."

She refilled his cup and sat at the end of his bed. She raised her goblet and nodded. "How about 'Princeling?'"

Min snorted.

"Why are you being this way?" Ankhmakis demanded.

She sipped her wine, deep in thought. During the day, when they weren't working together, Ankmakis kept busy receiving massages and baths from other healers, updates from the field, or visiting Weret and his son. Both Helena and Eleni spent hours by his side, and in addition to their energy work and meditation, Natasa sang and played the harp each afternoon during the quiet heat of the day, often putting him to sleep, which was what he needed most. At night, as the rest of them slept, Min was Ankhmakis's sole companion, and it appeared the prince was growing tired of his bedridden state. A man of action could be a danger to himself when bored.

"When was the last time you played the pandura?" she asked.

He shrugged. "I have no idea. I left mine in Abdju."

She turned to Min. "Go find an instrument, have it delivered to Iu-Amon's study, and then come back here."

"Why, my lady?" Min asked.

She looked at her beloved and smiled. "I think my princeling needs a night out."

Min left the room in a hurry, and for the first time in two years Natasa and Ankhmakis were alone. She remained quiet as she sat on her patient's bed, drinking her wine and gazing at him without shame. To her, he was the most beautiful thing in the world.

"Natasa, what are you planning?" he asked.

"The Houses of Healing never sleep," she explained. "Often, when our patients go to bed, I spend time in Iu-Amon's study. Ennaeus, Father, and Bastyre also join. We've sort of started our own club."

"A club? What sort of club?"

"Well," she said, embarrassed to admit her current state of affairs, "we're the misfits."

"Misfits? You're not a misfit."

Natasa shook her head and refilled his wine. "How's your pain?"

"You're changing the subject," Ankhmakis said. "Why is this group of yours considered misfits? Iu-Amon is the high priest of the Houses of Healing, Bastyre is the royal midwife, your father and Ennaeus are the pharaoh's advisors, and you are the spiritual companion to an heir to the throne."

She looked at him, her throat tight as she fought back her tears. She still wasn't used to the way her heart ached when in his company. "Was," she whispered. "I was a spiritual companion to the line of kings. Now, due to my Greek blood, I'm hiding here in the Houses of Healing, hoping Isidor and your mother don't remember I exist. My father and Ennaeus are in the same tenuous situation, and Bastyre has long been rejected by the court for her bloodline as well. Her mother, while Egyptian, was a concubine to the old king."

Ankhmakis leaned back against his pillows and sighed. "Iu-Amon protects each of you, doesn't he?"

"Yes, he does."

Ankhmakis balled his fists. "I should be the one protecting you."

"You protect Egypt," she said. Her heart felt as if it would burst. "You keep the entire kingdom safe."

"Why can't I keep you, the most important person in the world to me, safe?"

"Because, your love puts me in danger," Natasa admitted.

Ankhmakis stared at her, his jaw slack. She leaned forward and in spite of herself, kissed him on the top of his bald head. "Don't worry," she said, trying to comfort him, "Iu-Amon protects me, as does my father. It's going to be fine."

Ankmakis drew her closer and hugged her so hard he squeezed her ribs. The sound of Min clearing his throat behind them made her jump back in surprise.

"I did as you asked, my lady. Now what?" the guard said, pretending not to notice her intimate gesture with the prince.

"Pick the princeling up and follow me," she said as she walked toward the door. "We're going to a party, and I need you to carry him."

ɸ

When they arrived, the group was already well into their second pitcher of mead. Iu-Amon smiled as Min entered, carrying Ankhmakis in his arms as if he were a child.

"Do you have a place to set this guy down?" Min asked. "He weighs as much as an elephant."

Hecataeus snickered and jumped up from his chair by the small fire. "Here," the vizier offered, "take this one."

Min plunked Ankhmakis down in the seat, and Natasa found a stool and placed Ankhmakis's hurt leg on it. He winced as he shifted in his seat, attempting to find a comfortable position. Natasa put a pillow under his knee and relief crossed his face.

"Ankhmakis," Iu-Amon said, lifting his cup into the air as a greeting. "How nice of you to join us."

"I hope you don't mind," Natasa said, "but I can't leave him alone at night anymore. He's misbehaving."

"How so?" the older healer asked.

"It's nothing," Ankhmakis replied.

"He's a bit bored," Min added.

Bastyre rose and handed both men a mug of mead. "Welcome, Your Highness. As long as you play us some music, we'll tolerate your royal company."

The group laughed, and Natasa felt a sense of joy she'd long forgotten. She marched to her father and sat in his lap. He put his arms around her, and she relaxed in his embrace. Bastyre gave her a cup of mead. The pressures of the day had a way of fading when in good company.

"Play us a song, Princeling," Natasa said. She connected to his Ka and found layers of irritation. Her teasing hurt him. She sent him a wave of desire instead, and his eyes opened wide.

"As you wish," he replied as Min placed a pandura in his hands.

Ankhmakis plucked the strings, and Natasa leaned back in her father's arms, mesmerized as Ankhmakis's fingers danced on the instrument and beautiful notes filled the room. The song wasn't recognizable per se, but Natasa knew that he strummed the patterns playing in his head—the musings of his soul. She allowed herself to stare at him, drinking in his beauty as well as her mead. He looked down at the instrument itself, unaware of anything but the song he was composing. The notes rose and fell, became faster, and then slower, and then faster again, rising to a high point. Natasa connected to his energy field and saw images of war, death, and discomfort. She also saw the sunrise over the desert sands, their first kiss, Helena and Ankhmaat hugging, and a pair of hawks flying high in the desert sky. All of these things and more lived within Ankhmakis's heart, and he no longer filtered them from her. After struggling for weeks, he'd surrendered and broken down the wall around his heart.

As the song ended, Natasa smiled and caught his gaze. "Ankhmakis, I think you're ready to heal."

Ankhmakis beamed, and Hecataeus shifted beneath her.

"You're no small thing yourself," Hecataeus said with a grumble. "Not an elephant, but perhaps a jaguar?"

She jumped up from her father's lap to swat him and sat on the ground by the side of Ankhmakis's chair. She placed an arm next to his body and leaned in close, gazing up at his beautiful face. The energy flowed through them and each knew everything the other was feeling. Ankhmakis cocked his head, one eyebrow raised, as he took a sip of mead.

"Congratulations, Natasa," Iu-Amon said. Ennaeus's head rested upon the healer's shoulder. "The two of you have done well. I've never seen a wound heal with such speed. I knew your connection would help."

Natasa nodded and noticed Ankhmakis's expression of surprise as he looked at the intimate way Iu-Amon and Ennaeus sat. This was yet another thing the misfits guarded from the gossip of the court—the two men were lovers—a secret they had to keep.

Bastyre raised her glass to toast Ankhmakis. "Give us another song. This time something more vivacious. I feel like dancing."

Hecataeus picked up a drum. "Agreed," he said as he beat out a quick rhythm.

Natasa rose from her place, downed her mead, and held out her hand to Min. "Dance with me, soldier."

He shook his head, but she ignored him, dragging him out to the middle of the room as Hecataeus and Ankhmakis played a lively tune. She and the midwife danced circles around Min, shimmying and swaying their hips, a trick he couldn't resist, and the soldier gave in and joined them. The three spun round and round as the beat got faster, and Ankmakis sang at the top of his lungs.

Hours later, as she tucked Ankhmakis into bed, he drew her close to his face and whispered, "Thank you. I had a wonderful evening. Without fail, you know what I need."

"You're welcome," she replied, unwilling to pull away from him, even though their lips were mere inches apart.

"Am I correct in assuming Iu-Amon and Ennaeus are lovers?" he asked.

"Yes," she answered, her gaze locked upon his lips. Goddess, she wanted to kiss him. "Please, you must keep it secret. Iu-Amon took a vow of celibacy when he was seventeen, long before Ennaeus was even born."

"How long have they been together?"

"Since Ennaeus arrived in the court as Father's assistant, during Euergetes's rule. Almost as long as you've been alive," she replied, leaning into his neck and breathing in his scent. To be near him was heaven.

He tugged her even closer and her heart danced a jig under

her breasts. "How remarkable they can keep such a secret for so long," he noted.

"I think it's wrong when love must be kept a secret," she countered, nuzzling her head under his chin. "Any attempt to rule the human heart is shameful." She hear Min clear his throat, and she rose to stand, tugging the linen cloth up onto Ankhmakis's chest. "Sleep well, my lord. We start learning to walk in the morning."

"May I join you again?" he asked as she made to leave. "I want to be a part of your misfit club."

She turned and nodded. "Yes, I think our secret club will be very good for you. Now, good night."

☥

In the morning, Natasa found Ankhmakis ready to begin the next phase of their healing journey. Their days were now filled with strengthening exercises, spatial and imaginative work, as well as stretching and meditation. In the evenings, they spent hours in Iu-Amon's study talking, playing games and music, as well as sharing information. The misfits appreciated listening to Ankhmakis's tales of war and they brought him up to speed about the goings on at court and in the temples.

During their sessions she showed him how to place his hands on his thigh and command his Ka to regrow the tendons. He opened himself and allowed her access to his most intimate thoughts, where she taught him how to take the pain of his leg and turn it into the life-giving force of regeneration and growth. They worked day and night as a pair, and after weeks of labor, the moment arrived when he was ready to take his first steps.

"Scoot to the edge of the bed," she instructed. Ankhmakis did as was asked and she sat beside him on his right side.

"Put your arm around me," Natasa continued, and he obeyed. "Now, place your feet on the ground." He placed his feet on the stone floor, body tense and fists clenched. She murmured, "Close your eyes and feel the space around your body, dancing in streams, like the hands of the divine sculpting your muscles and bones. Can you see them?"

"Yes," he replied, his eyes squeezed shut.

"The space around our body is in constant motion, even if we're not aware of it. When we take the time to guide this force, we can build our bodies and repair even the most severe damage. Envision a stream coming from your knee, down behind and along the calf, across the bottom of your foot and into the earth below us. Feel your stronger leg extend into the ground," she whispered, "and send the energy down as you stand up. On three. One, two, and three..."

She rose from her place and Ankhmakis followed, their arms wrapped around one another as he kept his weight on his good leg. "Now shift the weight to your injured leg."

Ankmakis leaned into her grip, and she held him steady. He quivered, and as he sent a stream of energy down into the ground, he gained strength. Natasa slipped out from under his arm and let go of him. He stood, eyes closed, bearing weight on his injured leg. His joy filled the room, granting her a sense of success unlike any other. His eyes popped open as he held his arms out wide.

"I'm doing it," he cried, his smile as wide as the Nile itself. "I'm standing on my injured leg."

"Yes," she agreed, hugging him, unable to resist her own delight. "You are."

"My goddess," Ankhmakis yelled out loud. "We're going to do it, Natasa. I'm going to walk again."

"Not yet, my lord," she said as he made to try to take a

step. "Here, let me help you."

She held out her arm, and he took it as he moved forward. He was still in pain, but he transferred his weight from his right leg to his left. Ankhmakis's face was beautiful in its elation, and she felt her cheeks flush.

"What?" he asked.

"Oh, my love," she replied, still holding on to his arm. "I haven't seen joy upon your face in ages."

Ankhmakis grinned and hugged her close. "Yes, I am happy. Very, very happy, and it's all because of you."

18

Delicate Work

"Your hand is in my hand, my body trembles with joy, my heart is exalted because we walk together."
~ New Kingdom Love Poem, 16 Century BCE

Behdet, Egypt 201 BCE

Chanax followed the sounds of children laughing and screaming. As he rounded a large hedge, Helena, Senui, and Sethe skirted past him in a loud raucous.

"Catch her. Catch her," cried Senui.

How three children could make so much noise, Chanax would never know. He turned down the garden path from which they'd come and found his target—Ankhmakis. His brother had been home for three months, and Chanax had seen him only once. The Houses of Healing weren't the best place for a priest of Set right now, given Iu-Amon's very vocal hate of Isidor's purification laws. However, enough time had passed, and Isidor had given Chanax an assignment—to visit his brother, observe him, and report the state of his injury. They still hadn't figured out a way to attack his Ka. As a matter of fact, Ankhmakis was gaining in power and popularity. His injury had made him a legend among the troops, and the healing of his wound was nothing short of miraculous. Talk of "Ankhmakis the Savior" was flooding the land. Something had to be done to end the foolishness.

Sirius, their most sacred star, had risen beside the sun god, Ra, marking the beginning of the New Year and the season of Akhet. Rains poured down for days, and it appeared his brother was taking advantage of a rare sunny day by playing with his children. The pompous ass sat under a fig tree, a picnic spread out in front of him. Several small children, including Chanax's own toddler, Panas, and his chubby three-year-old daughter, Baktre, who was playing a hand clapping game with Silus's second son, Hor, surrounded the prince. On his lap sat Ankhmaat, now thirteen months and almost walking. In addition to the nursemaids, Ruia and Natasa sat in the shade, drinking cool, sweet ale and laughing in the morning light.

"What's this?" the red-robed priest asked as he glided into their midst. "A royal party?"

"Chanax, it's good to see you," Ruia said with a soft smile. At her breast nursed her infant girl, Anen, born just weeks before Ankhmakis had arrived injured from battle. "Come, join your brother in our women's work. You'll see it's quite enjoyable to play with the children."

"Why thank you, I'd love to join," Chanax lied. He'd rather dance with a horned viper than make small talk with Ankhmakis. The way his brother always seemed to come up the winner gave Chanax a headache. He sat next to the fiend and swept up his own little boy from the nursemaid's arms, pretending to look interested in the company. The art of deception was a necessary skill in the priesthood. He gazed around the loud group, noticing his own wife was missing.

"Where's Bithiah?"

"She never joins us," Ruia answered. "Thinks Natasa and I are foolish to do work our nursemaids could do for us. Weret should be here any minute though. Since Ankhmakis has taken an interest in his son, she doesn't leave us alone."

Ruia gave Natasa a knowing look and the two smiled. Their friendship was obvious. Chanax filed the realization away and decided he needed to tell Bithiah to join the women and children. The friendship between Ruia and Natasa could work against them, and he needed Bithiah to stir up some rivalry between the pair.

"How are you feeling today, brother?" he asked Ankhmakis.

"Wonderful," Ankhmakis replied, leaning back against an olive tree and pulling Ankhmaat closer to his chest. "I walked the whole way here with a cane."

"Remarkable," Chanax said. "You're healing faster than was expected. Whatever is your secret?"

Ankhmakis looked to Natasa, and Chanax could see the form of love between them, stronger than ever. Were they lovers again? Would Ankhmakis risk his very life for her sex? Chanax hated the look Natasa returned to Ankhmakis—one of complete adoration.

"I have a good healer," Ankhmakis replied with a lopsided grin.

Ruia hit Natasa on the shoulder. "She's the best all right."

Weret arrived, panting as if she'd run from the palace, adjusting her hair and necklaces as she approached. She sat next to Ankhmakis and gave him a kiss on the cheek. He didn't turn away and instead gave her his own quick kiss on the lips and handed her the baby.

"Good morning, Weret," Ankhmakis said. Chanax looked

to Natasa, still chatting with Ruia, nonplussed by the display of affection. "I'm glad you're here. I have work to do, and our son needs your loving care."

"What?" she whined as she picked up her toddler, who struggled to break free. "I arrived but a moment ago. I would have been here sooner, but the queen made me tend to the weavers today. Bithiah is still there. Mother makes her work, even though she's yet again with child."

"Well, I've been enjoying the company of the babies and royal toddlers for an hour and now have an appointment in the training ring," he explained as he struggled to stand.

"No, you don't," Natasa cut in, running to his side to assist him and handing him his cane, a carved piece of alabaster. "You aren't cleared for the training ring."

"No," he replied, "but you are."

She frowned. "I am?"

Weret rolled her painted eyes.

"Yes," Ankhmakis answered, eyes glittering in the sunlight. "I have a surprise for you. Besides, I need to see my men. Time to act like a general."

Natasa's eyebrows squished together, her mouth opening as if to speak. Chanax handed his son back to his nursemaid.

"A trip to the training ring sounds exciting. May I join you?" he interrupted, not wanting to go back to Isidor empty handed. Other than discovering that Ruia and Natasa were meeting in the gardens, and Ankhmakis was happy and healing, Chanax had nothing new to report. He needed to figure out how the man was making his remarkable recovery, as well as discover any weaknesses he might be hiding from everyone. It would be like the braggart to pretend everything was fine in order to get back to the front line and play the hero.

"If you'd like," Ankhmakis replied. "Let's talk while we

walk. It's been forever since I last saw you. I see you have two children now, and another on the way. You and Bithiah are quite an industrious pair. It appears priests have all the fun. I think I'm in the wrong business."

Ankhmakis winked at Weret as he spoke, causing the princess to blush. It appeared his brother had learned an important lesson—to get what he wanted, he needed to charm his wife. No wonder Bithiah hadn't been able to rouse Weret to anger since her husband's return—he was being kind. Yet another thing they'd have to remedy.

Chanax fell into place on the other side of Ankhmakis, and as they left the garden, the three eldest children zoomed past.

"Be careful, Papa," Helena screeched as she and Senui skipped by holding hands, Sethe at their heels, throwing olives at them. "We are very fast."

"Yes, you are fast, my precious one," Ankhmakis said, a glowing smile upon his doting face. "Much faster than I am, but soon I will catch you, I promise."

The rambunctious girl and boys giggled at Ankhmakis as he doddered past like an old man and continued the long walk to the training facilities. Despite the snail's pace, he made each step on his own. Natasa linked her arm with Ankhmakis's. Chanax hadn't seen him so vibrant in a long time.

"Brother," Chanax said as they shuffled along, "you look great. I must know how this can be. You were near death a few months ago."

"I told you, it's Natasa."

"No," she argued, "it's not me. It's you and your determination to cure yourself."

"Yes, about my wondrous healing," Ankhmakis continued, a gleam in his eye, "I'd like to leave the Houses of Healing and return to the palace."

"What?" she asked.

"Yes," Ankhmakis declared. "I can walk now, I miss my quarters, and it's closer to the war room, where I do most of my work."

Natasa remained quiet, considering his request. After a few silent steps, she agreed. "I imagine it would be fine for you to return to your chambers," she answered. "You'll need to post more guards to cover the entrances, for your protection."

"Protection?" Chanax asked. "What in the world do you need to be protected from here? You're hundreds of miles away from war. Behdet is very safe." Ankhmakis's glowing face fell.

"I was poisoned, Chanax. Didn't you know?"

The news took Chanax by surprise. "No, I didn't," he said, frowning. Too many secrets were kept inside the Houses of Healing. He'd need to visit more often if he and Isidor were going to crack the code and gain access to Ankhmakis's energy field.

"It's no matter," Natasa said, her narrow gaze penetrating Chanax as if attempting to read his mind. "I'm sure we can protect the prince as he continues his recovery within the palace. It's a good idea."

Ever since she'd been forced out of the temple of Isis and into the Houses of Healing, Natasa'd grown cold toward Chanax. No longer did she hug him or greet him with the enthusiasm of the past. Nor did she wear the bloodstone he'd given her. Something had changed.

They entered the ring and Ikui, the weapons trainer, approached, holding out his arms and bowing low to Ankhmakis.

"My lord, it has been too long," he said as he rose from the ground. Ankhmakis hugged the man and began to ask him questions about their troops. Several dozen men were sparring using various weapons. On the far side of the ring, a group of fifty Ethiopians was jumping up and down, doing pushups, and running the steps to the top of the amphitheater and back down again. Chanax was exhausted watching them.

"I should be out there," Ankhmakis said, his lips pouting.

"Soon," Natasa said, rubbing his arm. "You're very close."

Ankhmakis shook his head. "No, I'm not. No matter, we're not here for me. Ikui, did you make ready the knives?"

"Yes, sir," the old man replied, leading them to a corner of the training facility, where a table had been set up with several knives of different sizes. Their blades glistened in the sun. On a wooden target about fifteen feet away, someone had drawn a red figure of a human being. Chanax looked down at his red priest robe and back again at the red humanoid target. He crossed his arms.

"Your targets are made in the image of priests?" he asked.

Ankhmakis shrugged. "It's not intentional, but I imagine Natasa has more to fear from your kind than any other in the palace."

"You speak nonsense and you know it," Chanax replied, grinding his teeth. "How dare you say such a thing?"

Natasa again glared at Chanax as if she could see right through him and into his heart, where his evil plans originated, and the hair on his arms stood at attention. She *was* trying to penetrate his mind. In response, he blocked her mind. Her eyes grew wide at the action, and his lips curled into a sneer.

"We know what god you serve," Natasa said in a low voice.

Ankhmakis put his arm around Natasa and beckoned her closer. "Come. It's time for you to practice."

"Practice what?" she asked, taking a knife in her hand and running her finger along the blade.

"Protecting yourself," Ankhmakis answered. He eyed Chanax as he continued. "Our lives are in danger. If I die on the battlefield, the war will be over, and the entire kingdom will pay the price. They will come for the ones I love."

"You're being a bit dramatic," Chanax cut in. His brother's injury hadn't dampened the man's self-aggrandizing nature. "They're fighting right now without you."

"Because I still live," Ankhmakis said. "My life is their hope. If I die, the men will begin to surrender. Father's aware of this fact. He can't keep the army under his control if I perish. However, someone within the court wants me dead. Thus, I've taken it upon myself to protect my own. Weret and Ankhmaat have a new set of guards, but I can't place a guard upon you, Natasa, without upsetting my wife. Besides, guards won't be enough, should I die. You'll need to protect yourself and Helena, and escape Behdet. It makes sense to expand on a skill you have. I'm told you can use knives?"

She nodded, holding out the knife in her hand. "Yes, I've been taught some exercises with the short blades."

"Fine. Show me how well you can throw them."

Ankhmakis took a seat behind the table and Chanax stood by his side. Natasa lined up across from the target. She raised the knife, focused on the wooden, red figure, and threw it, piercing the center of the chest. Within moments she'd thrown the rest in a perfect circle around the first one. Her work was masterful.

"Well," Ankhmakis said, rising from his seat, licking his slightly open lips, "you can throw from a distance, which will come in handy. Now can you spar?"

"You mean fight someone with a knife?" she asked. "I learned techniques for sparring in my work as a dancer, but I've never practiced one-on-one combat."

"Have you, Chanax?" Ankhmakis asked.

"Yes," Chanax replied, "I was trained in weapons. All priests are."

"Wonderful," Ankhmakis said. "Since I'm disabled, you can fight Natasa. You're each to be armed, but don't hurt her. I need her functional if I'm to heal."

"I don't think it's appropriate for me to spar with Natasa," Chanax answered.

"Why not?" Natasa demanded. "Afraid you'll lose to a girl?"

"You think you can taunt me into this?" Chanax asked, wanting nothing more than to get out of this situation. He was there to figure out a way to breach Ankhmakis's energy field, not fight Natasa. "Such play is beneath my station."

Natasa drew two knives from their position on the target and handed one to Chanax. "Please."

Chanax felt a wave of excitement pass between the couple. Could they could speak to one another remotely? Perhaps they'd broken her vow of celibacy? His pulse quickened and he found he wanted to fight her, to punish her for giving her life to this useless man.

"Fine," he replied, "but don't get mad if I hurt you."

"My brother used to say the same thing when we were young," she answered with a wink. "I can handle it, trust me."

They took their positions in the center of a small ring and danced around one another. Chanax made to strike, but Natasa blocked him before kicking him in the side.

"Ow," he cried. "Not fair."

"Sorry," she replied, kicking at his knees.

The game was on.

Chanax was careful with the knife but struck and kicked her. He himself took several knocks. Their sparring was rough, and the dirt flew up from beneath their furious footwork. Years of anger and aggression poured out of her in waves. With each hit she thrust at him, he felt her blame him for her predicament, as if somehow she'd seen into his heart and understood it had been his jealousy, and not Weret's, behind her separation from Ankhmakis.

She kicked his ribs and he returned the kick with such force, she fell to the ground. Rather than feel empathy, he sent his own anger at her—anger at the rejection of his love and her obsession with Ankhmakis. He guided the form of his fury toward her heart and to his amazement she blocked it energetically with her own. As he lost himself in her fierce gaze, the true cause of her recent coldness toward him became clear, and it had nothing to do with Ankhmakis. She knew what he did for the priesthood of Set.

Natasa rose from the ground and made to slice at his elbow. As he raised his arm to block her attack, her eyes locked onto his and she connected to his Ka, probing his thoughts and revealing what he did for the god of chaos—the dark magic, the sacrifices, and the innocents slaughtered on the altar of his god. Natasa pushed further into his mind and became aware of their plans to kill the pharaoh and Ankhmakis and hand the crown to Chanax instead. He tried to block her, but she was too quick; she shoved him to the ground. He cowered in the dirt, ashamed as she searched his soul and saw his deeds. She knocked the knife from his hand, turned him to his back, and forced his arms to the ground, straddling his chest. He struggled to get out of her grip, but she wrapped her legs around his body and pressed the cool blade of her knife upon his throat.

"*I see you,*" she hissed within his mind.

He risked glancing at her and saw the fury in gaze. Her

weight against his body aroused him, and his body betrayed him, growing hard in between her legs, which she understood.

"I've got you," she said aloud.

Chanax struggled, and Natasa leaned closer to his face. Her mouth was mere inches from his. Nothing was more erotic than this moment, even though her anger surrounded him like a cage.

"And now I know what you do in secret." She spoke without speaking, yet her thoughts were loud and clear to Chanax—Natasa had mastered the art of energetic warfare, and neither he nor Isidor had noticed.

She thrust herself from his chest, wiping her hands on her robes as if she'd touched something vile. She turned to Ankhmakis, her body stiff and rigid, jaw clenched. "Long have the men of this court underestimated me."

Chanax rose from the ground and wiped the dirt from his mouth. Ankhmakis stared at her, slack jawed. Did he know what Natasa had just done? Chanax thought not. Like their father, Ankhmakis was no priest. The only warfare he understood was executed at the end of a bloodied blade.

"I tire of your games," Natasa said. "Remember this, Princelings, I see each of you, and your sisters, very, very clearly."

She turned and threw her knife at the target, now at least thirty feet away, and the blade struck the wooden figure right in the center of the head. She nodded, satisfied, and walked toward the exit.

"Ankhmakis, I expect you to report to me later today," she yelled at him without turning around.

"I expect you to start wearing a knife on your body at all times," Ankhmakis yelled back.

In a huff of dust, she was gone.

"What in the world?" Chanax asked, rubbing his shoulder. Several bruises were already starting to form on his body.

Ankmakis turned and slapped Chanax on the back. "I think my Natasa is more than capable of taking care of herself, don't you?"

Chanax shrugged from his brother and glanced at the red humanoid target, Natasa's knives surrounding its heart. Ankhmakis had no idea what that woman was capable of. No idea at all.

19

The Kiss

"The Egyptians appear to have reversed the ordinary practices of mankind. Women attend markets and are employed in trade, while men stay at home and do the weaving! Men in Egypt carry loads on their head, women on their shoulder. Women pass water standing up, men sitting down. To ease themselves, they go indoors, but eat outside on the streets, on the theory that what is unseemly, but necessary, should be done in private, and what is not unseemly should be done openly."

~ Herodotus, Father of Greek History, 400 BCE

Behdet, Egypt 201 BCE

"Come here," Natasa said, her hand waving to the spot in front of her, "let me check you one last time."

Ankhmakis stood before her, and she bent down on one knee to inspect his leg, her head inches from his groin. He ached for her to touch him the way she had when they were younger, and he was thankful she ignored how hard he was under his linen skirt.

Natasa drew her hand up and along his inner thigh, across

and to the outer side, feeling for signs of a tear or lingering injury. His vitals were clear, and he'd been able to run miles the previous day without any pain. If she gave the signal, he'd ride back out to war. Part of him wanted to return to the front line, for his army needed their general. The past months of rest and relaxation in Natasa's company at the Houses of Healing had been not only restorative, but also delightful beyond measure. The late nights with Hecataeus, Iu-Amon, Ennaeus, Min, Bastyre, and Natasa had awakened a sense of purpose within him. He was an even stronger general after having suffered and healed alongside his soldiers. Getting to know his children, Ankhmaat and Helena, was also a blessing. Helena was an amazing and captivating child, and Ankhmaat had started walking. Ankhmakis's chest ached watching his son tottle on unsteady legs behind his big sister around the garden as they hunted ladybugs together. Yes, Ankhmakis loved his children, and it would be difficult to ride out this time, for a part of him also longed for the war to end and to spend his days being a prince at court.

As Natasa cupped his thigh between her hands, electricity pulsed between them. His Ka responded with a surge of power, and the muscles of his leg tightened. He looked down at her and admired her beauty while she wasn't looking. Natasa was more powerful than ever, and Ankhmakis found he loved her even more for it. His throat began to tighten; the pain of being her friend rather than her lover felt like a knife to the heart. He balled his fists and stared at the ceiling, forcing his breath to slow. For her safety, he must not cross the line, but his body was betraying him.

She rose from her position. "You're healed, my prince. I clear you for battle."

"What if I don't want to leave?" he asked her.

"When have our desires ever mattered?" she replied, her kissable mouth turning into a slight scowl. She gathered her things. "I will let Iu-Amon know to release you and the other men as well. I imagine you'll go soon?"

"Yes," he answered, sorry that he'd have to leave her. "Not tomorrow, but the next day."

Natasa nodded but said nothing.

"Natasa," Ankhmakis began, not wanting the conversation to end, "what is the source of your power?"

"What do you mean?" she asked. "The Alchemies of Horus of course."

"Yes, but you're different. We've worked together in the other realms for many years," he said, hesitating as her lips parted before forming a slow smile that made his palms sweat. "We have discovered the highest points of bliss. However, the way you've taught me to heal myself goes beyond anything we experienced during ceremony, which is saying something, my love, considering how wonderful our Shadya..."

His voice trailed off, and he fought the urge to pick her up and carry her off and indulge in his desire. She tucked a bit of her short hair behind her ear and nodded, reading his thoughts, and a wave of heat passed between them.

"Yes," she agreed, "we're closer in a whole new way now, aren't we?"

She stared at him in silence, and he allowed himself to connect to her heart and lose himself in her love. They stood a foot apart and yet felt as one. He sensed the many thoughts flowing through her mind. He too had grown more powerful under her healing care.

"Do you remember the apiary?"

"Yes." He nodded.

"Come meet me tomorrow at sunrise," she offered, "and

I'll show you the source of my power."

He remembered Weret, and how he'd promised to have dinner with her later in the evening. He wouldn't stay overnight in her chambers. He never did. Sleeping alone was part of their tenuous agreement. They'd have a meal as a family, and when the servants took the child away—he didn't want to think about it for fear Natasa would know he'd returned to his sister-wife's bed.

"I'm glad you've reconciled," Natasa said, reading his mind anyway.

"Natasa, I'm not sure it's reconciliation. I don't trust her, but I need to have sex," he admitted. It felt good to be honest. "She lets me see my son, and I can take care of my needs. You have no idea how hard it is to be around you all day and not make love."

Her eyes lowered. "Do you think I have no idea what it's like to long for your touch? I've slept alone for so many nights, Ankhmakis, I've lost count."

"Oh, Natasa," he said, feeling guilty again, "I'm sorry, I can't seem to say anything right."

She placed her hand on his shaven cheek and shook her head. "No, don't apologize," she said. "I'm here by choice, and I know how to take care of myself. We priestesses of Isis are trained in self-pleasure you know."

Ankhmakis gulped and felt himself get hard again. "A bit too much information, my dear."

"After the intimate time you've spent as my patient," she continued, dropping her hand from his face, "I'm in the spotlight when it comes to Weret. I'll explain more tomorrow, but trust me, I don't want her near me, nor can I be her focus. If you can keep her happy, I'm safe. This is the way it is."

He grimaced at her words. "Khaleme believes sleeping

with a woman who doesn't want you is a sin. Thus, to seek out concubines, slaves, or whores is wrong. Weret is more than willing, begging for it even, so this arrangement is better than seeking out the concubines like a spoiled boy to ease my sexual needs, don't you think?"

"Of course," she said, but he could see tears forming.

"To be honest," he continued, "some part of me feels used after having sex with her. I don't love her, Natasa, and I don't think I ever will. Even without you in my bed, she and I don't get along. She threatens you in order to force me to give her what she wants so she might someday be queen. Maybe it's also wrong to make a man mate with a woman he doesn't love in order to produce heirs, or to keep her from hurting the ones he loves."

Natasa hugged herself. "You must feel like I did when given to Silus."

"I hate knowing he will be the last man to ever touch you," Ankhmakis replied, clenching his fists, wanting nothing more than to break his brother's nose again. "Khaleme also thinks Father sinned when he gave you to Silus to punish me. He told the pharaoh he was considering taking back his troops because the action made him question Father's right to rule Egypt. They take Anit-Shadya very seriously in Kush."

"What did Pharaoh Horwenefer say?"

"He admitted he'd been wrong to take you from me, but he stands by the purification of the temple law for now. Until the war is over, all Greeks, whether full blooded or not, can't hold leadership positions."

"I see," Natasa said. "Ankhmakis, I'm sorry your father has put you in this position. I wriggled out of my assignment to Silus with the help of Iu-Amon, but for the good of Egypt, there's no way for you to do the same. You need a queen, and several sons, to rule this land. It is your duty."

She blinked away the tears in her big green eyes, and he found himself transported to his twenty-year-old self in Alexandria when he first fell in love with her. His knees felt weak.

"Can you come to the apiary at sunrise?" she asked again. "I want to share my life with you in this way. Celibacy is hard, but what I do for the goddess now is both humbling and the greatest adventure of my life."

Ankhmakis wanted to know her secret. He gulped as he nodded. "I'd love nothing more."

"Tell no one and make sure you aren't followed. No one can know what I do." She bowed and walked away, leaving him wondering what she'd been able to hide so well from him.

☥

The next morning, he awoke before dawn and called for Min. "Make sure I'm not followed," he advised his guard. "This is important. Natasa has something to show me and no one else can know about it."

Min crossed his arms. "You best not touch her, my lord, because I can't support such treachery."

Ankhmakis's jaw hardened. "You'll do as you're told." Min gasped and stepped back. Ankhmakis continued, "I don't think sex is what she has in mind this morning, but I can't guarantee I won't succumb to my desire someday. It's too hard. I love her, more than anyone in the world, so don't make such a threat again."

Min nodded and followed him as he made his way to the apiary.

"The coast is clear," Min reported as they approached the old gates. "Where should I remain?"

"Along the path, about twenty feet over there," Ankhmakis said. "No one comes here. Most are scared of the bees."

"Aren't you?' Min asked.

"Of course, but somehow Natasa commands them."

Min's mouth dropped open, and Ankhmakis chuckled as a voice called inside his head.

"*Come,*" Natasa beckoned, "*I'm waiting.*"

He nodded to Min and rushed through the old gates and into the world of the bees. They hadn't yet awakened, and the entire garden droned with the sound of the sleeping insects. In the middle of the hives stood Natasa, in nothing but a white robe and her large golden earrings. She held something in each of her hands. She wore his ring, and he felt a sting in the back of his throat as he recalled the day he'd given it to her, just before the birth of their daughter. He'd marked her as his, only to lose her to his father's jealousy.

She glanced at her hand and smiled. "It works better when I wear your signet."

"What works better?"

She held out two short wands, one silver and one gold. "They're called the Wands of Horus," she explained. "Your father gave me the golden one on your wedding day. General Khaleme gave me the silver one before he headed out to join you in war. Together, they allow my consciousness to enter the realm of light. Much faster than any meditation we've ever done in ceremony."

"What?" Ankhmakis cried. "Nothing is better than Anit-Shadya."

"I didn't say better. I said faster, and in some ways, as delightful. You'll see. Come, stand here in the center of the apiary."

He stood inches from her and felt his heart beat faster.

"Take the silver rod into your left hand," she whispered into his ear. She was a hair's length from him, and his skin tingled as her breasts brushed his chest. "The golden one in your right. Hold them and take a step forward with your left foot. Allow Ra's golden kiss to bathe your face..."

She stepped away, giving him space, yet remained close enough for him to still smell her sweet, warm, amber-scented skin. "Let go," she instructed as she retreated from his side.

Ankhmakis clutched the wands in his hands and turned into the sun god's warmth. There was a tug at his navel as a sudden power surged around him. Images scattered about, and he attempted to focus on one, but none took hold.

"Go beyond the images," she said, her voice muffled, as if he were underwater. "Go to the realm of light, beyond our actions and emotions."

He allowed himself to drop beyond the feelings flooding him and found himself in the world behind the world. Light danced around him, like streams of silk. He was surrounded by people, not as themselves, but as eternities. He sensed events, millions of them, each a possibility waiting to happen. Information flowed into his soul—advice, strategies, ancient wisdom and pleas—coming from sources he couldn't identify. The experience was at once blissful and excruciating. He saw a world of men, dressed in strange clothes of pants and jackets, sitting before boxes made of metal. He knew without asking that they were machines, created with one purpose—to free man from his labors. Ankhmakis watched as they invented ways to illuminate homes without fire, to harness power in the palm of their hands, and control all intelligent life via their thoughts. The vision continued until he passed into oblivion, a place where the world of humanity no longer existed. After what felt like forever, he began to return to his body.

"Feel for your toes," Natasa instructed from somewhere in the distance.

When he opened his eyes, he looked around and felt like the whole world was different, the colors richer, and the scents stronger than ever before.

"What happened to me?" He gasped.

"I call it the Way," she replied.

"What?" he answered, handing back the rods. She took them and placed them in a box. She removed her ring, put it next to the rods, and made to close the lid, but the small, blue, paper flower he'd bought her in Alexandria caught his eye. He took it out of the box and held it in his hand, causing her to bite her lip. Her love swept through him, and he didn't block it. Instead, he allowed it to surge within himself.

"The rods take us to the realm of light," she explained, her voice shaking. "A realm where all things are connected and infinitely possible. Prayer is an asking, but if you can enter the Way, you don't ask; you command."

Ankhmakis nodded. "How do the rods work? It takes time for us to raise the serpents and gain access to the world behind the world. Holding these wands transported me there in an instant."

"I think it has to do with the crystal inside them," she answered. "Our thoughts connect to the crystals through the metals and are transported to the Way, which is a record of human activity stored as light."

He placed the paper flower behind her ear, causing her to gaze up at him. Goddess, he adored her. "Tell me more," he begged. He needed to understand.

"The realm of light is the All-One, where every event begins and ends. For example, I wanted you to heal, so I entered my own desire into the Way. Since you stand before me, battle ready, it appears my request was granted."

"Does everything happen as you wish?" he asked, sensing why this power needed to be kept secret.

"No," she replied. "If the request doesn't fit with the divine plan of the evolution of consciousness, it won't happen."

"I see," he murmured, now drawing her closer and putting his arms around her.

"Ankhmakis," she said, "do you understand what I've shown you?"

"I'm not sure," he admitted.

"The world behind the world is the origin of every action on Earth. We can approach it with humility, ask to be a part of it, and co-create with the divine. It requires great discipline. The realm of light isn't moral. It doesn't determine right from wrong. Millions of possibilities exist and at any time can become active. Which means some requests may seem to go unanswered, due to an incompatibility with the divine plan, but most are accepted and become a part of the Way, often with unintended consequences. Humans, by their nature, insert their will into the cosmic plan, whether they are aware of it or not. In terms of eternity, our decisions, no matter how foolish, can be balanced over centuries to serve the divine plan, but within a single lifetime, our wants and needs can cause great harm."

He stared at her face, understanding for the first time. "If the Way isn't moral, we must be very careful with our requests."

"Yes," she cried, her voice rising. "It takes time to study the nature of the Way. I spend hours every day observing this web of life. Each insertion of our will has consequences. Some are more devastating than others. To co-create with the divine means accepting the painful truth that what we want might not be best for the All-One."

Ankhmakis swallowed hard and nodded. What she did in the apiary was even more critical perhaps than what he was doing on the battlefield.

"You can see," she continued, "how the wands could be abused in the wrong hands, such as Isidor, Chanax, and their cult of Set. I've seen Isidor and his men in the Way. Through their evil, they do help you win battles, but often they try to manipulate you, the pharaoh, Silus, even Weret. They've killed people with their thoughts. I fear for the pharaoh's life, as well as yours. This is why no one can know about this. If Isidor, or anyone with such a dark heart, took these wands, chaos would follow, and Egypt would fall. The wands create an instant manifestation of thought into matter. This is why Weret must not fear me. Her neediness often draws attention to me, and as you can see, my work requires me to remain hidden."

"There's something else," he said, biting his lip and hesitating for a moment. He took a deep breath before continuing. "I saw the future just now."

Her eyes grew wide. "What have you seen?"

"A faraway future," he continued, his stomach turning as he searched for the right words to describe the wonders he'd just seen. His vision had been grand and terrifying at the same time. "Where men create complex tools, mimicking human limbs and thoughts, from metals and crystals, harvested from deep within the earth. Like the wands, their inventions will connect to the realm of light and allow them to do their work."

"Structures made of metal that will be like people?" she asked. "Why would they create such a thing?"

"To make life easier," he said. "Their inventions will do their labor, so they might be freed from their burdens. Not only the kings and queens, but also the peasants. Their tools of metal will send the requests to the All-One and co-create with the divine."

Ankhmakis paused, his heart now racing as if he were on the edge of battle, waiting for his enemy to strike, yet knowing that victory was at hand. "I want to be here on Earth in the age of metal servants. Promise me we'll come back and share that lifetime together."

"If your Ba wishes to return in that age, you must remember your duty," she advised. "In my work, I've seen that most men don't realize their thoughts are connecting to the All-One. They don't understand the nature of their requests. Everything we create sends commands to the All-One, which means the men of the future run the risk of creating a painful world for humanity. Those men of the future may be no different than Isidor, who would use the wands to manifest his own desires, regardless of the outcome for life as we know it."

He drew her into his arms again.

"Ankhmakis," she continued, now trembling, "in the hands of evil, the wands will create chaos. I watch the web of life before making a request. Evil men ask without any regard for the delicate way every being is interconnected. Don't become one of those men."

He kissed the top of her bald head. "I also saw something else," he said, his heart beating even faster. "I saw that we have been one, since the dawn of time."

"Yes," she whispered as she hugged him closer. "I've seen that as well."

"Have you seen what would happen if I kissed you now?" he asked, unable to stop the momentum now stirring within him.

She stepped back and smiled. "No. Perhaps you should show me?"

He cupped her cheeks and drew her into his passionate embrace. Three years was too long to go without the kiss of his beloved. As his mouth found hers, sparks flew through his entire being. He no longer knew where he ended and she started. Natasa returned the kiss, her nipples hardening against his chest, and he held her closer, his hands wandering down her back and to the bottom of her tunic. He picked her up into his arms and she wrapped her legs around his waist. He kissed her neck and she sighed.

"I love you, Ankhmakis."

He drew her closer and rocked back and forth, holding tight and whispering in her ear, "In your arms, I'm home. You are precious to me, Natasa, the greatest of jewels." Against his body's will, he placed her back on the ground, struggling to let her out of his embrace. For her safety, he needed to stop. "I must go. If I stay, I will make love to you."

Ankhmakis walked toward the gates and paused to look at Natasa one last time. She stood in the center of the apiary, the blue flower still behind her ear, her chin lifted high, exposing her long, elegant neck leading to her perfect shoulders and chest. A golden glow surrounded her. He bowed—for he was in the company of the goddess.

"I will become the pharaoh of our lands," he promised. "When I do, I will overturn the laws keeping you from my side. You will be my queen and right hand in all matters. Together we will create the next Egyptian dynasty. I promise."

Ankhmakis left his beloved in the garden as the new day's sun shone down upon the flowers, and the bees woke from their slumber.

20

A Father's Love

When Ankhmakis and his men returned to the front lines, the Upper Kingdom rejoiced, for the prince had been to the edge of death and returned an even greater man. They sang songs in the taverns and streets about Ankhmakis—their true king in heart and soul.

Behdet, Egypt 201 BCE

Ankhmakis sat at the King's Corner in the position of honor, Weret on one side, and Chanax and Bithiah on the other. In Silus and Horwenefer's absence, it fell upon him to host the evening's celebration in honor of the soldiers returning to battle. The dinner was a strange gathering. Rather than nobles in their finery and priests in their solemn robes, the great hall was crowded with tables of recovered soldiers, eager for a good meal before heading out to war the next morning.

Neferu-ankh-maat and the Ethiopian priest, Dardre, also sat in the King's Corner, as well as Ruia. Hecataeus and Queen Keket rounded out the company. After learning the truth about Isidor and his Invisible Hands, Ankhmakis refused to invite any of them, other than Chanax, who had warned him not to reject Isidor. Ankhmakis didn't care. Between Natasa's revelations and Khaleme's prediction that worshipping Set would do them great harm, he needed to use his moment as the highest-ranking royal in Behdet to show he wasn't aligned with the evil priest and his cult.

A group of priestesses entered the hall and danced for the men. Alexa was at the lead. When her daughter had been stripped of the position of high priestess-in-waiting, Neferu-ankh-maat had begun training Alexa for the position. Born of the great priestess Tyia and the old high priest Inebni, the young woman was of the purest of temple blood, just as Isidor and the queen wanted. Ankhmakis recalled the many times he'd sat in the hall watching Natasa dance in this way and daydreamed about their kiss in the gardens. Weret batted her eyelashes at him, and rather than encourage her, he drank from his goblet and pretended to appear interested in the priestesses of Isis. He couldn't bear to service himself with Weret again, for he wanted the taste of Natasa to linger upon his lips.

"*Come to me,*" a voice in his heart pleaded. He shook his head, unsure if Natasa was trying to contact him, or if his wishful thinking was playing tricks on him.

After the dancing, High Priestess Neferu-ankh-maat stood and blessed the men, asking the goddess Isis and her son Horus to watch over them as they set out to battle. Ankhmakis rose, golden goblet in his hand, and toasted the crowd.

"My dear men," he said, his voice booming across the great hall. "We ride out together at sunrise. The time has come to take Lycopolis. We will not stop until the city is in our hands."

The men cheered, and Ankhmakis's chest swelled. Yes, he loved these soldiers and hoped they'd soon be victorious in driving the occupiers from their lands. He was ready to come home and do the work of creating a new empire, rather than tearing an old one apart.

Weret stood beside him and waved to the men. They cheered the princess, which was a good thing. It felt false, but Weret was the best Ankhmakis had to offer right now. He looked to Chanax and Bithiah, both of whom sat with arms crossed at their seats. Extending his Ka to cover them, he sensed their jealousy. Did they think they stood a chance at being the king and queen of Egypt? Ankhmakis hugged Weret closer to his side and kissed her on the cheek, his gaze set upon his younger brother for good measure, before addressing the crowd.

"Come, men, it is time to retire. We ride out with Ra's ascent." He turned to Weret. "I must go."

"My dear," she begged. "Please stay the night in my chambers."

"No," he replied. "It's best I remain with the men. I'm their general."

"You're my husband, and I fear I won't see you again," she whined.

He kissed her once more on the cheek. "You might not. War makes my life uncertain. Take care of our son, and who knows, maybe the goddess has blessed us with another child?"

He patted her flat abdomen and was rewarded with a smile. He prayed to Hathor for another child—something for Weret to focus on other than her jealousy for Natasa and Helena while he was gone. He wasn't sure how long he'd be away.

"Goodnight, Weret, and take care," he said, and he marched to the floor and raised his arms. "Come, men."

There was some grumbling, but they followed him out of the palace and to the barracks. His things packed, Ankhmakis sat by the fire and played music as his men drank ale from wooden kegs and spun tales of battle. As the night wore on, the palace torches were extinguished, and when the stars were out in full bloom, many of his men wandered off to town to seek a pair of arms for the night. He didn't begrudge them; Khaleme wasn't there, and the men had gone months without the arms of a woman. Why not take pleasure on the eve of their return to battle?

"Come to me," the voice in his heart spoke once more. *"I need you."*

He quieted his mind and found her. Indeed, Natasa was trying to connect. Ankhmakis put his instrument back in his tent and found Min.

"Make sure I'm not followed," he whispered and set off to Natasa's apartment.

He was being foolish, but he told himself saying goodbye to his healer was the proper thing to do. The idea of riding off to war without one last moment in Natasa's embrace was unbearable. Min followed at a distance and didn't argue. As Ankhmakis approached the modest apartment Natasa shared with Hecataeus and Corinna, he skirted around to the small backyard and hid in the shadows. Checking he wasn't being followed, he slinked up to her bedroom window and climbed in.

The room was lit with candles, and in the center of her bed was Natasa, kneeling with her arms resting on her naked thighs. She smiled as he landed on the floor, trying his best to be quiet.

"I knew you'd come," she purred.

In response he removed his sword and skirt. Without speaking, he threw himself upon her, kissing her as he guided her backward onto the bed. He kissed her nose, her cheeks, her ears, her forehead, and her lips. He melded with her energy and felt an ache deep inside his body.

"I love you," he said over and over as he made his way to her breasts, taking the time to kiss and suckle each one. She groaned under her breath, so as to not rouse the sleeping household, and arched her back in delight. Her nipples grew hard upon his lips, and his skin flushed. He wanted to recall the taste of every part of her, for he'd forgotten her sweetness.

He thrust himself inside her, delighting in the luxuriousness of her body, uniting with her via mind, body, and soul. The two entered the realm of light and held each other for what felt like eternity, bliss rising and falling, worlds stretching out in all directions, love growing until they exploded within their ecstasy. As he climaxed, Ankhmakis cried, gentle and quiet at first and then, as he fell upon her chest in exhaustion, he sobbed. She wrapped her legs around him and cried as well. He shed tears for the way they'd been betrayed and forced into other relationships, he cried for their daughter and her safety, but most of all, he cried because what made him happiest in life could also now cost both of them their lives, if anyone were to know.

Ankhmakis pulled himself from inside her and rolled off. Perspiration covered her chest and it glimmered in the candlelight. "I don't want to leave you," he whispered. "I want to take you with me."

"You can take me with you." She touched a fingertip to his heart. "Call on me, and I'll be your lookout once more."

"I don't want you to merge with me in battle anymore," he replied. "I know it hurts you."

"Let's get creative," she suggested. "If I can be your eyes on the battlefield, I'm sure we can remotely unite in bliss as well."

He leaned in to kiss her, feeling the heat rise off their bodies yet again.

"I want it to be clear," she murmured as he kissed her neck, "I called you here because I needed your touch. Without it I'm nothing. I'm as guilty as you in this pleasurable sin. I'd rather die tomorrow than live an eternity without your sweet kiss."

"I feel the same," he replied, wanting to remain inside of her forever.

In response, Natasa rolled on top of him, thrust his sex deep within her own, and swayed her hips. "Stay in me," she whispered in his ear as she hugged him closer, "for this is the only way I feel complete."

Hours later, as she drifted into sleep, he kissed her and dressed himself. He needed to be in his tent before sunrise, lest he be seen by his other guards entering the campsite. Since the poisoning, the only one he could trust was Min. He leaned over his beloved and whispered into her ear, "I love you, Natasa."

She shivered and smiled under her drowsy eyelids. "Don't forget to call upon me as soon as you can. I'm merely a thought away."

"I will."

Ankhmakis tiptoed to her window and left her. As his feet hit the ground outside, a low voice startled him from behind.

"You know, I caught Chanax sneaking out of Natasa's window once."

Ankhmakis turned and found Hecataeus sitting on a rock outside of the window. Khons's silver boat shone over the landscape, illuminating the older man's features. His face was stern, large wrinkles cut across his forehead. He held a flask in his hand and rocked as he stood. He'd been drinking.

Beside Hecataeus sat a Siamese cat, about two feet tall, staring at Ankhmakis, blue eyes glowing under the moonlight.

"What?" Ankhmakis stuttered, fearful he'd been caught.

"I think they loved each other, back when they were children," Hecataeus continued as he stumbled closer. "When Chanax was Senmen, and Natasa was young and innocent—uncorrupted by the passion and politics of your court. Unaffected by the cruelty of war."

Ankhmakis's head began to pound. The last person he wanted to see right now was Natasa's father.

"I have no idea what he was doing in her bedroom," the old vizier continued. "I imagine giving Natasa her first kiss."

"She's never mentioned this to me," Ankhmakis objected, not wanting to hear any more.

"Why would she?" Hecataeus countered. "It was private, and a lifetime ago, when they were very different people."

"Why are you here, Hecataeus?"

"My guard cat told me something was amiss," he answered.

"Guard cat?"

"Yes," Hecataeus explained, petting the beautiful creature. "Sired by the ones who patrol your ancestor's tombs. I acquired him to keep watch over the girls. Comes to find me if strangers are near the house. Natasa named him Princeling."

Ankhmakis winced. "Why are you here, Hecataeus?"

"Do you mean, why am I here outside of my daughter's window, or why am I still here in Behdet, the last pale-skinned Greek left?"

"Both."

"Easy, since the answer is the same. I'm protecting my loved ones."

Ankhmakis glared at the man. "My father told me you were Ptolemy III Euergetes's man."

"Euergetes was a good man." The Greek took a drink from his flask. He held it out to Ankhmakis. "Would you like some? It's pure grain alcohol. Made from wheat. Bastyre's been experimenting. Though I'm not supposed to tell anyone."

Ankhmakis took the flask and drank it down. The taste made him want to vomit, but he swallowed the concoction, refusing to look weak in front of Natasa's father.

Hecataeus continued, "I was Euergetes's man from the start. Still am. I owe him my life. He helped me out of a tight spot, you see. I was a wanted man in Athens…"

Ankhmakis took another swig and handed the drink back, raising his eyebrow. "You were?"

"An affair with the wrong Senator's wife. I'm sure you can relate to the troubles created by a scorned woman," Hecataeus replied.

"Indeed. Go on."

"I needed to get out of Athens, and Ptolemy III made me an offer I couldn't refuse. Most Greek nobility thought Behdet was an unworthy assignment, but I disagreed. Deep in the south, far from Greece, this was my refuge. I tried my hardest to thwart your father's goal of rebellion. But when Philopater took the crown and killed Queen Bernice, his own mother, I had no choice but to avenge Euergetes. The man had saved my life. Destroying his murderous son was the least I could do."

Hecataeus took another drink and plopped down on the slope outside of the house. Ankhmakis joined him. The light of Khons's fullness lit the valley below, and beyond the city the Nile River flowed at a languid pace.

"Besides, I'd fallen in love with Neffa and we had a child. How could I leave?" He turned to the prince and smiled. "I couldn't imagine leaving Natasa to return to my homeland, and Neffa never would have left her station as the high priestess to join me. I remained in my post, and days turned into months turned into years, and I procured an army for the rebellion, and the rest is history."

"Father told me he gave you a chance to leave before the war began," Ankhmakis noted, holding out his hand and taking the flask once more. "This stuff isn't bad, by the way. It grows on you. Please give Bastyre my compliments."

Hecataeus smiled. "Yes, your father offered both Ennaeus and I safe passage out of Egypt to Greece. Ennaeus and I have attachments here. I could have taken Corinna and Eleni with me, but Natasa never would have left you, and I can't leave her. While you and Horwenefer are at war, I'm the one who keeps her safe."

"What are you suggesting?"

"The reason Isidor and Queen Keket haven't slaughtered everyone with even an ounce of Greek blood is Isidor's fear I will tear his heart out in his sleep," Hecataeus said. "Trust me, banishing Natasa from the temple was done to hurt Neferu-ankh-maat. Their real goal is to purify the nation, and they will if the pharaoh doesn't reign them in."

"Do you really think so?" Ankhmakis asked.

"Yes, I do. My days are numbered while your father spends his time in Thebes. Your war is taking too long."

"What are you implying?"

"This time, I am going to leave, and nothing will stop me. I've set the wheels in motion and contacted my countrymen. Getting passage out of Behdet won't be easy. Your rebellion makes travel along the river impossible. I may have to find another route, but mark my words, dear Princeling, I will get my family out of here. Especially since you've decided to give into your selfish desires with my daughter, even though it risks her very life."

"Do you no longer trust we can win this war?"

"No, I don't, and if you fail, all of us shall burn."

"I'm well aware of such an end," Ankhmakis said, a familiar fire building within his gut. "It's a burden I bear every moment of my life. I know if I fail, our people will be punished for my crimes. Natasa and Helena are the last rays of hope and joy I have. Would you deny me my sole delight in life?"

"You have no right to put her life in danger."

"All of our lives are in danger," Ankhmakis countered. "You said so but a moment ago."

Hecataeus's eyes narrowed. "Listen to me, king-in-waiting—the moment I sense Isidor will strike, I will flee, and all my family will join me. Is this clear?"

"Why are you telling me this?"

"Because when the time comes, I need you to convince Natasa to join me. You have to let her go, for the safety of your child. You can also make passage easier and help us escape. None of us can be here if Isidor has his way."

Ankhmakis stepped back and allowed the man's words to sink in. Hecataeus was right, both Helena and Natasa were in danger, but to imagine a life in which he could no longer see them was too painful to consider. How could he defend Egypt without his divine pair at his side? Yet, somewhere in the back of his mind, reason rang true, and the image of Behdet burning and Natasa trying to flee from the chaos with Helena filled his mind. They would punish her and kill their child.

"None of you can be here if I fail in battle," Ankhmakis admitted.

"You'll convince Natasa to listen to me?"

"Yes, and I'll see if I can help with the escape, but you have to promise me something," Ankhmakis answered.

"What?

"If I die on the battlefield, you will save her and Helena from the chaos sure to follow."

"If there's a way out, I'll be the first to flee, and I won't leave any of my family behind."

"I think we have a deal," Ankhmakis said as he made to leave.

"Not so fast," Hecataeus said.

"What now?"

"You know what I said to Chanax when I found him sneaking out of my daughter's window?"

"No."

"I told him if I ever caught him doing such a thing again, I'd kill him. The same goes for you. If I can corner you, you can be sure others will as well. There are spies everywhere. Be careful, Princeling, or I'll remove you myself."

"Yes, sir," Ankhmakis replied with a nod, before turning to follow the path back to camp and sneak into his tent, where he sat in silence considering what he'd learned from Hecataeus. When dawn covered the desert in its pale morning glow, he once more rode out to war.

PART TWO

The Unspeakable

"The birth of a child is a miracle of the highest order. It is a piece of the light of the cosmos pouring itself down and into matter. First, the child grows within the mother's body. After birth, it grows within her energy, nurtured by her vital élan. Last, the child grows within the community, infusing its customs, emotions, and songs until one day it steps forth and takes up its service, its calling, and its place in humanity. The birth of a human being and its progress is no small thing. For it is the act of a star, coming to know itself."

~ "The Star," by Finnian, Scribe of the North

21

Identification

The war continued, and Egypt remained split into two nations. The boy king, Ptolemy V, and his regent, the general Tlepolemus, controlled the Lower Kingdom. The Upper Kingdom was held by Horwenefer. The priests of Thebes had crowned their pharaoh. The priests of Memphis had not. They held out for Horwenefer to take their city, which was why he strived to obey them. However, priests are fickle men, and their loyalties are easily swayed.

Behdet, Egypt 201 BCE

"Metakryon tires of this war." Isidor sighed, staring into the torchlight and drinking his ale with slow, measured sips. He lounged on his chaise, a large leopard purring at his feet. His underground chambers were cool, and he delighted in the refuge from the desert heat. Chanax and his friends, Antonius and Qeny, as well as the other Invisible Hands, were present as well. Isidor had called them together for an important announcement.

"Everyone tires of the war," Antonius, the lone Greek member of the Invisible Hands, replied. "Your pharaoh was supposed to take Lower Egypt by now."

"Yes, but the army is still caught outside of Lycopolis," Isidor said. "The addition of the Ethiopians helped, and the surge gained us several more cities, yet the Greeks remain steadfast, and their archers line the banks of the Nile for miles. Horwenefer's troops can't breach them."

"What can we do about it?" Chanax asked. "We've spent hours in ceremony trying to break them, to no avail. What power protects the Greeks?"

Isidor gazed at Chanax, considering his words. There was much to tell them, but where to start?

"Memphis wants a new plan," he began. "They no longer believe Horwenefer will lead us out of this predicament. They've put off crowning Ptolemy V as Ptah because he's still too young. His general has squashed the latest Delta rebellion—thanks to Memphis they keep popping up like warts—and has turned his focus to our mission. The Greek general is pressuring Metakryon to do something, anything, to make it clear to the Lower Kingdom that Epiphanes, and not Horwenefer, is the true lord of our lands. We know the belief of the people is what gives the king power."

As he spoke, he never took his gaze from the youngest prince. "However, it's not Ptolemy V the people are beginning to worship in our kingdom. Thebes has crowned Horwenefer their pharaoh, yet the peasants see Ankhmakis, his son, as their savior."

"Which is ridiculous," Chanax replied, the grimace on his face betraying his annoyance. "How can anyone think him worthy of the crown?"

"Isn't it obvious?" Isidor replied. "The severity of his injury was exaggerated in tales and his miraculous recovery doubly so. Horwenefer grows old in the castle in Thebes as Ankhmakis rises from death's door and rides beside the mysterious Ethiopian general, taking three cities in less than a year. Yes, they've run into another stalemate, but their progress can't be denied. The Egyptians of the south are pressuring Thebes to give them a new pharaoh, while the Greeks of the north are breathing down Metakryon's back to crown their boy king. If there isn't a resolution soon, the rebellion will fail, and Egypt will be without any pharaoh. This must be avoided, for the chaos of such an eventuality would leave us open to invasions not only from Macedonia and Syria, but Rome as well."

"Why not convince Horwenefer to give the crown to Ankhmakis?" Antonius asked.

"Ankhmakis can't be pharaoh of Egypt," Isidor replied.

"Why not?" Antonius argued.

"Because he's not in our pocket," Isidor said through his clenched teeth. "He rejects Set; thus, he rejects our priesthood, as well as the priesthood in Memphis, who over decades created the conditions for this rebellion to occur in the first place. Horwenefer founded the temple of Set in Behdet as a condition for Memphis's support. If Ankhmakis closes us down, he loses Memphis and they will crown Ptolemy V, regardless of his age, and shut down their support for our war. Ankhmakis has already rejected Set; we have every reason to believe if he takes the throne from his father, he will break the contract with Memphis and the war will continue—or worse, the Lower Kingdom will call in their allies in Macedonia and Greece and destroy us."

Isidor looked to Chanax and smiled. "The best course of action is to continue our work against Horwenefer. We need to take advantage of his weariness and make him come down with a serious illness, and then, on his deathbed, have him name Chanax as his successor."

The men in the room turned to Isidor's most faithful pupil and nodded.

"What about my brothers?" Chanax asked. "The third son is a long shot to the throne."

"What have we been working on for years?" Isidor noted.

"The ruin of Silus," Chanax answered, rising taller in his seat. "He's become a raging alcoholic, thanks to my handiwork."

"Indeed," Isidor agreed, "and our work with the army as a group has also affected him. The men know he's spoiled and uncontrollable. He avoids Behdet for fear of being exposed. Better to hide his madness in the throes of battle. Yet he can't even get through the simplest exercises without help from Ankhmakis."

"Which leads us back to where we started," Antonius cut in. "We can't seem to make Ankhmakis falter, no matter what we do. True, after his spiritual companion was given to Silus it seemed he would self-destruct on his own, but he's become an even better man, with a male heir, and he still has the golden shield of protection around him. Who is protecting him?"

"Natasa," Chanax said, gripping the arms of his chair. "She's the one who healed him and somehow in the process made him even stronger."

"What do you mean?" Isidor asked.

"I told you," Chanax continued, his anger starting to rise, "she's mastered the art of energetic warfare. She can slip into your mind and twist everything around. She's more powerful than ever, and I'm sure her mother hasn't taught her these things. No, Natasa must have a different source, yet I can't discover it. None of our spies in the Houses of Healing have noticed anything unusual. She tends to the sick, makes medicines, cares for the bees, and spends hours in Iu-Amon's study."

"What do they do in the study?" Isidor asked.

"I can't get an actual witness into the room," Chanax answered. "Iu-Amon is no fool, and entrance is limited, but as far as I can tell, they get drunk together."

Isidor rose and paced the room. The entire situation was maddening. Even after years of planning and spell work on the pharaoh, they were no closer to Memphis, nor to destroying Ankhmakis. He had no choice but to reveal the truth. They needed to know what was slowing their progress. He sat next to Chanax and placed a hand on the younger man's thigh. The other men in the room shuffled in their seats.

"I too have attempted to spy on Natasa energetically," Isidor admitted. "I can't break the golden shield around her, but I have discovered its source."

Chanax looked up at his master, eyes glittering as he licked his lips, face open and eager, like a child's. "Is it the same source as Ankhmakis's?"

"Yes," Isidor replied, "it is. It appears the couple is protected by none other than their daughter."

"Helena?" Chanax gasped, brushing Isidor's hand from his leg. "She's but a child, not even six years old. Besides, she wasn't even born yet when we first attacked Ankhmakis."

"You aren't seeing the bigger picture," Isidor reprimanded. "I've studied her for years now, and even though it pains me to admit it, their child isn't a normal human. She's a being of light from the Halls of Amenti."

The room fell silent. Most of the men were well aware of what this meant. Even Chanax.

"No," Chanax replied. "It can't be. You said she wasn't the Golden Child."

"I lied," Isidor said, his irritation building. He rose and

paced the room once more. "I can't let the high priestess know she's right, but I've had my suspicions since her birth. Years ago, before Natasa and Ankhmakis were bonded, Neferu-ankh-maat told me the pair would give birth to the Golden Child, and she's never wrong about such things. Given the fact the child was female, I wasn't sure, but since Ankhmakis's healing, I know now Neferu-ankh-maat is correct. You may think Natasa's magic healed Ankhmakis, but it isn't the whole story. The child was also healing him every minute she was near him. I saw the connection and felt the power, but never could I even come close to breaking it. I've seen her mighty spirit."

"She's a female, and not even a true Egyptian," Chanax pointed out.

"I know," Isidor answered. "It's terrible such a perfect being decided to take on an inferior identity. The world yearns for a warrior to save us, and the gods send us a little, half-breed girl. Alas, even the gods can be wrong about these things. A child will be easier to sacrifice than a warrior like Ankhmakis."

"What do you mean?" Chanax asked, a deep line furrowing his brow.

"We must kill the child," Isidor said. The horrified looks on the men's faces irritated him. "What? After the numerous children we've sacrificed at our table, what's one more? Her death would put an end to Ankhmakis. We will drive the true arrow of destruction right into his heart, and when Horwenefer dies, Prince Chanax, loyal to Set and the priests of Memphis, will rise and take the throne."

"What about the army?" Chanax asked. "The men follow Ankhmakis. He said if he died, they would lay down their weapons and the rebellion would end."

Isidor thought for a moment. As much as he hated it, Chanax had a point. "This is true. Everything must be in perfect balance. Strike too soon, and the entire thing will fail."

"Sir," Qeny, who'd been silent the entire meeting, spoke up, "I won't sacrifice the prince's child on the altar of Set."

Isidor set his gaze upon the young man and sent a wave of fear over the room. Qeny anticipated the attack and blocked Isidor's magic, sneering. Isidor had taught him well, perhaps too well.

"I won't do it," Qeny continued. "You can't kill a child of the temple because you suspect her. In my observations, her mother is the one in our way. Her death would destroy Ankhmakis. Look what happened when his father took her from him and gave her to Silus. Imagine how he'd react if she were dead. Probably curl up and die himself. Kill the child and you might cause heartache, but her mother's power over Ankhmakis should not be underestimated. I think before anything else happens, we need to know who is training Natasa."

"True." Chanax nodded and Isidor winced. The man's adoration of Natasa would be his weakness, unto the end of time. "She is more powerful than ever, and she won't let us near Helena. Her skill with the blade combined with energetic mastery is unlike anything I've seen. She can read your mind, Isidor."

"No, you fool," Isidor hissed. "She can read weak minds, like yours." Chanax flinched and lowered his gaze. "Regardless, it appears we need to revise the plan. I want you to spy in a whole new way, Chanax. You will become her friend again."

Chanax paused, biting his lower lip. "I don't think she'll let me. She knows what we do in secret, and she doesn't approve."

"You best find out how she discovered us," Isidor warned, despising every minute spent in their company. Why couldn't these men see the importance of killing the child? Their ineptitude would be the end of his mission if he failed to get them behind his plan. "You need to befriend her. Nothing is more important. Get inside her trust again. Find out what she does when she's alone and get to know Helena. The two are key to Ankhmakis's undoing. Timing will be everything. Right now, we need our warrior prince to break through Lycopolis and get to Memphis before Horwenefer dies. Once he's taken the city, we strike Ankhmakis, either through Natasa or his daughter."

"I refuse to participate in the death of the child," Qeny said again.

Several others nodded. Isidor wanted to slap them but refrained. A vision of Ankhmakis and Natasa in a passionate embrace flashed through his mind and he turned to Chanax.

"Do you think they're lovers?" he asked.

Chanax shook his head. "Bithiah's spy told her the two were never alone the entire time he was in Behdet recovering. I don't see how they could have reunited. Even on his last night, Ankhmakis was seen entering his tent before midnight and leaving it at sunrise to join his army. Yet they're very close, and the forms of love and desire surround them now more than ever."

"Hmm," Isidor murmured. "Perhaps we won't have to kill the child."

He looked at his men and felt their emotions. Getting them to murder the Golden Child was going to be difficult. Perhaps he shouldn't have told them about it, as it appeared none were on his side in this matter.

"We could remain open to the possibility of Ankhmakis

getting himself killed on his own," he suggested. "If we can catch him in between Natasa's legs, the law would have them both hung in the public square for defying her vow of celibacy."

"That would be rather convenient," Antonius exclaimed.

"Yes," Chanax agreed, biting his lip, "but we'd need proof. One of us would have to witness it happening. Which will be hard, since he's at war and she's here in Behdet. Sex needs a closer proximity to take place."

"There's talk of a stalemate, which means the men will come home to Behdet to gather supplies and more troops," Isidor said, tapping the corner of his mouth. He pointed at Chanax. "You must discover Natasa's secrets before your brother returns. I can arrange to make hiding their affair much more difficult when he returns."

"*If* they're having an affair," Chanax pointed out.

"Trust me." Isidor smirked. "If they haven't yet, they will, and we'll catch them. I have faith in your abilities."

"Can we forget about hurting the child?" Qeny asked again. The man was insistent.

"For now," Isidor lied.

In truth, he had no intention of forgetting the child. Her death was more important than Horwenefer or Ankhmakis's. Of course, for Egypt's sake, the two men had to go. However, old age would take Horwenefer on its own, and the realities of war could destroy Ankhmakis tomorrow. More important was the removal of the half-breed Golden Child. The gods may have sent her, but Isidor saw her future without a doubt—Helena had been born to rebuild the nation beside her father and save Egypt from the cult of Set. As Set's most loyal servant, Isidor would stop at nothing to make sure she failed.

One thing at a time, he reminded himself. One thing at a time.

22

A Prince's Attention

The temples taught of the principle of matter as a field of existence responsive to and capable of being transformed by spiritual influences, refined through the evolution of embodied and individual consciousness. Thus, physical life forms were images of the gods, working within the field of matter, lifetime after lifetime, in order to know themselves. The Initiate's life was dedicated to this revelation, which is why the words are written on the temple walls, "The kingdom of heaven is within you; and whoever shall know himself shall find it."

Behdet, Egypt 201 BCE

"Hello?" a male voice cried out.

Eleni was in the garden, relaxing for once. Since the stalemate in the north, the steady stream of injured soldiers had dwindled, and the healers now had more free time on their hands. For her part, Eleni preferred to either rest in the garden alongside her mother and Helena or find the other young girls of the court to gossip down by the river. Overall, her life had become sweeter.

"Chanax," her sister's voice replied from inside the house. "What a surprise. Seeking me out at home now, are you?"

Natasa's voice was choppy and curt, something Eleni didn't understand. A visit from Chanax was special. Like his brother, he would give her and Helena gifts and dote upon them. Ankhmakis and his music were entertaining, but Chanax was a storyteller. He could make Eleni laugh so hard, once she nearly wet herself. Eleni jumped up from her mother's side and ran into the apartment to greet the youngest prince.

"What would you say if I told you I missed you?" he said to Natasa as Eleni entered the room.

"Chanax," Eleni said. "Ignore my sister. People her age are boring."

"She and I are the same age," Chanax noted with a smile. "There must be something else wrong." Natasa looked at Chanax, silent, arms crossed, and chin jutting forward under pursed lips. "I do miss you," Chanax continued, and he held out a white lily. Natasa took it and walked toward the table without a glance at the man.

"Fine." She waved her arms at the table. "Take a seat. If anything else, your visits help pass the time."

"What, too much time on your hands?" the prince asked, sitting at the head of the table. Eleni sat beside him as Natasa poured each of them a cool drink of ale. She placed a loaf of bread in front of their guest and sat down at the wooden table across from Eleni.

"No," Natasa replied. "Only wondering why you're interested in rekindling our friendship. It's a puzzle keeping me quite busy."

Chanax turned and looked to Eleni, and her stomach somersaulted. "What if I'm not here for your attention?" he said with a brilliant smile as he fished something from his pouch and nodded at Eleni. "Close your eyes and hold out your hands."

Eleni obeyed and Chanax placed something cool into her hands. When she opened her eyes, she found a pair of beautiful golden earrings glittering in her palms. A much nicer gift than anything Ankhmakis had given her—rather than toys for a child, Chanax presented her gifts fit for a queen.

"Chanax," Natasa reprimanded, "you shouldn't bring gifts."

"Why not?" Eleni said. "You never complained when Ankhmakis gave me presents."

Natasa eyed her, and Eleni shivered. She didn't like it when her sister didn't approve.

"Relax, woman. No need to get jealous. I'd give you jewelry as well, if I knew you'd appreciate it. I think time with Iu-Amon has turned you into a tetchy recluse. At least you've allowed your hair to grow back."

Eleni giggled and slid the earrings into her earlobes. She shook her head, which now had a layer of golden-brown hair falling around her blue eyes. The reduction of soldiers meant the reduction of lice in the healing complex, and they'd been given permission to grow their hair.

"You look beautiful," Chanax crooned. "Now tell me, lovely ladies, how are things for you these days?"

"Wonderful," Eleni said. "I haven't seen a man die for weeks."

Natasa gave a wry half-smile at the comment. "She's right. It's been such a relief. The war has shown our dear Eleni too many tragedies."

"Agreed," Chanax said as he wrapped his fingers around his mug. "Which is why the Invisible Hands are working hard at ending it."

"The Invisible Hands?" Natasa replied, her mouth narrowing. "You consider what you do in the temple of Set helpful to our cause?"

Chanax sighed. "Natasa, let's not argue. You don't approve of Isidor's methods, but trust me, we're making progress in the energetic realms. You should know how important such work is."

"Of course, I do. I also know how damaging it is to use dark methods to secure short-term advantages. There are consequences for everything you do."

Eleni shifted in her seat. They were ignoring her. Chanax noticed her discomfort and placed his hand on hers. "Your sister and I don't approve of one another's gifts. It's a shame because she and I are so similar. It's why we were best friends when we were your age."

"Best friends?" Eleni asked. "A boy was your best friend?"

Natasa grimaced, and her body stiffened. She folded and unfolded her hands as she spoke. "Yes, Senmen was my best friend. Chanax, however, is not the same person."

"Your words hurt, Natasa," Chanax replied, and Eleni saw him flinch.

"Memphis changed you," Natasa answered.

At the mention of Memphis, a dark expression fell across Chanax's face, and he narrowed his eyes. His mouth curled into a sneer.

"You have no idea what I endured in Memphis," he said, his voice deep yet wavering.

The look in his gaze scared Eleni.

"No, I don't," Natasa agreed, "because you've never told me. For years I've longed for your friendship, Chanax, but you shut me out. I miss our connection, our closeness, more than anything in the whole world, but I don't miss who you've become."

"Everyone changes," Chanax said, his face softening, the anger controlled. "We can't remain twelve forever, can we, Eleni?" He looked at her again, and she delighted in his attention. "Someday you'll be a woman. No one wishes to remain a child."

She grinned. "I can't wait to be a woman."

"Why?" Chanax asked.

"I want to wear beautiful jewelry and paint my eyelids with kohl and lapis."

"You'll be as powerful a healer as your sister," he continued. "I'm sure of it."

Eleni shrugged. "Natasa is powerful, but I'm not sure I could ever be what she is."

"Of course, you can," Natasa said, grasping Eleni's hands across the table and squeezing them. "You'll learn."

"Will you teach her your secrets, Natasa?" Chanax probed. "Because Eleni, if she does teach you the source of her knowledge, you must tell me. I'm dying to know how she's become a master at such a young age. Not even twenty-four, yet Natasa's ability to resurrect the great hero Ankhmakis from the dead is legend in every corner of Hugronaphor's land. They're writing songs about it in courts across the kingdom as we speak."

Natasa rose from her seat, her face reddening again. Eleni knew Chanax had somehow insulted her sister, but she wasn't sure why.

"You may stay if you wish to continue your visit with Eleni, but I'm to meet Bastyre. Bithiah will be entering the Birthing Rooms tomorrow to give birth to yet another one of your children, in case you're interested. I have to go make ready her accommodations."

Natasa left the room, and Eleni watched Chanax. His eyes followed Natasa as she walked away, and Eleni's tummy felt twisted into knots. She was nervous though she didn't know why. When Chanax turned to Eleni, his usual smile was back on his face.

"Eleni, I hope your sister's opinion of me doesn't influence you. I'm trying to rekindle our friendship because these are times of war, and in such times, friends are hard to come by. I may be failing in regaining her confidence but getting to know you has been delightful. I've never been in the company of such a mature young lady. You already surpass Natasa's talent when she was your age. Back then, she was still playing in the gardens with fools like me and throwing rotten figs at my older brothers, but you've already healed the sick and cured the lame. It would be an honor if you'd accept my friendship, whatever Natasa may think."

Eleni felt her chest swell and her cheeks grow warm. A prince wanted her friendship? She smiled. "Of course, Chanax. I like you a lot."

"Wonderful," he purred as he made to stand. "I must be going, but I'll visit you again soon. Perhaps without your sister. I think she's a lost cause. Promise me this, if you ever do discover the source of her power, let me know. Trust me when I say I want to help her. She needs me."

Chanax left Eleni alone at the table, her chin high and chest out. She wasn't sure how she could find out the source of Natasa's talent. Power wasn't something you found on accident, was it? Perhaps Chanax was wise about this. If Eleni wanted to be as successful as Natasa someday, she would need to understand what was going on, and the best way to learn was to pay more attention to her sister while in her company. Where was the harm in that?

23

Family Planning

"Put a rope around your neck, and many will be happy to drag you along."
~ Egyptian Proverb, approximately 1250 BCE

Behdet, Egypt 200 BCE

"Welcome, my dear friend," Corinna said as she opened the door, "and you as well, Dardre. Come in. You're right in time for supper."

Neferu-ankh-maat entered the small apartment, searching for Helena, who ran in from the back garden to greet her.

"Grandmother," Helena sang. "Dinner with us again?"

"Yes, my precious one," Neferu-ankh-maat replied. "Dardre and I hope to visit you much more often."

"Neferu," Hecataeus said in a gruff tone. "Dardre. Thank you for coming. Here, have a seat."

They took their places at the table as Corinna set to serving them a simple meal of warm bread, butter, honey, vegetables from her garden, cheeses, and olives. Natasa entered the room with a pitcher of wine and poured their glasses. She kissed Neferu-ankh-maat on the cheek before sitting down.

"This is nice," Natasa said, settling onto the bench at the table. "Better than meeting in Father's study."

"Much," Dardre agreed in his deep, melodic voice. "I enjoy family gatherings. It makes me feel at home."

Hecataeus nodded but said nothing as Helena sat on her grandmother's lap and chatted. "Eleni told me the men have stopped fighting."

Eleni looked up from her meal, frowning at Helena as if she'd just been served a rotten fig. She was twelve now, and Neferu-ankh-maat noticed the signs of womanly changes in her body. If these were times of peace, she'd be starting to work in the temple, or as a lady-in-waiting for one of the princesses. Thanks to Isidor and his horrible laws, neither of those paths were an option. Her only place was the Houses of Healing, and even there her safety looked dimmer with each day.

"Yes," Hecataeus answered, "they have. The Greeks have called a stalemate twenty miles south of Lycopolis. It's not surrender—they're fortifying the bank and hopes of a second surge on our part have fallen. The Upper Kingdom needs a new plan. They're heading to Aswan for a meeting with our Kush allies."

"Aswan?" Natasa asked. "Why not Behdet?"

Hecataeus eyed his daughter, his body stiff as he spoke. Neferu-ankh-maat sensed something wasn't right between them. "Aswan is more central between our two kingdoms, but they're stopping in Behdet along the way south."

As he spoke, Neferu-ankh-maat felt the tension grow between the two and wondered what the cause of it could be. Before she could ask, Corinna spoke, "It's time for the girls to go to bed."

"I'm not a baby like Helena," Eleni said, pouting. "I

don't see why I have to go to bed while the rest of you enjoy yourselves."

"See?" Hecataeus grumbled. "This is why I wanted to keep the meetings in my study in the palace."

"There are too many ears in the palace," Neferu-ankh-maat said. "Now, do as you're told, Eleni. We have adult things to discuss. They would bore you."

Eleni glared at Neferu-ankh-maat and crossed her arms. "I'm not going."

Helena jumped from Neferu-ankh-maat's lap, walked over to Eleni, and tugged at her sleeve. "Come, I'm tired."

"Go yourself," Eleni whined, brushing the little girl from her side.

"I've had it," Hecataeus yelled. "You best get to bed now, Eleni, and enjoy it, for soon you won't be able to sleep here anymore."

"Why, are you going to throw me out?" Eleni rose from the table, her hands on her hips.

"No, though your attitude makes the idea quite tempting, young lady," Hecataeus answered. "I stamped yet another law from our dear queen today requiring every woman and child of the palace, regardless of rank, to sleep together in the old harem."

"What?" Neferu-ankh-maat gasped. "The old harem hasn't been in use for generations."

"The queen feels Behdet is in danger, and while the men are traveling the country trying to create a plan for stability, the cities are advised to house their royal women, female servants, and children in the harem. Which means a curfew of sunset, whether any of you like it or not."

Eleni scowled at her father, and Neferu-ankh-maat shook her head. "I can't abide by such nonsense. My work requires access to the temple at night."

She glanced at Dardre and felt a rush of sexual need ignite in her belly. Their Anit-Shadya was wonderful and restorative on many levels. Dardre's lovemaking had cleansed her soul from the stain of Isidor's touch. She touched Dardre's cheek, and Hecataeus grumbled once more.

"I'm sure there will be exceptions, but for the most part everyone, including those in the Houses of Healing, is to figure out a way to do without women after dark, unless they're under strict supervision. The queen feels she shouldn't have to provide individual guards to the women of the court and thus one group of soldiers at the entrance to the harem will suffice."

"What does Pharaoh Horwenefer think of this?" Neferankh-maat asked.

"Who knows? Queen Keket doesn't pass anything by him anymore," Hecataeus admitted. "He'll be here soon, so you can ask him when he returns. I'm sure he'll request your company."

Neferu-ankh-maat felt the accusation in his voice. "Of course, I'm sure he will. He needs Anit-Shadya. It's been too long."

"I look forward to meeting your pharaoh," Dardre replied, running his finger along her jawline, causing her to shiver.

Hecataeus cleared his throat. "Now, Eleni, to bed. We have much to discuss and very little time."

Eleni frowned but didn't resist. She followed her mother and Helena out of the room. Hecataeus closed the door behind them before taking a seat. He slumped in his chair and rubbed his eyes, as if he hadn't slept in days, which was probably true. Neferu-ankh-maat knew he carried the weight of the kingdom on his shoulders.

"I can't believe we're forced to have a curfew," Natasa complained. "I don't want to sleep in the harem. Our home is the safest place in the royal complex." She grabbed a piece of cheese and plopped it in her mouth.

"It's a violation of our privacy," Neferu-ankh-maat agreed. "Will the princesses have to abide by it?"

"Yes," Hecataeus said. "Every woman and child under twelve in the entire palace. Of course, wives can stay in their husbands' chambers, if invited, and spiritual companions with their men." He turned to Natasa. "No one else."

"Good," Dardre said in a thick, heavy accent. "You may stay in my chambers, High Priestess."

"That doesn't help a celibate woman, does it?" Natasa declared, still starting at her father as if to challenge him.

Hecataeus drank down the contents of his goblet and refilled it, never taking his eyes from his daughter's. The tension danced between them like monsoon winds.

"What's going on?" Neferu-ankh-maat asked. "The two of you are acting strange."

"Are you going to tell her, or should I?" Hecataeus demanded.

"Why tell her at all?" Natasa snapped. "It's not pertinent to our meeting."

"The prince is on his way to Behdet as we speak, so I think it is pertinent," he answered.

Natasa downed her wine and refilled her goblet. The two stared at each other across the table like commanders of opposing phalanxes on the field at the moment of battle. Rather than wait for one of them to give in, for they were both as stubborn as mules, the high priestess sighed and expanded her Ka around the pair. Natasa was guarded of course, but Hecataeus was the open book he'd always been for her. A vision unfolded before her mind's eye—Ankhmakis in the garden outside of Natasa's window and Hecataeus approaching him, causing her heart to flutter. She looked to her daughter, shaking her head in disbelief.

"Oh, my dear goddess, how could you? How long have you kept this from me? All these meetings, all this work, and you risk it for sex?"

"Mother," Natasa replied through gritted teeth, her face now flushed. "I thought I'd never see him again, and I wanted to know him one last time."

"You'd put your daughter in danger like this?" Neferu-ankh-maat continued, slamming her palm on the table. "How dare you?"

"My love for Ankhmakis doesn't put Helena in danger. The law states he and I are the ones who will die, not our children. Each of us is willing to accept punishment for our love. You're protected by your pure blood, and you'll be able to take care of Helena in our absence, should we be discovered."

"The potential for death is all the more reason to live a life of discretion," Neferu-ankh-maat exclaimed.

"Which is what I do," Natasa yelled, rising from her seat. She paced the length of the table, her gaze shifting between Hecataeus and her mother as she continued her fit. She reminded Neferu-ankh-maat of a cornered cobra ready to strike. Never had she seen her daughter this unhinged. "I never leave the Houses of Healing. I work all day, tend to my child at night, and do as I'm told. For years I have lived as if I don't exist in this world, hoping the royals and their spies don't remember I'm alive. It's as if I'm dead already, I'm so hidden from view."

"Well, since the queen has instituted a curfew within the harem, the princeling can't come sneaking into your bedroom anymore," Hecataeus noted, a twisted smile upon his ruddy face. Natasa grabbed her empty mug and threw it at him.

He ducked, and it shattered on the wall behind him. "I've been in many bar brawls, my dear child. You'll have to improve your skills if you hope to leave your mark."

"Please," Dardre spoke up, causing both Hecataeus and Natasa to look his way. They wore surprised expressions, as if they'd forgotten anyone else was in the room. "Let's not fight about this. I agree with your concerns, Vizier, however, acts of love are not what we should fear. Acts of hate and jealousy are what we must guard against. Let's get to the business part of our meeting."

Neferu-ankh-maat nodded as her lover placed his hand upon hers. He continued in a calm, caring voice, "Tell me, Natasa, what the wands are revealing?"

Natasa started at the ceiling, struggling to gain control of her feelings and still panting hard. Neferu-ankh-maat sent her a wave of love and rather than block it, her daughter allowed the form to caress her. Her breathing slowed, and she sat back down at the table to join them.

"The web of life still pulses, and eventual success against Ptolemy V remains a strong possibility, but not soon and not clear," she said. "Isidor and his men continue to send their malicious spells at the Greeks, but sometimes their evil is also directed within the royal family. Pharaoh Horwenefer is their main target, and I'm convinced his health problems are tied to their dark magic. Bithiah keeps showing up as a fatal fragmentation in the way, though I'm not sure why she'd be involved in the Invisible Hands treachery, other than wanting to please Chanax."

"I imagine she's still mad at her father for forcing her to marry Chanax instead of Nefermaat," Neferu-ankh-maat said, shaking her head. "Oh, how I wish he'd listened to me. I'm sure she's helping them kill him."

"She's still angry she had to marry Chanax?" Natasa frowned. "She spends most nights in his chambers, and she's continuously pregnant. To me it seems she's resigned to her fate."

"Everyone takes his revenge somehow," Dardre said. "Divine Order will punish Pharaoh Horwenefer for manipulating his family, and in a way you'd least expect. Bithiah gives me pause though, for she's not waiting for divine order to issue its justice. Regardless of her outward behavior, the wands suggest she may have plans of her own."

"Makes sense to me," Hecataeus replied. "No use waiting around for the gods to do your work for you when you can do it yourself."

Dardre turned to Hecataeus. "It appears you have a suggestion, Hecataeus?"

Hecataeus cleared his throat and nodded. "The most practical plan is for us to flee."

"I agree," Dardre replied. "What do you have to report on that front?"

"There are three options right now," he said. Neferu-ankh-maat watched as he straightened in his seat. Being in charge had always made him more at ease. Hecataeus didn't like their talk of magic. He was a man of the flesh and needed action in the physical world.

"They are?" she prodded.

"The first is the easiest in the short term," he said. "We join the pharaoh and his men on their journey to Aswan and ask King Adikhalamani to allow us to emigrate to Kush. However, Pharaoh Horwenefer may see our actions as treason and have us arrested. There's no telling how he'd take our fleeing his country, and under the law he could have us hanged. In addition, if we lose the war, the Greeks will punish Kush in some way for their participation in the rebellion, and Ethiopia is surrounded by desert for hundreds of miles. The only way out is the Nile, through Egypt, and you can be sure it will be guarded. I believe the protection of Kush in the event of failure is part of what King Adikhalamani wishes to discuss during their time together. We have the upper hand right now, yet until Memphis is conquered, anything could happen."

Neferu-ankh-maat thought about it. "One of the main reasons for leaving is my belief the war will not be won," she admitted. "I've seen visions of Behdet burning. Trapping ourselves south doesn't make any sense."

Corinna entered the room and sat beside her husband. "The girls are asleep."

"Thank you, Corinna," Neferu-ankh-maat said. "Whatever would we do without you?"

Hecataeus kissed his wife on the cheek before continuing his report. "The other option is to sail one of Horwenefer's boats to Coptos and take the Wadi Hammamat toward the Red Sea. Traveling the desert trade route is difficult, even for men, much less with two children and three women. It's best to take a boat up the Nile through Lower Egypt, all the way to the sea."

"The pharaoh won't let us use one of his boats without issue," Neferu-ankh-maat pointed out. "Again, he could see my fleeing as an act of rebellion and send soldiers after us."

"True," Hecataeus agreed. "Which is why I've been looking for another boat. I have an Egyptian fisherman willing to take us up to Coptos, but he won't go any farther. I've contracted my old friend, Pistias, to meet us in Coptos. We will take the fishing boat from Behdet and meet Pistias, who will sail us up through Lower Egypt and to the Mediterranean to safety."

"How would he be able to dock his ship in Coptos if he's Greek?" Natasa asked. "Don't we control the port?"

"Ankhmakis will allow it," Hecataeus replied. Neferu-ankh-maat saw the surprise on her daughter's face. "He knows of our plan and has agreed to help. When he arrives in Behdet next week, we'll go over the final details. As it stands right now, Pistias and his men will arrive in Coptos sometime later this year."

"Later this year," Neferu-ankh-maat cried. "Why so long?"

"Because it takes time to round up his sailors and travel to Coptos from Athens," he replied. "Besides, Ankhmakis and company will be in Aswan for at least six months. By the time they return north, Pistias should be waiting for them, and Ankhmakis will provide him supplies and all permits, as well as armed guards, as he heads north to take Lycopolis. Pistias will remain in Coptos and wait for us. When I receive the signal, we'll make haste and head north ourselves. Hopefully, by the time we leave Coptos with Pistias, Ankhmakis will have cleared the Greek archers from Lycopolis and we'll be able to cross into the city and meet him. From there, the prince can grant us safe passage out of the Upper Kingdom, and Pistias can use his contacts in the Lower Kingdom to get us to the Delta, where we'll head for Pelusium and find passage on a sea vessel north."

"Why would Pistias help us in this way? What you ask is no small task," Neferu-ankh-maat said.

"He owes me. Besides, he's doing it for the gold."

"Gold? Do we have enough for such a mission?" she asked.

"The royal treasury is low due to the war, as we have yet to implement a proper taxation system, but Ankhmakis has agreed to fund the entire trip himself, using his private stock of Nubian gold."

Natasa's eyes grew wide and a smile twitched at the corner of her lips. "Ankhmakis is funding our trip?"

"Of course, he would," Neferu-ankh-maat replied. "He wants his loved ones safe."

"How far north will we travel?" Natasa asked.

"Does it matter?" Hecataeus said.

"Yes. I'll want to return to Egypt when the war is over and Ankhmakis is pharaoh."

Hecataeus shook his head. "You expect too much."

"He has to win," she cried. "Otherwise we can never come home. Lower Egypt isn't safe because we're Egyptian, and Upper Egypt isn't safe because we're Greek."

"There's nowhere in Egypt for you, my child," Hecataeus said, crossing his arms over his barrel chest. "Which is why I have to get you out of here."

"If I leave Egypt, I might never see Ankhmakis again," Natasa sobbed.

"My daughter." Neferu-ankh-maat put her arms around her daughter, but in her deep pain, Natasa shoved her away. "You've known this is a very real possibility. You can't remain here."

"I can if he takes the throne," she demanded, her cheeks now wet with her tears.

"*If* he takes the throne," Hecataeus replied. "Which isn't guaranteed. He wants you safe. If I get a boat here, you must get on it. Do you hear me?"

Natasa gripped her chair and Neferu-ankh-maat felt her pain. "What if he becomes pharaoh before Pistias gets here?" Natasa challenged her father.

"Impossible," her father argued. "The pharaoh would have to die and Silus concede the crown. The pharaoh may be ill, but Silus will be the one left behind with the army during the stalemate and we know the one who controls the army controls the crown."

"The men love Ankhmakis," Natasa said, her chest puffed out. "They will choose him. Besides, the crown, and the queen, are here in Behdet. Ankhmakis could sway her to crown him if Pharaoh Horwenefer dies."

"Natasa," Neferu-ankh-maat interrupted, "I wish I could believe in Ankhmakis, but I agree with your father. It will take Pistias less time to arrive than it will take for Ankhmakis to rise power and remove the anti-Greek clerics from the priesthood. The effort to purify the country extends farther than Behdet."

"The people love Ankhmakis," Natasa yelled, her hands balled into fists. "You hear the stories. They want him to be pharaoh now. They'll do whatever he asks."

"I know you both want this," Neferu-ankh-maat answered, "but I've seen the darkness in Isidor's heart, and I don't want to wait around to find out what he does next."

"How about we remain open to both plans?" Corinna suggested.

"What do you mean?" Hecataeus replied.

"Set the plan into motion and wait and see. If within the year Horwenefer has died and Ankhmakis has secured the throne, Natasa and Helena can join him by his side for all of Egypt to see."

Corinna drew Natasa's hands into her own from across the table as she continued, "If Pistias arrives in Coptos, and Horwenefer is still alive, we get on the boat together and leave Behdet before Isidor and the queen go further with their purification strategy. Either Ankhmakis will win it all and send for you, Natasa, or he'll die trying. Trust me when I say he'd rather die knowing you and Helena were far away from

Egypt."

Corinna stood and wrapped her arms around Natasa, who buried her head in the woman's chest and sobbed, clutching her nursemaid as if still a child. "Oh, Corinna, my heart stings as if pierced by a sword. I know I must take Helena out of Egypt, even though I might never see Ankhmakis again, but how can I live without him?"

"Don't worry, child," Corinna answered. "I'll be there every step of the way. Together, we can do this."

Natasa clutched Corinna even closer. Neferu-ankh-maat was grateful for all her old friend had done for her family over the decades. No one had ever been truer than Corinna. It was impossible to ever pay her back for her service. She glanced at Hecataeus and noticed he too had tears in his eyes. "Corinna, I don't know what we'd do without you."

24

The Song of Isis

"True teaching is not an accumulation of knowledge; it is an awakening of consciousness, which goes through successive stages."
~ Old Kingdom Proverb, 3000 BCE

Behdet, Egypt 200 BCE

Ankhmakis washed and dressed with the speed of a jackal running after its prey. Once again, he'd been gone over a year from Behdet, and there was so much to do. Helena and Ankhmaat would be different people by now, as would Eleni. What about Natasa, how would she have changed? Her work in the apiary must have transformed her in some way, even if the changes weren't visible to the eye. The years of fighting had changed him, except while he grew more like a monster with every stroke of his sword, Natasa was transforming into a goddess.

In spite of his failing health, Pharaoh Horwenefer had joined them on this trip. King Adikhalamani in Aswan required his presence—he had no choice but to oblige. As the general of the Egyptian army and the chief strategist, Ankhmakis was also required to attend, along with General Khaleme and a select group of his men. The rest of the army had been left twenty miles south of Lycopolis under Silus's charge. Their mission: to hunker down and keep the Greeks from launching a counter-offensive before the Aswan contingency returned. This was no easy task, and Ankhmakis wondered if Silus had it in him. His behavior was erratic these days, and even in battle he was often drunk or high. Ankhmakis knew well the pain that drove a man to use the substances, but what was Silus hiding from? What madness was eating away at his very spirit, driving him to take opiates daily?

"The pharaoh awaits you," Min announced, interrupting Ankhmakis's thoughts.

For his first appearance in Behdet in over three years, the pharaoh hadn't chosen a dramatic public entrance and instead asked his children to greet him in the throne room in private. Everyone agreed to hide his condition from the people. Ankhmakis knew this was his father's way of holding on to power when he should be handing it over to one of his sons.

"Father is very sick," Ankhmakis said to Min as they walked toward the throne room. "The trip here was arduous and slow due to his condition. What do you think ails him?"

Min shrugged. "I'm no healer, but he's with Iu-Amon and Natasa right now, perhaps they will know?"

Ankhmakis's heart skipped a beat. "Natasa? Will I get to see her?"

"My lord," Min said, winking, "of course you'll see her. The pharaoh wants you to hear from the healers what's wrong. This is why he called the meeting. Everyone, from Queen Keket to the smallest grandchild, is to be there when Iu-Amon and his favorite assistant, Natasa, give their assessment."

"Everyone except Silus," Ankhmakis grumbled. "He should let Father step down and hand me the crown."

"Ankhmakis," Min replied, his lips narrowed, "I don't disagree. Everyone in the kingdom wants you to be their king. Yet Silus is reckless and threatens to fight you for the crown, and your father can't risk a war within a war right now. I think in Aswan things will become clearer, both your path to the throne and the path to ending this war, for somehow they're connected."

"Of course they're connected," Ankhmakis moaned. The constant frustration was driving him mad.

"Why are you anxious to become pharaoh?" Min asked. "You're a strong general and becoming pharaoh would take time away from executing the war."

"Nonsense. Ramesses the Great was both pharaoh and general of his army. I can do both, but the war isn't the reason I want the throne. I'm not sure I even care about the rebellion anymore, except its end would mean peace in our lands."

"I still don't understand why it's so urgent for you to be crowned. Why not wait a few years?"

"I want to take the throne and overturn my mother's laws."

"So Natasa can be your spiritual companion again?"

They approached the throne room, and Ankhmakis noticed Ruia entering with her nursemaid and three children. Behind her stood Weret, holding a squirming Ankhmaat in her arms. Life had changed him. No longer a chubby toddler, the boy was now all arms and legs and itching to run and play, not sit still in a stuffy throne room, greeting his sick grandfather.

"Weret has given me a son," he continued, looking at her with as much kindness as he could muster, "but she can't give me a sacred union. I've tried, and it isn't there. She's a weak link in my chain of command. If I'm the one to unite the country, I need Natasa at my side, and the only way that can happen is for me to take the crown."

He left Min's side, walked toward his wife with his arms wide, and kissed her upon the lips. He patted his son's bushy head. "So much hair already?"

"Ankhmakis," Weret chastised. "He's well over two years old."

Behind Weret stood Bithiah and Chanax, their three children in tow. Alexa was on the other side of Chanax beside their son, Sethe. The fact he and Weret had produced one, single heir was never more apparent. Ankhmakis sighed, knowing what this meant. Pretending to be a caring husband for a woman he didn't love wasn't easy, and this visit would be brief and full of work, leaving little time for pleasure. Regardless, he held her arm and smiled at her. The throne room doors opened, and the pharaoh's guards called them in to greet their father and learn of his condition.

At the end of the hall sat Pharaoh Horwenefer in the golden Throne of Behdet, cleaned up and in his regal attire, but leaning to one side, slumped and lacking the strength to sit up straight. To one side stood Queen Keket, and Hecataeus flanked the other. Neferu-ankh-maat and Isidor, as well as the Kush priest Dardre, were also in attendance. Ankhmakis sought out Natasa and found her standing next to Iu-Amon. She wore the simple white tunic of the healer but had adorned herself for the occasion with gold bangles on her arms and jade earrings. She'd let her hair grow, and it now framed her face and hung to her chin in a blunt bob. She could've worn a wig—the royal women wore theirs—but next to the bald Iu-Amon, Natasa played her part.

Ankhmakis's heart beat like the thunder of his cavalry. He

recalled her naked flesh and the taste of her lips. He wanted nothing more than to run into her arms, but her energy toned neutrality and thus so did his. With each step he relaxed, knowing he could be near her and not betray his love. He had every intention of making her his second queen the moment he was pharaoh, but their moment of pubic reunion was not now, and his great need for her put both of them in danger.

"Family," the pharaoh called them to attention. "Please, come to me, so I may visit my grandchildren."

They gathered around the pharaoh and each took turns introducing their children. Ruia's boy, Senui, was the most vocal. At six years old, he held conversation quite well. Once their grandfather was done blessing them, the smaller children were let go to run around the room. Ankhmakis took a count as they buzzed around the hall. Eight children in total. His heart sank, for his own beloved daughter, Helena, hadn't been included.

"Now," Horwenefer began as the nursemaids led the children to the far end of the hall, so the adults could hear one another, "it's time to hear Iu-Amon's diagnosis. He and his assistant Natasa have examined my condition, and I assume they have something important to tell us."

Iu-Amon glanced at the gathered crowd before turning to the pharaoh to speak. "Natasa and I have done a thorough investigation, Your Majesty, and we've found several issues, some of which we may be able to repair, and others beyond our abilities."

Natasa bowed and stepped forward. "Your Majesty," she began, and Ankhmakis felt a rush of heat at the sound of her voice, "your digestion is poor. We have created a set of tonics and will send back a regimen to your healers in Thebes. They should help alleviate the pain in your abdomen. Your

Ka is very weak, my lord. Have you been disciplined with the Alchemies of Horus?"

Horwenefer shook his head. "I haven't had the time. The war is quite consuming."

"Even more reason to meditate and take ceremony, my lord," Natasa continued. She glanced out of the corner of her eye toward her mother. "Pharaoh Horwenefer, do you have a spiritual companion in Thebes?"

The queen clucked, "You haven't called the high priestess of Isis to your side for help? Interesting."

Horwenefer looked to Keket. "My dear queen, if you must know, I have concubines plenty to warm my bed, and I no longer participate in Anit-Shadya. I considered it unnecessary to send for my spiritual companion." He turned to the high priestess. "I'm sorry, Neferu-ankh-maat. I needed you here in Behdet. I couldn't leave both the city and the temple of Isis to the queen and her incompetence."

"I suggest the two of you take ceremony before heading to Aswan," Natasa said. "During war, men need the touch of the goddess. It keeps them whole."

Ankhmakis felt a wave of desire hit him and knew she was contacting him—in front of everyone. They'd resumed their astral connection over the past year, and it had helped him in battle and produced some pleasure. However, their astral lovemaking was nothing compared to her physical touch.

"*Meet me in the apiary in two hours,*" she said to his heart.

He glanced at Isidor and Neferu-ankh-maat, the other two in the room who could have heard her astrally communicate, but both were focused on the pharaoh, and neither noticed Natasa's call.

"*My pleasure,*" he answered her. How wonderful to be

able to speak without speaking.

"I agree, Natasa," Pharaoh Horwenefer replied. "Neferu-ankh-maat, let us begin this evening."

"Yes, my lord," the high priestess replied, bowing her head.

"Anything to revitalize your Ka is needed now," Iu-Amon continued. "A trip to Aswan is not advised until you've gained more strength."

"We must head out," Ankhmakis interrupted. "The king of Kush awaits us, and I don't have faith in Silus's ability to hold the line."

"He's correct," his father replied. "Iu-Amon, we need to heal me as fast as possible."

"My lord," Iu-Amon replied in a gentle voice. "I fear you can't be healed. We can delay your death a few more years at most."

Ankhmakis was shocked. A few years? Even after a lifetime of practicing Anit-Shadya and the Alchemies of Horus, death would still take his father at forty years of age. The realization was quite disturbing.

"There must be something you can do," Ruia cried out. "What ails him?"

"His heart is weak," Iu-Amon announced, "and a lingering infection from last Perit has destroyed part of his lungs."

"Father," Ruia said, tears forming in her concerned eyes. "What are we to do?"

Isidor stepped forward, raising his hand in a prayerful gesture. "I think Natasa's prescription of tonics and Anit-Shadya will ready our pharaoh for his trip to Aswan. We need his physical body capable of performing the duties required of the pharaoh of our great land."

As he spoke, the throne room door burst open, and

against protocol, in walked Helena, barefoot and dressed in a beautiful tunic of green linen, her thick, braided dark hair hanging about her shoulders. She walked toward the pharaoh without a care in the world. In her hands she held a tiny bird. Several guards followed her, one of them Min, who was shrugging.

"I'm sorry, Your Majesty," Min said. "I know this is unusual, but Helena insists she must see you. She has a gift for her grandfather."

The queen and Weret both frowned at the child.

"She isn't one of the royal children," Weret demanded. "She's not invited. This is for family only."

"I'm her father, am I not a part of this family?" Ankhmakis said to his wife, rounding on her.

Weret shrunk in her place. "But Ankhmakis—"

"Let her in," Horwenefer answered, a soft smile gracing his lips. "Until your mother passed her purification laws, Helena was my granddaughter and heir to the high priestess. What title could be more royal?"

"What's a law?" Helena asked as she walked toward the throne.

"A law?" Horwenefer replied with a chuckle. "Why, law is what governs the world. Laws tell us how to behave and how to live. Without them, we would live in chaos."

Helena approached the throne and sat at her grandfather's feet. Ankhmakis was both afraid for her and yet proud. She was beautiful, radiant, and quite clever.

"You believe laws are more powerful than blood?" she asked.

The room was still. Isidor stared at the girl with unnatural interest, but no one spoke.

"Yes," the pharaoh said. "We must answer to the law first

and above our feelings for our family."

"You believe law is greater than love," Helena said, her voice singing like a soft, spring song. Horwenefer swallowed and didn't answer. "I found this little bird," Helena continued as she opened her palms to reveal a small starling. "It has been abandoned by its mother, or lost, I can't tell."

"How very sad, my child," Horwenefer replied, opening his arms to beckon her closer. "Is this what you're here to tell me?"

She looked up at the pharaoh and shook her head. Her eyes glimmered with tears as she spoke, "No, Grandfather. I'm here because I love you."

Helena rose from his feet as she let the starling fly from her hands. It soared to the top of the throne room and out toward the window. The other children in the room followed its path below, each trying to catch it. As the starling made its way to freedom, Helena sang "The Song of Isis," the same song the goddess sang to Osiris to shepherd him back to life after his brother Set had destroyed him. Helena's sweet voice filled the hall with joy and life, each note telling the story of resurrection, devotion, and power, and also surrounding the humans in the room with the form of love. Ankhmakis could see the streams of light as they wove their way through the room, from heart to heart. Ankhmakis looked to his father, now surrounded in a pale golden haze, his eyes closed. Helena continued to sing, and when the older man opened his eyes to gaze upon his granddaughter, tears were pouring down his cheeks. He rose taller in his throne and grinned. Ankhmakis's heart beat like thunderclaps across the hot desert landscape— he hadn't seen his father this happy since he was a boy.

When Pharaoh Horwenefer stood to stand before his granddaughter, his head was high and his legs sure. Helena held out her arms toward him and sang her last words, "The Queen of Heaven speaks to you...know my love and you will know yourself."

She hopped up and down before her grandfather, small and tiny compared to his large, masculine frame, and he swept her up in his arms. He was no longer weak. Instead, the pharaoh looked once more like the ruler he was born to be. Ankhmakis had no idea what was happening, but somehow his daughter had renewed the man's energy.

"My goddess," Iu-Amon exclaimed as he put his hand to the pharaoh's neck, searching for his pulse. "Your heart is beating stronger. 'The Song of Isis.' Of course, why didn't I think of it?"

"Because," Helena said, holding her grandfather tight and kissing his cheek, "you don't love him, Iu-Amon, so sometimes you miss things."

Horwenefer spun his granddaughter in the air before placing her upon the ground with tenderness, as if she were the most precious object in the entire kingdom.

"Well," Horwenefer exclaimed, "it looks like I'm going to be busy the next few days. Ankhmakis, prepare to ride out within the week. Hecataeus, I want you to join us in Aswan. Natasa, get me those tonics, and Neferu-ankh-maat, I think I'll meet you for ceremony within the hour, if you don't mind."

Ankhmakis blushed at his father's obvious desire as it swept around him. Queen Keket, however, grimaced.

"Most important," Horwenefer said, looking down at Helena, "I want you to sing to me every day until I leave. Will you do this?"

"Of course, Grandfather," she replied, grinning from ear to ear. "I was born to sing for you."

Ankhmakis felt a chill sprint down his back. He looked

up from his daughter and found Natasa's face, now no longer radiant, but pale, lips tight, and grim. He followed her gaze across the room and noticed Isidor and Chanax staring at their daughter, covering her with the form of malice.

After wondering for years, Ankhmakis was now certain who within the court wanted him, and his daughter, dead.

25

Marital Bliss

"You will free yourself when you learn to be neutral and follow the instructions of your heart without letting things perturb you. This is the way of Maat."
~ Ancient Egyptian Proverb

Behdet, Egypt 200 BCE

"I can't believe this," Bithiah whined as she paced Chanax's chambers. "We've been working together to take down Father our entire marriage, and with one song, a mere child ruins everything."

Chanax threw himself on his sedan and covered his face with his hands. "How did the little girl cure him? I've never seen anything like it. Do you know how long it will take to establish the magic? Father could live forever now, especially if the child sings to the bastard every day."

"What do we do now?" Bithiah cried out, wringing her swollen, ring-covered hands. "Father will never discuss handing you the crown. Worse, what are we going to do about your public perception?"

"What are you talking about?" he demanded.

"The way the public sees you," she explained. "The peasants don't even know your name. Instead, they sing heroic songs about our horrible brother. They cry for him in the streets. Ankhmakis and his remarkable warriors. Ankhmakis and his return from death. Why, he was near death's door because of me."

"What do you mean?" Chanax asked, rising from the couch and rounding on his sister. How dare she keep information from him?

"I had my spy poison the fool," she replied.

Bithiah eyed him under her painted brows, and then turned to walk toward his private baths. The last thing he wanted was to touch her—her constant demands were starting to repulse him. She threw off her robe and walked down the frescoed steps into the pool of hot water and sighed. "Ah, much better."

He followed her to stand beside the pool. "You had your spy try to kill our brother?"

"Yes," she answered. "You weren't doing anything about it, so I decided to take the matter into my own hands. Ankhmakis is a problem, Chanax, and you know it. If he were out of the way, Isidor and the priests in Memphis would arrange for Silus's undoing the moment Father died. Mother would make you king of Behdet, and the priests in Thebes would crown you pharaoh. Given how little the people care about you, and that the soldiers think you're weak, I see no other way."

"What do you mean the soldiers think I'm weak?"

"Haven't you heard the stories about how Natasa bested you in a fight?"

"What? How do you know?"

"Everyone knows," she yelled at him, her strident tone echoing off the marble walls. "You were in the training ring, with a girl who took you down within minutes. How you fell into a trap of Ankhmakis's I'll never know. Even I respect his cunning for that one."

"Do not speak to me that way. I am your husband." Chanax's anger rose within him and rather than diffuse it, he allowed it to permeate the room.

"I'll speak to you how I please," his wife continued. "I've done everything for this relationship, caring for three children, constant energetic work on Weret and the queen, spying on our brother, and even arranging for his murder. What do you do? Sit around in Isidor's study staring at the fire, smoking herbs, or rutting with your priestess whore."

"I said, do *not* speak to me that way."

Chanax sent his anger out toward her. He'd taught her much, but never how to block his curses, and within moments, she was struggling to breathe. She rose from the tub, the water and oils dripping off her gasping, trembling, chubby body. He focused on her with his malice and could see her fear. "Your constant state of pregnancy is destroying your figure, which is a shame. You used to be quite beautiful."

She flinched at his cruel words, and he released her from his energetic grip. She fell back into the water, choking for air, and started to cry.

"I think it's time you told me who this spy is of yours," Chanax hissed.

"Nefermaat," she said between sobs.

"If you want to do something useful, woman, use him to find out if Ankhmakis and Natasa are having an affair," he commanded. He was done taking orders from her. "No need to murder our brother if he can't keep his desire in check. I'm surprised you never thought of it."

Chanax turned to leave the room.

"Where are you going?" Bithiah cried out.

"To indulge in my priestess's perfect body," he answered. "You'd best be out of my quarters by sunset, since Alexa will need a place to sleep tonight, other than the harem."

26

Love in the Realm of Light

"The god Re wept, and the tears from his eyes fell on the ground and turned into a bee. The bee made his honeycomb and busied himself with the flowers of every plant and so wax was made and also honey out of the tears of Re."
~ Inscription from an Ancient Egyptian papyrus

Behdet, Egypt 200 BCE

Natasa paced back and forth between the beehives. The afternoon was approaching, and Ankhmakis still had not yet arrived. Waiting for him was driving her mad. To know he was alive and near, but not in her arms, was agonizing. How was she going to manage this? She allowed her gaze to soften and focused on the entrance to a hive ten feet away, turning her attention to the honeybees flying in and out, each one busy and yet unhurried. To the hive, there was no time; nothing but the sun god's kiss, the light of Ra, existed. Natasa relaxed and allowed her thoughts and anxiety to flow away from her. Her heart aligned with the bees, and she was both connected and yet apart from the world.

"My, it's good to see you," her lover murmured from

behind her. His deep voice sent waves of pleasure throughout her entire body. She smiled and turned to gaze upon him.

Ankhmakis stood inches away, no longer dressed up, but instead in a simple skirt. His windblown hair hung around his elegant face. As was his habit, his sword was at his side. He wore nothing else. Natasa touched his bare chest, her fingers dancing across his nipples.

"Your body is my favorite thing in the whole world," she groaned as she kissed his neck.

"I've stationed three guards down the path outside of the ancient gates. Are there any other entrances?" he asked. He grew hard under his skirt as she removed his sword and scabbard from his waist.

"No," she murmured, now kissing his collarbone, "there's one entrance and exit. Besides, in an attempt to keep my wand work a secret from the men of Set, we let go of any beekeeper except myself and Bastyre, and when I'm on duty, she leaves me alone to do Our Lady's work."

Natasa removed his loincloth, and he stood naked before her. Her breasts ached.

"Is this the Lady's work?" he asked as he drew her close and kissed her.

She melted at the taste of his lips.

"The holiest of work," she murmured as she led him to a small shaded area, surrounded by old hives in disrepair and long ago abandoned, where she'd laid out a blanket, wine, and a picnic. It provided some shelter from his guards' lustful spying as well as protection from the elements.

Ankhmakis lowered her to the ground and entered her within moments. Nothing was more delightful than the fullness of her lover inside her. The mixture of desire, peace, and power was intoxicating. As he grew harder with each thrust, her own passion exploded around them, encircling their bodies and entering their hearts. Natasa fell into her ecstasy, the one place in all the cosmos where they were perfect. Her lover joined her in her climax, and they cried out in glory. When they finished enjoying one another's bodies, she lounged in his arms and fed him figs as he sipped from his wine and stroked her cheeks, neck, and breasts. There was nothing else to say—their lovemaking had done the talking.

"I'm expected at the palace this afternoon. I have a meeting with your father and Khaleme."

"Of course," she replied, "I know how you spend your days. Nothing has changed."

"I used to have my nights with you," he answered, running his fingers through her short hair, "and now I sleep alone. A few stolen moments is not enough time in your arms."

"I know, but you're not hurt, so there's no reason for you to come to the Houses of Healing," she admitted. "I've been trying to figure out a reason to call you in for inspection but can't. Everyone knows you're healed."

"Well, if you want to inspect me, you can now," he suggested, his wicked grin gracing his handsome face. "I still have an hour, and everyone else is resting in the heat of the day."

She leaned over and looked at his thigh. The wounds were healed but had left two small whitish scars where the arrow had entered and exited, each in the shape of a butterfly. She kissed each scar and brushed his thigh with her breasts before using her mouth to examine the rest of his lower half. She kissed his inner thighs, making her way between his legs, and put him in her mouth. He cried out her name as Natasa allowed his desire to rush across her skin and Ka, feeding on it as if his ecstasy was the nectar of the gods.

"Yes," she purred after he finished climaxing, "everything has healed."

"My goddess, woman," he moaned as she crawled into his lap, and he wrapped his arms around her. "How can it be this good?"

"Love," she whispered as she nuzzled closer to his neck to kiss it. "Love makes everything, including Shadya, much better."

He nodded, and she rested her head under his chin. "What did Helena do today for Father?"

"She sang," she replied.

"You know what I mean."

Natasa leaned back a bit and gazed at her beloved. "Helena is a wonder. She can speak to me remotely, the way you and I do."

"She can?"

"Yes, and after this morning, I now know for a fact Isidor has some sort of magical connection to your father and is siphoning away his vital life force. I believe he's cast an etheric cord to the king's Ka in order to drain his energy bit by bit, over time. When Helena sang, she somehow cut Isidor's connection, allowing your father the freedom to heal. The ancient songs are nourishment for the Ka."

"Which would explain Isidor's reaction when she sang," Ankhmakis said, frowning.

"Yes, I fear Isidor now knows of Helena's power, and this isn't good. If he discovers the truth—" Natasa gulped down the lump of fear in her throat. "Ankhmakis, she's not a normal human child. Khaleme suggested that I let her work with me, and she's shown me how to use the wands to connect to the material world around me. To speak to the animals, flowers, all of life. You saw her with the bird today. She's taught me to do the same with the bees."

Ankhmakis looked at her with a strange grimace.

"What's wrong?" she asked, lowering her gaze as she picked at her nails, wondering if he still loved her after this revelation.

"I do love you," he said, knowing her thoughts, "but sometimes both you and Helena scare me. Not because of your blood, but because of your power. The pair of you are surreal and out of this world, too precious for a man like me and far too precious for a court like this."

"Father tells me you're sending us away," Natasa replied, hot frustration roiling in her stomach. Part of her wanted him to fight her father and keep her by his side.

"Yes, I am," he admitted. "I'd rather you stay here in Behdet, but my father's not giving up the crown, Silus has threatened a war within a war if he does crown me, and after the way Isidor and Chanax looked at our daughter today, I believe they want to see the three of us dead. I can't bear it, and if there's a way to preserve the two of you and send you somewhere safe while I try to clean up this mess, I'll do everything I can to make it happen."

"When will you call me home?"

"When I have the crown," he promised, "and the war has ended."

"Both?" she cried. "I'm sure Horwenefer will die before the Ptolemies are put down."

"I don't want you anywhere near Egypt if we fail to take Memphis."

Ankhmakis squeezed his eyes shut and rubbed his temples. Natasa connected to his mind and saw his greatest fear—Behdet burning, and her and Helena being sold into slavery.

"The Greeks would punish us in such a horrific way?" she whispered.

"Worse," he said, eyes popping open wide as he took her hands into his. "Do you see? My own family wants to hurt you, and the nation I fight against will punish you if I fail. It makes no sense to bring you home when I grab the crown if I haven't finished the war. You and Helena would be targets and used against me. Why would I want to see my precious queen and child sold into slavery? No, you need to be far, far away until the coast is clear."

"It could take years," Natasa complained. "I don't want to be away from you for years."

"Natasa, I can't bear it knowing you're in danger. Please take the boat when it comes."

She looked at him and stroked his cheek, losing herself in his loving gaze. Somehow, she knew if she left Egypt, she'd never return, but he wouldn't want to hear it. He needed to think she was safe, and thanks to Isidor and Chanax, Behdet was becoming more dangerous by the minute. "As you wish, my lord."

He drew her closer for another long, languid kiss. "What I wouldn't give to take you out on the boat right now. Someday, you and I will spend days on the Nile, doing nothing but making love and fishing."

"Fishing?" She giggled.

"Yes," he replied, "for our food. That way, we could be alone. You do realize we're never alone, correct? Servants as well as my guards are watching me, even when I sleep."

"Indeed," Natasa said. "I can't imagine never having a moment to myself. I spend most of my days here in the gardens, with no one but Helena, or the flowers and bees for company."

"I'm sorry you have to hide like this," he answered, his lips turning into a frown. "I imagine you feel quite alone."

She shook her head and kissed him on the forehead. "No, I'm not alone. I love nature much more than people, with the exception of you and Helena of course. Everyone else seems strange to me, each one caught up in their own drama, unable to see how little any of it matters to the evolution of consciousness."

"What matters most, Natasa?"

She answered him with the deepest, most intimate kiss she'd ever given him. A kiss so sweet and pure, it left each of them breathless. Ankhmakis withdrew from her embrace and rubbed his eyes with the back of his hand.

"I need to go," he croaked, running his hands over her breasts, neck, and through her hair. "Same time, same place tomorrow?"

"Yes, if you can manage it."

"Oh, I'll be here," Ankhmakis promised. "I wouldn't miss it for the world."

27

A Series of Conversations

The Ancients had many different ways of transmitting information from one generation to the next. Their temples and pyramids were books in and of themselves. The Ptolemys wanted to build great temples but failed to understand that a monument isn't a building; rather, it's a testament to the knowledge and consciousness of the people who built them.

Behdet, Egypt 200 BCE

Four days into their brief stay in Behdet, and Nefermaat was growing tired of Ankhmakis's games. As he stood yet again in the ancient, forgotten olive grove outside of the apiary, guarding his brother while the idiot indulged in Natasa, Nefermaat recalled his last conversation with Bithiah. She wanted to know if Ankhmakis and Natasa had reunited. Of course, he'd told her yes, but without a witness, there wasn't any proof. He refused to testify against the prince. A guard took an oath to remain true to his lord above all things, and if he testified against his lord in any court, his own life was forfeit, even if his lord was guilty. This was the law, and he felt no desire to die for Bithiah.

He'd spy for her, even poison the prince, but give up his life for the woman? Never. His mother's disinterest in him as a child taught him long ago that women weren't worth it. Besides, it appeared Bithiah was doing fine without him. Every time he returned home, she'd given birth to yet another child. Obviously, she didn't avoid her brother's bed the way Ankhmakis avoided Weret's.

"Ouch," he cried as he slapped his neck.

"What?" Min asked, leaning against a tree and sharpening his sword.

"A damn bee bit me."

Min snickered. "How strange. We're nowhere near the hives here."

Nefermaat glared at his captain and swallowed the bile now forming at the sight of him. How was it that Min, a man born of a nursemaid and a priest, had a higher rank than himself? Born of the high priestess, Nefermaat should have become the high priest of Set, but his father had denied him his inheritance, forcing him instead to guard the king's precious second prince in times of war. Nefermaat hated all the royal men in equal measure.

"I tire of this," Nefermaat spat. "Why should soldiers such as us sit in an olive grove while he breaks the law with his whore?"

"Nefermaat, watch yourself," Min warned.

Nefermaat turned to Pontius, Min's fraternal twin brother. "Do you enjoy guarding the royals as they mate with their women?"

"Well," Pontius said, "we guard them when they sleep. Sex is no different. Though I must say watching Ankhmakis and Natasa is much more exciting than when he mates with Princess Weret. Goodness, it's in and out, no foreplay, no moaning, and no passion. I'm grateful to have been spared from such horrible sex so far this trip."

"Enough," Min commanded.

"Are you blushing?" Pontius asked.

"What? No, but we shouldn't talk about our prince's private matters. We serve him."

"I think you have a shine for Natasa," Pontius teased his brother. "It's why you peek when he rides her. You like to watch."

"That's it," Min replied and took a step toward his brother but stopped short at a noise heard in the distance. He hushed them. "What was that sound?"

The three stood at attention. Even though Nefermaat hated both Ankhmakis and Natasa, he didn't want the prince to get caught on his shift. The soft and rhythmic sounds of quick footsteps could be heard around the far corner of the ancient wall.

"Nefermaat," Min commanded, "go see what it is."

Nefermaat shrugged. Investigating was better than guarding the couple. He crept low, walking the length of the apiary, and turned the corner, his sword at the ready. The garden complex was surrounded by an olive grove long ago left untended and overgrown. He looked around and at first didn't see anything and was turning back when a person leaning at the far end of the wall caught his attention. He walked toward the figure, ducking under the overgrown trees, trying to be as silent as possible. He hugged the vine-covered wall and drew closer, discovering a young girl standing on a wooden bucket and looking through the wall. He drew closer and stepped on a branch, which cracked, causing the girl to look his way.

"Eleni?" he called.

She made to run, but he lowered his sword and put a finger

over his mouth to shush her. He had no idea if Ankhmakis could hear him out here on the other side of the wall, which had to be at least ten feet high and several feet thick, but one never knew. Nefermaat walked toward the girl, who was trembling. As he drew closer, he discovered the girls's secret. There were bricks missing from the wall, and she'd shifted aside the vines to peek through them.

"Spying, are we?" he whispered.

He looked through the peephole and saw it afforded a much better view of the goings on inside the apiary than his station at the front gates. In spite of himself, a flush of desire raced through his body as he witnessed his sister on top of Ankhmakis, head thrown back and sun shining down upon her naked breasts. She was in a state of bliss.

"I see," he said as he drew away from the peephole.

"I'm sorry," Eleni explained. "I didn't know they'd be..." She stopped speaking, picking at her fingernails. She tugged at her hair as she peeked up from under her eyelashes at Nefermaat. "I mean, I've been watching my sister as she works with the bees, but today, when I arrived, this was happening and..." Once more her voice trailed off.

"Don't worry," Nefermaat said, trying to hide his delight as he imagined the look on Bithiah's face when he gave her this lead. "I won't tell Natasa. I promise. Now go away."

Eleni ran through the olive grove with the speed of a rabbit being chased by a coyote. Nefermaat jerked the vines over the peephole to hide it and made his way back to the front gates, where both Min and Pontius still stood at attention.

"Well?" Min asked.

Nefermaat shrugged and answered. "It was nothing. Only a small animal sniffing around."

♱

Hours later, Nefermaat sat beside Bithiah in a small, secluded alcove deep within an area in the Temple of Horus which had been under construction when the war broke out. Since his father killed the Greek masons working on Ptolemy's dear project, this part of the temple still remained unfinished and thus unused by everyone except Bithiah and Nefermaat, who would meet in the abandoned space from time to time. They had the place to themselves.

She leaned against him and sighed, running her fingers along his collarbone, sending chills across his flesh. "Well, my dear, why did you call me here? Your scent is still strong upon my skin from this morning's pleasures."

Bithiah kissed him, and Nefermaat recalled their lovemaking earlier in this very same place. Even though Bithiah and Chanax's constant mating made him angry, he still loved her very much and could never refuse her when he returned to Behdet. She was his great weakness.

"I have a witness for you," he answered, his chest constricted as he spoke.

She leaned toward him, her round breasts rising and falling with her shallow breaths. "You do?"

"Yes," Nefermaat answered, his groin aching. "If you want someone to testify for you, I'd suggest you speak to Eleni."

Bithiah frowned, unsure of whom he was talking about. After a moment, her eyes grew wide and she nodded, clasping her hands. "Eleni? Natasa's younger sister?"

"The one and only. Trust me, she's seen everything. I'll tell you no more, so don't ask any more questions. This can't lead back to me."

"Oh, my love," Bithiah cried. "I knew you'd come through."

Bithiah leaned in close and kissed Nefermaat with the passion of a lover who wasn't allowed to be in love. Tumbling onto the cold stone floor, Nefermaat entered her for the second time that day.

☥

After dinner, Bithiah paced in her chambers. She'd called for her useless husband hours ago, and the man still hadn't arrived. He was trying to punish her for her cruel but honest comments. Oh, how she wished she could have married Nefermaat. Why did she have to give herself to such an indulgent man as Chanax?

"My lady," her servant announced, "Lord Chanax has arrived."

"Let him in," she replied.

She turned and watched as her husband entered the room, his red robes flowing around his ankles. In spite of his failures, he was handsome—as well as her ticket to becoming the high queen of Egypt and getting back at her father for denying her Nefermaat as her husband. After her time in Nefermaat's arms today, she was closer than ever before to destroying the bastard, for if he lost Ankhmakis, Horwenenfer's plans would fail, and he'd be killed on the battlefield within weeks. Her revenge was so near, she found it hard to contain her excitement.

"Well," Chanax demanded, arms crossed, "what is it?"

She threw back her shoulders and tossed her hair. "I have a witness."

Chanax rose to the balls of his feet. As a triumphant smile crossed his full lips, Bithiah remembered why she desired him, even though she didn't love him. Of all people she'd ever known, Chanax was the most charismatic, and his power was absolute. When he got his way, his joy was contagious, and she found his elation addicting.

"You need to talk to your friend Eleni," she continued. "Turns out, she's a bit of a voyeur."

Chanax ran to her and drew her close. "Eleni? Your source is reliable?"

"Yes, husband," she whispered.

Chanax kissed her and picked her up. "You, my dear, deserve to be rewarded."

Before she could protest, he dropped her on the bed, tore back her skirts, and threw himself upon her. Rather than resist, she surrendered to his passion, allowing him to fill her with his seed yet again. To her surprise, Bithiah rather enjoyed the experience of making love to more than one man in the same day.

28

Demands

Weret's birth had led to her mother's death, and deep down she'd always known that something was terribly wrong with her.

Behdet, Egypt 200 BCE

Weret stood outside of Hecataeus's office, staring out the great, open window, watching the servants work in the garden. They weeded and watered as the sun beat down upon their sweaty, glistening black backs. These people were like her. They slaved away in the heat, making her gardens beautiful, and she struggled to make herself beautiful so that her husband might notice her. In many ways, the workers were freer than she was. They returned home to loving arms when Ra set for the night, yet she slept alone in the harem, wondering if and when her husband would call upon her.

Damn the queen for enforcing the harem, and damn Ankhmakis for spending so much of his time in meetings. Well, Weret was done waiting. The time had come for her husband to make good on his duty. He'd made love to her the last time he was in Behdet. Why not now?

The low voices of men saying goodbye filled the hall as the door to the vizier's office opened. The Ethiopian general was the first to leave, several of his men following in his wake. He nodded as he passed by but didn't stop to talk. He often ignored her, as if she didn't even exist. Next Min and company strode out the door, followed by Ankhmakis. Her husband noticed her, and a slight grimace crossed his otherwise pleasant face. She rubbed her sweaty palms along her white shift and nodded his direction, holding her head higher despite the anxiety in her heart.

"Weret," he said. "How are you?"

"I need to speak to you," she answered, her voice tiny. Why did he make her feel so small? "I've sent many requests to call on me, but you haven't replied."

Hecataeus and Ennaeus now stood in the doorway, their eyes darting between her and her husband.

"Well, men," Hecataeus said, running his hands through his hair. "We'll gather tomorrow one last time before we head out to Aswan." He and Ennaeus lunged back into the study and shut the door.

"Yes," Ankhmakis answered, face tight as he rubbed the back of his neck, "as you can see, we've been quite busy. This isn't a pleasure stop. More like a refueling before heading on to the real goal."

"I need to see you now," she said, trying to keep a sense of dignity.

Min, Nefermaat, Pontius, and several other men stood beside them at attention, but not at ease. Her own private guard was waiting down the hall.

"Fine," her husband said.

She led the way to her chambers, unable to speak. The entire situation felt wrong. It had felt wrong since the beginning. After five years of marriage, they still hadn't bonded. Ankhmakis blamed the war, as well as her own spoiled nature. She'd become the woman he wanted, and he still paid her no attention. Even after the removal of his whore Natasa, he continued to ignore her. When they arrived at her apartments, she asked the guards to wait outside. She didn't want the men see her grovel.

"Well," Ankhmakis demanded, "what is it?"

"What is it?" she exclaimed. "How can you not know?"

"I'm not a mind reader, Weret."

"Of course," she said, unable to quell the hysteria rising within her. "Even after all these years you still don't understand, do you?"

"Weret, what's going on?"

"How many days have you been here?"

"Four," he replied.

"Yet you haven't called on me?"

Ankhmakis remained silent.

"Don't tell me you've been busy," she cried. "It's not natural for a man to be away at war for over a year, return home, and not seek out his wife."

"Weret, I told you, this isn't a pleasure trip."

"Of course not," she continued as she paced her room, wringing her hands as she spoke. "I mean, I wondered. Why wouldn't a man seek out a woman for comfort? You're cold to me, I know, and you have an heir, so your needs have changed. Yet you don't even seek out the concubines like your soldiers do."

"How do you know how I spend my nights?" he asked. His nostrils flared on his otherwise controlled face.

"As I've told you before, husband, I have spies everywhere."

His posture changed. He wasn't open, but he was listening.

"Oh, yes," she continued. "I know you sleep alone, but why, when I sleep in the horrid harem, wondering when you'll call? If you don't allow whores in your bed, who is it who pleases you?"

Ankhmakis walked to the window and took a deep breath. His entire form looked like a bow strung too tight. In a flash, it dawned on Weret what was happening.

She gasped. "You and Natasa have renewed your relationship, haven't you?"

He snapped around to face her. "Do not make such dangerous accusations," he said, his jaw tight and fists clenched. "How dare you suggest such a thing?"

"Ankhmakis, how do you think I feel? I have one child as my sisters' arms overflow with little ones. It's true Silus never comes home anymore, but he has already given Ruia three children. Chanax and Bithiah mate like barn animals. What do I do? I'm the most beautiful, the kindest, yet I suffer so. Why can't you help me be who I'm supposed to be? Why can't you love me? If you refrain from my bed, I can only suppose it's to be with her, the one you're not allowed to touch."

He trembled as if fighting some unseen foe, and she feared him more than ever before. "Fine," he said, gulping as he swiped his hands along his tunic. "I've been wrapped up in meetings and have been a very poor husband. Thank you for making me aware of my failing. I will make time for you. I have yet another engagement right now but can join you after dinner."

"Thank you." She tossed her hair and smiled, delighted to have him understand her needs.

"Shall I come to you? We can dine with Ankhmaat and send him away like the last time I was home."

"I have to be in the harem at sunset," she answered. "New

law."

His eyebrows raised as he rubbed the back of his neck. "Oh, right."

"I'd love to come to you," she suggested, overjoyed at this turn of events. "I despise sleeping in the harem. Wives are allowed to stay with their men. Bithiah does it when Chanax doesn't have Alexa in his chambers."

Her husband trembled again and tightened his fists. She feared he would say something cruel, but he swallowed hard and smiled at her. "Of course, you can join me in my chambers."

"Wonderful," she said, her chest bursting. She hadn't been invited to his private rooms since their wedding night. "I'll have my guards escort me at sunset."

☥

Later in the evening, as Natasa retired in the harem to sleep next to her daughter and the other women of the court, she looked at Weret's bed and found it empty. Once her child was breathing with eyes closed and dreaming, Natasa sat against the cold, stone wall, keeping watch. When at midnight Weret's bed was still empty, she hugged herself close and cried.

29

Boundaries

"A phenomenon always arises from the interaction of a complementary. If you want something, look for the complement that will elicit it. Set causes Horus. Horus redeems Set."

~ Ancient Egyptian Proverb

Behdet, Egypt 200 BCE

When Ankhmakis arrived in the apiary the next day, he found Bastyre, covered in bees from head to toe as she harvested honey.

"Looking for someone?" the midwife asked.

"No," he answered, standing out of the range of the swarming bees. "I mean yes. I thought Natasa would be here."

"She didn't come to work today," Bastyre answered, brows furrowed. "Not like her, but sometimes, even the best of us fail to rise to our duties."

Ankhmakis felt dread in the pit of his stomach. Of course, Natasa knew Weret had spent the night in his quarters. The harem made it impossible to keep anything from the women. He ran to her apartment and found Corinna and Eleni repairing a pot together at the table.

"Hello?" he called as he entered the room.

"Why, Ankhmakis." Corinna smiled as she rose to give him a hug. "It's a pleasure to see you."

He embraced her and turned to Eleni, who remained at the table, refusing to look at him, which struck him as odd. "Where are Natasa and Helena?" he asked, trying to hide his panic. "I want to visit them before I head to Aswan tomorrow."

"They left a few moments ago," Corinna replied. "Though I'm not sure where they went. Helena loves the stables. You might check there."

"Thank you," he said and took his leave.

As he approached the stables, he extended his Ka, searching for Natasa, finding her, and feeling nothing but her shame. He followed the trail of sadness to the area of the barn where the old mares lived. The sounds of children's laughter greeted him as he walked in and saw Helena, Senui, and Sethe running in the dusty corral and playing games with the old horses. Natasa stood to the side, her arms crossed, leaning against the stable wall.

"Natasa," Ankhmakis said as he approached. She didn't turn to look at him. He drew closer and stopped inches from her side. He could feel her pain and hurt covering her like a thick, woolen blanket. "My love, please look at me."

She continued to stare at the children, a wistful look on her face. "When I was young, I too played in a threesome—Senmen, Alexa, and I. We were inseparable."

Ankhmakis turned to the three children, each approaching six years of age, hugging and feeding the mares various tree fruits.

"I loved both of them very much," she continued, "but Senmen grew into Chanax, a person I could never again know, and Alexa became his spiritual companion. I was left out."

"Natasa," he began. How could he explain himself?

"You already have." She sighed, yet again reading his mind. "A million times over. We both know why you must make Weret happy. Why you must make love to her, why she matters more than me."

"No one matters more than you."

Natasa turned to face him, and his heart broke at the look of shame in her gaze. "I can't do it, Ankhmakis. I can't be your lover."

"What?" He shifted in his place, trying to hide his panic.

"I sat in the harem last night and marveled at the fact that Weret, a spoiled child of a woman, passed the evening in the arms of the man she loved, while I, a healer and devotee of the goddess Isis herself, spent yet another night alone. Why must I sneak around, yet Weret is awarded love at her command? What is the purpose of such merciless punishment?"

Unable to speak, he felt as if she held his heart in his hand and was squeezing tighter with every word she uttered.

"My entire life I've played by your father's rules," she continued, digging her fingernails into her biceps, arms still crossed over her chest, protecting her own heart from his love. "I've done everything the court has asked of me. I delivered myself into your arms as a young woman and taught you of love, and then went to your brother when I was forced into his arms and learned I couldn't do the same for him. I fled to Iu-Amon in order to avoid becoming a slave to Isidor and your mother's depraved desires. When you arrived injured, I healed you without question to my own needs, or my desire to keep my child and myself safe. Why must I, the one most loyal and true to the royal family, pretend I have no needs? Why must I sit alone at night, knowing the love of my life takes another woman to his bed?"

"Natasa," he said, unable to even breathe.

She gazed toward the children, eyes unfocused, staring through them as if they weren't there. "You asked if I felt alone, Ankhmakis, and I lied to you. The truth is I'm the loneliest woman in Egypt. A woman in love with a man who belongs to another. I've become the most pathetic creature, and my soul is dying. Please, you need to go away, for I can no longer bear to be near you. If you ever loved me, let me go."

"Natasa," he begged again. His legs felt weak as he grasped for her. "Weret suspected something, and I needed to play husband to protect you."

He placed his hands on her shoulders and turned her body to face him. His heart raced as he tried to connect to her. She threw off his embrace. "I told you I tire of the games of the court," she replied. "I can no longer do this. Don't seek me out ever again."

Ankhmakis grabbed her again and hugged her close against her will, no longer able to hide his panic and fear. "I can't lose you. You're the one who keeps me going. Please don't do this to me."

She fought against him, shoving him away from her side, and walked toward the corral. "Helena, come and say goodbye to your father."

The child halted her play and skipped up past her mother and into his arms. "You're leaving again, Papa?"

"Yes," he answered, holding her close. He breathed in her scent and smelled horses, rosemary, and dust. She was perfect.

"Oh," Helena replied as she planted a small, wet kiss upon his cheek, "you must figure out how to end this war. That way, we can spend more time together. I should like to get to know you, Father."

The child jumped from his embrace and skipped back to her friends as if he'd already gone.

Natasa looked toward the stable entrance. Her voice wavered as she spoke. "Yes, I hope you do win the war. Now please, go."

"I will be away for at least six months, maybe more," he replied, hoping for one last moment of connection. "When I return, I will have a plan to take Lycopolis and get you and Helena to safety."

Her face was pale as a ghost and she spoke without emotion. "Fine. Good luck."

"Natasa, don't do this." How could he be losing the one thing he loved in the world? "I was trying to protect you."

She tugged up her dress, exposing her thigh and the knife she kept in a leather strap above her knee. She drew it out of its sheath, held it up in the sunlight, and spun it as if it were a toy. The lost look she wore scared him, and her voice was thick. "I think I'm safer if you stay away."

He made another attempt to energetically connect to her, but she refused him. He allowed her despair to wash over him. Ankhmakis turned to leave and found he couldn't. To be disconnected from her was too painful. He remained beside her, sending her unconditional love, hoping to connect. Her defenses held strong, and she refused to meet his gaze.

"Have you been lying to me?" he asked.

"Lying?" she replied. "About what?"

"About how much you love me?"

She whipped her head around, green eyes wide and color forming in her cheeks. Now he had her attention. He continued to open his own heart. To leave without hearing her say she loved him would be wrong—he needed to hear it once more.

She slipped her knife back into the garter, fingers shaking as she fought to control her emotions.

"I've always loved you. Even as a girl, I was hiding in the trees watching your every move," she cried, her lower lip trembling. "Since I can remember, I've never been able to keep my eyes off you."

The wall around her heart burst open and they were connected. The truth of what hurt her—the pain of being the other woman whom he had to pretend didn't exist—washed over him, and she placed her head in her hands and continued to cry.

"My love for you is why I can't do this anymore," she sobbed. "The happiest years of my life were the ones I spent as your spiritual companion. There were no secrets and no lies. We were one, and everyone celebrated it. Now I hide in the shadows, like a dog, hoping for a bit of you when you can manage to sneak away from prying eyes, while Weret, a woman you don't even care for, gets to parade around the city on your arm."

He stepped forward to hold her, but rather than surrender, she brushed him away with her arm as she spoke. "If I can't be yours in public, without shame or fear, there's no place for me any longer in Egypt. I must go away, Ankhmakis, or I will go insane."

Ankhmakis grabbed her into his rough embrace, regardless of the looks from the stable hands or his guards, who were stationed at the far end of the barn. "Now I understand," he whispered into her ear, holding her closer as she continued to fight against him, refusing to let her escape. "I will see what I can do in Aswan. Maybe I can get Father to allow me to take you once more as my spiritual companion. It's a law, and any law can be overturned." She stopped struggling and nuzzled her head under his chin, giving him the courage to continue. "However, I don't hold out much hope. When I return from Aswan, I will have a boat ready for you and Helena in Coptos. My family's dysfunction isn't safe for either of you. Nor is this country."

She pulled back and wiped her eyes. "This country isn't safe for any of us," she said, glancing at the young boys kicking up dust and chasing his laughing daughter around in circles.

"True." Ankhmakis sighed. "Everyone will die if the tides turn against us, but if I can't save everyone, the least I can do is save the two I love the most."

He wanted to kiss her but held back. Too many were watching; even the little ones could betray them. Instead he bowed to her and radiated his love. "Don't shut your heart to me, Natasa. You and I are more powerful united than apart, even if we can't be together in the flesh, and we both need our wits about us right now." She lowered her head, avoiding his gaze. He placed a finger under her chin and lifted her face toward his. "Natasa, don't ever doubt the love I have for you. There is no other in the world who will inhabit this heart of mine. I need you to live, you must know this?"

"Yes, and I need you," Natasa whispered, her mouth turned down, tears still running down her cheeks. "Which is why it hurts me to be the other woman."

Ankhmakis hugged her one last time and called across the arena to Helena. "Goodbye, dear one. Take care of your mother while I'm gone."

"I will, Papa," the child replied as Senui threw his arms around her and tickled her. Her smile lit up the entire world. "I know she needs me."

In spite of the guilt he felt for hurting Natasa, Ankhmakis

smiled as he walked away to prepare for his departure.

He spent the night in camp, beside his men, refusing Weret's demand to join him in his chambers. Natasa needed to know he'd heard her pain. Once again, with the rising sun, Ankhmakis marched out to war.

30

The Seeds of Deception

"I am the most beautiful tree in the garden
And for all times, I shall remain.
The beloved and her brother
Stroll under my branches,
Intoxicated from wines and spirits
Steeped in oil and fragrant essences."
~ Turin Papyrus 1150 BCE

Behdet, Egypt 200 BCE

Later in the week, after the men, including Hecataeus, were well on their way to Aswan, Chanax invited Eleni for a picnic by the river. She'd accepted and was full of excitement when he met her at her apartment. She was wearing the earrings he'd given her, and he smiled.

"You look stunning and very grown up," he said, bowing. "Whoever gave you those earrings has wonderful taste."

She punched him on the shoulder and smiled. "Chanax, you say the funniest things. I like the way you make me laugh."

She looked so much like the young Natasa, and Chanax swallowed, his throat constricted. Flashbacks to picnics held years ago by the river flooded his mind. His chest tightened as he considered his mission.

"Chanax?" Eleni asked, noticing his sudden mood shift. "What's wrong?"

"Nothing," he said, his emotions now under control. "I was thinking of how Natasa, Alexa, and I would have picnics down at the river when we were young."

"You did?" she asked. "Do tell me. I never get to play at the river."

Chanax held out his arm and Eleni took it. "Come," he said, now smiling and light-hearted, "I'll tell you while we walk. Though mind you, most of our picnics consisted of over-ripe figs, stale bread, beer stolen from the kitchen, and almost always ended in a mud fight. I promise our event will be much more civilized."

As they walked through the exquisite palace gardens and down toward the royal boathouse, Chanax told Eleni a few stories, and by the time they'd arrived at the river, she was laughing at his every word, and he knew he had her in the palm of his hand.

"I can't imagine it," she cried as he placed a blanket on the ground under a sycamore tree. Eleni plopped down without invitation. The low Nile River drifted past under the Perit sun. "Natasa is very serious now."

"Well," Chanax replied, "Natasa believes it was my training in Memphis that changed me, but her training with the priestesses of Isis also changed her. Becoming my brother's spiritual companion is what ruined our friendship."

A dark look crossed Eleni's face. Chanax knew why, but now was not yet the moment to bring up her sister's perfidy. She needed to relax a bit more. He offered her a plate of food and listened to her chatter as she ate. He paid attention to every detail about her—from the way she shook her hair from her forehead, to her tone of voice when talking about a certain person. She was a gorgeous child and would be very beautiful when grown. Once she was comfortable, he placed a hand on her arm, knowing the time had come to approach the subject of her sister's love life.

"Eleni," Chanax began, handling her with as much care as a glassblower casting a fine vase for the king, "I understand you have some important information about Natasa and my brother." The form of fear surrounded her. Chanax answered with the form of peace to calm her, taking her hands unto his. "Please, don't be afraid. I've come to help you, but you're going to have to be honest."

"Chanax," the girl squeaked, "I don't know what you're talking about."

She'd never testify for him in front of the priests. It was too much to ask of a child, and though sometimes under pressure one could force a child to confess, more often, they'd lie. Unlike adults, children didn't quite understand the true power of the law.

"Eleni," he tried again, "I know you've witnessed your sister and my brother having sex. I want to know where and when."

"Why?" She gasped.

"Because," he continued, "I want to help them. If you can spy, so could others, and I don't want them to get in trouble. You do know what the penalty is for lying with a woman who has taken the vow of celibacy?"

She swallowed hard, and Chanax now drove up her fear one more notch. She responded to his energetic touch with a cracked whisper, "Death."

"Yes," he said. "Please tell me, Eleni. Where did you see

them do this?"

"In the apiary," she confessed.

"The apiary?" He should have known. The remote part of the garden was the perfect place to hide an affair. "I haven't been there since I was a child roaming the palace grounds, but if I remember there's a ten-foot wall around the entire garden, with one way in and hundreds of bee hives. I'm sure my brother would have posted guards. He's an idiot, but not a fool."

She winced at the words, and he toned it down. He might have Eleni's confidence now, but Ankhmakis had long been important to her family. "I'm sorry, I shouldn't call him names. Now, how did you see them in the apiary?"

"Through a hole in the wall," Eleni admitted, "but it's hard to find."

"Can you show it to me?" Chanax begged.

"Why?" she asked.

"I must have the wall repaired," he lied. "It's important that no one else catches them."

"But," Eleni whined, "I use the hole to spy on my sister when she's working."

"You spy on her?"

"Yes," she answered. "I took your advice and started following Natasa around and noticed she spent a lot of time in the apiary. I wondered if the bees were the source of her power. I remembered the hole in the wall I found last year when playing chase with the healers' children. I've been going there every now and then to watch her, and she does remarkable things, Chanax."

She sat up straighter and clapped her hands.

"Oh," Chanax replied, now very curious. "Tell me."

"Well, I can't," she replied. "Not because I don't want to,

but because I'm not sure I understand it. She stands in the garden and holds these two metal cylinders in her hands and works with the plants and animals in strange ways. I once saw her command the bees swarming her to go to the other side of the apiary and wait for her to finish harvesting their honey. They did it, Chanax, I swear it. Another day, she made seeds sprout. Oh, and she can make it cloudy around the apiary, so she is shaded from the sun as she works."

She was exaggerating, but his heart was racing anyway. "Metal cylinders? Tell me more." Was it possible she'd found the mate to the golden wand his father had given her? Isidor would be delighted if this were true.

"Yes, one gold and one silver," Eleni replied. "She stands with them in her hands and meditates, sometimes for an hour. It's sort of boring, but what she does the rest of the time is exciting."

"Such as making love to my brother?"

Eleni's face turned red, and she covered her mouth with her hands.

"I know you stumbled upon them," he continued.

"Yes," Eleni cried, voice muffled from behind her palms. "I didn't plan it. I didn't know they'd be sinning together. My sister works in the apiary at the same time every day. I showed up to watch as usual, but he was there and..."

She dropped her hands to her lap and looked away as her voice trailed off. Yes, watching the pair make love was more than Eleni's pure mind ever could have imagined. Chanax felt his groin ache as he envisioned it, and hoped he'd have his chance. He'd need to see them in the act if he was going to get rid of his brother.

"What time does she work in the apiary?" he asked. "Because I don't want to disturb her when I fix the wall.

She mustn't know that we know about her secret. It would embarrass her."

"She arrives before the midday heat," she replied, her voice going low as she spoke. "Sometimes she remains there for hours."

Eleni lowered her gaze, biting the inside of her cheek as she tugged at the end of her long hair. Chanax put a hand on her shoulder. "I know you want to continue learning from your sister in this way," he said with an air of authority, "but you mustn't anymore. I will have the hole in the wall sealed as soon as possible, so don't bother trying."

"If you don't like your brother," she said with a frown, "why would you help him in this way?"

"I'm not helping him, silly," Chanax replied, ruffling her hair. "I'm helping Natasa. I told you, she's my friend."

"She was your best friend."

A memory crossed his mind—this time the two of them were on a wall in Abdju, throwing corn husks at the Pigs of Perit. It was the same day he'd kissed her. As he recalled the feel of her lips, Chanax's heart hurt. "Yes, she was my best friend, until my brother stole her from me."

Eleni dropped her head to one side, as if to ask a question, but she remained silent.

"Now," he said, rising from his seat. "Show me where the hole is in the wall, so I can have it fixed."

"Yes, Chanax," she answered. "You are a good friend. Of course, I'll show you."

31

The Arrangement

"These drugs of subtle virtue the daughter of Zeus was given by an Egyptian woman, Polydamna, wife of Thon; For the rich earth of Egypt bears many herbs mixed together, which have the power to cure, or to kill."

~ Homer, *The Odyssey*, as quoted by Herodotus in his Histories

Behdet, Egypt 200 BCE

After months of enduring curfew, Natasa found herself on duty late at night in the Houses of Healing. Iu-Amon had sent for her, regardless of the queen's rule. She relaxed in a settee near his desk and allowed him to pour her a drink. Ennaeus and Bastyre were also in attendance.

"I've decided our evening frivolity must continue, even if the queen desires to control the nightlife of the female population," Iu-Amon announced before he gulped down his mead. He made a slurping sound, then slammed his empty mug on the table. "Truth is, I find you ladies to be some of my favorite companions."

"What about me?" Ennaeus asked. Iu-Amon kissed his

lover's cheek in response.

Natasa felt her heart ache. Would she have to remain in the shadows with Ankhmakis the rest of her life? Did it even matter, now that her flight from Egypt had been set in motion? Pistias and his crew had arrived in Coptos and were waiting for Ankhmakis's return from the south. Knowing the time to flee was at hand made Natasa's heart ache even more. She didn't know what was worse, having to hide her love for the man, or leaving him behind. Yet her love for him no longer was enough—getting Helena out of Behdet was what mattered now.

"Yes, well, I miss you ladies, which is why I've petitioned for you to work the night shift. This is when we get to be ourselves, isn't it?"

"Oh, yes," Bastyre exclaimed as she tipped the jug of her mysterious grain alcohol to her lips. Gulping down the swill, she offered the flask to Natasa, who waved the concoction away. Something was amiss, Natasa could tell. The midwife wasn't known to abuse spirits like this.

"No, thank you," Natasa said. "I think the mead is enough for me."

"You don't know what you're missing, Priestess," the midwife proclaimed. "I'm glad no one is in labor this evening. I need some time to relax, and to train another midwife. I'm getting too old for this job. These princesses breed with great ambition. Long have the royal women used their bodies as weapons against one another."

Natasa laughed at the thought. "Well, their entire purpose is to ensure succession for their husbands."

"Both Weret and Bithiah are due as Sirius rises with the dawn," Bastyre continued, raising her eyebrow. "Two babies as the New Year begins. They will enter the Birthing Rooms at the same time. It's as if they both conceived on the same day. Bithiah makes sense, she spends most of her nights in Chanax's bed, but how did Weret manage to conceive when her husband is nowhere to be seen, eh?"

Natasa glanced at Bastyre and turned away, not wanting her mentor to know what she'd done. It was true, she'd placed a request in the Way for Weret to conceive, though it was a long shot, considering the pair had spent a single night in over twelve months in each other's arms. Perhaps Weret also kept a secret lover? Doubtful given how badly she wanted to bear Ankhmakis's heirs. Natasa had found that the manifestation of certain things within the realm of light had become quite easy these days. Natasa wished she could manifest the end of the war, but it appeared a ceasefire was beyond her abilities. Conception of a child was one thing—the cosmos apparently longed for human birth—but the resolution of a civil war was more difficult.

"Well," Iu-Amon said, "I'm glad to spend my evenings in this way. Expect more night shifts, even if they're spent right here, in my office."

"How did you manage to get around the whole curfew thing?" Natasa asked.

"The queen and I have an arrangement," he replied.

Natasa felt a chill run across her skin as she looked to Bastyre, her usually pleasant face twisted into a grimace, dark eyes squinting at the firelight. Natasa wanted to inquire what was wrong, but the midwife rose and told them the story of Hatshepsut, the great female pharaoh of Egypt who built several ships and sailed the Red Sea in hopes of establishing trade with Punt and the lands of the Israelites.

"Can you imagine," Bastyre said in closing, "how wonderful life must have been to have a woman ruling Egypt?"

Iu-Amon gazed at his old friend. "Yes, as long as she's not Queen Keket."

Bastyre frowned and took a seat. Iu-Amon leaned forward to nuzzle Ennaeus's neck and after a moment, the pair said goodnight, and Natasa swallowed down her jealousy as the lovers retired to Iu-Amon's quarters, wishing more than anything that Ankhmakis wasn't a prince. Better to love a guard or tutor than an heir to the throne when three brothers were fighting for it.

"Well," Bastyre said, interrupting her thoughts, "looks like the forbidden lovers have gone off to do the forbidden." Natasa sipped her mead and stared into the fire as the old woman continued, words slurring. "You do know most of the court has sex illegitimately."

"Yes, they do," Natasa replied, her mouth twisting into a knowing sneer as she considered it.

"Even the high queen," Bastyre offered. She put her flask to her mouth and drank again.

"Keket?" Natasa's jaw fell. It couldn't be true.

"Why do you think she and Iu-Amon have an arrangement?"

"The two of them are lovers?" Natasa gasped. "What about Ennaeus?"

"No, foolish girl," the midwife answered. "He knows her secret."

"Queen Keket has a secret?"

"Oh, yes, child, she does. It's a very big secret."

"Do tell."

Bastyre poked Natasa in the chest with a harsh jab. "This is not the mindless gossip of children, or even the princesses. What I'm about to tell you has already cost lives."

Natasa flinched away, now sure that whatever Bastyre

was about to say would change her life. "Why do you mention it if it's dangerous?"

"Because the time has come for you to know. The queen's last son, Chanax, isn't Hugronaphor's child."

Natasa's stomach tightened as she considered her mentor's words. "That can't be true."

Bastyre rose and stumbled around Iu-Amon's study. "It is true. I remember the day he was born as if it were yesterday. Twenty-three years ago, tonight, which is why it's on my mind. The day Chanax entered the world was the day I lost my beloved teacher, Nyla."

Bastyre halted and stared into the candlelight. "She was a wonderful woman. Knew everything there is to know about the power of birth, babies, and the All-One."

Natasa gulped. She wasn't sure she wanted to hear this but held her tongue to let Bastyre continue.

"An unnatural chill had settled upon Behdet that day. Mafuane, Horwenefer's second queen, had died giving birth to Weret at dawn, and the palace was still in silence and mourning. Keket began to labor later that evening, at least two moons too soon, according to the dates she'd given us for conception. Nyla wasn't fooled. She knew the truth."

Bastyre turned and gazed at Natasa, grimacing, voice quavering.

"You see, after your dear Ankhmakis was born, Keket began refusing her husband's sexual invitations. She never sought his bed. Years later, she called him back to her side, and out of the blue, she was pregnant and giving birth two months too soon to a healthy infant boy. Never had I seen such a big baby. Someone like the pharaoh would pass it off as coincidence, he's not too bright, but Iu-Amon and Nyla knew Keket had been sniffing around the garden for years prior, stealing herbs to prevent pregnancy, even though she stayed clear of her husband's bed. Which meant one thing—she was bedding someone else."

"I'm unsure your claims are proof of an affair, Bastyre," Natasa noted. "Perhaps Keket returned to her husband to have a child because she longed for a daughter?"

"No." Bastyre shook her head. "The moment Chanax was born, she begged both Iu-Amon and Nyla to hide his birth from the court until the official due date. Mafuane had already been confirmed pregnant with Weret long before Keket returned to her husband. The two babies never should have been born on the same day. The most damning evidence is this—on the day Chanax was born, Nyla took me into meditation in the All-One and together we greeted the boy. Both his mother and father's spirits presented themselves, and the father was not Horwenefer."

"Who was it?" Natasa asked.

"Isidor."

Natasa's heart skipped a beat.

"Yes, Isidor. Nyla knew the truth and confronted the queen. The next morning, my beloved teacher was found dead in the river, and I became the royal midwife. I also knew the truth, yet I'm a coward and said nothing to the queen. I've kept the woman's secret for decades."

"What did Iu-Amon do?"

"After Nyla's death, Iu-Amon approached Keket, and confronted her about the child's true paternal lineage. He agreed to keep it secret, and in exchange for his aid in her deception, the queen has had to obey his every command for decades. She wants no one to know the truth of Chanax's parentage, not even Isidor himself. She must protect herself and Chanax. If the court discovered he wasn't a prince, his life would be over."

"Why? If his father is Isidor, he should be the high priest-in-waiting, which is what Isidor has been preparing him for all these years."

"You'd think so," Bastyre agreed. "However, Isidor and the priests of Memphis want Chanax to be the next pharaoh. Which is why they strive to take Ankhmakis down. If Chanax has no blood claim to the throne, their scheming will have been for nothing. The queen's bastard doesn't qualify for the royal throne."

Isidor and the Invisible Hand's plans now made sense. This was why they were killing Horwenefer and Silus with their dark magic. They'd forced her out of the temple, not because of her Greek blood, but because they desired to deny Ankhmakis the source of his power by destroying her.

"Ankhmakis is the better king," Natasa exclaimed, swallowing down her anger with a swig of Bastyre's awful concoction. She choked down the burning sensation in her throat. "Chanax has no right to claim the title."

Bastyre gripped Natasa's shoulder, swaying in her place and waving a finger in the younger woman's face. "Queen Keket cares for nothing but herself, and of all her children, she loves Chanax most because the only man she's ever loved is Isidor. I have no idea if their affair has lasted until today. I think not, but the queen remains under his thumb. If anyone ever found out Chanax was Isidor's son, all three of them—Chanax, Keket, and Isidor—would find themselves in trouble. No man may touch the queen except her husband. Do you see the power Iu-Amon has over her, knowing what he does?"

"Why does she let him have this power?"

"She has no choice," Bastyre replied. "She thinks he's the only person in the world who knows."

The midwife stumbled into the settee and Natasa covered the older woman in blankets, poured herself another cup of mead, and settled down on the floor by Bastyre's feet. She didn't want to return to the harem. She drank and gazed at the fire dancing in the brazier as a chill, night breeze whispered across the study, considering her predicament. Chanax and Isidor were a threat—her work in the realm of light had revealed this to her numerous times, and the reason was because Chanax desired to be pharaoh of Egypt after Horwenefer. Yet Chanax wasn't even a legitimate heir to the throne. The irony of the situation would be laughable if her daughter's life wasn't in danger.

Perhaps she and Chanax could also have an arrangement? One in which she promised not to tell anyone about his parentage and in exchange, he left her, Helena, and Ankhmakis alone? It seemed a stretch, but she needed to buy herself some time and ensure Ankhmakis's success when she left on the boat. The sooner he took the crown, the sooner she could return home.

She swallowed hard at the realization that it was Chanax who posed the greatest threat, which hurt Natasa all the more, because deep down, she still loved him very much.

32

Two Sides of the Same Coin

Within the Way of the universe, all events leading to the evolution of consciousness are of equal potential. As choices are made, specific events become active and others disappear forever. Such situations are called collapses, and a series of collapses creates a path that can be seen by those who have the eyes to see it. Yet sometimes an event occurs which is far off the path and can't be predicted, but changes the course of history. Natasa called these events fragmentations. The sages called them destiny, and avoiding them was impossible, even for the greatest of seers.

Behdet, Egypt 200 BCE

"The lady Natasa awaits you in your chambers," Chanax's guard announced as he approached the golden doors to his rooms.

"Natasa?"

She'd never been near his private apartments before. Not to visit and, much to his disappointment, not for pleasure. His stomach tightened as he nodded to his guard and entered his parlor. She stood near the window, the breeze tossing her now chin-length hair and blowing the scent of her jasmine perfume around the room. In spite of her constant rejection over the years, to gaze upon her was heaven. Even after months of spying on her in the apiary, he still hadn't tired of it. Perhaps she'd discovered him? Why else would she pay him a visit?

"Good morning, my lady," Chanax said with as much charm as he could muster. "What a pleasant surprise to find you here."

She turned, and his pulse raced as he caught her eye. She scanned him with her energy, and this time he held his own, blocking her attempt.

"Do you have a minute?" she asked him, the tone of her voice neutral. He couldn't pick up any emotions.

"Yes, please, have a seat," he replied, gesturing to a small table in the corner. He called to his servant and asked for some refreshments to be served.

Natasa walked to the table, head high and back straight. She sat, staring at him, her full, red-painted lips drawn into a wry, contemplative smile. Chanax felt the familiar desire that had built within him each day as he took his place outside of the wall to watch her work with the wands. He'd learned much from his experiences, but still hadn't told Isidor of his discoveries. He wasn't ready to reveal the secret because he enjoyed watching her and didn't want to stop.

Besides, Chanax wanted to keep the wands from Isidor for an even more simple reason—he desired them for himself. He wanted to steal them, but he didn't know where she hid them when she wasn't using them. He'd asked Eleni to search the apartment, to no avail. During the brief moments when he dared to go into the apiary, he'd found no sign of them. Of course, knowing Natasa, she hid them inside the busiest beehive in the garden, and no one except her or Bastyre would be able to gain access without suffering the stings of thousands of angry bees.

He smiled at her as he considered her cleverness. Natasa shook her head, shaking her hair around her face. "Well, where to begin?"

"How about explaining your purpose for seeking me out in my private chambers?" he suggested, swallowing hard as he gazed at her, his pulse beating like thunder in his ears. "I must be honest, this is something I never could have predicted, even in my wildest dreams."

Natasa shifted under his gaze—he knew his desire gave her pause. "Chanax, my dear, I'm not here for pleasure."

"Of course not," he replied, acting as if her constant rejection meant nothing. "Healers don't allow themselves such indulgences. Perhaps you're here to accept my offer of friendship? I do miss you."

The hard expression on her face caused him to shiver. "I'm here to settle things," she said.

"What do you mean, settle things?"

"I know you seek to destroy Ankhmakis," she replied.

"What? How can you accuse me of such a thing?"

"I see you for who you are, Chanax," she continued. "I know your Invisible Hands drain the energy of the pharaoh in order to kill him and drive Silus to madness so he'll be incapable of inheriting the throne when his father dies. I also know you plot to kill Ankhmakis and take the throne yourself."

"Those are serious allegations, Natasa," he replied, trying to keep a casual tone. "Even if you did speak the truth, I wouldn't admit any of it to you."

"Of course, you wouldn't," she agreed. "Like your mother, you're good at lying and hiding the truth."

He narrowed his eyes at her. What was she getting at?

"What does my mother have to do with anything?"

"High Queen Keket is the reason I'm here today."

"My mother is the reason for your visit? Do you think I can convince her to lift the Purification Law that stripped you of your title? I'll have you know I was never in favor of assigning you to my men. I love my mother, but her intentions crossed a line. I promise you, I never would have let it happen."

Natasa shook her head. "I no longer care for the temple of Isis. I love being a healer. It suits me more than the role of high priestess."

"Does Ankhmakis know this? I mean, pleasuring him was your main duty, wasn't it? Oh wait, you were Silus's companion when the Purification Law was passed, weren't you?"

He smirked and winked. She tipped her head and poured herself a drink of ale.

"No need to be nasty, Chanax."

"Nasty? You're the one here accusing me of treason and killing my own father and brothers for the throne."

Natasa sipped her ale for a moment, her gaze soft yet condemning. She was keeping something from him. She placed her mug on the table, rose from her seat, and stood behind him. She rested her hands on his shoulders and leaned forward into his ear, causing his stomach to turn cartwheels. A wave of heat passed between them. He could feel her warm breath against his neck as she spoke. The scent of jasmine and her hot flesh was intoxicating.

"I understand the desire to be pharaoh," she cooed, allowing her hands to caress his neck. Chanax gulped back his need. "After all the hard work your father has done to gain control of the Upper Kingdom, it's natural for his sons to covet the position."

She ran her fingers across his bald head and leaned in

even closer. Chanax struggled to keep her out of his mind. She was manipulating him, and yet he longed for her to continue to touch him.

"The problem is," she breathed into his ear, "only a son of the pharaoh and his high queen can take the throne. Which means your efforts to kill your brothers to secure the throne for yourself are useless, since you, Chanax, are not one of Horwenefer's sons."

Desire melted into hot anger, and Chanax thrust himself from his chair to face her. "What are you suggesting? I am High Queen Keket's son.

"Yes," Natasa agreed as she stepped away from him, her beautiful lips drawn into a smirk, "of course you are. Yet it doesn't make you Horwenefer's son."

Hate filled his vision, and her taunting face blurred. "Do you dare accuse my mother of adultery?"

"Yes, and I have proof. I'm sorry, Chanax, but you don't share the same father as Silus and Ankhmakis. Go ahead, ask your mother. She won't be able to hide it from you; your sight is too powerful."

She was correct. If he confronted Keket, she would, of course, say Horwenefer was his father, but he'd know if she was lying or not. He pointed at Natasa and cried, "I don't have to ask her. I know you're the liar."

"You know I'm telling the truth," Natasa challenged. "Go ahead, search my mind with your Ka. You'll see, Chanax."

He glared at her, unable to do as she suggested because he didn't want to know the truth. If his mother had indeed been unfaithful to the pharaoh, he was useless in the eyes of Memphis, and Isidor for that matter. His sacrifice in Memphis as a child would have been for nothing.

"Why do you tell me this now, Natasa?" he demanded.

"Because, it's time we made a deal," she answered. "You and Isidor both see me as a means to an end when it comes to Ankhmakis, and it needs to stop. I want to be left alone to do my work and raise my child. The Invisible Hands must end their quest against both of us, and you will remove yourself from the pursuit of the throne. You aren't an heir, Chanax, and if you destroy Ankhmakis in an attempt to gain the crown, I will reveal the truth to everyone."

"What is the nature of your truth?" He snarled, plunking his hands on his hips.

"Your father is none other than Isidor himself, and as I said, I have the means to prove it."

He choked for air and stepped away from her, searching for something to hold on to. What she said was blasphemy, and yet...

"Isidor?"

"Yes, Isidor," she replied. "Let this be our arrangement, Chanax. You will drop every plot against myself and Helena and support Ankhmakis in his quest to create peace in this land, and I will carry this secret to my grave."

"What if I don't agree to your terms?"

"I will tell the pharaoh the truth myself—you are not his heir and his queen has been unfaithful with his high priest for decades."

Chanax sent his anger forth in wisps, trying to surround her, but the golden shield surrounding her held true.

Natasa held up her hand and laughed, her voice mocking. "You may be able to curse Horwenefer and Silus, but don't even try it with me. You were right, Chanax, when you said the two of us are similar. We're evenly matched. For every talent you have in darkness, I can counter with one from the light. We're two sides of the same coin. Oh, how I wish it had been different, and we were working together. Imagine the world we could have created."

"What you speak of," he whispered, allowing the form of love to permeate the room, "is what I've longed for my whole life."

She bit her lip, and he saw the form of regret surround her, but she gripped her fists and quieted her emotions with a toss of her hair. "Too late, Chanax. Now, do we have a deal, or do you need to check with your mommy first?"

Her cruel voice felt like a blade to the heart, and any love he felt for her sputtered out. He would ask Keket, but he already knew the answer. Natasa spoke the truth, and he hated her for it.

"We have a deal, for now. The Invisible Hands will leave you and your child alone."

"Lastly, you will inform Isidor and the priests of Memphis that you no longer desire the throne yourself," she added. "They'll have no choice but to support our current pharaoh by stopping their efforts to kill him, as well as Ankhmakis, the true heir, in his mission."

"You have no business trying to manipulate the outcome of the war. Love and chaos don't mix, Natasa," he said through clenched teeth. "I thought you knew better."

"I think we're done here."

She turned and left him alone by the table. He grabbed a handful of grapes, stuffing them into his mouth. He needed to see his mother.

Chanax rushed through the palace and found her sitting in one of his father's studies, weaving a small blanket on a vertical loom. Several servants were helping her, and Weret sat in the corner, resting her hands on her swollen abdomen. The women looked up as he entered the room in a flurry of robes. His breaths were shallow as he fought to put on a calm face.

"Chanax." Keket smiled. "How nice to see you."

"I need to talk to you, Mother," he demanded.

"Not right now," she answered. "I'm busy making Weret's new baby a blanket."

"What I need to discuss is a matter of national security."

Keket rose from her place and cocked her head. "Well, what is it?"

"Everyone leave," Chanax commanded. "I demand privacy."

Weret moaned from her chair. "Whatever you can say to Mother, you can say to me."

"Wrong," Chanax replied. "Mother is the pharaoh's wife; you, however, are a woman of the court. I'm not at liberty to discuss matters of the state in front of you."

Weret pouted and jutted out her chin. "I am the general's wife—"

Keket clucked her tongue at the woman, rolling her eyes as she waved her hands at the youngest princess. "Oh, Weret, do as you're told, and Chanax, why can't you be nicer?"

Weret called a servant over to help her get out of her seat, groaning and moaning as if she were ready for labor, which was nonsense since she wasn't due to enter the Birthing Rooms for two more months, with Bithiah, who was up and about chasing their three children. After the room emptied, Chanax sent out his Ka to surround his mother with his watchful sense.

"Well, what is it? Has something happened to your father?"

He didn't find any genuine concern in her energy field; rather, her face was bright and her smile wide, as if she hoped the man was in trouble. He drew closer and grabbed her arm.

"Why didn't you ever tell me?"

"Tell you what?"

"The truth about Isidor. He's my father, isn't he?"

She covered her mouth and stepped back. "Who told you?"

She wasn't even going to try to lie. She couldn't, not with the hold his Ka exerted upon hers.

"Natasa," he replied.

"Natasa? How could she know?"

"She says she has proof."

Keket bit her lip, her eyes narrow and voice low and dangerous, growling like a rabid dog. "Iu-Amon. He has broken our arrangement. I shall have him pay for this."

"Mother," Chanax said as he grasped her shoulders, "Iu-Amon isn't the problem. It's Natasa. She's threatened to tell the pharaoh if I don't do as she says."

"Yes, of course she would. She's learned a lot from her time in the Houses of Healing. I should have signed an order to have her and all her kind killed long ago, but no, I refrained because your father doesn't want to kill Hecataeus and his spawn. What a weak man."

"Which father?" Chanax demanded. "Horwenefer or Isidor?"

Keket wriggled from Chanax's grip. "I can't believe this is happening. Oh, Chanax, you can't let her tell anyone. You must do whatever she requests."

"I will not let her, or any woman, tell me what to do," he answered. "Does Isidor know about me?"

"No, and he can't. He would hate me, knowing I allowed myself to conceive, and worse, lied about it to the court. He'd be hung for touching the king's wife. Chanax, no one can know."

"Natasa says I must stop fighting for the crown and abdicate to Ankhmakis, since I no longer qualify for the position."

"What are we going to do? Isidor's plans hinge on you becoming pharaoh. He would be angry if you were against him. You have to do as he says."

"Why do you fear him if he's your lover?" Chanax asked.

"He's no longer my lover," she admitted. "He hasn't been for years. He gave me up when I failed to steal that damn golden wand from the pharaoh before he gave it to Natasa." So Isidor did covet the wands. All the more reason he should tell his master about the pair, yet he wanted them for himself. His mother continued, wringing her hands as she spoke, "He never forgave me for not procuring it for him. Besides, he's more interested in younger women."

Chanax probed her energy further and saw this was true. Isidor no longer found Keket attractive in her old age, and it broke his mother's heart.

"I see," he replied.

"The high priestess's half-breed child must die. There must be a way to make it look like an accident. It's what I did to the midwife who refused to lie to Horwenefer about your birth."

"You killed someone to hide this secret?"

"Yes," she answered. "I would've killed more if Iu-Amon hadn't stepped in. Oh, I will make him pay for this."

"You'll do nothing of the sort," Chanax commanded. "Leave this to me. I'll let Natasa think she has won and do as she says. I can call off some of the plans and make it seem I no longer aspire for the throne."

He gazed at Keket and saw how time had affected her. She

appeared much older than her forty-four years. It seemed she was as much a victim as he.

"I will take care of Natasa," he continued, "but you'll let me do it my way. Don't try any of your immature tricks. I've been working for months to ruin her and soon will have my chance."

"How?" she asked.

"I can't tell you," he answered. "Trust me, I'll take care of it. You will stay out of my way. Agreed?" She nodded. "I need to go," he said as he strode to the door, stopping before he opened it to look at her one last time. "Did you love him?"

"Who?"

"Isidor."

Her lower lip trembled as she spoke. "He's the only man I've ever loved."

33

Strategies and Requests

In the beginning, Egypt was two countries, with the Red King in the North and the White King in the South. Until Narma, the man considered the first pharaoh of Egypt, united the kingdoms and the two became one. As the Egyptian Revolt of 200 BCE progressed, many in the south considered the splitting of kingdoms as a way forward and to peace. Yet Memphis still remained a great prize to Horwenefer, for being the White King wasn't enough—he coveted the entire nation.

Aswan, Egypt 199 BCE

"General Khaleme, you say the strangest things." Horwenefer chuckled, clutching his stomach.

"What do you mean?" the general asked, unsure of why they were laughing. "I don't intend to be strange."

Ankhmakis patted his good friend on the back. They were enjoying dinner after another long day of strategy and training, and the discussion had turned to death, which was not unusual, given the amount of war they'd all been through.

"You bury your noblemen in crystal tombs?" Horwenefer

continued.

Eight months of hard work had passed in Aswan, and as the rains of Akhet were ushering in another New Year, the pharaoh still looked radiant. It seemed the combination of Helena's singing and the high priestess's Anit-Shadya had done wonders. Ankhmakis knew his chance to take the throne sooner than later had passed. The man wasn't dying anytime in the near future.

"We have much crystal in Kush," Khaleme explained. "It is the finest in the world, and very pliable. We dry out the body, as your priests do, and remove the internal organs. When the body is ready, we paint it to look the way it did in life, and we encase it in crystal. First the body is shown in the eldest son's home. After the mourning period is over, we place it on the street leading to our royal palace."

King Adikhalamani added, "Not all bodies are welcome on the King's Road. Only the noblest are preserved in this way."

Horwenefer took a drink of mead and nodded. "Well, I stand corrected, but I still find it strange."

"Yet paying priests to leave gifts of food for eternity beside your dead body in tombs the size of cities isn't strange?" the king of Kush asked.

Ankhmakis's father opened his mouth to speak and then shut it. For once, the man was speechless. Surrounded by this light-hearted company, Ankhmakis found his courage. Perhaps he might be able to ask his father to overturn the laws keeping Natasa from his side? Khaleme supported him; why not challenge Horwenefer in front of the other king?

"Father," Ankhmakis began, "I have something I wish to discuss."

"What is it, son?" Horwenefer asked.

"I want you to remove the Purification of the Temple

Laws," he said, rising up in his seat to appear tall and confident.

Horwenefer stared at him, but Ankhmakis couldn't read his face. "Why?"

"Because I want Natasa as my spiritual companion once more," he blurted out before he lost the courage.

"This is a good idea," Khaleme replied. "It is important."

"Enough," Horwenefer answered, his voice firm. "I may think your mother is a zealot in many ways; however, I agree with the law. We can't have any Greek blood in our leadership ranks if our mission is to take control away from the Greeks. We must be consistent, son."

"You keep Hecataeus as your vizier. He's full-blooded Greek."

At the mention of Hecataeus, the pharaoh quieted for a moment. Ankhmakis felt caution emanate from his father.

"Hecataeus and I have an agreement," he replied. "He convinced Philopater to grant us our army, as well as the best men from Greece to train us. I have no choice but to protect him. He can't leave us for the Lower Kingdom. He's a traitor and a wanted man there. Thus, I must provide him a safe home. It's the least I can do."

Ankhmakis thought about how Hecataeus planned on traveling through the Lower Kingdom to save his family and worried the vizier might be the weak link. Yet there was no other way out.

"What about Natasa? She's his child. Don't you owe it to Hecataeus to allow her to become the high priestess?"

"I used to," Horwenefer admitted, "but no longer. The truth is, there's a reason why I leave Hecataeus behind in Behdet. I'd love to have him by my side in Thebes as he's the smartest man I know, and the best advisor I've ever employed. Which is why I made him join us here in Aswan. Yet I can't be seen in public with a Greek by my side, any more than my son can."

"Natasa is also our blood," Ankhmakis demanded, struggling to hide his trembling lower lip.

"Yes, but the color of her eyes and lighter skin tone give away her Greek heritage. Ankhmakis, if you're to lead this rebellion, you can't be associated with a mixed-blood woman. It's not good for you. Besides, Natasa is safe in the Houses of Healing. The peasants love her. They even sing songs about her amazing ability to heal your injuries. I think I've lived up to my end of the bargain."

"No," Ankhmakis demanded, his heart breaking and hope faltering, "you haven't. She's the love of my life. You tore her from my side as punishment years ago, and now I want her back. I've done everything you've asked of me—commanded our army, followed your orders, and produced heirs with Weret. Why can't you grant me this one wish?"

Horwenefer gave him a lazy, unconcerned look, as if he were dealing with a schoolboy and not a general of his army. "You can't have her, I'm sorry. I'm willing to remove the law prohibiting you from the priestesses of Isis. You can choose a new, pure-blooded, spiritual companion if you wish. I agree you've earned it."

"Oh, splendid," Ankhmakis said, spitting his words at the man as if they were venom. "Yet another woman I don't love in my bed. No thank you."

Khaleme looked to his king and cleared his throat. "You know how I feel about this. It is a sin to divide a divine pair."

"Where do you get this divine pair nonsense?" The pharaoh laughed as he stretched across the table and took a handful of nuts from a golden bowl. He popped them into his mouth, chewing with such enthusiasm, the smacking of his lips irritated Ankhmakis.

"From our ancestors," Khaleme explained. "It is written in the most ancient Egyptian teachings. The divine pair is what humanity longs for. No man should have to settle for less. If you wish to usher in an age of glory in Egypt, you would allow your son to have Natasa as both his spiritual companion and as his queen. You would see a change in the momentum of the war."

Ankhmakis nodded at Khaleme. Perhaps he could change Father's mind?

"Nonsense," Horwenefer cried. "It would be a violation of the oldest of our laws. Our royal men marry their sisters. Our heirs are pure."

"Your second queen wasn't your sister," Ankhmakis noted. "Queen Mafuane was a priestess born of your cousins. Natasa and I share more of the same blood than you two did."

"If I don't want Greek blood in my priesthood, it can't be in our queens. Second, third, or fourth queen, it doesn't matter. The queen is a leadership position. Mafuane's father was a pure-blooded priest and her mother a pure-blooded cousin of mine. Natasa's father isn't Egyptian. She doesn't qualify, even if I do remove the purification laws."

"What is a law?" Ankhmakis begged. "Why can't it be broken?"

"I see where Helena gets her ideas," Horwenefer answered, jaw clenched. "However, she is much more enchanting in her requests. The purity laws with regards to the line of kings are as old as our nation. I won't change them. They're as sacred as the celibacy law. These things cannot be negotiated."

Ankhmakis glared at his father, clenching his fists and digging his fingernails deep into the palms of his hands.

"You need to let her go, son," Horwenefer said. "Focus on

winning this war. I know you don't like Weret, but you don't need to bother with her any longer. She's given you a son, with a second child on the way. If it's a boy, she'll no longer cling to you. Keket started refusing my advances the moment you were born. Marriage isn't about love."

"Which is why you took a second queen," Ankhmakis noted.

"Yes, and look where it got me," Horwenefer answered. "Three more children and a broken heart. Trust me and take refuge with the concubines; they expect nothing from us."

"Sex with a woman who doesn't want it is no better than sex with an animal," Ankhmakis accused.

"You have such lofty ideals, son," Horwenefer said, waving a finger at him.

"He speaks the truth," Khaleme interrupted. "It is bad energy. A woman's embrace is powerful when she welcomes you with joy."

"Ah, now I understand where you get these thoughts," Horwenefer said, shifting his shoulders away from them, as if trying to escape the conversation. "I appreciate your wisdom with regards to military engagement Khaleme, yet I'd rather you keep your cultural values to yourself."

"Military engagement is a direct reflection of cultural values," the general replied.

Horwenefer rose from his seat. "I tire of this conversation. Forget Natasa. She isn't the future of Egypt."

"You're telling me the finest woman in your court, the smartest and most talented, the high priestess Neferu-ankh-maat's own daughter, has no place at our side?"

"She does have a place in my court, as a healer. We need her there. She does great work, and Iu-Amon adores her. Leave her be." Horwenefer looked to his guests. "Is there anything else? If not, I think it's time to retire for the evening. There are women waiting for me in my quarters. Aswan has such fine whores, and the best part is, I won't have to see them again once we leave. Goddess knows women are even more work than running a rebellion."

"There is one more thing," King Adikhalamani declared as he rose from his seat. He towered over Horwenefer. "We wish for you to close the temple of Set in Behdet.

The pharaoh threw back his head, choking back his mad laughter. "You're insane. The temple of Set operates in Behdet as a blood pact made with Memphis. If I close it, they will crown Ptolemy V Pharaoh, even if he is still a child. We are at war, and we need the god of chaos on our side. Moreover, I need those priests. They are what give me my crown, not the other way around."

"You keep the dark cult open at your own peril," the king of Kush replied. "All societies fall once they practice blood magic."

"You worry too much," Horwenefer answered, moving to stand beside the Kush king, even though he was dwarfed by the Ethiopian's majesty and height. "They've ushered in nothing but luck thus far."

Ankhmakis winced. King Adikhalamani shook his head, turned away from the pharaoh, and paced the room. "You speak of law as the highest order yet ignore the most important law of all—the Law of Divine Order—as above, so below. You cannot avoid this law, for it is the foundation of all things. The progress of the war reflects the order within your own house. Withholding love from your sons and allowing human sacrifice are liabilities, not strategies. You fail to break the Greek frontline because you fail to understand the nature of the universe. The laws of man cannot compete with the Law of Divine Order."

"The laws of men are quite efficient," said Horwenefer, slamming his fist on the table. "They are the agreements keeping our rebellion together. I cannot lose the support of the priests in Memphis. They started this war, and I will need them to finish it. It's their order, not divine order, which gives authority to my crown. Now, if you'll excuse me, I need to rest."

The pharaoh and his guards left the room and Ankhmakis felt his entire being deflate. The war, as well as his very own life, no longer held any meaning.

"At least you tried," Khaleme said. "Your Natasa would make a very fine queen."

Ankhmakis looked to his friend, his mouth trembling as he fought his despair. He lowered his head to his hands and started to cry.

"My dear warrior," King Adikhalamani said. "Why do you cry?"

"Because my heart hurts," Ankhmakis replied. "Everything hurts."

Khaleme held him close to his chest, and Ankmakis surrendered to the loving gesture as he sank deeper into his despair. There was nothing left to do but get Natasa on Pistias's boat and send her and his daughter far away. Yet the idea of living in a world where they no longer existed triggered the ever-familiar pain he now carried, as if a blade were embedded in his gut. Perhaps he should flee with them? As Khaleme patted him on the back and squeezed him closer, Ankhmakis considered leaving his father and Egypt to their fate. His could live his own life far away, free for the very first time.

As the idea took hold within his mind, he began to breathe

and felt a darkness lift from his soul. He imagined living in Athens, Natasa as his wife and several more children running around their home. He would be a rhapsodist entertaining the merchants by the sea, and Hecataeus would grow old by their side. With each thought, Ankhmakis fell deeper and deeper into bliss and knew, as he did long ago in Alexandria, that Natasa was all that mattered, and he would follow her to the ends of the earth.

As Ankhmakis gave into his resolution to leave Egypt behind, Hecataeus rushed into the room, his face pale and eyes wide.

"Where is the pharaoh?" the vizier demanded.

"He's retired for the night," Ankhmakis answered. "Why?"

"A messenger has arrived from the north. The Ptolemaic army has launched a mighty counter-offensive strike," Hecataeus explained.

Ankhmakis, Khaleme, and the king of Kush leaped from their places, jostling the low table at which they sat.

"What?" Khaleme exclaimed.

"Silus has fallen back to Abdju," Hecataeus continued. "Every city taken in last year's surge has been lost, and he struggles at this moment to keep the enemy north of Thebes. He needs more backup, or we will lose the royal city as well."

"If this is true, none of our work here in Aswan will amount to anything," Ankhmakis cried.

"We must inform the pharaoh," Khaleme said as he strode toward the door.

If Thebes fell, the efforts of the past five years would have amounted to nothing as well. Ankhmakis couldn't allow a full retreat. Events linked together within his mind, like pieces in a puzzle. "Call a meeting. We need to use this to our advantage."

"How?" Hecataeus asked.

"Thebes," Ankhmakis replied as he expanded his awareness out in the six directions and connected to the All-One. "The Greeks need her, and Coptos as well. They covet the Wadi Hammamat trade route to the Red Sea, and the power of the Theban priesthood. Why not use both as bait?"

The men in the room looked at him as if he were crazy, but in Ankhmakis's mind the way forward was clear, and a new plan of cat and mouse took shape. It would mean delaying Natasa's flight from Egypt, but it might grant him Lycopolis at last.

34

The End of All Things

"Vital suffering is consciousness undergoing the process of surpassing itself."
~ The Temple of Man, R.A. Schwaller de Lubicz, 1949 CE

Behdet, Egypt 199 BCE

The men paced Hecataeus's study, zigzagging across the room, their anxiety filling the space with turbulent emotions. Even Hecataeus could feel the tension. Each one was afraid, for if they failed this mission, all would die. There was no mercy in the Ptolemy court.

Horwenefer had taken five Ethiopian regiments to Thebes. There they would hold the city with the rest of their army, twenty thousand men total, until they received a signal from Ankhmakis to retreat, and fall back to Hierakonpolis, a city fifty miles north of Behdet, where they would rally with thousands more Ethiopian and Nubian warriors, waiting for the moment to strike. To allow the war to come closer to their central city was risky, but such a risk was their only chance at success.

Hecataeus looked at the prince, lines of concentration

now etched upon his young forehead. He was twenty-eight years old and bore the weight of the world upon his shoulders. Everything rested on the timing of his plan—including Hecataeus's flight out of Egypt. Part of him regretted leaving the pharaoh and his family at this crucial moment, but there was nothing left for him, or his loved ones, to do. He'd help the royals this one last time, and then run like the wind, for Hecataeus knew now more than ever he needed to get his children and granddaughter out of Behdet or suffer the consequences.

"After our retreat from Thebes," Ankhmakis explained to the nervous men, "the Greeks will think we're on the verge of surrender. They'll take the time to force the Theban priests to crown the boy king as their pharaoh before heading south, toward Behdet to issue their justice."

A large map sat upon the table and Ankhmakis slid an onyx figure from the city of Thebes to the south and over the city of Hierakonpolis, at the same time sliding a second figure, this one made of ivory, from Hierakonpolis, across the desert, and up to Lycopolis.

"If all goes as planned, my cavalry and I will be well on our way through the desert to Lycopolis. We can't get there by boat. They'll have archers along every bank north of Thebes. We will ride the sands. It will be difficult, but they'll never expect this. When we hit Lycopolis from behind, they'll be heading south up the river, leaving it unattended and vulnerable to our forces."

"It is over two hundred miles away, maybe more," one of the men argued. "Through the desert without any forage or water. How can we get ten thousand men to Lycopolis without running out of supplies?"

"We will go to the Kharga Oasis first, approximately

one hundred and fifty miles as the crow flies," Ankhmakis explained. "Given the size of our army, it should take three days, but to ensure we make it, we'll have six days' worth of supplies. We'll take the oasis from the residents by force to re-supply and rest for a few days before heading out to Lycopolis for the final attack."

The soldier crossed his arms and looked to the others. "It will take another hundred miles through the desert. It's risky."

The men shifted in their places. Hecataeus admired Ankhmakis for his poise and intelligence. On papyrus, this plan might work.

"Once we've taken Lycopolis and fortified the line, we'll recruit able-bodied natives from the city into our ranks and ride south toward Thebes along either side of the Nile, clearing out the archers in our path. This will be your signal to advance," Ankhmakis continued, one hand on the white piece, the other on the black. He drew the pieces closer toward one another. "You will meet much resistance as you draw their attention toward you, but we'll be close behind, growing in size as we take each city to the north, meeting in the middle..."

He slapped the figures together with a loud crack north of Thebes, in Coptos. Hecataeus sighed. The one place he needed to go would be ground zero for the battle.

"...crushing them from both directions."

There followed a stiff silence, each man weighing the significance of the plan. Ankhmakis's proposal was risky and hinged on two things—the Greeks sending the majority of their troops south to Thebes, leaving the northern cities, including Lycopolis, easy targets, and timing. Everything had to be perfect.

"We ride out this evening," Ankhmakis informed them. "Cavalry and infantry, as well as supplies, are gearing up as we speak. When we get to Hierakonpolis, those of us taking the desert route will continue and the rest will wait for the pharaoh and his troops to arrive from Thebes. Are there any questions?"

The men shook their heads.

"Well," Ankhmakis said, looking at General Khaleme. "What do you think?"

The solid man stood silent, considering his words. Hecataeus liked this quality about the general—he was as peaceful and contemplative as he was fierce. Hecataeus would miss him when he left.

If he ever left.

"It is a clever plan," Khaleme replied, "and there is much hope of success. As long as no one in the court gets in the way."

"What?" Ankhmakis asked. "Why would anyone in the court interfere? Everyone has signed off on it."

"My high priest, Dardre, believes something is amiss in the temple of Set. With permission from the highest leadership in your court, they plot to strike against you."

Ankhmakis rubbed his chin, and Hecataeus nodded to the general. "This has long been true—Chanax, Isidor, and the high queen harbor their own agendas, and it wouldn't surprise me if they wanted Ankhmakis dead. Be on guard, Prince, and you'll be fine."

Khaleme looked at Hecataeus and shook his head. "I wouldn't ignore this warning," the general said. "This—"

"I won't," Ankhmakis interrupted. "I appreciate what you have said and will spend time considering it. Anything else?"

When the men remained silent, Ankhmakis dismissed everyone, and as soon as the room was clear, he sent his guards outside and shut the door. This next part of the meeting was for the two of them alone. Ankhmakis looked to Hecataeus from under his brow, forehead tight and face pale.

"How long will this operation of yours take?" Hecataeus asked. "I understood Khaleme's warning, and I'm sure the threat isn't on the battle field, but right here in Behdet."

"Agreed," Ankhmakis replied. He sat at the table and poured himself a drink. "I have no idea. We have planned for at least nine months to secure the area."

"Nine months?" Hecataeus cried. He placed his hands on the table and leaned into the prince. "We don't have nine months."

"Hecataeus," Ankhmakis replied, exhaling as he spoke, "we've been working on the escape plan for over a year already. What's another nine months?"

Hecataeus sat and slumped in his chair. He wanted to scream at the young man but found he couldn't. Ankhmakis wasn't the reason the war was taking too long, nor was he responsible for the Greeks kicking off the New Year with a massive, surprise surge at the exact same time Pistias and his men arrived in Coptos. It was, however, Ankhmakis's fault his daughter was in danger.

Yet Hecataeus couldn't begrudge the prince, for he'd been a witness to the day the young man fell for Natasa, and there was no stopping the momentum of such an event. "I remember the day you arrived at my door in Alexandria, asking to escort Natasa to the library. I sometimes think she would've made the best archeologist, or even historian, but research wasn't her destiny."

Ankhmakis's shoulders slumped, and his eyes fell to the floor. Hecataeus placed a hand on the prince's knee. "You were her destiny, and the very reason she was on that trip. Everyone had hoped the two of you would throw off your childhood animosities and fall in love, and everyone got their wish. Everyone but me, who'd wanted her to be a celibate healer from the beginning."

"I also wished for her to desire me." Ankhmakis replied, a faraway look in his eyes. "For I was already in love before I knocked on her door."

"You're a fine pair of lovers," Hecataeus replied. "The injustice of your situation is unbearable, and yet the betrayal of your family has now turned your beautiful, precious love into the one thing to be used against you."

"I can't have you near the battle, Hecataeus. It's too risky, I'm sorry. Pistias managed to secure his boat in Coptos before the city fell and will wait in the harbor biding his time. Being Greek, he's safer there now than he will be when it's back under my control." Ankhmakis leaned forward in his chair, rubbing his head and wiping his eyes. "Why can't I get this to work? Every way I look at it, there is danger. If you stay here, something terrible might happen, but if you go, you enter the battlefield where you are surrounded by danger every moment. Can you, a politician, take yourself, three women, and two children, into a war zone and get everyone out alive? What are your chances of success?"

Hecataeus put his hand on Ankhmakis's shoulder. "Less than a month. My boat leaves Behdet at the next full moon."

"I will leave my personal guard behind." Ankhmakis sighed. "They will protect you as far as Hierakonpolis and then make to join my father. Afterward, you'll be on your own."

"I've been on my own for a long time, son," Hecataeus grumbled.

A look of understanding crossed the prince's face, and he nodded. "Thank you for saving Natasa and Helena. I owe you my life."

"No," Hecataeus replied, "I think we're even."

He grabbed Ankhmakis and embraced him, squeezing the young man and starting to weep himself. "I'm not sure I'll ever see you again, son. I don't plan on returning to Egypt. It's been an honor watching you grow to become a brilliant and commanding general—the exact man Egypt needs right now to lead her forward. I'll miss you."

Ankhmakis drew him even closer into his embrace. "Please," he begged, "get Natasa and Helena to a place far away from both Isidor's reach and Ptolemaic law. Keep them safe, so I might retrieve them and usher them home when I rule these lands."

"I will do whatever it takes," Hecataeus promised. "Who knows, maybe this will be part of the tales they sing of you in the future? Someone will write a song, and they'll call it, 'The Flight of Natasa.'"

Ankhmakis shook his head. "The only song I want to hear is, 'The Return of Natasa,' where she lives by my side for all of time."

The two men continued to hold one another, until there was nothing more to be said. Once the honest quiet settled deep within their hearts, they let go of each other and rose from their places. Hecataeus walked the prince to the door. He turned to the young man and bowed to him, one last time.

"Goodbye, Lord Ankhmakis," Hecataeus said with a soft smile, in spite of the nervous ache in his gut. "Rebel King of Egypt."

35

Promises

Reincarnation and renewal—these were the tenants of the Pharaonic faith. The belief that the human Ba returns to Earth over and over, renewed by the experience and each time coming closer to transcendence—a moment in time where the blessed gift of reincarnation is no longer necessary. Twin flames often weave through eternity, passing sometimes like two ships in the night and at other times slamming right into one another in joyful reunion. Regardless, their karma as a pair is intertwined for eternity.

Behdet, Egypt 199 BCE

When Ankhmakis arrived in the apiary, Natasa stood shaking, barely able to stand upon her wobbly legs. The rawness of the moment washed over her entire being. Her heart was racing, her mind no longer serene, for it had never been clearer—this was the moment when she and Ankhmakis would say goodbye forever. She would never again touch him, or smell his warm flesh, or luxuriate in his loving gaze.

The likelihood of both of them surviving the next year was slim. His counter-offensive put him in grave danger, and her escape put her in the center of the battle. Yet remaining in Behdet was dangerous for Natasa. The world was falling down around her, and any way out seemed shut. To stay still was to be a target. To flee was to enter chaos.

"My love," she said as she grasped his face to hers and kissed him. She surrendered to the anger surrounding each of them—a brilliant, glowing fury at the injustice of their separation. This anger had been brewing in her for years. The moment Horwenefer had stripped her from Ankhmakis's side, Natasa began to harbor a sense of outrage that had grown as the war progressed and the pharaoh's court began to hunt her and her daughter. She clawed at Ankhmakis—his heart hammered against her chest—and knew his heart beat the same turbulent song as her own.

No words were needed as they threw themselves upon each other. Natasa spread her legs wide, clutching her lover's hips to draw him closer. Ankmakis lifted her into his arms and swept her up against the wall, thrusting himself deeper. Theirs was an angry, forceful, and fearful lovemaking, Natasa meeting her lover as if to both punish him for leaving her and at the same time, raging against the world for forcing her to part from him. She yanked at his hair and scratched him as he bit and kneaded her flesh, his own frustration hot upon his skin.

As they climaxed, they screamed like a pair of bobcats in the night, cursing the universe for its cruel joke. Of course, his guards heard them, but she didn't care. She'd be willing to go the gallows for this—better than having never known his touch, his scent, his sex deep within her, their life force intertwined in the most beautiful of forms, his spirit forever one with hers. There might be other men in the world to adore, but Natasa loved Ankhmakis beyond all imagination.

Nothing could explain it, and she would never forget loving this man for all of eternity.

They panted and Ankhmakis dropped her down onto the blanket. "What a fantastic warm-up," he whispered.

She pulled him down on top of her and kissed his neck. "How much time do we have?"

"Not much," he answered. "We ride out before sunset."

Natasa removed herself from his embrace. "I'll be brief with my instructions, and you must listen well. I'm leaving the wands behind for you."

"Why?"

"Because I've discovered what the Resurrection Bath of the Osirion is for, and the wands are the key."

"What?" Ankhmakis asked, raising up on one elbow and looking at her, his gaze steady.

"Father and I found the Resurrection Bath a decade ago and even though the experts believed the well was nothing but a purification room, I knew it was special. In my meditations, I have discovered that the wands are what make the room function. When you retake Abdju, you must return to Behdet and retrieve the wands. Bastyre will collect them for you. Trust me, don't go looking yourself, or you'll be attacked by thousands of honey bees."

She wrinkled her nose as she imagined her bees swarming Isidor to protect her wands and noticed Ankhmakis gazing up at her from under his eyelashes, a crooked smile upon his face.

"What?" she asked.

"You're quite cute when you think of a hive of bees attacking a man."

She ran her hands through his thick hair. "Take the wands to Seti's temple. Go to the Osirion, which is well marked on Hecataeus's notes and schematics. My father spent years documenting, and everything is still in our house near the temple complex. Remove your clothes and enter the pool, holding the wands as I have instructed. Remain quiet and let them renew your Ka to the perfection point of birth, thus regenerating every cell in the body and reducing the effects of aging."

"Turning back time in my physical body and ultimately preventing death," Ankhmakis replied, sitting up straight and scratching his head. "How does it work?"

"Our Ka is energy pulsing throughout the body," she explained. "It grounds us to the earth and marks our way back to the material when we travel outside of our bodies. It is also magnetic, and as such as time passes, begins to degrade. This loss of energy within the Ka begins to age the body and ushers in death. If you balance your magnetic Ka with the energy of the earth, you reset the process of aging by infusing your physical body with the vital élan of the universe. Anit-Shadya does this as well but soaking in the Resurrection Pool deep within the Osirian while holding these wands takes hours instead of years, and you can do it on your own. Somehow the wands complete the energy around us and guide it to renew us."

"The wands close the circuit," he whispered.

"What?" she asked. "I don't know the word, circuit."

"It's nothing," he said, shaking his head and instead removing her tunic. He rose from the blanket, dropped his loincloth, and stood naked before her in all his beauty. She stood as well and clutched him close, their dark, bare bodies sliding against each other to the beat of the longing within their hearts.

"Go to Abdju with the wands," she advised as he began to kiss her neck. "This is the power of the old kings, and with this ancient power, you will win the war."

"I will do as you ask," he whispered into her ear. "I'm leaving my guard behind to keep you safe until you get on the boat. I trust Min will protect you from Isidor's plans. Knowing you are gone from this place makes my life possible—if I fail this fight, you'll have fled from Behdet and be harder to capture, and if I succeed, I will call you home. I promise."

Natasa nodded, but it felt as if someone were stabbing her in the chest. She didn't want to travel so far from home without him. She didn't want to leave the Nile Valley, for the land is what makes the people, and Natasa was a part of Kemit, The Black Land. However, none of those things mattered. She needed to protect Helena from the temple of Set. Their flight out of Egypt was inevitable. Natasa drew her lover closer and kissed him, guiding him down upon the ground and climbing on top, feeling his masculinity inside her one last time, and enjoying the instant sensations of bliss surrounding them. They would make love like the gods, encountering the ecstasy of the divine pair one last, beautiful time.

Natasa stored each of those precious moments deep within her eternal memory, leaving trails of their bliss in the realm of light, so one day, she might find him again.

☥

"I think I've seen enough," Bithiah said, her voice cold and harsh. "We got what we wanted."

Chanax put his finger over his mouth to shush her, wanting nothing more than to watch the pair as Natasa rocked on top of his brother, her breasts bathed in sunlight and her naked hips swaying to the rhythm of their intense lovemaking. Never had Chanax seen such sex, and jealousy grew in his heart with every moan they uttered.

"Chanax," Bithiah said again, "let's go."

He elbowed her away, angered at her pestering. "Go on without me," he insisted. "I'll send for you when it's time to testify."

She tugged at his robe. "You plan to stay and watch? You've already seen them have sex."

"They might reveal more information about the wands, or her escape. I need every bit of information I can collect. You understand, don't you?"

She put her hands on her round hips and frowned. The lovers' sighs and moans filled the air, and he turned to look through the wall again.

"You're a pervert," she replied as she waddled away, heavy with child, leaving him alone to watch his brother make love to the most beautiful woman in the world.

This time when they climaxed, Chanax looked away. There was no anger, no fear, no victim, and no perpetrator. The entire apiary was filled with the form of perfect, unconditional love, and in his shame and self-pity, Chanax wanted to weep. After a few moments, the desperate cries of Natasa filled the air, and he turned to look back through the peephole.

The couple was dressed and Ankhmakis was making to leave the apiary.

"I love you," she cried, tears streaming down her face.

Ankhmakis kissed her again before extracting himself from her embrace and walking away. Natasa ran forward, threw herself to the ground, and grabbed him by the legs.

"Don't go, don't go, don't go," she repeated over and over as she sobbed at his feet. Ankhmakis dropped to his knees and embraced her, holding her close to his chest as if she were the most delicate of glass, the form of grief surrounding them. Chanax turned away again, for fear he'd cry out. Their pure love left no room for him, or anyone else, and the realization tore a horrible hole deep within his heart.

"Please, don't forget me," Natasa cried. "No matter what happens. Even if the long sleep of death takes us, you must find me when you wake up. Please, don't forget me."

"I promise," Ankhmakis replied, the cracks in his voice revealing the full pain of his soul's agony. "Whether in this life or the next, I will find you and call you home."

Chanax had asked the same of her, in Abdju years ago, before he'd set out to Memphis—to remember him. She'd made a promise, one she still had to make good on. Chanax turned away from the wall and yanked the vines over the peephole. He'd seen enough. As he made his way back toward the palace, he found his heart growing cold. Any bit of sympathy he'd held for Natasa vanished, because now Chanax knew Natasa was a liar and a cheat. She'd forgotten Chanax and fallen into the arms of Ankhmakis. She could have been his mate and run the temples at his side. Instead she'd become nothing more than a concubine worthy of sacrifice upon the altar of war.

"Good luck trying to find her, dear brother," Chanax hissed through his clenched teeth under the afternoon sun. "She's going where you can't follow, and in your despair, you will lose her trail. Off you will fly, into oblivion, and you'll never find each other, in this lifetime, or any to come."

Chanax waited two days before reporting the act to the temple authorities, to ensure Ankhmakis was far enough away to not be able to turn back to Behdet and save Natasa from her fate, and yet not too far into his military charge that the police would have trouble catching him and escorting him home for his own trial. How wonderful for Ankhmakis to come home in chains, a criminal on the way to the gallows, for all to see. Under normal circumstances, his soldiers would fight to the death for him, but if he were arrested for breaking the celibacy law with a healer, they'd have no choice but to submit to the king and the law of the land. Everyone would know what a criminal his brother was, and Natasa and her horrible secret would be gone forever, paving Chanax's way to the throne.

36

Accusations in the Night

"From the ashes of the phoenix rises the golden eagle of Egypt. But where is his mate? He flies to the west, searching for her over the sands of time, but comes home alone. For the river god Hapy took her, and never shall she return."
~ The Flight of Natasa

Behdet, Egypt 199 BCE

"All rise."

There were five in attendance—Isidor, an old priest from the temple named Zethus, Queen Keket, a scribe, and Chanax—the bare minimum for a temple council. Held after dinner, as Ra slipped under the horizon, and the rest of their leaders, such as the vizier, the high priestess, and Iu-Amon, were preparing for slumber. This was the in-between time of the evening, when bellies were full and wine skins empty, and Isidor had thought it best to use this moment to their advantage.

"We're now in session," he continued.

They took a seat, and Zethus peered around the table. "Where are the vizier and the high priestess Neferu-ankh-maat?”

"Given the nature of the charges, we thought it best to do the initial hearings without them," Isidor replied. "It's their daughter who broke the law."

"Natasa broke the law?" the queen asked, a slight smile upon her thin lips. She had no idea what Chanax was about to reveal, and he was eager to share the glorious news. She eyed the scribe. "Let's begin, shall we?"

The scribe nodded, and Isidor nodded to Chanax. Biting his lip, Chanax turned to his mother and spoke, picking at his nails and shifting his eyes between her and Isidor, as if he were nervous. "I would like to make an accusation. I witnessed Natasa the healer, a sworn member of the celibate cult of Sekhmet, making love to Prince Ankhmakis, my brother and second son of our Lord Pharaoh Horwenefer."

"No," Keket cried. Her answer wasn't the reaction Chanax had been expecting.

"Yes," Chanax continued.

"I don't believe you," the queen continued.

"Mother," he replied, shocked at her stubborn refusal. "I saw them."

She crossed her arms and turned her shoulder away from him. "I said I don't believe you."

Isidor grinned like a fox in the hen house, and Chanax panicked, his breaths shallow and forced. What was she doing? She should be delighted at how easy it would be to remove Natasa and her threat from the court.

"No matter," Chanax answered. "Bithiah saw them as well. Call her in."

A moment later, Bithiah arrived, rocking back and forth as she approached the table, waddling to her chair like a sphere, not a woman.

"Why are we doing this now?" she whined. "It's time to retire."

"Because," Isidor said, "the less people who are involved, the better."

"Fine." She sat, shifting to try to get comfortable.

"Well?" Zethus asked. "Did you also witness Natasa the healer breaking her vow of celibacy with Prince Ankhmakis?"

Bithiah nodded. "Oh yes, I did. The two of them were yelling and screaming and acting like they'd never have sex again. Their performance was quite dramatic, wasn't it, husband?" She smiled at him and batted her eyelashes. "Chanax was so captivated, he stayed to watch them make love a second time."

"Bithiah," Keket cried. "Watch your manners, young woman."

Bithiah sighed and placed her hands on her round stomach. "Mother, you amaze me. Your son has been accused of breaking the celibacy law, and all you care about are my manners?"

"My queen," Isidor purred, and Chanax noticed his mother's tension dissipate. "I know this is hard for you to hear, but we have two witnesses. At this point there's enough evidence to arrest them both and put them to trial. We can arrest Natasa as soon as you give the word and send the police out to fetch Ankhmakis. Natasa can wait in the dungeon until her lover arrives, and they will have their say together, before the full court of law."

"I will not put my son to death." The queen wrung her hands, trembling like a field mouse.

Chanax ground his teeth together. Why wasn't she following orders? "Mother, Natasa must be stopped, remember?"

Isidor looked at the two of them, his eyes pinched. Chanax blocked him from reading his mother's thoughts. She wore her guilt upon her sleeve and was vulnerable to the man.

"I will not have my son put to death," she repeated, the form of anxiety now swirling around her.

"There may be another way to deal with this unfortunate situation," Isidor said, and Chanax sensed his master sending his mother a wave of peace. The queen's shoulders dropped.

"What do you mean, Isidor?" his mother asked, rising up in her seat.

"There is the law of tribute," the high priest of Set continued. "Where another individual can take the place of the accused and pay the price of the crime of a nobleman. Often it is a slave or lower-ranked servant, but it can also be a child of the accused."

Queen Keket's eyes widened, as did Bithiah's. Chanax felt a sense of rage swell within him.

"What?" he cried. "A child? You suggest we proxy one of Ankhmakis's children as his tribute?"

"Why not? We keep our general at a time of need, and yet the crime has been paid for. Seems like the best solution."

"Helena," Keket whispered. "Helena can be the tribute."

Realization of Isidor's maleficence hit him like a marble wall, and Chanax understood Isidor had been using him the entire time. He'd sent Chanax searching for a way to get rid of Ankhmakis, yet in reality, Isidor had been focusing on the girl, and Natasa was caught in the crossfire.

"You'd kill a child in order to save a grown man?" Bithiah said, slamming her palms to the table and causing the high queen to flinch. She raised a finger to the high priest, her arm trembling as she spoke. "The child did nothing. It's her father who sinned. How dare you?"

"Bithiah, I know it sounds cruel," Isidor said, "but the tribute rule exists for these situations, where the ruler's life can't be spared, but the punishment must be administered to maintain balance within the law. The girl is the perfect proxy. She won't go on trial. We'll instead hold her in the dungeons during her mother's trial. When Natasa's found guilty, the two will be sent to the gallows and a message can be delivered to Ankhmakis, letting him know what happened. I suggest we hold out informing him until we know he's taken Lycopolis. We don't want to ruin his military plans, for our lives rest upon his success."

"Are we sure about this?" Zethus asked, rubbing his forearm, his face twisted as if he'd eaten something rotten.

"Ankhmakis and Natasa have broken her vow of celibacy," Isidor replied. "They must be punished, and in this moment, killing the prince isn't prudent. We need him to win the war."

"I think it's a wonderful idea," the queen exclaimed. "Scribe, write up the arrest, and I'll sign it. We don't need Hecataeus for this part. I have sovereign rights to the arrest of criminals."

"Mother, how could you do this?" Bithiah said, her eyes filling with tears. "How can you kill an innocent child?" She turned to Chanax, trembling like a fragile river reed. "If I had known this was your plan, I never, ever would have helped you."

"Bithiah, I had no idea—" he began.

"You're dismissed," the queen interrupted. "Thank you, daughter, for your testimony."

Bithiah stood and sprinted toward the door in spite of her pregnant state.

"Bithiah," Chanax called out. "I suggest you take the night in my chambers."

She turned to him, her wet eyes narrow and glittering, mouth drawn tight, and he knew she hated him in that moment, yet she understood—he couldn't have her talking about this to anyone. "Yes, husband," she whispered before fleeing the room as if it were on fire.

"You too, Zethus," Isidor said. "You're no longer needed here. Sign as a witness to prove that proper protocol was followed."

Zethus rose from his seat, his hand wavering as he signed the document, and turned to Isidor, shaking his head. "What would your father, my master, the high priest Inebni, think of your evil deeds?" Shoulders hunched, he pulled the collar of his robe up over his head and exited the room with the scribe.

"There's one more thing," Chanax added as the door shut. "Hecataeus plans on taking Natasa and Helena out of Behdet via the river."

"What?" Isidor exclaimed. "How long have you known this?"

"A few days," he replied. "I heard Natasa and Ankhmakis talking in the garden. It's why he left Min and the rest of his guard behind. They're to make sure Natasa and Helena leave without issue."

"When will they go?" Isidor asked, his eyes wide and mouth open. It pleased Chanax to find the man unhinged for once.

"I have no idea." Chanax shrugged. "They didn't say. Could be tonight for all I know."

"Why would they flee?" Queen Keket cried out.

"Because, foolish woman," Chanax said, his patience with her long gone, "Ankhmakis thinks he might lose the war and wants Natasa and their child hidden from the Greeks."

"He means to leave the rest of us to burn?" His mother

gasped.

Chanax waved his hand. "I wouldn't take it as an insult, Mother."

"Enough," Isidor said, his words harsh, like a curse. "We can't let them flee. The child must not leave Egypt."

"Nor can Natasa," the queen said. "She must be taken care of."

"I suggest we arrest them this evening," Isidor said. "You've experienced how well Natasa can fight, and we can't risk it in front of others. Send the guards to arrest her while they sleep."

"Fine," the queen said, signing the order.

"We'll schedule the trial for first thing tomorrow. She can spend the night in the dungeon. It'll scare her and make her more vulnerable to our cause."

Keket stamped the order and rose to leave. "I trust this will be over without drawing attention to me?"

"Indeed, Your Majesty," Isidor replied. "Now send in Nefermaat and Pontius. I need to discuss the handoff. They're here to protect Natasa, and we need to make sure they let us do our job."

Keket nodded and left the room.

When they were alone, Isidor eyed Chanax. "I know you'd rather it be Ankhmakis who dies tomorrow but killing him isn't possible right now. Trust me when I say the key is Helena. Kill her, and when he gets the news, he will crumble like our ancient temples."

Chanax bit the inside of his cheek. He'd thought cornering Natasa would give him a sense of satisfaction, but Ankhmakis would get away with something yet again, a fact which stole his brief moment of happiness. As he stewed in his disappointment, Nefermaat and Pontius arrived. They stood at attention, refusing to meet Isidor's gaze.

"Your master has been foolish," Isidor began, "and his crimes haven't gone unnoticed. He has been seen having sex with Natasa the healer. I know you're both well aware of this, having to endure witnessing his sexual perfidy for years as his guard, but I need you to keep the other men, especially Min, out of the way tonight. Natasa and her daughter, Helena, are to be arrested in the harem, after curfew, and you must be sure Ankhmakis's other guards do not interfere."

The two men nodded, still both staring at the wall across the room.

"Use whatever means," Isidor commanded as he grabbed Nefermaat's arm, forcing the guard to look at him. "One more thing—I don't trust the woman and child together in the dungeons. They're too powerful, and I fear they would escape if we leave them unattended, even behind bars. They know the ancient magic. We can't hang them until a proper trial occurs, but perhaps there could be an accident? One in which the child dies?"

"Before the trial?" Chanax asked, unable to believe his own ears. To suggest such a thing was madness.

"Yes," Isidor said. "If Helena dies in the arrest, Natasa will be ruined and putty in our hands, yet even the child's accidental death can be used to spare Ankhmakis's life. This way we prevent the pair from fleeing with Hecataeus into the night."

"That's cruel," Chanax replied, his insides churning as if a stew full of hate for his master were simmering within him. "Even for you."

"Trust me when I say the Golden Child cannot leave Egypt," Isidor said, rubbing his hands across his bald head. "Be sure to kill the child during the arrest. Is this understood?"

The men nodded but didn't speak. Chanax knew the plan bothered them, but no one would defy Isidor. No one, that is, except Neferu-ankh-maat. A sudden realization dawned on Chanax as the two guards departed—Isidor cared not about the Golden Child nor prophecies. What he wanted most was to punish Neferu-ankh-maat for refusing his love, the way Chanax wanted to punish Natasa for the same crime. It appeared both men would have their desire for revenge come true.

Like father, like son.

37

The Unspeakable

"My masters taught me to live in the now, for this is where the door to my power lies open. Yet the now is too painful to bear, because you do not exist here. Our love is bound to the past, haunting me from lifetime to lifetime, from body to body, for all of eternity."

~ Lament of the King

Behdet, Egypt 199 BCE

Min's baritone laughter filled the kitchen as he drank his ale.

"I'm sure you were high," he said to Ansel, who'd also been left behind to protect Natasa. Twelve men in total to guard their master's loved ones.

"No," Ansel replied, wiping his mouth after taking a long sip of beer, "she did have three breasts, I tell you. Things are strange in Carthage."

Min slammed his thick beer mug on the table and shook his finger at his old friend. A three-breasted woman was too outrageous. He glanced at Pontius and Nefermaat, neither of whom was laughing. Instead they fiddled with their mugs without drinking, which was unusual. "Brother?" he asked. "What is troubling you?"

Pontius looked at him in such a strange way, it gave Min pause. Something was wrong. Nefermaat patted Pontius on the back and smiled, almost as if mocking him, making Min's stomach turn. As a matter of fact, his stomach didn't feel well at all.

"He hates how Ankhmakis left us behind to guard Natasa rather than join him on the battlefield. This is the turning point of the war. Either we succeed and continue north to Memphis, or we fail and pay the price. It's wrong that he left us behind."

"You doubt our prince," Min accused, putting his hands to his stomach and fighting the nausea. "Why is it so hard for you to honor his wishes?"

Nefermaat grinned again, and Min felt the room start to spin. His fingers tingled, and he looked to Ansel and the other men and noticed their faces were pale and sweaty. As the room faded out of focus, Min heard Nefermaat laugh. "Because no one has ever honored my wishes."

The next thing Min knew was darkness.

☥

"Come," Nefermaat said, standing as the rest of the men fell to the floor. Pontius cracked his knuckles as he kicked at his brother, who lay prone on the floor. Min didn't even twitch. The herbs had worked. "We're expected at the harem. The women should be asleep by now."

The two left the other guards passed out in the antechamber and walked without speaking through the dark, torch lit halls, out through the garden where the light of Khons cast shadows upon the hedges, and on to the harem, where the temple guards stood at attention.

"Good evening, men," Nefermaat said, nodding to the captain. "We're here on the high queen's orders to arrest a woman and her child." He held out the paper signed by the queen to the head guard, who read the document carefully and then nodded.

"Fine. This way."

Nefermaat followed the men into the darkness of the harem. He grabbed a torch from the wall and shoved it in front, illuminating the room. Weret appeared before him.

"What are you men doing?" she blurted out, fighting a sleepy yawn. One hand rested on her pregnant belly and her eldest son clung to her legs, looking so much like his father, Nefermaat felt a moment's hesitation. He shrugged his shoulders to clear his mind.

"We've come with orders to arrest Natasa the healer," he admitted.

"Arrest her?" Weret asked. "Whatever for?"

"Breaking her vow of celibacy with your husband, Prince Ankhmakis," he answered, watching as she placed her hands upon her stricken face. It was good to see her squirm.

She jumped away, waving her hands in the air as if to stop them. "No, this cannot be. He would never—"

Nefermaat grabbed her loose tunic and drew her close. "Now tell me, Princess, where does Natasa sleep?" Weret shook her head, unable to speak. "Don't worry," he continued. "Our brother is safe. Tell me where she sleeps and don't make any noise."

Weret glanced to the far west side of the room. "She sleeps with the other healers and their children," she whispered, pointing to a dark corner filled with sleeping women, their arms wrapped around their precious children.

The guards turned and followed her directions, leaving the princess and her little prince trembling in their wake.

☥

Natasa and Ankhmakis's spirits soared together in the All-One, which was how they passed most of their nights. Deep in a trance-like state, she bonded with her lover and rested in the peace of their out-of-body experience. It made their parting much less painful and kept each of them up to date on their actions. He would arrive in Hierakonpolis late the next day, and the troops were camping along the river. All was quiet in the Nile Valley.

"*My love,*" he said to her heart, "*I wish we could be in this place forever. Why must we ever live in our bodies?*"

"*So we can make love and experience bliss,*" she answered.

"*This is bliss,*" he replied

A second Ba joined them in their place outside of time. "*Mother,*" Helena cried, interrupting their union. "*You must wake up. They're here.*"

Startled, Natasa felt her body wrenched from the floor. As she woke, her connection to Ankhmakis severed, leaving her disoriented. Her arms were tied behind her back, and around her women and children were screaming as men held them against the ground. She struggled like a fish under the water; everything was blurry and chaotic. She searched for Helena and found her, trembling like a stable mouse in the grip of one of the temple guards. A second man held Natasa to his chest.

"You are arrested, Natasa of the Houses of Healing, for breaking your celibacy law with Prince Ankhmakis," a familiar voice accused.

Her lungs clamored for air as she gained clarity. She needed to act.

"I'm sorry," her brother said as he strode to stand before her, his dark gaze glittering in the torch light.

"Nefermaat," she cried. "Ankhmakis left you here to protect me."

"You shouldn't have broken the law, sister," he replied, his mouth twisted into a vicious sneer. "This is your fault."

Pontius tore Helena from the guard's hands and a glimmer of hope filled her mind. Perhaps they would save her?

Instead, Pontius raised his knife and held it against Helena's small throat. The fear in her child's gaze shocked Natasa to the core—they were going to kill her baby in cold blood.

"Let her go," yelled Corinna, screaming as she threw her guard from her back and rushed forward to try to save Helena. Nefermaat struck the woman from behind, and their beloved nursemaid fell to the ground at Natasa's feet, Nefermaat's knife planted in her back.

"Now," Nefermaat yelled and Pontius drew his weapon across her beautiful daughter's throat. Helena's precious body fell limp and Pontius dropped the child to the ground, his expression frozen, as if shocked by the horrible, unspeakable act he'd committed. Her innocent blood poured about his feet.

As her child died, Natasa felt the energetic connection of mother-and-child between them snap, sending shockwaves in all directions of time. The breath left Natasa's lungs, and the world stopped. There were people around her, streaking past her vision like ghosts, yet silent for she could no longer process sound. Guards, women, and children, all cowering and running in different directions. Before her mind's eye stretched the events leading up to this moment in full clarity, and in the center of the dreadful deed stood Chanax, as triumphant as he was devastated. As this knowledge settled within her heart, Natasa felt nothing but a dark, evil pain strangling her from the inside out before she passed out cold, going limp in the guard's arms.

Helena had died for her crimes.

☥

Beside Natasa, Eleni struggled, screaming and crying as a huge guard sat on top of her, holding her against the hard, cold floor. She watched the men drag her limp sister away. One of them grabbed a blanket from the floor and wrapped it around Helena's small body, before taking her from the room. Another heaved her mother from the floor and slung her over his shoulder. Blood was everywhere, thick and gooey on the floor and in her bed. The man released her from his grip and followed his commander out of the harem.

"No one may leave until sunrise," a guard cried out. "Queen's orders."

The door slammed behind them, and Eleni heard them place the wooden latch with a loud boom that echoed across the harem. They were locked inside.

"Mother," she screamed, her vision going dark, blood rushing her head and breath coming in shallow gasps. She'd been left behind. How could this be? She ran toward the door, arms flailing, her thoughts disjointed and dizzying.

"Eleni," a woman cried from behind her. She felt Bastyre drawing her closer, trying to calm her down. "Hush, child. There, there. I'm sure it's going to be fine. Let me hold you and we'll get through the night. We'll go to your mother in the morning. She's hurt, and they've taken her to Iu-Amon, who will fix her."

Eleni looked at Bastyre's face and knew the women was lying. The events of the evening became clearer in her mind.

Helena was dead, her mother was dead, Natasa was arrested for breaking the celibacy law with Ankhmakis, and Nefermaat was in charge of the entire thing. She recalled the afternoon when he'd caught her spying on her sister—and knew without a doubt she was the reason everyone had been punished. She fell to the floor sobbing. There was no way out. Her world had ended.

♀

Ankhmakis awoke to a pain in between his shoulder blades, as if he'd been stabbed from behind. The astral connection with Natasa had been cut with such force, his neck and head ached. What was Helena trying to tell them? He sent out his Ka toward his beloved and felt nothing. He tried again but met a dark void. Not a wall or a block, but nothingness, like the deep emptiness of the desert.

Ankhmakis jumped up from the ground and ran out of his tent, grabbing his weapons and a small pack of water and food. As he passed Khaleme's tent he called out, "I must return to Behdet. Lead the men on without me."

Khaleme exited his tent and followed him to the horses. Ankhmakis struggled to get Biriq ready to ride, dropping the riding blanket as his hands trembled. Khaleme put his firm hand on Ankhmakis's shoulder to stop him. "Your horse is already tired," the general said, his voice thick with sleep. "Why do you go back when the way is forward?"

"Something has happened to Natasa," Ankhmakis answered, his heart pounding in his chest.

"You may be walking into a trap," Khaleme said, taking the riding blanket from Ankhmakis's hands and securing it to Biriq himself.

"It doesn't matter. I have to help her."

"I shall join you."

"No, the men need you."

"No, they need you. They can wait here until we return," Khaleme replied as he returned to his tent to prepare his things.

Ankhmakis glanced at the quarter moon in the sky. He'd been gone only a few days; what was going on? He tried again to energetically connect once more to his beloved and choked as an evil, cold chill filled his soul. There was no trace of Natasa, and he feared she was dead.

38

Confessions

Behold, Set the wretched, is on his way back. He has returned, in order to rob with his hand he thinks of seizing violently as if he were as he used to be when destroying the sites, when tearing down their temples, when uttering screams in the sanctuaries. He has inflicted grief, he has repeated hurt, he has caused...to come into being again."
~ The Book of Victory over Set, 1000 BCE

Behdet, Egypt 199 BCE

Chanax slunk down the dark, dank corridors of the dungeon, the smell of sweat, death, and dust penetrating his senses. Where was Natasa? He'd expected her pain to be great, like an energetic beacon for him to follow in this place of despair. Instead, when he extended his Ka to locate her, he sensed only empty space. No, empty wasn't the word. Void. Natasa's energy field was missing.

He raised the torch above his head and peered down a hallway, illuminating a series of cells inhabited by decaying, yet still alive prisoners. She wasn't down there. He continued until he found a quiet, deserted corridor and knew Isidor would put her there. A place where no one could find her, where no one could help her.

"Natasa?" he called out, not expecting an answer.

He lifted the torch and saw her, lying on the floor in a heap, her shift covered in her daughter's blood. They hadn't even bothered to clean her.

Chanax shuffled toward her, drawn to her pain and emptiness. He'd been this empty before. He knew how to leave the world of the flesh and enter the Void. Some experiences in the body were too painful to endure. He crouched in front of her cell and saw her face. Eyes open, but not seeing. The only movement was her index finger, digging in the dirt floor, listless yet purposeful.

"Natasa, it's Chanax." Her mouth opened and closed, but no words could be heard. "Natasa, what happened?"

He knew the answer, and yet couldn't find it in him to believe Nefermaat had carried out Isidor's instructions. Why would he murder a child? Nefermaat had never hidden his disdain for his mother. Perhaps he also considered killing Helena as a way of destroying the high priestess, the way Keket and Isidor had?

"I'm sorry," he said, not expecting Natasa to hear. If she'd indeed left her body to avoid her pain, she wouldn't remember any of this. "I didn't think they'd kill Helena. They were supposed to kill Ankhmakis, but not your child." Her finger stopped moving. "What about you? Yes, they were supposed to kill you as well. That's why I told them about your affair, so that the two of you would die."

Again, her mouth opened and closed without words, yet he heard the soft sound of her finger as she began scratching back and forth again in the dirt, making a small hole, deeper and deeper. He stuck his arm through the prison bars and was delighted to discover he could touch her. He ran his finger down her face, her filthy flesh cold against his warm fingertip. If Natasa felt him, she didn't show it; her gaze remained vacant and unfocused.

"Why would I kill you?" he asked, hoping a small part of her was listening. "Remember when I kissed you, in Abdju? You said you liked it. You promised you'd never forget me. You didn't remember me, did you Natasa?" He brushed her hair from her forehead and cupped her face. The gesture was tender, and his blood rushed through his veins. His sex hardened as he recalled those sweet and innocent kisses, wishing yet again he'd never been taken from her side to train in Memphis. "You were supposed to cleanse me from my pain, Natasa, with your undying love, and heal me from the filth I endured at the hands of Philopater. Instead you became my brother's whore."

Chanax's rage stoked the passion in his groins. He looked at Natasa's helpless form and found himself swooning—he could enter her without any protest, stealing her sex the way Ptolemy IV and his men had stolen his. She couldn't refuse him in her state. He could kiss her and make love to her over and over, for no one else even knew she was here. Chanax rose and called for the guard to unlock her cell. They wouldn't deny him, the future pharaoh, would they? He imagined how exquisite it would feel to be inside Natasa after wanting her for so long...

"Chanax?" a cruel voice called from the dark. "Whatever are you doing?"

Isidor sauntered toward him, wearing not his red robes, but a dark, hooded one. His jaguar followed at his feet. The pair were nearly invisible with the exception of the golden chain Isidor wore around his neck and the large cat's yellow eyes, glowing in the torchlight.

"Sir," Chanax said, feeling his passion go limp. "I was making sure the deed was done. To report to you, of course."

"Why did you call to the guard to open her cell?" Isidor challenged.

Chanax gulped and fought hard against his master's astral attack. Isidor was trying to read his mind, but Chanax refused. He couldn't let Isidor know he'd been planning to use Natasa's body. He slipped past his master's magical grip, out of his own body, and into the Void, where nothing existed. There he guarded himself from Isidor. He could see his own body standing at attention as Isidor continued questioning him, but felt and heard, nothing.

"*I see you,*" a voice whispered.

He found Natasa in the Void beside him, in a form more terrifying than any he'd seen. Her Ka rose before him, not beautiful and powerful as she'd been in life, but shattered into thousands of pieces, held together by the smoky form of grief. Chanax only recognized her by the familiar way his soul yearned to be near her.

"*I see you, Chanax,*" she continued, her mouth in several parts, scattered before him. "*I know what lives in the darkness of your heart.*"

In a panic, he thrust himself out of the Void and into his body, collapsing at Isidor's feet. Chanax opened his eyes, coughing up dust from the floor, and found himself level with Natasa's tear and blood-stained face, eye-to-eye. She stared at him, her dazed expression gone, and fresh tears now running down her bloodied cheeks. Her Ka pulsed around her, broken and torn, but alive nonetheless. The form of her love surrounded him, and Chanax found it unbearable to meet her gaze.

"But, Chanax, I did love you," she whispered, her voice hoarse. "You were the first..." She trailed off as she blinked away her tears.

Isidor startled at the sound of Natasa's voice and peered down at his prisoner. She tilted her head toward the high priest, eyes rolling back in her head, mouth twisted into a wicked grin. Isidor grabbed Chanax by the shoulder, heaving him from the ground, and turning him away from his beloved. "Do not look at her. What's done is done. Now, come with me. We will hang her in the morning."

Chanax wanted to protest, wanted to beat the man and free Natasa. She'd said she loved him. He had to save her, had to make up for his betrayal. However, when he glanced back and saw the madness in her expression, he shrank into Isidor's grip. Gone was the love of a moment ago, replaced with anguish pouring from her very being. To face her accusing glare, to see the hate, malice, and contempt now surrounding her, was too much.

"I shouldn't have come here," he whispered.

"No, you shouldn't have," Isidor agreed. "Since childhood you've had a weakness for the half-breed. Let's go. Your part in this is finished."

"You're wrong," Natasa said in a low growl. Her eyes were now clear and focused upon them. She licked the drying blood and dirt from her lips. "This will never be finished. Until the end of time, your betrayal will haunt us both, Chanax."

She rolled and turned her back on them, retreating from the world as she drew into the Void, leaving her breathing, yet lifeless body behind. They remained still for a moment within the emotionless silence, until Isidor tugged him away. Chanax followed his master, the ghost of Natasa's grief clinging to his soul, settling deep inside him and taking up residence. Rather than fight it, he embraced her pain as his curse. He was willing to carry it for eternity—his guilt was the closest thing to love they'd ever share.

39

The Flight of Natasa

I have come unto thee, O my Lord, and I have brought myself hither that I may behold thy beauties. I know thee, I know thy name, I know the names of the Forty-two Gods who live with thee in this Hall of Maat, who live by keeping ward over sinners, and who feed upon their blood on the day when the consciences of men are reckoned up in the presence of the god Un-Nefer.
~ The Egyptian Book of the Dead, 1240 BCE

Behdet, Egypt 199 BCE

Neferu-ankh-maat awoke to a hysterical pounding at Dardre's chamber doors. His guards answered, and Min stumbled into the room. Her stomach turned—he would only be there if the worst had happened.

"They've taken her," Min cried, his voice hoarse.

"What?" Neferu-ankh-maat asked as she rose from her lover's bed and put on a robe.

"Hecataeus sent me," the guard said as he gasped for air. He must have run the entire way to find her. "Grab your travel bag. You leave tonight."

"Where is he?" she demanded.

"With Iu-Amon," Min said, tears streaking through the sweat on his face. "Saying goodbye to Corinna and Helena."

"What has happened?" Neferu-ankh-maat yelled as she grabbed the young man by the arm. "Tell me now."

"They entered the harem, on the queen's orders, in the middle of the night to arrest Natasa for breaking her vow of celibacy with Ankhmakis."

"Why didn't you stop them?" she accused. "Ankhmakis left you here for just this reason."

"Because," he sobbed, "Nefermaat put something in our drinks to knock us out. When I regained consciousness, Hecataeus was shaking me and commanding me to get you and meet him at the dungeons. Somehow both Helena and Corinna died in the arrest attempt, and now Natasa sits in jail awaiting trial at sunrise."

"Helena is dead?" Neferu-ankh-maat's mind shut down. Her heart slowed. She looked to Min and knew he spoke the truth. "Corinna as well? How could this have happened?"

"I'm sorry," Min said. "I've failed you."

"Yes, you have," she replied, grabbing the travel bag she'd had ready for weeks—ready to flee at a moment's notice. "Yet if we can still save Natasa, we must. Can I bless the bodies before I go?"

Min shook his head. "We have to get Natasa out of prison before Isidor or the queen wakes up and sends reinforcements. As of now, they think I'm still passed out. We need to go straight to the dungeons."

"How will we save her?"

"My guards await," Min answered. "We will kill anyone who stands in our way. We may have failed Helena, but if we can save Natasa, we will have still served our prince."

Neferu-ankh-maat turned to Dardre. "What will you do?"

"Remain behind. Khaleme will return when Ankhmakis discovers what has happened. I will travel to Kush after reporting to him. There is nothing left for me here. The spirit of Kemit has abandoned these lands."

She hugged him close. "No," she whispered in his ear. "The men of Egypt have abandoned the goddess."

"Which is why the land no longer has its soul," Dardre said as he drew her close and kissed her. "Now go and flee while you can."

She followed Min through the palace and a courtyard to a part of the compound she'd never seen before. As they crawled through the midnight shadows, a whistle called out and she turned to see Hecataeus standing behind a pillar, holding two bags, his sword glimmering in the torchlight at his side. As she approached, he grabbed her by the shoulders.

"Is it true?" She struggled for breath. Too much was happening at once. "Are both Corinna and Helena dead?"

"Yes," he said, his voice cracked and eyes puffy.

"What will happen to the bodies?"

"Iu-Amon will give them a proper burial. He's already accused Keket of treachery and sent for Ankhmakis to return. We can't wait, for he's too far away to get here before they hang her. We have to leave now if we're to save Natasa, for they have two witnesses, and she will be convicted. The trial is scheduled for dawn."

Neferu-ankh-maat stared at the quarter moon. They were leaving too soon. "What about Eleni?"

Hecataeus's face fell. "She's locked in the harem till morning. We can't get in without risking Natasa's escape. Iu-Amon has promised to take care of her as soon as he can get her out of there. Now, we must go, or we will lose yet another loved one."

He slung the bags over his shoulder, and Min led them to the entrance to the prison, where the rest of Ankhmakis's guards—minus the betrayers—waited. Several of the king's men stood at a hesitant attention, their eyes shifting to one another and their commander.

"Drop your weapons," Min declared as he raised his sword. "We demand the lady Natasa to be freed."

"We follow the orders of the pharaoh, not captains," the leader of the guard answered.

Hecataeus yanked Neferu-ankh-maat out of the way as the men sliced at each other. She'd never been this close to violence, and she cradled her queasy stomach as she ran around the fallen men and followed Hecataeus and Min toward the prison entrance, sliding inside as the battle continued behind her. Min chopped off the hand of a guard who held the door and let it slam, bolting it shut to keep anyone else from pursuing them farther.

"Where is she?" Neferu-ankh-maat asked, unable to peel her eyes from the gruesome sight of the bloody hand lying in the dirt at her feet.

"This way," Min said as he turned to lead them deeper into the complex.

They wandered down a dark, empty corridor and stopped before a small cell. The air smelled of dirty, dying men. In the center of the cell Natasa lay facedown and unmoving.

"Get her out of there," Neferu-ankh-maat cried, grasping the bars and shaking them.

Min took a key from his pocket and unlocked the door. Natasa didn't stir as the three of them entered.

"Natasa?" Neferu-ankh-maat cried. "Natasa?"

Hecataeus leaned over and shook his daughter. "Come

on, little hawk," he begged her. "It's time to fly. Get up now." He heaved his daughter from the floor, and she stared at them with glossy, deadened eyes, unable to stand on her own two feet. Neferu-ankh-maat felt her pulse and saw her chest rise and fall, but otherwise the young woman was lifeless.

"She's in shock," Neferu-ankh-maat assessed. "You'll have to carry her."

"Fine," Hecataeus said, handing her the bags. "You take those, and I'll take her. Min, you lead the way. The exit will be guarded. I'll need you to lead the fight."

"Yes, Vizier," Min replied, and the three of them continued on through the dungeons. The pharaoh's prisoners called out for them to stop and rescue them as well. Neferu-ankh-maat looked at them, their pale skin and hallowed out eyes ghost-like in the torchlight, bodies thin and starving. This was the justice of the court of Horwenefer. She shivered, grateful to be released from the service of such people.

They entered a small tunnel and continued walking. The noises of fighting and prisoner's cries faded, and their own footsteps echoed off the granite walls as they hurried through the dark corridor. Still Natasa didn't rouse.

"Darling," Neferu-ankh-maat whispered. "Come on, darling. Wake up. Wake up."

Her daughter remained silent in her father's arms. He carried her like a baby, and she gripped his neck, hiding her face within the folds of his tunic. She didn't cry. Neferu-ankh-maat extended her own Ka and felt nothing. How could this be? Her eyes were open; thus, her Ka must still pulse somewhere?

Neferu-ankh-maat didn't have time to ponder the anomaly further because they'd arrived at their destination. As Min heaved open the door, three men jumped at him.

Ankhmakis's young captain struck them; the sounds of their blades clashing startled Neferu-ankh-maat, and she hid her face. Hecataeus placed Natasa on the ground and joined in the skirmish. The guards fell dead in a pool of blood. Sensing the fight was over, Neferu-ankh-maat heaved the rucksacks on to her shoulders and walked over the fallen men and out into the night. They continued in silence, about ten feet from the river, hidden by reeds and brush. Behind them, the palace torches were illuminating one-by-one, signaling some sort of emergency. Perhaps Isidor had discovered Natasa missing? Had the queen let the women out of the harem? Neferu-ankh-maat had no idea. The only thing that mattered now was getting on the boat.

A small man wearing linen pants and a white wrap around his head appeared out of nowhere and bowed low. "Hecataeus, I'm at your service."

Hecataeus, still cradling Natasa in his arms, nodded at the man and glanced at the river, where a fishing boat made of Syrian cedar rocked in the shallows. "Thank you, Atalan. Is this our boat?"

"Yes. Come now, we can get far on our journey before the docks fill with the morning fishermen," the small man said.

Neferu-ankh-maat tugged up her skirts and walked into the muddy river toward the boat, grateful that the blood stains on her feet were washing away.

"This is where I leave you," Min called out.

She turned to look at him one last time, noting the form of shame surrounding him. She wanted to forgive him for his failure but found she didn't have the words. She was too angry.

"Thank you, Min," Hecataeus replied, his voice cracking. "Avenge Helena and Corinna."

"I will do nothing less," Min answered before turning to

sprint back toward the palace.

"Get in," Hecataeus said to Neferu-ankh-maat.

She climbed up onto the deck and followed him down under it, into a small space carved out in the bottom of the boat. Here she put their travel packs and fell exhausted onto a wooden seat. Hecataeus plopped Natasa beside her. The girl was shivering in spite of the humid heat. Neferu-ankh-maat checked her forehead. No fever. Natasa was going even deeper into shock.

"My dear Natasa," she pleaded. "It's me, your mother. Papa and I are taking you away where you will be safe. I promise."

She wrapped a blanket around the trembling woman and drew her closer to her own body. As the boat joined the flow of the river northward toward the war, Neferu-ankh-maat glanced at Hecataeus. Rather than engage with her, he dropped his head into his hands, his strong body heaving silent sobs. She wanted to hold him, but instead leaned her head upon her unresponsive daughter and allowed her own tears to fall. Natasa gazed at the wall, her eyes still unfocused and hazy, oblivious to her father's pain.

"Neferu-ankh-maat?" Hecataeus choked. "How could this happen? I thought you could see into the future."

She looked at him, tears flooding her vision. "We knew Isidor was evil. I saw it in his heart, but I wanted to believe otherwise. Why did they try to arrest Helena, when she wasn't the guilty party?"

"The queen," he groaned. "She used Helena as tribute for Ankhmakis's offense, to keep him from being executed himself."

"Is that legal?"

"Yes." Hecataeus sighed. "Proxy. It's an old law."

"An innocent child in exchange for a guilty man," she whispered. "What sort of a world do we live in? What happened to Corinna?"

Hecataeus shook his head, new sobs quaking through his body. He didn't speak for what seemed like hours, and when he did, his voice was rough and thick. "Nefermaat killed her as she tried to save Helena."

"Oh, Hecataeus," Neferu-ankh-maat said. "Why was she in the harem and not in bed with you?"

"Because she feared Eleni and Natasa were in danger," he replied, wiping his tears. "She wouldn't leave their sides."

Corinna had been willing to give up her comfy bed to be near her children and died doing what she must. Neferu-ankh-maat felt ashamed.

"Neferu-ankh-maat," he began again. "How did I not see this coming? We had your sight and my knowledge of the law, and still we failed."

"Don't call me that," she said.

"Call you what? A failure?"

"Neferu-ankh-maat," she replied. "That is the name of the high priestess of Behdet, but I've left her station behind me."

He raised his head, red eyes hallow and empty, and leaned back against the wooden wall of the boat.

"Call me Neffa. For now, I'm a mother and a woman in exile."

40

The Crowning of the King

"The people of his time will be joyful, and the gentleman will make his name, for eternity and all time! Those who fall into evil and those who plot rebellion have fueled their own speech for fear of him... The Ureaus which is on his forehead now quietens the malcontents for him."
~ The Prophecy of Neferti, 12th Dynasty

Behdet, Egypt 199 BCE

Ankhmakis rode his already exhausted horse nonstop, throughout the night and day in order to arrive in Behdet as the sun set. His legs were jelly as he dismounted the panting, struggling horse. Trying once more to connect with Natasa, he still felt a cold nothingness. Either she had fled, or she was dead. Yet, if she'd fled, why hadn't she contacted him? She'd promised to let him know the moment she headed north.

"Lord Ankhmakis," a young man standing near Biriq's stall called out as he and Khaleme dragged their weary selves and horses into the stables. "The high priest Iu-Amon requests your presence in the Houses of Healing."

The look on the servant's face was grave. Ankhmakis

remembered him from his days recovering from his injury. The boy was an acolyte of Iu-Amon's, who'd lost an arm on the battlefield and now served the dying soldiers. Ankhmakis gestured to Khaleme, and they followed the young man to the Houses of Healing. As they entered the main sick bay, he found the room filled with weeping women and injured men staring at the floor, wringing their hands. A fearful hush fell upon the room as he entered. No one would meet his gaze.

"My lord," cried Bastyre, who was sitting with the mourners, "you've returned. Come, follow me."

"What has happened?" Ankhmakis demanded. "Why are the healers crying? Why do the soldiers look shaken?"

Tears streamed down the old midwife's face, but she did not speak. He followed her a few more steps to the royal wing of the healing center—the exact room where Natasa had healed him from his injury and the two of them had fallen in love again, after years of separation.

Iu-Amon sat holding a sobbing Eleni under his arms beside two flat tables, each covered in beeswax candles, silken cloths embroidered in gold, and a body, clean, shaven and pale, wearing a funeral cloak. The sight of the smaller figure—it was a child—made the prince fall to the floor. His heart felt as if clenched in the palm of Set himself, and Ankmakis became light-headed.

Iu-Amon turned and rose from his place. "My lord," he said, as he helped Ankhmakis up to his feet, "I'm very sorry."

The old man held Ankhmakis in his arms, and the prince's body quaked as he stumbled, daring a quick look at the second body—Corinna lay dead beside his child, not Natasa—and drew nearer to Helena's small corpse. A jagged red knife wound ran across her delicate neck. She'd been murdered in cold blood.

"No," he wept as he knelt before her and took her small frame into his arms. Sobs rose up from within his soul and racked his body. He held her corpse to his chest and rocked back and forth. "No, Helena, no, no, no, no, no, not my Helena."

He cried out her name over and over, sometimes as a scream, sometimes as a whisper. Iu-Amon's embrace remained firm, holding the prince as he held his dead child. Ankhmakis again searched his energy field for Natasa and felt nothing. Where was she?

After many long minutes, his sobs ended, and he placed Helena's small, lifeless body back on the funery table before turning to the others in the room. Min had arrived, as well as most of his personal guard, and stood beside Khaleme. Eleni clutched Bastyre's waist, her face streaked with tears. Ennaeus sat in a chair by the window, biting his nails.

"Why was my child murdered?" Ankhmakis spoke, his voice hoarse from his mourning.

"Your mother took Helena's life as tribute in exchange for yours," Iu-Amon answered, fists balled, ancient face grimacing, obviously trying to hide his own pain and fury. "To balance your crimes with Natasa."

Ankhmakis felt as if he'd vomit. "She arrested Natasa for breaking her vow of celibacy and killed Helena in my stead?"

Iu-Amon nodded. "Hecataeus and Neferu-ankh-maat managed to free Natasa before her trial, and they now head north to Coptos."

Ankhmakis's head snapped toward Min, and he glared at his captain with dark, unreasonable fury. "How dare you let this happen?"

Min's body tremored, and he spoke in rasping breaths. "My lord, Nefermaat drugged us so we'd be out of the way when they arrested her. We came to after the deed was complete."

"What? My brother drugged all of you? Where is Pontius?" Ankhmakis demanded.

"My lord," Min continued, "Nefermaat and Pontius work against you. As do your younger brother and sister, Chanax and Bithiah, who testified against you."

"How did they know about us?" Ankhmakis asked.

The stricken face of Bastyre caught his eye, and he recalled the hole in the apiary wall she'd shown him years ago. He'd forgotten about it. His head dropped into his hands and he wept.

"I've failed," he sobbed, turning toward Helena's dead body. How could anyone take an innocent life such as hers? What sort of monster would suggest such a thing? Prickly heat flashed across the surface of his skin. The hairs on his arms stood at attention. The image of his mother and Chanax filled his mind. He would make his mother pay by slaughtering her youngest son while she watched.

"Where is the queen right now?" he demanded.

"In the throne room, with the rest of the court and High Priest Isidor," Min replied. "Dozens of the queen's retinue guard them. They're expecting you."

Ankhmakis glared at his men and nodded to Khaleme. "I need you to fight for me," he said. "I will make every person who betrayed me pay for their hideous treachery. Starting with my mother."

"We will fight for you," Min answered. "After the murder of Helena, we no longer serve Pharaoh Horwenefer, nor his queen."

Ankhmakis drew his khopesh sword by its hilt and stormed from the room, making his way toward his mother's lair. As he approached, several guards blocked his entrance with long spears.

"The queen will see you tomorrow morning," the lead guard announced, but the tremble in his lower lip exposed his fear.

"No." Ankhmakis drew to his full height and raised his gleaming sword. "She will see me now."

The man's continued objections were silenced as Ankhmakis cut off his head and spun to stab two other men. The guards fell to the floor, and Ankhmakis stepped over their warm corpses, taking deep, steady breaths as he approached the golden doors of the throne room and kicked them open. High Queen Keket sat in the throne, and at either side of her stood her sniveling priests, Chanax and Isidor. Weret, Bithiah, and Ruia huddled to the side, clutching one another, eyes wide and cheeks stained with eye makeup and tears. Ankhmakis saw nothing but red as his mother's guards—at least forty of them in total—advanced upon him. He allowed his Ka to fill the room, growing stronger and more violent with each man he sliced down, and he felt his sisters struggle under the force of his rage as it sank into their very being. Hating them, and everyone in his family, he screamed in their faces as he passed by, forcing the three women to jump out of his way and cower even farther into a corner.

He took life after life, and around him, his men did the same, creating a trail of bodies and blood as he slaughtered his way toward his mother. Min battled his own brother, Pontius. Ankhmakis charged toward the queen and her priests, but Nefermaat placed himself between Ankhmakis's blade of death and his mother.

"Enough," Nefermaat called. "You may go no farther. Killing the King's Guard is against the law, and you won't be shown mercy."

Ankhmakis looked him in the eye. "Did you kill my daughter?"

"I did as was ordered by the king," Nefermaat answered.

"The king?" Ankhmakis yelled, his voice echoing off the marbled walls and floor. "There is no king here. Instead I see a weak queen, cowering upon her throne. I will ask you again. Did. You. Kill. My. Daughter?"

"I did as was ordered by the high queen of Upper Egypt," his half-brother replied. "What does it matter who issued the order?"

"Because, Nefermaat," Ankhmakis answered in a low tone. "I'm king now."

Ankhmakis raised his sword and sliced Nefermaat's throat. As his brother's body fell, Bithiah cried out, and Ruia held her back. Ankhmakis turned to his mother, who clung to Isidor's side. Pontius held Min in a death grip on the floor, his knife against his twin's throat, but before Ankhmakis could help his friend, Khaleme stabbed the traitor through the heart from behind. Pontius stared at the gleaming tip of the blade protruding from his breast, his blood dripping onto Min's face. Khaleme tugged his sword from the man's body, and Min scrambled to stand as his brother fell to the floor. The women's whimpers and moans filled the air.

Ankhmakis sensed his friend's grief but continued to walk through the blood now puddling across the gilded floor toward his mother. "Do you think your priests are going to save you?" he said as he stepped across Nefermaat's corpse and stood before the throne. "Everyone knows even a girl can defeat Chanax."

Isidor and Chanax energetically attacked him, but he parried their attack with his Ka the way Natasa had taught him. He raised his sword and placed it at his mother's throat. Khaleme grabbed Isidor, and Min held Chanax back. Ankhmakis swallowed his bile, tempering his desire to kill her on the spot, and instead allowed the blade to cut her skin the tiniest bit.

"Ankhmakis," Ruia cried. "Don't kill her."

He never took his attention from his mother's, relishing in her terror. "Crown me king of Behdet," he demanded. "Or I'll kill you and crown myself."

"Ankhmakis," Keket begged, her wide eyes darting briefly to Isidor's. "I was following the law. You had sexual relations with a celibate healer. You know the punishment is death. I saved you from your crime by taking your daughter as proxy. You should be grateful."

The room spun around Ankhmakis as his hate poured out of his body. "Crown me king," he repeated. "Or I'll kill you and crown myself."

"What about your father?" she asked, her voice a broken whisper.

"Horwenefer has made a poor pharaoh," Ankhmakis declared. "The time has come for him to step down."

Keket shook her head in dismay. She looked to Isidor for advice.

"Don't do it," the high priest answered. "Arrest him instead."

Ankhmakis turned and placed his sword at Isidor's temple.

"For my first act as the king of Behdet," Ankhmakis said, "I declare your cult closed. You and your priesthood have twenty-four hours to flee my kingdom. I ride out in the morning to Thebes. If you are here, I will have my men tear you apart, limb from limb. If I find you on the road to Thebes,

I will slaughter you there instead. Be sure I never see your face again."

He turned to Chanax. "You included, little brother."

"You can't exile me," Chanax demanded as he managed to free himself from Min's hold. The youngest prince hurled his body at Ankhmakis, knocking the sword from his hands. The two tumbled to the ground, rolling across the hard granite floor through puddles of blood. Nefermaat's corpse—still warm to the touch—stopped their momentum, and Ankhmakis felt his rage build to a storm. He shoved his dead brother out of the way and pinned Chanax to the ground, wrapping his hands around the weasel's neck. Chanax sent his curses to his brother, but his petty magic was no match for Ankhmakis's anger and hate now pouring into the room like a swarm of hornets in the heat of the day.

"I despise you," Ankhmakis hissed as clenched his grip harder around Chanax's thin neck, and his brother's eyes rolled to the back of his head, his dark skin turning pale as he struggled to cling to his life. "I will kill you and send you into the eternal darkness."

Isidor wrangled in Khaleme's grip, but the Ethiopian held his squirming captive to his chest. His mother ran forward but slipped in her guards's blood and fell to the floor, begging Ankhmakis to stop from all fours like a pathetic, broken dog.

"Please, Ankhmakis, don't kill him," Queen Keket screamed, reaching out her blood-stained hand.

Ankhmakis heard nothing but the slowing of Chanax's heart, and he tightened his grip around the villain's neck. As Chanax's life force faded, Ankhmakis felt peace. Chanax's life for Helena's was a balanced payment. It was fitting that his mother watch her son die, that she too may suffer as Ankhmakis did. As Chanax's last breaths wheezed out his dying body, someone grabbed Ankhmakis's leg, and a desperate female voice began to plead, "Stop, brother. Please don't kill him. He isn't worth it."

He tried to kick her off, but Ruia clung to his leg, her face twisted, and stained cheeks reddened with splattered blood.

"Please, Ankhmakis," she begged, tugging his leg into her blood-stained robes. "You've already killed enough men."

Something in her voice reminded him of Natasa, and Ankhmakis let go of Chanax's throat. Ruia rose and grasped his bloody arms to help him stand over their brother. She wrapped her arms around him and sobbed into his chest. Ankhmakis stared down at Chanax, rolled in the fetal position, clutching his neck and choking for air. Such a weak and pathetic excuse of a man. How was it possible that this despicable person could have destroyed him in such a powerful way?

"You will leave now, Chanax," Ankhmakis said, his rage still brewing like a storm blowing in across the desert. Ruia drew him closer into her embrace. "Never return to my kingdom, or else I shall rip off your head with my bare hands. Is this clear?"

Chanax gasped and struggled to stand. His neck was red and starting to bruise. "You can't do this," he croaked.

"Watch me," Ankhmakis replied. He released Ruia, picked up his sword from the slippery, gilded floor, and rounded on his mother, placing the bloodied hilt in her hands. His guards surrounded them as he commanded her, "Now, woman, place my sword on my shoulder and crown me king. You have two minutes, or Khaleme will chop off your hands."

"Ankhmakis," she begged. "This isn't right."

"Do it," he growled.

She placed the sword on his right shoulder as tears ran down her tired, exhausted face.

"By the powers vested in me," she said as if under a spell. "I, the queen of Behdet and high queen of Upper Egypt, now crown Ankhmakis, second son to my husband, Pharaoh Horwenefer, King of Behdet and our noble house."

Ankhmakis yanked the sword from her hands. "You are banished to our estate in the south, where you will remain under house arrest for the rest of your life."

"Ankhmakis," his mother sobbed, "I was trying to save you."

"What sort of man would prefer his innocent and pure daughter pay the price of his crime?" he answered. "I was willing to die for Natasa's love, and you should have let it happen. Whom you see before you is no longer your son, but a beast of a man with a heart set on vengeance. Now go, all three of you, before I turn my guards upon you."

Isidor and Chanax grabbed Keket and led her out of the room, stepping over the dead guards as they hobbled away.

"You can't do this," Chanax barked at him before leaving. "You can't be king."

"Dear brother, I am the king of Behdet. Soon to be pharaoh of all of Egypt."

The golden doors slammed behind them, and Ankhmakis turned to his elder sister, who tapped his shoulder.

"Ankhmakis?" Ruia asked. "What about us?"

"Ruia," he said, trying to be calm, taking her hands into his, "I plan to name Silus as the steward of Behdet and send him home as soon as we have secured Lycopolis. Until then, you will rule here with Ennaeus as your guardian. Do whatever he tells you and make no laws yourself. Is that clear?"

"What about me?" Weret cried, waddling her pregnant body around Ruia and pushing her out of the way. "If you are the king, then I am the queen."

His heart sank. What would he do with her? He placed a hand on her swollen belly. "You remain here as well. It may be years before I gain military control over Ptolemy's armies, and Behdet is the safest place for the children. Your greatest, most important duty is to care for our children, do you hear me? Protect them at all costs, so my son can join me at my side when he's old enough."

Weret winced. "Yes, husband."

"As for you, Bithiah," Ankhmakis said, glaring at his female betrayer. "I strip you of your titles. Your husband, Prince Chanax, has been exiled from the Upper Kingdom. You can either follow him or remain here at court and raise your children in relative safety. We will provide your food and shelter, but you will be Ruia's lady-in-waiting. Your sons will be taken into the military at age ten and your daughters will remain at court to serve the other princesses. None of your line shall have claim to the throne of Egypt."

"Ankhmakis, I had no idea they would kill Helena," she said from behind her hands, shielding her face from Nefermaat's dead body.

"You thought you could take my life from me with no consequences?" he demanded. "Kill my daughter and lover with ease? Bithiah, your ambition has been your ruin. I was destined to become pharaoh of Egypt, no matter what you did. You should have left well alone. If you had, Helena would still be alive and Natasa at my side. You ignorant, evil woman."

Ankhmakis spat at Nefermaat's body, then turned and left the room, his men following at a short distance. He was overdue in Thebes—he had unfinished business with his father.

41

Slipping Through the Cracks

"This land is in commotion, and no one knows what the result may be, for it is hidden from speech, sight, and hearing because of dullness, silence being to the fore.

"I show you the land in calamity, for what had never happened has now happened. Men will take weapons of war, and the land will live in confusion. Men will make arrows of bronze, men will beg for the bread of blood, men will laugh aloud at pain; none will weep at death, none will lie down hungry at death, and a man's heart will think of himself alone. None will dress hair today; hearts are entirely astray because of it, and a man sits quiet, turning his back, while one man kills another."

~ The Prophecies of Neferti, 12th Dynasty

Thebes, Egypt 199 BCE

Isidor stood on the docks of the west bank of Thebes, hands behind his back, surveying the busy river before him. They'd traveled nonstop for days, hoping to remain ahead of Ankhmakis while also trying to catch up to Hecataeus and Neferu-ankh-maat. He had no idea what the vizier's plans were but didn't want to leave any loose ends. Letting Neferu-ankh-maat flee Egypt to freedom was not an option.

Chanax stood by his side. The rest of their priesthood awaited them on the boat. They'd removed their red robes and now wore the simple leopard-skin uniform of the local priests. The disguise was working. Everywhere they stopped, people gave them food and drink, as was custom. Throughout the kingdom of Egypt, priests were revered.

"Any news?" Chanax asked.

"Yes," Isidor replied. "According to the old lady at the market, a man fitting Hecataeus's description passed by here two days ago. Not a lot of Greek men showing their faces this far south these days."

"Was Natasa with them?" the young man continued.

"The woman said he was alone. I imagine she and the high priestess didn't leave the boat. Why do you ask?"

"Because," Chanax replied, "I don't sense her Ka anymore. Even though I could never breach it, I could sense it whenever I tried. Helena's Ka is deleted from the record of life, but Natasa's is as well. I think she might also be dead."

"Ah, I see," Isidor murmured. "How interesting. I myself have searched Ankhmakis's field, and the Golden Child no longer shields him. Her death was worth it."

"Are you sure?" Chanax replied, crossing his arms over his chest. "The protective shield is gone, but have you been able to penetrate his Ka or manipulate his emotions?"

Isidor looked at his student, knowing he couldn't hide his failure from his pupil. Chanax was powerful, perhaps too much so. "I have tried."

"Well? Can you even come close to an attachment like we've done with Father or Silus?"

"Not yet," Isidor admitted.

"You won't, old fool." Chanax shook his finger in the air. "Ankhmakis is surrounded by his righteous anger, and now he's slicing his way north toward Thebes, protected from us by his very rage. He may turn against his own self, but until such a time, he's out of our control. Even more out of control than when Helena was alive. At least then we had something to threaten him with. Now he rides to take the crown from Father and will surf the wave of his anger until he arrives in Lycopolis and kill every Greek in sight. What do you think he'll do if he discovers us along the way? The plan failed, Isidor. I gave up Natasa for nothing."

Isidor allowed the younger man to rant. He was hurting.

"Come," the high priest said, placing his arm around the angry prince. "I have contacts in Coptos who will get us to Memphis. One way or another, we will arrive there, and when we do, you'll see how Ankhmakis will never be pharaoh of Egypt. He may be crowned pharaoh in Thebes, but not in the North. We'll bide our time in Memphis, grow in strength, and when the day comes, we will overthrow Ankhmakis, and you will be crowned. I promise."

Isidor gazed into Chanax's eyes, noting the look of madness the young man wore. Isidor had seen that look once before, after the boy had been molested by Ptolemy IV Philopater. He worried that awash in his grief and guilt, Chanax was becoming unhinged, and paused for a moment, wondering if his acolyte was still under his control.

"Chanax," Isidor said, measuring each word with great care, "we will win this war. I promise. Now come, we mustn't tarry."

To Isidor's relief, Chanax followed him onto the boat, and Isidor gave the sailors the signal to continue on their way and into Greek territory.

☥

Across the river, on the eastern banks of Luxor, Hecataeus watched Isidor's craft sail away. They'd camped along the far bank for two days, holding back to give Ankhmakis time to clear their path. Hecataeus was quite surprised when he awoke that morning to see Isidor standing on the docks. At first, he'd wanted to kill the man, but decided against the act. Better to let the villain go in front.

"I can't believe he's following us," Neffa said from behind.

"I don't think he's following," Hecataeus said. "The old lady in the village told me he traveled with a group of priests. They've been advancing their way down the Nile."

"The entire priesthood of Set is heading north on a ship?" she murmured. "How strange."

"It tells me Ankhmakis has taken the throne," he replied, turning to his daughter, in hopes the news would break through her shock. Her eyes remained vacant, staring into the river without emotion—she didn't even blink. "I wish Natasa would connect with him in that way."

"Astral communication?" Neffa asked.

"Yes. We'd have some idea of what we're up against. Their unusual connection had been a key piece of the escape plan, but now it's like she's not here. She hasn't spoken for days, and barely lets you feed and clean her. It's starting to scare me."

"I know," Neffa said, her voice shaking. "She's still in shock. I'm sure she'll return soon, but she's lifeless, as if her vital élan has vanished. I don't know what to do."

He put an arm around her and joked, "Well, only one vocal woman makes for a quiet day."

She shoved him and glanced down at her basic brown robe. Around her waist she wore a crocodile-skin pouch filled with herbs and tinctures. She'd removed her jewelry, including the silver snake upon her upper arm, and now wore the clothing of a potions seller. Hecataeus smiled. She was far too elegant for such a disguise.

"My clothes are dirty. We'll need to wash."

"Yes," he agreed. "Why don't you go into Thebes and pick up new robes, shoes, and supplies? I'll stay here and guard Natasa. Ankhmakis left us several pounds of gold before he left. Best to do our shopping now."

Hecataeus glanced up the river. Isidor's boat was now nothing but a small image surrounded by many others. Trade was restricted, but Ankhmakis's army used the river for the procurement of food and supplies, providing a steady stream of traffic in both directions.

"After this we're in Greek territory," he said, "and you won't be allowed out on deck for quite some time. I think you should buy some Macedonian servant's clothing."

"Why?" she asked.

"The two of you will need to dress as my attendants. Might as well use my pale face to my advantage."

"I thought you were a wanted man?"

"I am," he replied, "but everyone knows you Egyptians think all Greeks look the same."

He winked at her and was rewarded with a smile. Neffa got into the small reed raft, and he shoved her into the current. Corinna and Eleni entered his mind, and he wondered if he should risk turning back and fetching them, when it hit him that Corinna was no longer of this earth. He had no idea what the situation was in Behdet. Could he get to Eleni, or did the pharaoh already have men headed this way to arrest him? He'd committed several crimes punishable by death by killing the dungeon guards and stealing a prisoner. His life was forfeit.

At least he was with Neffa. They traveled well together. As she rowed the raft across the river to the docks of Thebes, Hecataeus sighed and turned to his eldest daughter, who sat on the prow, staring out at the reeds as they blew in the wind.

"Natasa," he murmured as he approached her, "why won't you speak?"

She didn't answer. He touched her shoulder. "You know, it would be helpful if you could connect to Ankhmakis. He's worried about you and if you answered, we'd know what to do next."

A dragonfly alighted on her finger. She looked at it but didn't attempt to shake it off.

"I love you, little hawk," he tried once more.

Her focus remained on the reeds, but as the dragonfly lifted from her finger, she crossed her arms to hug herself, her teeth chattering as if she were cold.

Hecataeus took off his cloak and wrapped it around her. Pulling her close to his chest, he wondered if he'd ever speak to either of his daughters again.

42

A Father's Love—Revisited

"If you are wise, look after your house; love your wife without alloy."
~ Ptah-Hotep

Thebes and Coptos, Egypt 199 BCE

Ankhmakis stormed into his father's bedchambers. The pharaoh had been injured on the frontline and now lay in his bed in his palace in Thebes, unable to sit up and greet his son. He was dying, and in his moment of weakness, his son had come to take his crown.

"This is an unfortunate situation," Horwenefer croaked as his son stood beside him and yanked the bed screen aside. Ankhmakis wore a white kilt, his royal collar, and the crown of Behdet. His body tense yet quaking. He was formidable.

"It is," Ankhmakis replied, looking him up and down as his guards surrounded the bed. Ankhmakis looked to the healer who stood wide-eyed beside the ailing pharaoh. "You're dismissed."

The healer nodded and ran from the room.

"Where is my guard?" Horwenefer asked, his voice

cracked and almost inaudible.

"Dead," Ankhmakis said, voice flat. "Well, not all of them. Many surrendered and are now under my charge. I take it you received my message?"

Horwenefer coughed and grabbed his stomach. He'd suffered a sword wound in the spleen that was now infected— his life was almost over. The fact both terrified him and gave him great relief. As he looked up into his son's fierce face, a sense of failure sucked the last bits of life out of him.

"Yes," he croaked, "and I'm sorry. The entire situation is horrible."

Ankhmakis drew his sword. "Have your priests crown me pharaoh," he said.

"Why should you be pharaoh of Upper Egypt?" Horwenefer asked, coughing up blood this time.

"Because you killed my daughter," he replied.

"No," the pharaoh said. "Your mother killed the child, and she had every right within the law."

"She had no right to kill her without a trial," Ankhmakis replied, his voice monotone. "You know this to be true."

Horwenefer winced in pain. His son was correct. "This isn't how I envisioned this moment. I've long planned to make you king. Silus isn't too bright, and Chanax is too unstable. The crown in either hands would be one of misery for the people. You, however, are the genius, the one who sees a plan where none exists. I was going to crown you sooner or later, but you weren't patient enough."

"Nonsense," Ankhmakis answered, his eyes alight as he drew his sword. Hugronaphor noted a vein bulging in his son's corded neck and drew his covers to his chin for fear the man would slay him. "I have been nothing but patient for years while you waged this war like an ass. We'd have the entire empire under our control if you'd ever listened to me. I was patient for far too long, and since your queen has killed my daughter, I'm no longer willing to let you control me. It's I who controls you now. Hand me your crown and tell your damned priests to name me pharaoh of the Upper Kingdom."

"I wouldn't disrespect the priesthood." Horwenefer coughed. "You need to honor the priests, son, or they'll retaliate. I'd think your experience with Isidor would have already taught you this."

"Give me your crown."

"Again, son," Horwenefer lamented. "I'm very sorry." He removed the blue Khepresh crown of the Upper Kingdom from his wrinkled, bald head and handed it to his son. "Go," he whispered. "Thebes won't hold for much longer and soon this place will be crawling with Greeks. Have Setep crown you and head out to Lycopolis."

"What about you?"

"Silus has agreed to let me remain behind," Horwenefer replied.

"What?" Ankhmakis asked. "They'll execute you."

"I'm going to die any moment now, and I want to leave this world in my bed, right here in Thebes, next to the monuments of my forefathers."

"They won't give you a proper burial."

"I'm willing to be left to rot," Horwenefer replied, unable to hide the fear in his voice. To be refused proper burial was to give up the afterlife. He'd never reincarnate into the line of Egyptian kings again. So be it. "My time in Egypt is over, son. I'd like to be an Oriental in my next lifetime, or a Roman, or wherever my Ba ends up. If there's anything I've learned this time around, it's that the world beyond our lands is large, and I'd like to experience more than the Nile Valley."

Horwenefer reached out and grasped Ankhmakis's hand in his own. "I never should have separated you from Natasa. It was a rash decision fueled by an old man's foolish pride and the greatest mistake of my life. It might have even cost us the rebellion. The least I can do is lie here in this bed and let the Greeks think they captured the pharaoh, when in reality, the true pharaoh rides north to sweep them out of the Nile Valley like flies from a sweet cake."

"That is very brave, Father," Ankhmakis replied, his face nonplussed, still not displaying any emotion. Much to Horwenefer's dismay, his son took the crown in his hands and left his father behind to die among strangers without so much as a backward glance.

☥

In 199 BCE, the Theban priesthood crowned Ankhmakis, who took the name Ankhwenefer, "The Good Being of Isis." Once crowned, the new pharaoh ordered his troops to withdraw from the city and sent a message to Pistias in Coptos, informing him that the river wouldn't be safe for quite some time, yet they needed to get out, as the city would soon be overrun with Greek soldiers making their way to Thebes.

"Take the desert road to the Red Sea," he wrote. "The Wadi Hammamat is the only way. Get Natasa out of Egypt, and tell her I'm a thought away, should she wish to connect. Always I am seeking her. Her pharaoh will call her home as soon as he can."

Pharaoh Ankhwenefer and his army rode north through the desert toward the Kharga Oasis. Along the way, they happened upon remnants of cities long ago buried by the desert. His was an ancient nation, his people makers of monuments to gods and kings. As they marched toward their goal, every step the army took was a journey across the sands of time. Ankhwenefer and his men retraced the steps of their forefathers, trying to reclaim what had been lost to them for centuries—trying to find a way back to glory.

ɸ

Pistias was a tall man, with wavy brown hair and a rough beard to match. His two front teeth were made of gold, and upon his shoulder he wore a mongoose. The first thing Hecataeus thought was how much Helena would have loved the animal, and a pain flamed within his heart. Pistias handed Hecataeus a note from the pharaoh. Hecataeus shook his head and ran his fingers through his hair.

"The Wadi Hammamat, eh?" he asked.

"There's nothing for it," the sailor replied. "We'd have to remain here for months, maybe even years, if we wanted to take the river as it's become a warzone. The Egyptians have surrendered Thebes, and the Greek army is sailing from the north to take the city and drive them to final surrender in Behdet."

"Where they will run into a trap of over ten thousand angry Kushmen." Hecataeus smiled. "And the rest of the Upper Kingdom's army."

"It's a brilliant plan," Pistias agreed. "Ankhmakis is quite the strategist, isn't he?"

Hecataeus looked to his daughter to see her reaction. Nothing. He read her Ankhmakis's letter and she stared into space, as if his name meant nothing.

"I thought you said she was your daughter," Pistias asked. "Strange your child would be quiet."

"She's in shock," Neffa explained. "I'm sure she'll come out of it."

"Can she walk?" Pistias asked.

"Yes, she'll follow right along, without complaint," Hecataeus said.

"Good," Pistias replied. "Because we have a lot of walking in front of us. One hundred and twenty-four miles along a dry ancient riverbed to be exact, to get to the port of Quseir."

"What?" Neffa asked. "Can we take pack animals?"

"Yes," the man replied. "I've arranged for a wagon and animals, and there are stops along the way, but it won't be easy. Trust me."

Hecataeus glanced at his daughter. He was worried she might not make it. She ate nothing but the ale Neffa forced her to drink, or boiled water when they could get it. At least the Wadi Hammamat contained several oases with fresh, natural springs. They must go on. Dying in Coptos wasn't an option. Hecataeus wanted nothing more than to get out of Egypt and fast.

He looked to Pistias. "It's fine. We're ready to head out whenever you are. I need to send a letter to the new pharaoh first."

"There are scribes down the street still running messages through enemy lines. It's the way the soldiers keep in touch with their families, and a great way for a scribe to make a living, if he has the courage."

In a crowded tavern off the harbor, Hecataeus found a scribe and gave him a golden nugget to deliver a message north to an old friend named Janus, in Lycopolis, who would hold the message for Ankhmakis. To use the pharaoh's name would give away the army's plan.

"My friend," Hecataeus wrote. "We received your letter and are taking the desert road with our ally. Natasa is alive, but not living. She hasn't spoken since Helena's death, so don't expect her to contact you anytime soon. From the Red Sea, we will head to Pelusium. Send any news there. If we don't hear from you, we will leave Egypt and head to Gaul the moment the winter seas have cleared."

Satisfied, Hecataeus returned to camp, where Pistias and his men were taking down their tents. Natasa and Neffa stood to the side of the commotion.

"I think we'll walk first," Neffa said as he approached. "My legs need to stretch. After days of hiding in the boat, it's good to see Ra's face again."

Natasa gazed out at the horizon. The desert stretched beyond them as far as the eye could see. She wore simple linen pants, and a dress that wrapped up around her head to protect her from the sand and wind. Only her shocking green eyes, vacant and lifeless, could be seen through the veil. It gave Hecataeus the chills.

"We're going on an adventure," he said to his daughter, the first person to steal his heart. "Across the desert and to the sea. I've long wanted to take you to Quseir. I think you're going to like it."

Natasa crossed her arms and shivered, yet still she didn't speak.

☥

The next morning, Chanax sprinted along the docks of Coptos, the wind blowing his leopard-skin robes. The city was in a panic, and boats from the north crowded the harbor as Egyptians were rounded up for questioning. His priestly attire had enabled him to escape the Greek onslaught.

"They were here," he cried as he jumped onto the boat. "Hecataeus and two small, dark servants. They must be Natasa and her mother. That means Natasa lives."

Isidor nodded at Chanax, his gaze flickering to the action on the river.

"They've taken the Wadi Hammamat. Left yesterday."

"We've been here several days." Isidor frowned. "How did we miss them?"

"They never approached the docks. A cook saw them walk into town and head out the same day with a bunch of Greek traders. If we hurry, we can catch them."

Isidor shook his head. "The desert road takes us too far out of the way. I've secured safe passage north along the river." He stretched out his hand to reveal a beautiful golden ring, the Ptolemaic seal embossed upon it. "A gift from Metakryon. We are priests seeking asylum with our father and friend, Ptolemy V, the true pharaoh of Egypt. Hecataeus was forced to take the Wadi Hammamat because he's a wanted man by the Ptolemy family, and the only Egyptians heading north are those like us, with friends in high places."

"Do we tell them of Ankhmakis's plan?" Chanax asked as more Greek ships rowed upriver past them. They were one of the few going north.

"I've considered it," Isidor said, "but I think we should let Ankhmakis fail on his own. We've interfered enough—for now. We'll decide when we arrive at Lycopolis."

Chanax nodded. "I still think we should follow Hecataeus."

"Why?" Isidor asked. "They're nothing to us."

Chanax looked at Isidor and grimaced. If only he knew what secret Natasa carried.

"Yes, Father," Chanax said, not realizing he'd let the word slip until it was out of his mouth.

"What did you say?" Isidor asked.

"What?" Chanax stuttered. His cheeks burned and he dropped his head. "Nothing, sir."

Isidor eyed him for a moment before turning to talk to the captain. Chanax took a seat near the prow and looked to the east, where the desert filled the horizon. Natasa was out there somewhere. He tried again to find her with his Ka but felt nothing but a dark void, more horrible than Set himself. She might never return from such a state of madness. He wasn't sure he'd recovered from his time separated from his body to avoid the pain of being passed around the room to be used by Philopater's men. Knowing Natasa's fate caused him even more guilt and shame.

He touched his neck, still sore from his brother's attempt to kill him, and considered the guilt now gnawing at his heart. Natasa had admitted she loved him. Had she meant it? The possibility tortured him as he contemplated his betrayal. Had he destroyed her for nothing? As he looked out at the docks where men and women ran in various directions, each one afraid of what was happening, Chanax realized he was never going to see Natasa again.

In spite of all she'd done to hurt him, the thought of losing her forever made him weep.

To be concluded in...
Song of the King's Heart
Book Three
Civilization's End

About the Author

Nicole Sallak Anderson is a Computer Science graduate from Purdue University, and former CTO for a small Silicon Valley startup, turned novelist and blogger, focusing on the intersection of technology and consciousness. She currently lives in the beautiful Santa Cruz Mountains in California with her husband, where she raises goats and bees. She enjoys spinning, knitting, playing the bass, and dancing, particularly the tango. You can keep up with all her latest writing by following @NSallakAnderson on Facebook, Twitter, and Medium or her blog, nicolesallakanderson.com. Feel free to contact her. She almost always answers any query or comment!

www.ingramcontent.com/pod-product-compliance
Lightning Source LLC
Chambersburg PA
CBHW060949190726
48286CB00005B/1499